Essex*Works.*

For a better quality of life

Please return this book on or before the date shown above. To
renew go to www.essex.gov.uk/libraries, ring 0845 603 7628 or
go to any Essex library.

Essex County Council

Atonement by Ian McEwan

The Road Home by Rose Tremain

Money by Martin Amis

The Woman in Black by Susan Hill

The Wind-Up Bird Chronicle
by Haruki Murakami

Irène Némirovsky was born in Kiev in 1903, the daughter of a successful Jewish banker. In 1918 her family fled the Russian Revolution for France where she became a bestselling novelist. She was prevented from publishing when the Germans occupied France and moved with her husband and two small daughters from Paris to the safety of the small village of Issy-l'Evêque (in German occupied territory). It was here that Irène began writing Suite Française. She died in Auschwitz in 1942.

IRÈNE NÉMIROVSKY

Suite Française

TRANSLATED FROM THE FRENCH BY
Sandra Smith

VINTAGE BOOKS
London

Published by Vintage 2011

2 4 6 8 10 9 7 5 3 1

The publisher makes grateful acknowledgement to the French
Cultural Attaché for a Burgess Grant for translation

First published in France by Editions Denoël as *Suite Française* in 2004

First published in Great Britain in 2006 by
Chatto & Windus

First published in Vintage in 2007

Random House, 20 Vauxhall Bridge Road,
London SW1V 2SA

www.vintage-books.co.uk

Addresses for companies within The Random House Group Limited
can be found at: www.randomhouse.co.uk/offices.htm

The Random House Group Limited Reg. No. 954009

A CIP catalogue record for this book
is available from the British Library

ISBN 9780099563181

The Random House Group Limited supports the Forest Stewardship
Council® (FSC®), the leading international forest certification
organisation. All our titles that are printed on Greenpeace approved
FSC® certified paper carry the FSC® logo. Our paper procurement
policy can be found at www.randomhouse.co.uk/environment

Printed and bound in Great Britain by
CPI Bookmarque, Croydon, CR0 4TD

ïi institut français

This book is supported by the French Ministry for Foreign Affairs, as
part of the Burgess programme headed for the French Embassy in
London by the Institut Français du Royaume-Uni

I dedicate this novel to the memory of my mother and father,
to my sister Elisabeth Gille,
to my children and grandchildren,
and to everyone who has felt
and continues to feel
the tragedy of intolerance.

Denise Epstein

Translator's Note

Irène Némirovsky wrote the two books that form *Suite Française* under extraordinary circumstances. While they may seem remarkably polished and complete, 'Storm in June' and 'Dolce' were actually part of a work-in-progress. Had she survived, Irène Némirovsky would certainly have made corrections to these two books and completed the cycle she envisaged as her literary equivalent to a musical composition.

Translation is always a daunting task, especially when the translator has so much respect and affection for the author. It is also a creative task that often requires 'leaps of faith': a feeling for tone, sensing the author's intention, taking the liberty to interpret and, sometimes, to correct. With *Suite Française*, I have made slight changes in order to correct a few minor errors that appear in the novel. In particular, I have altered characters' names when they were inconsistent and could prove confusing. However, I have retained other anomalies that pose no real problem to the reader, such as the incorrect proximity of Tours to Paray-le-Monial. Perhaps the most striking error for the English reader is the misquotation of Keats, when Némirovsky writes: 'This thing of Beauty is a *guilt* for ever'. I have deliberately retained this mistake in the text as a poignant reminder that Némirovsky was writing *Suite Française* in the depths of the French countryside, with a sense of urgent foreboding and nothing but her memory as a source.

The Appendices in this edition provide important details regarding Némirovsky's plans for the remaining three books, along with poignant correspondence that reveals her own family's terrible situation.

This translation would not have been possible without the support, advice and encouragement of many people. I am very grateful to my husband Peter, my son Harry, Rebecca Carter at Chatto & Windus, Anne Garvey, Patricia Freestone, Philippe Savary, Paul Micio, Jacques Beauroy and my friends and colleagues at Robinson College, Cambridge. It has been a privilege to translate *Suite Française*. I am sure Irène Némirovsky would have been happy that so many years after her tragic murder, so many thousands world wide can once again hear her voice. I hope I have done her justice.

I wish to dedicate this translation to my family: the Steins, Lantzes, Beckers and Hofstetters, and to all the countless others who fought, and continue to fight, prejudice and persecution.

Sandra Smith, Cambridge, March 2006

Contents

ONE

Storm in June

1

War

Hot, thought the Parisians. The warm air of spring. It was night, they were at war and there was an air raid. But dawn was near and the war far away. The first to hear the hum of the siren were those who couldn't sleep – the ill and bedridden, mothers with sons at the front, women crying for the men they loved. To them it began as a long breath, like air being forced into a deep sigh. It wasn't long before its wailing filled the sky. It came from afar, from beyond the horizon, slowly, almost lazily. Those still asleep dreamed of waves breaking over pebbles, a March storm whipping the woods, a herd of cows trampling the ground with their hooves, until finally sleep was shaken off and they struggled to open their eyes, murmuring, 'Is it an air raid?'

The women, more anxious, more alert, were already up, although some of them, after closing the windows and shutters, went back to bed. The night before – Monday 3 June – bombs had fallen on Paris for the first time since the beginning of the war. Yet everyone remained calm. Even though the reports were terrible, no one believed them. No more so than if victory had been announced. 'We don't understand what's happening,' people said.

They had to dress their children by torchlight. Mothers lifted small, warm, heavy bodies into their arms: 'Come on, don't be afraid, don't cry.' An air raid. All the lights were out, but beneath the clear, golden June sky, every house, every street was visible. As for the Seine, the river seemed to absorb even the faintest glimmers of light and reflect them back a hundred times brighter, like some multifaceted mirror. Badly blacked-out windows, glistening rooftops, the metal hinges of doors all shone in the water. There were a few red lights that stayed on longer than the others, no one knew why, and the Seine drew them in, capturing them and bouncing them playfully on its waves. From above, it could be seen flowing along, as white as a river of milk. It guided the enemy planes, some people thought. Others said that couldn't be so. In truth, no one really knew anything. 'I'm staying in bed,' sleepy voices murmured, 'I'm not scared.' 'All the same, it just takes one . . .' the more sensible replied.

Through the windows that ran along the service stairs in new apartment blocks, little flashes of light could be seen descending: the people living on the sixth floor were fleeing the upper storeys; they held their torches in front of them, in spite of the regulations. 'Do you think I want to fall on my face on the stairs! Are you coming, Emile?' Everyone instinctively lowered their voices as if the enemy's eyes and ears were everywhere. One after another, doors slammed shut. In the poorer neighbourhoods there was always a crowd in the Métro, or the foul-smelling shelters. The wealthy simply went to sit with the concierge, straining to hear the shells bursting and the explosions that meant bombs were falling, their bodies as tense as frightened animals in dark woods as the hunter gets closer. Though the poor were just as afraid as the rich, and valued their lives just as much, they were more sheeplike: they needed each other, needed to link arms, to groan or laugh together.

Day was breaking. A silvery blue light slid over the cobblestones, over the parapets along the quayside, over the towers of Notre-Dame. Bags of sand were piled halfway up all the important monuments, encircling Carpeaux's dancers on the façade of the Opera House, silencing the Marseillaise on the Arc de Triomphe.

Still at some distance, great guns were firing; they drew nearer, and every window shuddered in reply. In hot rooms with blacked-out windows, children were born, and their cries made the women forget the sound of sirens and war. To the dying, the barrage of gunfire seemed far away, without any meaning whatsoever, just one more element in that vague, menacing whisper that washes over those on the brink of death. Children slept peacefully, held tight against their mothers' sides, their lips making sucking noises, like little lambs. Street sellers' carts lay abandoned, full of fresh flowers.

The sun came up, fiery red, in a cloudless sky. A shell was fired, now so close to Paris that from the top of every monument birds rose into the sky. Great black birds, rarely seen at other times, stretched out their pink-tinged wings. Beautiful fat pigeons cooed; swallows wheeled; sparrows hopped peacefully in the deserted streets. Along the Seine each poplar tree held a cluster of little brown birds who sang as loudly as they could. Deep beneath the ground they heard the sound everyone had been waiting for, a muffled, faraway call, like a three-tone fanfare. The air raid was over.

2

In the Péricand household they listened in shocked silence to the evening news on the radio, but no one passed comment on the latest developments. The Péricands were a cultivated family: their traditions, their way of thinking, their middle-class, Catholic background, their ties with the Church (their eldest son, Philippe Péricand, was a priest), all these things made them mistrustful of the government of France. On the other hand, Monsieur Péricand's position as curator of one of the country's national museums bound them to an administration that showered its faithful with honours and financial rewards.

A cat held a little piece of bony fish tentatively between its sharp teeth. He was afraid to swallow it, but he couldn't bring himself to spit it out either.

Madame Péricand finally decided that only a male mind could explain with clarity such strange, serious events. Neither her husband nor her eldest son was at home: her husband was dining with friends, her son was not in Paris. Charlotte Péricand, who ruled the family's daily life with an iron hand (whether it was managing the household, her children's education or her husband's career), was not in the habit of seeking anyone's opinion. But this was of a different order. She needed a voice of authority to tell her what to believe. Once pointed in the right direction, there would be no stopping her. Even if given absolute proof she was mistaken, she would reply with a cold, condescending smile, 'My father said so . . . My husband is very well-informed.' And she would make a dismissive little gesture with her gloved hand.

She took pride in her husband's position (she herself would have preferred a more domestic lifestyle, but following the example of our Dear Saviour, each of us has his cross to bear). She had come home between appointments to oversee her children's studies, the baby's bottles and the servants' work, but she didn't have time to take off her hat and coat. For as long as the Péricand children could remember, their mother was always ready to go out, armed with hat and white gloves. (Since she was thrifty, her mended gloves had the faint smell of stain remover, a reminder of their passage through the dry-cleaners.)

As soon as she had come in this evening, she had gone to stand in front of the radio in the drawing room. Her clothes were black, her hat a divine little creation in fashion that season, decorated with three flowers and topped with a silk pom-pom. Beneath it, her face was pale and anguished, emphasising the marks of age and fatigue. She was forty-seven years old and had five children. You would have thought, to look at her, that God had intended her to be a redhead. Her skin was extremely delicate, lined by the passing years. Freckles were dotted over her strong, majestic nose. The expression in her green eyes was as sharp as a cat's. At the last minute, however, it seemed that Providence had wavered, or decided that a shock of red hair would not be appropriate, neither to Madame Péricand's irreproachable morals nor to her social status, so she had been given mousy brown hair, which she was losing by the handful since she'd had her last child. Monsieur Péricand was a man of great discipline: his religious scruples prohibited a number of pleasures and his concern for his reputation kept him away from places of ill repute. The youngest Péricand child was only two, and between Father Philippe and the baby, there were three other children, not counting the ones Madame Péricand discreetly referred to as the 'three accidents': babies she had carried almost to term before losing them, so that three times their mother had been on the verge of death.

The drawing room, where the radio was now playing, was enormous and well-proportioned, with four windows overlooking the Boulevard Delessert. It was furnished in traditional style, with large armchairs and settees upholstered in golden yellow. Next to the balcony, the elder Monsieur Péricand sat in his wheelchair. He was an invalid whose advancing age meant that he sometimes lapsed back into childhood and only truly returned to his right mind when discussing his fortune, which was considerable (he was a Péricand-Maltête, heir of the Maltête family of Lyon). But the war, with its trials and tribulations, no longer affected him. He listened, indifferent, steadily nodding his beautiful silvery beard. The children stood in a semi-circle behind their mother, the youngest in his nanny's arms. Nanny had three sons of her own at the front. She had brought the little boy

7

downstairs to say goodnight to his family and took advantage of her brief entry into the drawing room to listen anxiously to what they were saying on the radio.

The door was slightly ajar and Madame Péricand could sense the presence of the other servants outside. Madeleine, the maid, was so beside herself with worry that she came right up to the doorway. To Madame Péricand, such a breach of the normal rules seemed a frightening indication of things to come. It was in just this manner that the different social classes all ended up on the top deck during a shipwreck. But working-class people were highly strung. 'How they do get carried away,' Madame Péricand thought reproachfully. She was one of those middle-class women who generally trust the lower classes. 'They're not so bad if you know how to deal with them,' she would say in the same condescending and slightly sad tone she used to talk of a caged animal. She was proud that she kept her servants for a long time. She insisted on looking after them when they were ill. When Madeleine had had a sore throat, Madame Péricand herself had prepared her gargle. Since she had no time to administer it during the day, she had waited until she got back from the theatre in the evening. Madeleine had woken up with a start and had only expressed her gratitude afterwards, and even then, rather coldly in Madame Péricand's opinion. Well, that's the lower classes for you, never satisfied, and the more you go out of your way to help them, the more ungrateful and moody they are. But Madame Péricand expected no reward except from God.

She turned towards the shadowy figures in the hallway and said with great kindness, 'You may come and listen to the news if you like.'

'Thank you, Madame,' the servants murmured respectfully and slipped into the room on tiptoe.

They all came in: Madeleine, Marie, Auguste the valet, and finally Maria the cook, embarrassed because her hands smelled of fish. But the news was over. Now came the commentaries on the situation: 'Serious, of course, but not alarming,' the speaker assured everyone. He spoke in a voice so full, so calm, so effortless, and used such a resonant tone each time he said the words 'France', 'Homeland' and 'Army', that he instilled hope in the hearts of his listeners. He had a particular way of reading such communiqués as 'The enemy is continuing relentless attacks on our positions but is encountering the most valiant resistance from our troops.'

He said the first part of the sentence in a soft, ironic, scornful tone of voice, as if to imply, 'At least that's what they'd like us to think.' But in the second part he stressed each syllable, hammering home the adjective 'valiant' and the words 'our troops' with such confidence that people couldn't help thinking, 'Surely there's no reason to worry so much!'

Madame Péricand saw the questioning, hopeful stares directed towards her. 'It doesn't seem absolutely awful to me!' she said confidently. Not that she believed it; she just felt it was her duty to keep up morale.

Maria and Madeleine let out a sigh.

'You think so, Madame?'

Hubert, the second-eldest son, a boy of seventeen with chubby pink cheeks, seemed the only one struck with despair and amazement. He dabbed nervously at his neck with a crumpled-up handkerchief and shouted in a voice that was so piercing it made him hoarse, 'It isn't possible! It isn't possible that it's come to this! But, Mummy, what has to happen before they call everyone up? Right away – every man between sixteen and sixty! That's what they should do, don't you think so, Mummy?'

He ran into the study and came back with a large map, which he spread out on the table, frantically measuring the distances. 'We're finished, I'm telling you, finished, unless . . .'

Hope was restored. '*I* see what they're going to do,' he finally announced, with a big happy smile that revealed his white teeth. 'I can see it very well. We'll let them advance, advance, and then we'll be waiting for them there and there, look, see, Mummy! Or even . . .'

'Yes, yes,' said his mother. 'Go and wash your hands now, and push back that bit of hair that keeps falling into your eyes. Just look at you.'

Fury in his heart, Hubert folded up his map. Only Philippe took him seriously, only Philippe spoke to him as an equal. 'How I hate this family,' he said to himself and kicked violently at his little brother's toys as he left the drawing room. Bernard began to cry. 'That'll teach him about life,' Hubert thought.

The nanny hurried to take Bernard and Jacqueline out of the room; the baby, Emmanuel, was already asleep over her shoulder. Holding Bernard's hand, she strode through the door, crying for her three sons whom she imagined already dead, all of them. 'Misery and misfortune, misery and misfortune!' she said quietly, over and over again, shaking her grey head. She continued muttering as she started running the bath and

9

warmed the children's pyjamas: 'Misery and misfortune.' To her, those words embodied not only the political situation but, more particularly, her own life: working on the farm in her youth, her widowhood, her unpleasant daughters-in-law, living in other people's houses since she was sixteen.

Auguste, the valet, shuffled back into the kitchen. On his solemn face was an expression of great contempt that was aimed at many things.

The energetic Madame Péricand went to her rooms and used the available fifteen minutes between the children's bath time and dinner to listen to Jacqueline and Bernard recite their school lessons. Bright little voices rose up: 'The earth is a sphere which sits on absolutely nothing.'

Only the elder Monsieur Péricand and Albert the cat remained in the drawing room. It had been a lovely day. The evening light softly illuminated the thick chestnut trees; Albert, a small grey tomcat who belonged to the children, seemed ecstatic. He rolled around on his back on the carpet. He jumped up on to the mantelpiece, nibbled at the edge of a peony in a large midnight-blue vase, delicately pawed at a snapdragon etched into the bronze corner-mount of a console table, then in one leap perched on the old man's wheelchair and miaowed in his ear. The elder Monsieur Péricand stretched a hand towards him; his hand was always freezing cold, purple and shaking. The cat was afraid and ran off. Dinner was about to be served. Auguste appeared and pushed the invalid into the dining room.

They were just sitting down at the table when the mistress of the house stopped suddenly, Jacqueline's spoon of tonic suspended in mid-air. 'It's your father, children,' she said as the key turned in the lock.

It was indeed Monsieur Péricand, a short, stocky man with a gentle and slightly awkward manner. His normally well-fed, relaxed and rosy-cheeked face looked, not frightened or worried, but extraordinarily shocked. He wore the expression found on people who have died in an accident, in a matter of seconds, without having had time to be afraid or suffer. They would be reading a book or looking out of a car window, thinking about things, or making their way along a train to the restaurant car when, all of a sudden, there they were in hell.

Madame Péricand rose quietly from her chair. 'Adrien?' she called out, her voice anguished.

'It's nothing. Nothing,' he muttered hastily, glancing furtively at the children, his father and the servants.

Madame Péricand understood. She nodded at the servants to continue serving dinner. She forced herself to swallow her food, but each mouthful seemed as hard and bland as a stone and stuck in her throat. Nevertheless, she repeated the phrases that had become ritual at mealtimes for the past thirty years. 'Don't drink before starting your soup,' she told the children. 'Darling, your knife . . .'

She cut the elderly Monsieur Péricand's filet of sole into small strips. He was on a complicated diet that allowed him to eat only the lightest food and Madame Péricand always served him herself, pouring his water, buttering his bread, tying his napkin round his neck, for he always started drooling when he saw food he liked. 'I don't think poor elderly invalids can bear to be touched by servants,' she would say to her friends.

'We must show grandfather how much we love him, my darlings,' she instructed the children, looking at the old man with terrifying tenderness.

In his later years, Monsieur Péricand had endowed various philanthropic projects, one of which was especially dear to his heart: the Penitent Children of the 16th Arrondissement, a venerable institution whose goal was to instil morals in delinquent minors. It had always been understood that the elder Monsieur Péricand would leave a certain sum of money to this organisation, but he had a rather irritating way of never revealing exactly how much. If he hadn't enjoyed his meal, or if the children made too much noise, he would suddenly emerge from his stupor and say in a weak but clear voice, 'I'm going to leave them five million.'

A painful silence would follow.

On the other hand, if he'd had a lovely meal and a good sleep in his chair by the window, in the sunshine, he would look up at his daughter-in-law with the pale, distant eyes of a small child, or a newborn puppy.

Charlotte was very tactful. She never replied, as others might, 'You're absolutely right, Father.' Instead, she would say sweetly, 'Good Lord, you have plenty of time to think about that!'

The Péricand fortune was considerable, but it would be unjust to accuse them of coveting the elder Monsieur Péricand's inheritance. They didn't care about money, not at all, but money cared about them, so to speak! There were certain things that they deserved, including the Maltête-Lyonnais millions; they would never manage to spend it all but they would save it for their children's children. As for the Penitent Children of the 16th Arrondissement, they were so involved with this charity that, twice a year, Madame Péricand organised classical music concerts for the unfortunate children; she would play the harp and was gratified to notice that, at certain passages, sobbing could be heard in the darkened concert hall.

Monsieur Péricand followed his daughter-in-law's hands attentively. She was so distracted and upset that she forgot his sauce. His white beard waved about alarmingly. Madame Péricand came back to reality and quickly poured the parsley butter over the ivory flesh of the fish, but it was only after she placed a slice of lemon at the side of his plate that the old man was calm again.

Hubert leaned towards his brother and muttered, 'It's not going well, is it?'

'No,' he replied with a gesture and a look. Hubert dropped his trembling hands on to his lap. He was lost in thought, vividly imagining scenes of battle and victory. He was a Boy Scout. He and his friends would form a group of volunteers, sharpshooters who would defend their country to the end. In a flash, his mind raced through time and space. He and his friends: a small group bound by honour and loyalty. They would fight, they would fight all night long; they would save their bombed-out, burning Paris. What an exciting, wonderful life! His heart leapt. And yet, war was such a savage and horrifying thing. He was intoxicated by his imaginings. He clutched his knife so tightly in his hand that the piece of roast beef he was cutting fell on to the floor.

'Clumsy oaf,' whispered Bernard. He and Jacqueline were eight and nine years old respectively and were both thin, blond and stuck-up. The two of them were sent to bed after dessert and the elder Monsieur Péricand fell asleep at his usual place by the open window. The tender June day persisted, refusing to die. Each pulse of light was fainter and more exquisite than the last, as if bidding farewell to the earth, full of love and regret. The cat sat on the window ledge and looked nostalgically towards an horizon that was the colour of green crystal.

Monsieur Péricand paced up and down the room. 'In a few days, maybe even tomorrow, the Germans will be on our doorstep. I've heard the High Command has decided to fight outside Paris, in Paris, beyond Paris. No one knows it yet, thank goodness, because after tomorrow there will be a stampede on the roads and at the train stations. You must leave for your mother's house in Burgundy as early as possible tomorrow morning, Charlotte. As for me,' Monsieur Péricand said rather proudly, 'I will share the fate of the treasures entrusted to my care.'

'I thought everything in the museum had been moved out in September,' said Hubert.

'Yes, but the temporary hiding place they chose in Brittany isn't suitable; it turns out it's as damp as a cellar. I just don't understand it. A Committee was organised to safeguard national treasures. It had three sections and seven subsections, each of which was supposed to appoint a panel of experts responsible for hiding works of art during the war, yet just last month an attendant in the provisional museum points out that suspicious stains are appearing on the canvases. Yes, a wonderful portrait of Mignard with his hands rotting away from a kind of green leprosy. They quickly sent the valuable packing cases back to Paris and now I'm waiting for an order to rush them off to somewhere even further away.'

'But what about us? How will we travel? By ourselves?'

'You'll leave tomorrow morning, calmly, with the children and the two cars, and any furniture and luggage you can carry, of course. We can't pretend that, by the end of the week, Paris might not be destroyed, burned down and thoroughly pillaged.'

'You are amazing!' exclaimed Charlotte. 'You talk about it so calmly!'

Monsieur Péricand turned towards his wife, his face gradually returning to its normal pinkish colour – a matte pink, the colour of pigs who have been recently slaughtered. 'That's because I can't really believe it,' he explained quietly. 'Here I am, speaking to you, listening to you; we've decided to flee, to leave our home, yet I cannot believe that it is all *real*. Do you understand? Now go and get everything ready, Charlotte. Everything must be ready by tomorrow morning; you could be at your mother's in time for dinner. I'll join you as soon as I can.'

Madame Péricand's face wore the same resigned, bitter look as when the children were ill and she was forced to put on an apron and nurse them; they all usually managed to be ill at the same time, though with different maladies. When this happened, Madame Péricand would come out of the children's rooms with a thermometer in her hand, as if she were brandishing the crown of martyrdom, and everything in her bearing seemed to cry out: 'You will reward your servants on Judgement Day, kind Jesus!'

'What about Philippe?' was all she asked.

'Philippe cannot leave Paris.'

Madame Péricand left the room, head held high. She refused to bow beneath the burden. She would see to it that the entire household was ready to leave in the morning: the elderly invalid, four children, the servants, the cat, plus the silver, the most valuable pieces of china, the fur coats, food and medicine in case of emergencies. She shuddered.

In the sitting room, Hubert was pleading with his father. 'Please let me stay. I can stay here with Philippe. And . . . don't make fun of me! Can't you see that if I went and got my friends we could form a company of volunteers; we're young, strong, ready for anything . . . We could . . .'

Monsieur Péricand looked at him. 'My poor boy!' was all he said.

'It's all over? We've lost the war?' stammered Hubert. 'Is . . . is it true?'

And suddenly, to his horror, he felt himself burst into tears. He cried like a baby, like Bernard would have cried, his large mouth twisted, tears streaming down his face. Night was falling, soft and peaceful. A swallow flew by, lightly brushing against the balcony in the dark night air. The cat let out a frustrated little cry of desire.

3

The writer Gabriel Corte was working on his terrace, between the dark, swaying woods and the golden green setting sun fading over the Seine. How peaceful everything was around him! Beside him were his well-trained faithful friends, great white dogs who were awake yet motionless, their noses pressed against the cool paving stones, their eyes half closed. At his feet his mistress silently picked up the sheets of paper he dropped. His servants, the secretary, were all invisible behind the shimmering windows; they were hidden somewhere in the background of the house, in the wings of his life, a life he desired to be as brilliant, luxurious and disciplined as a ballet. He was fifty years old and had his favourite games. Depending on the day, he was either Lord of the Heavens or a miserable writer crushed by hard work and labouring in vain. On his desk he had had engraved, 'To lift such a heavy weight, Sisyphus, you will need all your courage.' His fellow writers were jealous of him because he was rich. He himself bitterly told the story of his first candidature to the Académie Française: one of the electors implored to vote for him had sarcastically replied, 'He has three telephone lines!'

He was handsome, with the cruel, languid movements of a cat, expressive soft hands and a slightly full Roman face. Only Florence, his official mistress, was allowed to remain in his bed until morning (the others never spent the night with him). Only she knew how many masks he could put on, this old flirt with dark circles under his eyes and thin arched eyebrows, too thin, like a woman's.

That evening he was working as he normally did, half-naked. His house in Saint-Cloud had been specially built to be hidden away from prying eyes, right down to the vast, wonderful terrace, planted with blue cinerarias. Blue was Gabriel Corte's favourite colour. He could only write if he had a small glass bowl of deep lapis lazuli beside him. He would look at it now and again, and caress it like a mistress. What he liked best in Florence, as he often told her, were her clear blue eyes, which gave him the same feeling of coolness as his glass bowl. 'Your eyes quench my thirst,' he would murmur. She had a soft, slightly flabby chin, a contralto voice that was still beautiful and, Gabriel Corte confided to his friends, something cow-like in her expression. I like that. A woman should look like a heifer: sweet, trusting and generous, with a body as white as cream. You know, like those old actresses whose skin has been softened by massage, make-up and powder.

He stretched his delicate fingers in the air and clicked them like castanets. Florence handed him a lemon, then an orange and some glacé strawberries; he consumed an enormous amount of fruit. She gazed at him, almost kneeling before him on a suede pouffe, in that attitude of adoration that pleased him so much (though he couldn't have imagined any other). He was tired, but it was that good tiredness which comes from doing enjoyable work. Sometimes he said it was better than the tiredness that comes after making love.

He looked benevolently at his mistress. 'Well, that's not gone too badly, I think. And you know, the midpoint.' (He drew a triangle in the air indicating its top.) 'I've got past it.'

She knew what he meant. Inspiration flagged in the middle of a novel. At those moments, Corte struggled like a horse trying in vain to pull a carriage out of the mud. She brought her hands together in a gracious gesture of admiration and surprise. 'Already! I congratulate you, my dear. Now it will go smoothly, I'm sure.'

'God willing!' he murmured. 'But Lucienne worries me.'

'Lucienne?'

He looked at her scornfully, his eyes hard and cold. When he was in a good mood, Florence would say, 'You still have that killer look in your eye . . .' and he would laugh, flattered. But he hated being teased when in the throes of creativity.

She couldn't even remember who Lucienne was.

'Of course,' she lied. 'I don't know what I was thinking!'

'I don't know either,' he said in a wounded voice.

But she seemed so sad and humble that he took pity on her and softened. 'I keep telling you, you don't pay enough attention to the minor characters. A novel should be like a street full of strangers, where no more than two or three people are known to us in depth. Look at writers like

Proust. They knew how to use minor characters to humiliate, to belittle their protagonists. In a novel, there is nothing more valuable than teaching the lesson of humility to the heroes. Remember, in *War and Peace*, the little peasant girls who cross the road, laughing, in front of Prince Andrei's carriage? He speaks to them, directly, and the reader's imagination is at once lifted; now there is not just one face, not just one soul. He portrays the many faces of the crowd. Wait, I'll read you that passage, it's remarkable. Put the light on,' he said, for night had fallen.

'Planes,' Florence replied, looking up at the sky.

'Won't they leave me the hell alone?' he thundered.

He hated the war; it threatened much more than his lifestyle or peace of mind. It continually destroyed the world of the imagination, the only world where he felt happy. It was like a shrill, brutal trumpet shattering the fragile crystal walls he'd taken such pains to build in order to shut out the rest of the world.

'God!' he sighed. 'How upsetting, what a nightmare!'

Brought back down to earth, he asked to see the newspapers. She gave them to him without a word. They came in from the terrace and he leafed through the papers, a dark look on his face. 'All in all,' he said, 'nothing new.'

He didn't want to see anything new. He dismissed reality with the bored, startled gesture of a sleeping man awakened abruptly in the middle of a dream. He even shaded his eyes with his hand as if to block out a dazzling light.

Florence walked towards the radio. He stopped her. 'No, no, leave it alone.'

'But Gabriel . . .'

He went white with anger. 'Listen to me! I don't want to hear anything. Tomorrow, tomorrow will be soon enough. If I hear any bad news now (and it can only be bad with these c**** in government) my momentum will be lost, my inspiration blocked. Look, you'd better call Mademoiselle Sudre. I think I'll dictate a few pages!' She hurried to summon the secretary.

As she was coming back to the drawing room, the telephone rang. 'It's Monsieur Jules Blanc phoning from the Presidential Office, wishing to speak to Monsieur Corte,' said the valet.

She carefully closed all the doors so that no noise could filter through to where Gabriel and his secretary were working. Meanwhile, the valet went to prepare a cold supper for his master, as he always did. Gabriel ate little during the day but was often hungry at night. There was some left-over cold partridge, a few peaches, some delicious little cheeses (which Florence herself had ordered from a shop on the Left Bank) and a bottle of Pommery. After many years of reflection and research, Corte had come to the conclusion that, given his poor digestion, only champagne would do. Florence listened to Jules Blanc's voice on the telephone, an exhausted, almost imperceptible voice, and at the same time heard all the familiar sounds of the house – the soft clinking of china and glass, Gabriel's deep, languid voice – and she felt as though she were living a confusing dream. She put down the phone and called the valet. He had been in their service for a long time and trained for what he called 'the workings of the house', an inadvertent pastiche of seventeenth-century parlance that Gabriel found quite charming.

'What can we do, Marcel? Jules Blanc himself is telling us to leave . . .'

'Leave? To go where, Madame?'

'Anywhere. To Brittany. The Midi. It seems the Germans have crossed the Seine. What can we do?' she repeated.

'I have no idea, Madame,' said Marcel frostily.

They'd waited long enough to ask his opinion. 'They should have left last night,' he thought. 'Isn't it just pathetic to see rich, famous people who have no more common sense than animals! And even animals can sense danger . . .' As for him, well, he wasn't afraid of the Germans. He'd seen them in '14. He'd be left alone; he was too old to be called up. But he was outraged: the house, the furniture, the silver – they hadn't thought about anything in time. He let out a barely audible sigh. *He* would have had everything wrapped up long ago, hidden away in packing cases, in a safe place. He felt a sort of affectionate scorn towards his employers, the same scorn he felt towards the white greyhounds: they were beautiful but stupid.

'Madame should warn Monsieur,' he concluded.

Florence started walking towards the drawing room, but she had barely opened the door when she heard Gabriel's voice. It was the voice he assumed on his worst days, when he was most agitated: slow, hoarse, inter-rupted now and again by a nervous cough.

She gave orders to Marcel and the maid, then thought about their most valuable possessions, the ones to be taken when there's danger, when you have to escape. She placed a light but sturdy suitcase on her bed. First she hid the jewellery she'd had the foresight to get out of the safe. Over it she put some underwear, her washing things, two spare blouses, a little evening dress, so she'd have something to wear once they'd arrived – she knew there'd be delays on the road – a dressing gown and slippers, her make-up case (which took up a lot of space) and of course Gabriel's manuscripts. She tried in vain to close the suitcase. She moved the jewellery box, tried again. No, something definitely had to go. But what? Everything was essential. She pressed her knee against the case, pushed down, tried to lock it and failed. She was getting annoyed.

Finally, she called her maid. 'Do you think you can manage to close it, Julie?'

'It's too full, Madame. It's impossible.'

For a second Florence hesitated between her make-up case and the manuscripts, chose the make-up and closed the suitcase.

The manuscripts could be stuffed into the hatbox, she thought. I know him, though! His outbursts, his crises, his heart medicine. We'll see tomorrow, it's better to get everything ready tonight and not tell him anything. Then we'll see . . .

4

Along with their fortune, the Maltête family of Lyon had bequeathed to the Péricands a predisposition to tuberculosis. This illness had claimed two of Adrien Péricand's sisters at an early age; his son, Philippe, had suffered from it a few years earlier. Two years in the mountains, however, seemed to have cured Father Philippe, his recovery coinciding with the moment when he was finally ordained a priest. His lungs were still weak, so when war was declared he was exempt. Nevertheless, he looked strong. He had good colour in his cheeks, thick black eyebrows and a healthy, rugged appearance. His parish was a little village in the Auvergne. As soon as his vocation had become apparent, Madame Péricand had given him up to the Lord. In exchange for this sacrifice, she had hoped for a bit of worldly glory and that he might be destined for great things; instead, he was teaching the catechism to the small farmers of Puy-de-Dôme. If the Church was unable to find some greater responsibility for him, even a monastery would be better than this poor parish. 'It's such a waste,' she would say to him vehemently. 'You are wasting the gifts the Good Lord has given you.' But she consoled herself with the thought that the cold climate was good for him. He seemed to need the kind of air he'd breathed in the high altitudes of Switzerland for two years. Back on the streets of Paris, he strode along in a manner that made passers-by smile, for it seemed out of keeping with his cassock.

And so that morning he stopped in front of a grey building and entered a courtyard that smelled of cabbage. The Penitent Children of the 16th Arrondissement were lodged in a small private residence set behind a tall administrative building. As Madame Péricand explained in her annual letter to the Friends of the charitable institution (Founding Member, 500 francs per year; Benefactor, 100 francs; Member, 20 francs), the children lived in the best possible material and moral conditions, were apprenticed to a variety of trades and participated in healthy physical activities: a small glass lean-to had been built on to the house, providing a carpenter's work-shop and a cobbler's bench. Through the window-panes, Father Péricand saw the round heads of the little inmates look up for a second when they heard his footsteps. In one part of the garden, between the steps and the lean-to, two boys aged fifteen and sixteen were working with a supervisor. There were no uniforms. The Institution hadn't wanted to recall the prisons already known to some of them. They wore clothing made by charitable people using leftover wool. One of the boys had on an apple-green cardigan that revealed his long, thin, hairy wrists. In perfect discipline and silence, he and his companion were digging the earth, pulling out grass, repotting flowers. They nodded to Father Péricand who smiled at them. The priest's face was calm, his expression stern and a bit sad. But his smile was very sweet, slightly shy, with a kind of gentle reproach: 'I love you,' it seemed to say. 'Why don't you love me?' The children were watching him, saying nothing.

'What beautiful weather,' he murmured.

'Yes, Father,' they replied, their voices cold and forced.

Philippe said a few more words to them, then went into the house. Inside it was grey and clean, and the room where he found himself was almost bare, containing only two cane chairs. It was the reception room, where the charges could have visitors, a practice tolerated but not encour-aged. In any case, almost all of them were orphans. From time to time some neighbour who had known their dead parents, some older sister living in the country, would remember them and come to visit. But Father Péricand had never met a living soul in this room. The director's office was on the same floor.

The director was a short, fair man with pink eyelids and a pointed nose that trembled like an animal's snout when he smelled food. His charges called him 'the rat' or 'the tapir'. He stretched both arms out to Philippe; his hands were cold and clammy. 'I simply do not know how to thank you for your kindness, Father! You are really going to take charge of our boys?'

The children had to be evacuated the following day. He'd just been called urgently to the Midi, to his sick wife's side . . .

'The supervisor is afraid he'll be snowed under, that he won't be able to manage our thirty boys all alone.'

'They seem very obedient,' Philippe remarked.

'Oh, they're good boys. We get them into shape, teach the rebellious ones how to behave. But without wishing to seem proud, I'm the one who keeps everything going here. The supervisors are afraid. In any case, the war has claimed one of them and as for the other . . .' He pouted. 'Excellent if he follows a rigid routine, but incapable of taking any initiative whatsoever, one of those people who could drown in a glass of water. Anyway, I was wondering which Saint to pray to in order to evacuate these boys when your good father told me you were passing through, leaving tomorrow for the mountains and that you wouldn't refuse to help us.'

'I'll gladly do it. How are you planning to get the children out?'

'We've been able to get hold of two trucks. We've got enough petrol. They're going somewhere that is only about fifty kilometres from your parish, you know. It won't take you too far out of your way.'

'I'm free until Thursday,' said Philippe. 'One of my Brothers is replacing me.'

'Oh, the journey won't take that long! Your father tells me you are familiar with the house one of our benefactresses has placed at our disposal. It's a large estate in the middle of the woods. The proprietor inherited it last year and the furniture, which was very beautiful, was sold just before the war. The children can camp in the grounds. They will enjoy doing that in this lovely weather. At the beginning of the war they spent three months camping in another château in Corrèze kindly offered to us by one of these good ladies. We didn't have any heating at all there. Every morning we had to break the ice on the jugs. The children have never behaved so well. The days of peacetime luxury and ease,' said the director, 'are over.'

The priest looked at the clock.

'Would you do me the honour of having lunch with me, Father?'

Philippe declined. He'd arrived in Paris that morning having travelled through the night. He was worried that Hubert might do something hotheaded and had come to get him, but the family was leaving that very day for Nièvre. Philippe wanted to be there when they left: an extra pair of hands wouldn't go amiss, he thought, smiling.

'I'll go and tell the boys you'll be taking my place,' said the director. 'Perhaps you'd like to say a few words to them to get acquainted. I had intended to speak to them myself, to tell them the whole country's at war, but I'm leaving at four o'clock and . . .'

'I'll speak to them,' said Father Péricand.

He lowered his eyes, joined his hands and placed his fingertips on his lips. His face took on an expression of harshness and sadness as he looked into his heart. He disliked these unfortunate children. He walked towards them with all the kindness and goodwill he was capable of, but all he felt in their presence was coldness and disgust, not a single glimmer of love, nothing of that divine feeling which even the most miserable of sinners awoke in him when begging for forgiveness. There was more humility in bragging atheists, in hardened blasphemers, than in the eyes and words of these children. Their superficial obedience was terrifying. Despite being baptised, despite the holy sacraments of Communion and penance, no divine light illuminated them. They were children of Satan, without even enough spirituality to elevate themselves to a point where they desired divine light; they didn't feel it; they didn't want it; they didn't miss it. Father Péricand thought tenderly of the good little children to whom he taught the catechism. He had no illusions about them, of course. He knew very well that evil had already planted solid roots in their young souls, but at certain moments they showed such promise of kindness, of inno- cent grace, that they trembled with pity and horror when he spoke to them of the Passion of Christ. He was eager to get back to them. He thought of the First Communion they would celebrate the following Sunday.

Meanwhile, he followed the director into the hall where the boys had been assembled. The shutters were closed. In the darkness, he tripped on one of the steps near the doorway and had to grab on to the director's arm to avoid falling. He looked at the children, waiting, hoping for some stifled laughter. Sometimes a ridiculous incident like this breaks the ice between students and teachers. But no. Not one of them reacted. They stood in a semicircle against the wall with the youngest – those between eleven and fourteen – in front; their faces were pale, their lips tightly clenched, their eyes lowered. Almost all of them were small for their age and scrawny. The older ones, aged fifteen to eighteen, stood at the back. Some of them had the low brow, the thick hands of killers. As soon as he was in their presence, Father Péricand again felt a strange sensation of aversion, almost fear. He must overcome it at all costs. He walked towards them and they stepped back imperceptibly, as if they wanted to sink into the wall.

'My sons, from tomorrow until the end of our journey, I shall be looking after you instead of the director,' he said. 'You know that you are leaving Paris. Only God knows the fate in store for our soldiers, our dear country; He alone, in His infinite wisdom, knows the destiny of each of us in the days ahead. It is, alas, immensely likely that we shall all suffer dearly, for public misfortunes consist of a multitude of private misfortunes and this is the only time when, poor blind ungrateful creatures that we are, we feel the solidarity which unites us, forms us into a single being. What I would like to have from each of you is a gesture of faith in God. Our lips form the words "May His will be done", but deep in our hearts we cry out "May *my* will be done, oh Lord". Yet why do we seek God? Because we hope for happiness: it is man's nature to desire happiness and if we accept His will, God can give us this happiness, right now, without making us wait for death and Resurrection. My sons, may each of you entrust yourself to God. May each of you seek Him as your father, place your life in His loving hands, so divine peace can fill your hearts.'

He paused for a moment, looked at them. 'Let us say a little prayer together.'

Thirty shrill voices indifferently recited 'Our Father'; thirty thin faces surrounded the priest. As he made the sign of the Cross over them they lowered their heads sharply, mechanically. Only one lad turned his eyes towards the window. He had a large bitter mouth and the ray of sun that slipped through the closed shutters lit up his delicate freckled cheek, his thin pinched nose.

Not one of them moved or spoke. When the supervisor blew his whistle, they lined up and left the hall.

5

The streets were empty. People were closing their shops. The metallic shudder of falling iron shutters was the only sound to break the silence, a sound familiar to anyone who has woken in a city threatened by riot or war. As they walked to work, the Michauds saw loaded trucks waiting in front of the government buildings. They shook their heads. As always, they linked arms to cross the Avenue de l'Opéra to the office, even though the road, that morning, was deserted. They were both employees of the same bank and worked in the same branch, although the husband had been an accountant there for fifteen years while she had started only a few months earlier on a 'temporary contract for the duration of the war'. She taught singing, but the previous September had lost all her students when their families took them to the country for fear of the bombings. Her husband's salary had never been enough to pay their bills and their only son had been called up. Thanks to this secretarial job, they just about managed. As she always said, 'We mustn't ask for the impossible, my dear.' They had been familiar with hardship ever since they left their families to get married against their parents' will. That was a long time ago. Traces of beauty still remained on her thin face. Her hair was grey. He was a short man, with a weary, neglected appearance, but sometimes, when he turned towards her, looked at her, smiled at her, a loving teasing flame lit up his eyes – the same, he thought, yes, truly, almost the same as before. He helped her across the road and picked up the glove she'd dropped. She thanked him by gently pressing her fingers over his as he handed it to her. Other employees were hurrying towards the open door of the bank. One of them came up to the Michauds and asked, 'Well, are we finally leaving?'

The Michauds had no idea. It was 10 June, a Monday. When they had left the office on Friday, everything had seemed under control. The executives were being sent to the countryside but nothing had been said about the employees. Their fate was being decided in the manager's offices on the first floor, on the other side of two large green padded doors; the Michauds walked past them quickly and in silence. At the end of the corridor they separated. He went upstairs to Accounting, she remained on the managerial floor: she was secretary to one of the directors, Monsieur Corbin, the head of the branch. The second director, the Count de Furières (married to one of the Salomon-Worms), was responsible for the foreign affairs of the bank, whose clientele was most select, and limited, preferably, to wealthy landowners and the most important names in the metalworking industry. Monsieur Corbin hoped that his colleague, the Count de Furières, would make it easier for him to get into the Jockey Club. For several years now he had lived in hope. However, the Count deemed that favours such as invitations to dinner parties and to join the de Furières hunting party were ample compensation for the generous credit facilities allowed to him. In the evening, Madame Michaud would amuse her husband with impersonations of the meetings between the two directors, their sour smiles, Corbin's grimaces, the look on the Count's face. It relieved a bit of the monotony of their working day. But for some time now even this distraction had failed them: Monsieur de Furières had been sent to the Alpine front and Corbin was running the branch alone.

Madame Michaud collected the post and went into the small room next to the manager's office. A faint perfume lingered in the air, a sign that Corbin was busy. He was patron to a dancer: Mademoiselle Arlette Corail. All his mistresses were dancers. He seemed not to be interested in women of any other profession. Not one secretary, no matter how pretty or young, had ever managed to lure him away from this particular penchant. Whether beautiful or ugly, young or old, he treated all his female employees in the same aggressive, rude and mean-spirited manner. His odd little voice emerged from a head that sat on top of a fat, heavy, well-fed body; when he got angry his voice became as high-pitched and feverish as a woman's.

The shrill sound Madame Michaud knew so well was filtering through the closed doors today. One of the employees came in and said quietly, 'We're leaving.'

'When?'

'Tomorrow.'

In the corridor, whispering shadows passed by. People were gathering near the windows and outside their offices. Corbin finally opened his door and saw the dancer out. She was wearing a candy-pink cotton suit and a large straw hat covered her dyed hair. She was slender, with a good figure, but beneath the make-up, her face was hard and tired. Red patches had appeared on her cheeks and forehead. She was obviously furious.

'Do you want me to leave on foot?' Madame Michaud heard her say.

'Will you never listen to me? Go back to the garage at once. Offer them money, promise them whatever they want and the car will be fixed.'

'But I'm telling you it's impossible! Impossible! Don't you understand?'

'Look, my dear, what do you want me to say? The Germans are at the gates of Paris and you're talking about taking the road to Versailles. Why on earth would you want to do that? Take the train.'

'Do you have any idea what's going on at the train stations?'

'It won't be any better on the roads.'

'You have . . . you have no conscience at all. You're leaving, you have two cars . . .'

'I need to move the files and some of the staff. What the hell do you want me to do with the staff?'

'Oh, please! Must you be so rude? You have your wife's car!'

'You want to go in my wife's car? What a wonderful idea!'

The dancer turned her back on him and whistled for her dog, who bounded in. She put his collar on, her hands trembling with indignation. 'My entire youth sacrificed to a . . .'

'For goodness sake! Stop making a scene. I'll phone you tonight, I'll see what can be done . . .'

'No, no. I see very well that all I can do now is go and die in a ditch at the side of the road . . .'

'Oh, do shut up, you're making me furious . . .'

They finally realised that the secretary was listening to them. They lowered their voices and Corbin, taking his mistress by the arm, walked her to the door.

He came back and glanced at Madame Michaud who, finding herself in his path, was the first target of his fury. 'Get the section heads together in the meeting room. Right now, if you don't mind!'

Madame Michaud went out to pass on his orders. A few moments later the employees filed into a large room containing a marble bust of the bank's founder and a full-length portrait of the current president, Monsieur Auguste-Jean, who had been ailing for some time with a softening of the brain caused by his great age.

Monsieur Corbin received them standing behind the oval table where nine sheets of blotting paper marked the Board of Directors' places. 'Gentlemen, we are leaving tomorrow morning at eight o'clock to go to our branch in Tours. I will take the Board's files in my car. Madame Michaud, you and your husband will accompany me. As for those who have a car, be in front of the bank at six o'clock to pick up other staff members, that is, the ones I have selected. I will see what I can do for the others but, if necessary, they will have to take the train. Thank you, gentlemen.'

He disappeared and immediately the murmur of anxious voices buzzed around the room. Only two days before, Corbin had declared he could foresee no reason to leave, that the hysterical rumours were the work of traitors, that the bank, *the bank*, would remain where it was, would fulfil *its* obligations even if others did not. Given that the 'withdrawal', as it was discreetly called, had been decided so suddenly, all – without doubt – was lost! The women wiped the tears from their eyes. Through the crowd the Michauds found each other. Both of them were thinking about their son Jean-Marie. His last letter was dated 2 June. Only a week ago. My God, anything could have happened since then! In their anguish, their only comfort was being together.

'How lucky we are not to have to be apart,' she whispered to him.

6

Night was falling but the Péricands' car was still waiting outside their door. Tied to the roof was the soft deep mattress that had adorned their marital bed for twenty-eight years. Fixed to the boot were a pram and a bicycle. They were trying in vain to cram in all the family's bags, suitcases and overnight cases, as well as the baskets containing the sandwiches, the thermos flask, bottles of milk for the children, cold chicken, ham, bread and the boxes of baby cereal for the elder Monsieur Péricand. There was also the cat's basket. At first they had been delayed because their clean linen hadn't been delivered and the laundry couldn't be reached by telephone. Their large white embroidered sheets were part of the Péricand-Maltête inheritance, along with the jewellery, the silver and the library: it was impossible to leave them behind. The whole morning had been wasted looking for things. The launderer himself was leaving. He had ended up giving Madame Péricand her sheets in damp, crumpled bundles. She had gone without lunch in order to supervise personally the packing of the linen. It had been agreed that the servants, along with Hubert and Bernard, would get the train. But at all the train stations the gates were already closed and guarded by soldiers. The crowds were hanging on to them, shaking them, then swarming chaotically back down the neighbouring streets. Women in tears were running with their children in their arms. The last taxis were stopped: they were offered two thousand, three thousand francs to leave Paris. 'Just to Orléans . . .' But the drivers refused, they had no more petrol. The Péricands had to go back home. They finally managed to get hold of a van, which would take Madeleine, Maria, Auguste and Bernard, with his little brother on his lap. As for Hubert, he would follow the cars on his bicycle.

All along the Boulevard Delessert, groups of people appeared outside their houses – women, old people and children, gesticulating to each other, trying, at first calmly and then with increasing agitation and a mad, dizzy excitement, to get the family and all the baggage into a Renault, a saloon, a sports car . . . Not a single light shone through the windows. The stars were coming out, springtime stars with a silvery glow. Paris had its sweetest smell, the smell of chestnut trees in bloom and of petrol with a few grains of dust that crack under your teeth like pepper. In the darkness the danger seemed to grow. You could smell the suffering in the air, in the silence. Even people who were normally calm and controlled were overwhelmed by anxiety and fear. Everyone looked at their house and thought, 'Tomorrow it will be in ruins, tomorrow I'll have nothing left. We haven't hurt anyone. Why?' Then a wave of indifference washed over their souls: 'What's the difference! It's only stone, wood – nothing living! What matters is survival!' Who cared about the tragedy of their country? Not these people, not the people who were leaving that night. Panic obliterated everything that wasn't animal instinct, involuntary physical reaction. Grab the most valuable things you own in the world and then . . . ! And, on that night, only people – the living and the breathing, the crying and the loving – were precious. Rare was the person who cared about their possessions; everyone wrapped their arms tightly round their wife or child and nothing else mattered; the rest could go up in flames.

If you listened closely, you could hear the sound of planes in the sky. French or enemy? No one knew. 'Faster, faster,' said Monsieur Péricand. But then they would realise they'd forgotten the box of lace, or the ironing board. It was impossible to make the servants listen to reason. They were trembling with fear. Even though they wanted to leave too, their need to follow a routine was stronger than their terror; and they insisted on doing everything exactly as they had always done when getting ready to go to the countryside for the summer holidays. The trunks had to be packed in the usual way, with everything in its correct place. They hadn't understood the reality of the situation. They were living two different moments, you might say, half in the present and half deep in the past, as if what was happening could only seep into a small part of their consciousnesses, the most superficial part, leaving all the deeper regions peacefully asleep. Nanny, her grey hair undone, her lips clenched, her eyelids swollen from crying, was folding Jacqueline's freshly ironed handkerchiefs with amazingly firm, precise movements. Madame Péricand, already in the car, called her, but the old woman didn't reply, didn't even hear her.

Finally, Philippe had to go upstairs to look for her. 'Come along, Nanny, what's the matter? We have to leave. What's the matter?' he repeated gently, taking her hand.

'Oh, leave me be, my little one,' she groaned, forgetting suddenly that she now only called him 'Monsieur Philippe' or 'Father', and instinctively returning to the past. 'Go on, leave me be. You're kind but we're lost!'

'Come now, don't get so upset, you poor thing, leave the handkerchiefs, get dressed and come downstairs quickly. Mother is waiting for you.'

'I'll never see my boys again, Philippe!'

'But you will, you will,' he said, then he himself tidied up the old woman's hair and put a black straw hat on her head.

'You'll pray to the Holy Virgin for my boys, won't you?'

He kissed her gently on the cheek. 'Yes, yes, I promise. Come along now.'

The driver and the concierge passed them on the staircase as they went up to collect the elder Monsieur Péricand. He had been kept away from all the commotion until the very last minute. Auguste and the male nurse were just finishing dressing him. The old man had had an operation a short while ago. He was wearing a complicated bandage and, given the cold night air, a flannel girdle so big and so wide that his body was swaddled like a mummy. Auguste buttoned his old-fashioned boots and pulled a light but warm jumper over his head. As he put on his jacket, Monsieur Péricand, who until now had wordlessly let himself be manipulated like an old, stiff doll, seemed to wake up from a dream and mumbled, 'Wool waistcoat . . .'

'You will be too warm, Sir,' Auguste remarked, trying to pay no attention.

But his master stared at him with his pale, glazed eyes and repeated more loudly, 'Wool waistcoat!'

He was given it. They put on his long overcoat, the scarf that went twice round his neck and fastened at the back with a safety pin. Then they sat him in his wheelchair and took him down the five flights of stairs. The wheelchair wouldn't fit in the lift. The nurse, a strong, red-headed man from Alsace, went down the stairs backwards and took the brunt of the weight while Auguste respectfully supported from behind. The two men stopped on each landing to wipe away the sweat running down their faces, while Monsieur Péricand calmly contemplated the ceiling and quietly nodded his beautiful beard. It was impossible to imagine what he thought of this hasty departure. However, contrary to what they might have believed, he was fully informed about recent events. He had murmured while being dressed, 'A beautiful, clear night . . . I wouldn't be surprised if . . .'

He seemed to have fallen asleep and only finished his sentence a few seconds later, at the doorstep: 'I wouldn't be surprised if we were bombed on the way!'

'What an idea, Monsieur Péricand!' the nurse exclaimed with all the optimism befitting his profession.

But already the old man had resumed his look of profound indifference. They finally got the wheelchair out of the house. The elder Monsieur Péricand settled in the right-hand corner of the car, well sheltered from any draughts. His daughter-in-law, hands trembling with impatience, wrapped him up in the Scottish shawl whose long fringes he liked to twist.

'Is everything ready?' Philippe asked. 'Good, get going.'

'If they make it out of Paris before tomorrow morning, they'll have a chance,' he thought.

'My gloves,' said the old man.

They gave him his gloves. It was difficult getting them to fit over his wrists, made thicker by the layers of wool. The elder Monsieur Péricand refused to leave a single button undone. Finally everything was ready. Emmanuel was wailing in his nanny's arms. Madame Péricand kissed her husband and her son. She didn't cry, but as she held them tight they could feel her heart beating fast against their chests. The driver started the car. Hubert got on his bicycle.

The elder Monsieur Péricand lifted up his hand. 'Just a minute,' he said in a calm, quiet voice.

'What is it, Father?'

But he made a sign that he couldn't tell his daughter-in-law.

'Did you forget something?'

He nodded his head. The car stopped. Madame Péricand, white with frustration, leaned out of the window. 'I think Papa has forgotten something?' she shouted in the direction of the small group left on the pavement, made up of her husband, Philippe and the nurse.

When the car had reversed back and stopped in front of the house, the old man, with a small discreet gesture, called over the nurse and whispered something in his ear.

'What is going on? This is madness! We'll still be here tomorrow,' exclaimed Madame Péricand. 'What do you need, Father? What does he want?' she asked.

The nurse lowered his eyes. 'Monsieur wants us to take him back upstairs . . . to do pee-pee . . .'

Charles Langelet was kneeling on the parquet floor of his empty drawing room, wrapping up his porcelain himself. He was fat and had a heart condition; the sigh he let out from his heavy chest sounded like a groan. He was alone in the apartment. The servants, who had been with him for seven years, had panicked when, with the rest of Paris, they had woken to a thick man-made fog raining down on them like a shower of ashes. They had left early to get provisions, but had never come back. Monsieur Langelet thought bitterly of the generous wages and all the presents he had given them since they had come into his service, money which had allowed them to buy, no doubt, some peaceful cottage, some secluded little farm in their native towns.

Monsieur Langelet should have left long ago. He admitted that now, but he had been unable to deviate from his normal routine. Frosty, scornful, the only things he loved in this world were his apartment and the objects scattered around him on the floor: the rugs had been rolled up with mothballs and hidden in the cellar. All the windows were decorated with long strips of pink and baby-blue adhesive tape. Monsieur Langelet himself, with his pale, fat hands, had arranged them in the shape of stars, ships and unicorns. They were the envy of his friends, but how could he possibly have lived with a drab, common decor? All around him, in his house, everything consisted of fragments of beauty. Sometimes modest, sometimes valuable, these fragments combined to form a unique atmosphere of soft luminosity – the only one worthy of a cultured man, he thought. When he was twenty he had worn a ring with an inscription inside: *This thing of Beauty is a guilt for ever* (Monsieur Langelet happily spoke English to himself: the language, with its poetry, its force, suited certain of his moods). It was childish and he had got rid of this trinket, but the maxim remained with him and he remained faithful to it.

He pushed himself up on to one knee and looked around with a piercing, hopeless expression that took in many things: the Seine beneath his windows, the graceful curve of the wall between his two reception rooms, the fireplace with its antique andirons and the high ceilings where light floated, a clear light coloured green and as transparent as water because it was filtered through almond-coloured canvas blinds on the balcony.

Now and again the telephone would ring. There were still indecisive people in Paris, idiots who were afraid to leave, hoping for some kind of miracle. Slowly, with a sigh, Monsieur Langelet picked up the receiver. He spoke in a calm, nasal voice, with a detachment, an irony, that his friends – a small, very exclusive, very Parisian group – called 'inimitable'. Yes, he had decided to leave. No, he was not afraid of anything. They would not defend Paris. Things would hardly be different anywhere else. Danger was everywhere but it was not danger he was fleeing. 'I have seen two wars,' he said. He had in fact spent the war of '14 at his property in Normandy, exempt from military service because of his heart condition.

'My dear friend, I am sixty years old, it is not death I fear!'

'Why are you leaving, then?'

'I cannot bear this chaos, these outbursts of hatred, the repulsive spectacle of war. I shall withdraw to a tranquil spot, in the countryside, and live on the bit of money I have left until everyone comes to their senses.'

He heard a little snigger: he had the reputation of being miserly and cautious. 'Charlie?' people said about him, 'He sews gold coins into all his old clothes.' He smiled, an icy, bitter smile. 'He knew very well that people envied his luxurious, comfortable life.

'Oh, you'll be fine!' his friend exclaimed. 'But not everyone has your money, unfortunately . . .'

Charlie frowned: he found her lacking in tact.

'Where will you go?' the voice continued.

'To a little house I own in Ciboure.'

'Near the border?' asked his friend, who was clearly losing her composure.

They parted coldly. Charlie again knelt down next to the half-full packing case and caressed, through the straw and tissue paper, his Nankin Cups, his Wedgwood centrepiece, his Sèvres vases. As long as he lived he would never part with them, never. But his heart was aching; he would not be able to take the dressing table in his bedroom, made of Dresden china, a museum piece, with its trumeau mirror decorated with roses. That would be left to the wolves. He remained still for a moment, squatting down on the floor, his monocle hanging almost to the ground by its black cord. He was tall and strong; on the delicate skin of his head, his fair hair was arranged with infinite care. Usually his face had the smooth, defiant look of an old cat purring by a warm stove, but he was so tired from the previous day that it couldn't but show and his weak jaw suddenly drooped like a corpse. What had she said, that stuck-up madam on the telephone? She had insinuated that he wanted to flee France! What an imbecile! Did she think she would upset him, make him ashamed? Of course he would leave. If he could just get to Hendaye, he could make arrangements to cross the border. He would stay briefly in Lisbon and then get out of this hideous Europe, dripping with blood. He could picture it: a decomposing corpse, slashed with a thousand wounds. He shuddered. He wasn't cut out for this. He wasn't made for the world that would be born of this rotting cadaver, like a worm emerging from a grave. A brutal, ferocious, dog-eat-dog world. He looked at his beautiful hands, which had never done a day's work, had only ever caressed statues, pieces of antique silver, leather books, or occasionally a piece of Elizabethan furniture. What would he, Charles Langelet, with his sophistication, his scruples, his nobility – which was the essence of his character – what would he do amid this demented mob? He would be robbed, skinned, murdered like a pitiable dog thrown to the wolves. He smiled slightly, bitterly, imagining himself as a golden-haired Pekinese lost in a jungle. He wasn't like ordinary men. Their ambitions, their fears, their cowardice and their complaints were foreign to him. He lived in a universe of light and peace. He was destined to be hated and betrayed by everyone. He then remembered his servants and snorted. It was the dawn of a new age, a warning and an omen! With difficulty, for the joints in his knees were painful, he stood up, rubbed the small of his back with his hands and went to his office to get the hammer and nails to close up the packing case. He took it down to the car himself: there was no need for the concierge to know what he was carrying.

8

The Michauds got up at five o'clock in the morning to have enough time to clean their apartment thoroughly before leaving. It was of course strange to take so much care over things with so little value and destined, in all probability, to be destroyed when the first bombs fell on Paris. All the same, thought Madame Michaud, you dress and adorn the dead who are destined to rot in the earth. It's a final homage, a supreme proof of love to those we hold dear. And this little apartment was very dear to them. They'd lived here for sixteen years. No matter how hard they tried, they could never take all their memories with them: the best memories would remain here, between these thin walls. They put their books away at the bottom of a cupboard along with the sentimental family photographs, the kind you always promise to put into albums but which are left in a mess, faded, caught in the groove of a drawer. The picture of Jean-Marie as a child had already been slipped deep inside the suitcase, in the folds of a spare dress. The bank had firmly instructed they take only what was strictly necessary: a bit of clothing and some toiletries. Everything was finally ready. They'd eaten. Madame Michaud covered the bed with a big sheet to protect its slightly faded pink silk upholstery from the dust.

'It's time to go,' her husband said.

'Go ahead, I'll catch up with you,' she said, her voice faltering.

He went out, leaving her alone. She went into Jean-Marie's room. Everything was silent, dark, funereal behind the closed shutters. She knelt for a moment beside his bed, said out loud 'Dear God, protect him', then closed the door and went down.

Her husband was waiting for her on the stairs. He drew her close, and then, without saying a word, hugged her so tightly that she let out a little cry of pain: 'Maurice, you're hurting me!'

'Sorry,' he murmured, his voice husky.

At the bank, the employees assembled in the large entrance hall, each one with a little bag on his knees, whispering the latest news to each other. Corbin wasn't there. The manager was giving out numbers: they had to get into the car assigned to them when their number was called. Until noon, departures were carried out in an orderly fashion and in almost total silence. Then Corbin came in, impatient and sullen. He went down to the basement, into the room where the safes were kept, and came back up with a package which he held half hidden beneath his coat.

'That's Arlette's jewellery,' Madame Michaud whispered to her husband. 'He took out his wife's two days ago.'

'As long as he doesn't forget us.' Maurice gave a sigh that was both ironic and anxious.

Madame Michaud deliberately stood in Corbin's way. 'You're still planning to take us with you, aren't you, Monsieur?'

He nodded yes and asked them to follow him. Monsieur Michaud grabbed their suitcase and the three of them went outside. Monsieur Corbin's car was waiting, but as they got closer, Michaud narrowed his short-sighted eyes. 'I see our seats have been taken,' he said quietly.

Arlette Corail, her dog and her luggage were piled up in the back of the car. Furiously, she opened the door and shouted, 'Are you going to throw me out on to the street, then?'

The couple started bickering. The Michauds moved back a few steps, but could still hear every word.

'But we're supposed to meet my wife in Tours,' Corbin finally shouted, kicking the dog.

It gave a little yelp and hid under Arlette's legs.

'You brute!'

'Oh, do shut up, will you! If you hadn't been gadding about the day before yesterday with those English pilots . . . two more I'd like to see at the bottom of the ocean . . .'

'You brute! Brute!' she repeated over and over again, her voice growing shriller and shriller. Then suddenly, with the utmost calm, she said, 'I have a friend in Tours. I won't need you once we get there.'

Corbin gave her a savage look but seemed to have made up his mind. He turned towards the Michauds. 'I'm sorry, there isn't enough room for you, as you can see. Madame Corail's car was in an accident and she has asked me to take her with me to Tours. I cannot refuse. There's a train in an hour. It will probably be a bit of a crush but it's a very short journey

. . . Whatever happens, make sure you manage to join us as soon as possible. I am counting on you, Madame Michaud. You are more energetic than your husband and, speaking of which, Michaud, you must really try to be more dynamic' – he stressed the syllables 'dy-nam-ic' – 'than recently. I will no longer tolerate your attitude. If you want to keep your job, take this as a warning. Both of you must be in Tours the day after tomorrow at the latest. I must have all my staff.'

He waved them away, got into the car next to the dancer and drove off. The Michauds were left standing on the pavement, looking at each other.

'Well, that's the way to do it,' Michaud said, lightly shrugging his shoulders, his voice nonchalant. 'Give the people you should be apologising to a good telling off, that's it!'

In spite of themselves, they started to laugh.

'What are we going to do now?'

'We're going to go home and have lunch,' his wife said, furious.

It was cool back in their apartment, the kitchen without many provisions, the furniture covered up. Everything seemed secretive, friendly and sweet, as if a voice had whispered from the shadows, 'We were expecting you. Everything is as it should be.'

'Let's stay in Paris,' Maurice suggested.

They were side by side on the sitting-room sofa and, with a familiar gesture, she stroked his forehead with her thin, delicate fingers. 'My poor darling, that's not possible. We have to live and we haven't any savings left since my operation, as you know only too well. I only have 175 francs in my account. Don't you think Corbin would jump at the chance to get rid of us? After a blow like this, all the branches are going to reduce their staff. We must get to Tours at all costs!'

'I think that will be impossible.'

'We have to,' she repeated.

She was already standing up, putting her hat back on, picking up the suitcase again. They left and headed for the train station.

They would never manage to get inside the large departure area; it was closed, locked, blocked off by soldiers and by the jostling crowd crushed against the barriers. They stayed until evening, struggling in vain. All around them people were saying, 'Too bad. We'll have to walk.'

Everyone spoke with a kind of devastated astonishment. They clearly didn't believe what they were saying. They looked around and expected some miracle: a car, a truck, anything that would take them. But nothing came. So they headed out of Paris on foot, past the city gates, dragging their bags behind them in the dust, then on into the suburbs, into the countryside, all the while thinking, 'This can't be happening! I must be dreaming!'

Like all the others, the Michauds started walking. It was a warm June evening. In front of them a woman in mourning, wearing a black crêpe hat askew over her white hair, stumbled on the stones in the road and, gesturing like a madwoman, muttered, 'Pray and give thanks that we're not fleeing in winter . . . Pray . . . Just pray!'

9

Gabriel Corte and Florence spent the night of 11 June in their car. They had arrived in the town at about six o'clock in the evening and the only accommodation left was two hot little rooms right under the roof of the hotel. Gabriel strode angrily through the rooms, pushed open the windows, leaned out for a moment over the bright safety rail, then pulled his head back in, saying in a curt voice, 'I am not staying here.'

'We have nothing else, Monsieur, I'm very sorry,' said the manager, his face pale and exhausted. 'Just think, with all these crowds of refugees, people are even sleeping on the billiard table. I was trying to do you a favour!'

'I am not staying here,' Gabriel repeated, stressing each word as he did at the end of discussions with editors when he shouted at them from the doorstep: 'Under these circumstances, it will be impossible for us to reach an agreement, Monsieur!' The editor would then weaken and increase his offer from 80,000 to 100,000 francs.

But the manager just shook his head sadly. 'There's nothing else, nothing at all.'

'Do you know who I am?' Gabriel asked, dangerously calm all of a sudden. 'I am Gabriel Corte and I'm telling you that I would rather sleep in my car than in this rat hole.'

'When you leave, Monsieur Corte,' replied the offended manager, 'you'll find ten families on the landing, begging on their knees for me to rent them these rooms.'

Corte let out a loud laugh, overdramatic, icy and scornful. '*I* certainly won't be fighting for them. Adieu, Monsieur.'

To no one, not even to Florence who was waiting downstairs in the lobby, would he ever admit the real reason he had turned down the rooms. In the fading light of the June evening, he had seen a petrol depot from the window; it was close to the hotel and, a little further away, what looked like tanks and armoured cars were parked in the town square.

'We'll be bombed!' he thought, and he started trembling all over, so suddenly, so profoundly that he felt ill. Was it fear? Gabriel Corte? No, he couldn't be afraid! Don't be ridiculous! He smiled with pity and scorn, as if replying to some invisible person. Of course he wasn't afraid, but as he leaned out of the window once more, he looked up at the dark sky: at any moment it could rain fire and death upon him, and that horrible feeling shot through him again, first the trembling right down to his bones, then the kind of weakness, nausea and tensing in the stomach you feel before you faint. He didn't care whether he was afraid or not! He rushed outside, Florence and the maid following behind.

'We'll sleep in the car,' he said, 'it's just one night.'

Later on, it occurred to him that he could have tried another hotel, but by the time he'd made up his mind, it was too late. An endless, slow-moving river flowed from Paris: cars, trucks, carts, bicycles, along with the horse-drawn traps of farmers who had abandoned their land to flee south, their children and cattle trailing behind. By midnight there wasn't a single free room in all of Orléans, not a single bed. People were sleeping on the floor in cafés, in the streets, in the railway stations, their heads resting on suitcases. There was so much traffic that it was impossible to get out of the city. People were saying that a roadblock had been set up to keep the road free for the troops.

Silently, with no lights on, cars kept coming, one after the other, full to bursting with baggage and furniture, prams and birdcages, packing cases and baskets of clothes, each with a mattress tied firmly to the roof. They looked like mountains of fragile scaffolding and they seemed to move without the aid of a motor, propelled by their own weight down the sloping streets to the town square. Cars filled all the roads into the square. People were jammed together like fish caught in a net, and one good tug on that net would have picked them all up and thrown them down on to some terrifying river bank. There was no crying or shouting; even the children were quiet. Everything seemed calm. From time to time a face would appear over a lowered window and stare up at the sky for a while, wondering. A low, muffled murmur rose up from the crowd, the sound of painful breathing, sighs and conversations held in hushed voices, as if people were afraid of being overheard by an enemy lying in wait. Some tried to sleep, heads leaning on the corner of a suitcase, legs aching on a narrow bench or a warm cheek pressed against a window. Young men and women called to each other from the cars and sometimes laughed. Then a dark shape would glide across the star-covered sky, everyone would look up and the laughter would stop. It wasn't exactly what you'd call fear, rather a strange sadness – a sadness that had nothing human about it any more, for it lacked both courage and hope. This was how animals waited to die. It was the way fish caught in a net watch the shadow of the fisherman moving back and forth above them.

The plane above their heads had appeared suddenly; they could hear its thin, piercing sound fading away, disappearing, then surging up again to drown out the thousand sounds of the city. Everyone held their breath. The river, the metal bridge, the railway tracks, the train station, the factory's chimneys all glimmered; they were nothing more than 'strategic positions', targets for the enemy to hit. Everything seemed dangerous to this silent crowd. 'I think it's a French plane!' said the optimists. French or enemy, no one really knew. But it was disappearing now. Sometimes they could hear a distant explosion. 'It didn't hit us,' they would think, sighing with happiness. 'It didn't hit us, it's aimed at someone else. We're so lucky!'

'What a night! What a terrible night!' Florence groaned.

In a barely audible voice, which slipped through his clenched lips with a kind of whistle, Gabriel hissed at her as you would to a dog, '*I'm* not asleep, am I? Do what I'm doing.'

'For heaven's sake, we could have had a room! We had the unbelievable luck to find a room!'

'You call that unbelievable luck? That disgusting attic, which reeked of lice and bad drains. Didn't you notice it was right above the kitchen? *Me*, stay there? Can you picture me in there?'

'Oh, for heaven's sake, Gabriel, don't be so proud.'

'Leave me alone, won't you! I have always felt it, there are nuances, there is a . . .' he was looking for the right word '. . . a sense of decency which you simply cannot feel.'

'What I can feel is my painful arse,' shouted Florence, suddenly forgetting the past five years of her life and slapping her ring-covered hand vigorously against her thigh in the most crass way. 'Oh, for goodness sake, I've had enough!'

Gabriel turned towards her, his face white with fury, nostrils flaring. 'Get the hell out! Go on, get the hell out! I'm throwing you out!'

At that very moment a bright light lit up the town square. It was a missile shot from a plane. The words froze on Gabriel's lips. The missile disappeared but the sky was filled with planes. They flew back and forth above the town square in a manner that seemed almost lazy.

'What about *our* planes, where are ours?' people groaned.

To Corte's left was a miserable little car carrying a mattress on its roof, along with a heavy round gueridon table with vulgar bronze mounts. A man in a peaked cap and two women were sitting inside; one woman had a child on her lap and the other a birdcage. It looked as if they had been in an accident on the way. The car's bodywork was scratched, the bumper hanging off and the fat woman holding the birdcage against her chest had bandages wrapped round her head.

On his right was a truck full of the kind of crates villagers use to transport poultry on Fair days but which now were full of bundles of old clothes. Through the car window right next to his, Gabriel could see the face of an old prostitute with painted eyes, messy orange hair, a low angular forehead. She stared at him long and hard while chewing on a bit of bread. He shuddered. 'Such ugliness,' he murmured, 'such hideous faces!' Overcome, he turned round to face inside the car and closed his eyes.

'I'm hungry,' Florence said. 'Are you?'

He gestured no.

She opened the overnight case and took out some sandwiches. 'You didn't have dinner. Come on. Be sensible.'

'I cannot eat,' he said. 'I don't think I could swallow a single mouthful now. Did you see that horrible old woman beside us with her birdcage and bloodstained bandages?'

Florence took a sandwich and shared the others with the maid and driver. Gabriel covered his ears with his long hands so he couldn't hear the crunching noises the servants made as they bit into the bread.

10

The Péricands had been travelling for nearly a week and had been dogged by misfortune. They'd had to stay in Gien for two days when the car broke down. Further along, amid the confusion and unimaginable crush, the car had hit the truck carrying the servants and luggage. That was near Nevers. Fortunately for the Péricands, there was no part of the provinces where they couldn't find some friend or relative with a large house, beautiful gardens and a well-stocked larder. A cousin from the Maltête-Lyonnais side of the family put them up for two days. But panic was intensifying, spreading like wildfire from one city to another. They had the car repaired as best they could and set out once more, but by noon on Saturday it was clear the car could go no further without a thorough overhaul. The Péricands stopped in a small town just off the main highway where they hoped to find a room. But all sorts of vehicles were already blocking the streets. The sound of creaking brakes filled the air and the ground next to the river looked like a gypsy camp. Exhausted men were sleeping on the grass, others were getting dressed. A young woman had hung a mirror on a tree trunk and was putting on make-up and combing her hair. Someone else was washing nappies in the fountain.

The townspeople had come out on to their doorsteps and surveyed the scene with utter amazement. 'Those poor people! But honestly, they look so awful!' they said, with pity and a secret feeling of satisfaction: these refugees came from Paris, the north, the east, areas doomed to invasion and war. But *they* were all right, time would pass, soldiers would fight while the ironmonger on the main street and Mlle Dubois, the hatmaker, would continue to sell saucepans and ribbons; they would eat hot soup in their kitchens and every evening close the little wooden gates that separated their gardens from the rest of the world.

The cars were waiting for morning to fill up with petrol. It was already becoming scarce. The townspeople asked the refugees for news. No one knew anything. 'They're waiting for the Germans in the Morvan Mountains,' someone said. Such an idea was greeted with scepticism.

'Come on, they didn't get that far in '14,' said the fat chemist, shaking his head, and everyone agreed, as if the blood spilled in '14 had formed some mystical barrier to keep the enemy out for ever.

More cars arrived, and still more.

'They look so tired, so hot!' everyone kept saying, but not one of them thought to open their doors, to invite one of these wretches inside, to welcome them into the shady bits of heaven that the refugees could glimpse behind the houses, where wooden benches nestled in arbours amid redcurrant bushes and roses. There were just too many of them. Too many weary, pale faces, dripping with sweat, too many wailing children, too many trembling lips asking, 'Do you know where we could get a room? A bed?' . . . 'Would you tell us where we could find a restaurant, please, Madame?' It prevented the townspeople from being charitable. There was nothing human left in this miserable mob; they were like a herd of frightened animals. Their crumpled clothes, crazed faces, hoarse voices, everything about them made them look peculiarly alike, so you couldn't tell them apart. They all made the same gestures, said the same words. Getting out of the cars, they would stumble a bit as if drunk, putting their hands to their throbbing temples. 'My God, what a journey!' they sighed. 'Hey, don't we look gorgeous?' they asked with a giggle. 'They say things are a lot better over there,' they would say, pointing over their shoulders to somewhere lost in the distance.

Madame Péricand's convoy had stopped at a little café near the railway station. They got out their basket of food and ordered some beer. At the next table, a beautiful little boy, very elegantly dressed but whose green coat was all crumpled, was calmly eating some bread and butter. On a chair next to him was a clothes basket in which a baby lay crying. With her experienced eye, Madame Péricand could tell immediately that these children came from a good family and that it would be all right to speak to them. So she talked kindly to the little boy and made conversation with the mother when she came back; she was from Reims, and looked enviously at the substantial snack the Péricand children were eating.

'Can I have some chocolate with my bread, Mummy,' said the little boy in green.

'My poor darling!' said the young woman, putting the baby on her lap to try to calm him down, 'I don't have any. I didn't have time to buy some. You'll have a lovely dessert tonight at grandmother's.'

'Would you allow me to offer you some biscuits?'

'Oh, Madame! You are too kind!'

'Don't mention it . . .'

The two women conversed cheerfully and graciously, with the same gestures and smiles they used when being offered a *petit four* and a cup of tea on any ordinary day. Meanwhile, the baby was screaming; one after the other, refugees with their children, their baggage, their dogs poured into the café. One of the dogs smelled Albert in his basket and, barking excitedly, rushed under the Péricands' table where the little boy in green was calmly eating his biscuits.

'Jacqueline, you have some lollipops in your bag,' said Madame Péricand, with a discreet gesture and a look which meant 'You know very well you should share with those who are less fortunate than you. Now is the time to put into practice what you have learned at catechism.'

She got a feeling of great satisfaction from seeing herself as possessing such plenty and, at the same time, being so charitable. It was a credit to her foresight and kindness. She offered the lollipops not only to the little boy but to a Belgian family who had arrived in a truck jammed with hen-coops. She threw in some *pains aux raisins* for the children. Then she had some hot water brought to prepare the elder Monsieur Péricand's herbal tea.

Hubert had gone to try to find some rooms. Madame Péricand went out of the café to ask directions to the church in the middle of the town. There, families were camping out on the pavement and on the church's large stone steps.

The brand-new church was white and still smelled of fresh paint. Inside, it embraced two different worlds: the normal world of daily routine and another existence, strange and feverish. In one corner, a nun was changing the flowers at the feet of the Virgin Mary. A sweet, calm smile on her face, she slowly removed the shrivelled stems and replaced them with big bouquets of fresh roses. You could hear her scissors clicking and her gentle footsteps on the flagstones. Then she put out the candles. An elderly priest walked towards the confessional. An old woman was sleeping on a chair, holding her rosary beads. Many candles were lit in front of the statue of Joan of Arc. Little flames danced in the strong sunlight, pale and clear against the dazzling whiteness of the walls. Between two windows the golden letters of the names of people who had died in 1914 shimmered on a marble tablet.

Meanwhile, an ever-increasing crowd rushed towards the church like a wave. Women, children, all came to thank God for having arrived safely or to pray for the journey ahead. Some were crying, others were wounded, their heads or arms wrapped in bandages. Their faces were mottled with red blotches, their clothes wrinkled, torn and filthy, as if they had slept in them for several nights. Some were sweating, large drops of sweat falling like tears through the grey dust on their cheeks. The women pushed their way inside, threw themselves into the church as into some inviolable sanctuary. Their agitation, their frenzy, was so great that they seemed incapable of staying still. They moved from one altar to another, knelt down, got up, bumped into chairs with a timid, terrified look like night owls in a room full of light. But little by little they calmed down, hid their faces in their hands and, exhausted and with no tears left, finally found peace in front of the large black crucifix.

After saying her prayers, Madame Péricand left the church. Once outside, she decided to restock her supply of biscuits, which had been greatly diminished by her lavish generosity. She went into a large grocer's store.

'We've got nothing left, Madame,' said the employee.

'What? No shortbread, no gingerbread, nothing?'

'Nothing at all, Madame. It's all gone.'

'Then let me have a pound of tea, Ceylon tea?'

'There's nothing, Madame.'

They pointed out some other food shops to Madame Péricand, but nowhere could she buy a thing. The refugees had cleaned out the town. Hubert met her near the café. He hadn't been able to find a room.

'There's nothing to eat, the shops are empty!' she exclaimed.

'Well,' said Hubert, '*I* found two shops full of goods.'

'Really? Where?'

Hubert burst out laughing. 'There was one that sold pianos and the other, things for funerals!'

'You're such a silly little boy,' said his mother.

'At the rate we're going,' Hubert remarked, 'I imagine pearl crowns will soon be in great demand. We could stock up on them, what do you think, Mother?'

Madame Péricand shrugged her shoulders. She could see Jacqueline and Bernard on the doorstep of the café. Their hands were full of chocolate and sweets that they were giving out to everyone around them. Madame Péricand leapt towards them.

'Get back inside! What are you doing out here? I forbid you to touch the food. Jacqueline, you will be punished. Bernard, your father will hear about this.' Grabbing the two stunned culprits firmly by the hand, she dragged them away. Christian charity, the compassion of centuries of civilisation, fell from her like useless ornaments, revealing her bare, arid soul. She and her children were alone in a hostile world. She needed to feed and protect them.

11

Maurice and Jeanne Michaud walked one behind the other on the wide
road lined with poplar trees. Around them, behind them, in front of them,
people were fleeing. Occasionally the road rose more steeply and they
could see clearly the chaotic multitude trudging through the dust, stretching
far into the distance. The luckiest ones had wheelbarrows, a pram, a cart
made of four planks of wood set on top of crudely fashioned wheels,
bowing down under the weight of bags, tattered clothes, sleeping children. These were the poor, the unlucky, the weak, the sort who don't
know how to manage, who are always pushed to the back; the frightened,
too, and the stingy, who had put off buying a ticket until the last minute
because of the price, the expenses involved and the dangers of the journey,
but who had suddenly been gripped by panic just like everyone else. None
of them knew why they were bothering to flee: all of France was burning,
there was danger everywhere. Whenever they sank to the ground, they
said they would never get up again, they would die right there, that if
they had to die it was better to die in peace. But they were the first to
stand up when a plane flew near. They were compassionate and kind,
offering that active and attentive sympathy that working people normally
reserve for their own families or the poor, and even then only at moments
of the most exceptional fear and misery. Nearly a dozen times, some of
these big, strong women had offered to help Jeanne Michaud to walk.
Jeanne herself held children by the hand while her husband carried bags
on his shoulders: sometimes a bundle of clothing, sometimes a basket with
a live rabbit and potatoes, the worldly possessions of a little old woman
who had left Nanterre on foot. In spite of the exhaustion, the hunger, the
fear, Maurice Michaud was not really unhappy. He had a unique way of
thinking: he didn't consider himself that important; in his own eyes, he
was not that rare and irreplaceable creature most people imagine when
they think about themselves. He felt pity towards his fellow sufferers, but

his pity was lucid and detached. After all, he thought, these great human migrations seemed to follow natural laws. Surely such occasional mass displacements were necessary to humans, just as the migration of livestock was to animals. He found this idea oddly comforting. The people around him believed that fate was tracking them down, them and their pitiable generation; but not Maurice: he knew there had been exoduses throughout history. How many people had died on this land (on land everywhere in the world), dripping with blood, fleeing the enemy, leaving cities in flames, clutching their children to their hearts: no one gave a thought to these countless dead, or pitied them. To their descendants they were no more important than chickens who'd had their throats slit. As he walked along, he imagined their plaintive ghosts rising up, leaning towards him, whispering in his ear, 'We've been through all this already, before you. Why should you be more fortunate than us?'

'There's never been anything as horrible as this!' a big woman next to him groaned.

'On the contrary, Madame, on the contrary,' he replied quietly.

They had been walking for three days when they saw the first regiments in full flight. Confidence was so ingrained in the heart of the French that when they saw these soldiers, the refugees thought a battle was about to begin, that the High Command had given orders for small groups to head for the Front by a circuitous route, that the armed forces were still intact. This hope kept them going. The soldiers wouldn't say much. Almost all of them were depressed and pensive. Some slept in the backs of trucks. Tanks plodded forward in the dust, camouflaged with thin branches. Between the leaves faded by the burning sun, you could see their pale faces, weary, angry and exhausted.

Madame Michaud kept thinking she saw her son among them. Not once did she see his regiment's number, but a kind of hallucination took hold of her. Every unfamiliar young face or voice caused her to tremble so fiercely that she had to stop dead in her tracks, clutching her heart and softly muttering, 'Oh, Maurice, isn't that . . .'

'What's wrong?'

'No, it's nothing . . .'

But he was no fool. He shook his head. 'You see your son everywhere, my poor Jeanne!'

All she did was sigh. 'He does look like him, doesn't he?'

After all, it could happen. He could have cheated death; he could suddenly appear at her side, her son, her Jean-Marie; he would call out to them joyfully, tenderly, in that sweet masculine voice she could still hear, 'But what are you two doing here?'

Oh, just to see him, to hold him close, to feel his cool rough cheek beneath her lips, to see his beautiful eyes shining close to hers, his deep expression, so alive. He had hazel eyes with long eyelashes like a woman, eyes that saw so many things! She had always taught him to see the funny and moving side of people. She liked to laugh and felt sympathy for others. 'It's your Dickensian spirit, Mother,' he would say. How well they knew each other! They would cheerfully, sometimes cruelly, make fun of people who had been unkind to them; then a word, a gesture, a sigh would make them stop. Maurice was different: he was more serene, cooler. She loved and respected Maurice, but Jean-Marie was . . . Oh, my God, he was everything she wanted to be and everything she dreamed of and everything that was the best of her: her joy, her hope . . . 'My son, my little love, my Jeannot,' she thought, calling him by the nickname he'd had when he was five, when she would take his head gently in her hands and kiss his ears, tilt his head back and tickle him with her lips while he laughed and laughed.

Her thoughts became more and more feverish and confused the longer she walked. She was a good walker: when she and Maurice were younger, they had often gone rambling in the countryside during their short holidays. When they didn't have enough money to stay in a hotel, they would set off like this with food and sleeping bags in their rucksacks. This was why she suffered less fatigue than her companions. But this incessant kaleidoscope, these strange faces passing endlessly before her, then fading and disappearing, was much more painful than physical exhaustion. 'A herd of horses,' she thought, 'trapped.' In the crowd, cars were tangled up like those reeds you see floating on the river, anchored by invisible knots while floodwater rushes all around them. Jeanne turned away so she couldn't see the cars. They poisoned the air with their petrol fumes, deafened the people on foot with their futile honking as they tried in vain to clear a way through. Seeing the impotent rage or the gloomy resignation on the drivers' faces was a comfort to the refugees. 'They're not going any faster than us!' they would say to one another, enjoying the feeling of shared misfortune.

The refugees were walking in small groups. Chance had thrown them together at the edge of Paris and now they stayed together, though they didn't even know each other's names. With the Michauds was a tall, thin woman, wearing a cheap, shabby coat and a great deal of costume jewellery. Jeanne vaguely wondered what would possess someone to flee wearing enormous earrings encrusted with fake pearls and diamonds, large red and green stones on her fingers and a paste brooch with small bits of topaz.

Then there was a concierge and her daughter, the mother small and pale, the child big and heavy. They were both dressed in black and dragged along amid their luggage a portrait of a large man with a long black moustache. 'My husband,' the woman said. 'He's the caretaker at the cemetery.' Her sister was with her, pregnant and pushing a sleeping child in a pram. She was very young. As each convoy of soldiers passed by, she too would tremble and search the crowd. 'My husband is out there somewhere,' she would say; out there somewhere, or perhaps out here . . . anything was possible.

And Jeanne would say, for the hundredth time no doubt – she really had no idea what she was saying any more – 'So is my son, so is my son . . .'

They hadn't yet been shelled. When it happened, they didn't know what was going on at first. They heard the sound of an explosion, then another, then shouting: 'Run for it! Get down! Get down on the ground!' They immediately threw themselves face down.

'How grotesque we must look!' Jeanne mused. She wasn't afraid, but she was short of breath and her heart was pounding so violently that she pressed both hands to it and pushed it down against a stone. She could feel a bell-shaped pink flower brushing her lips. Later, she would remember that while they were stretched out on the ground, a small white butterfly was lazily flitting from one flower to another.

Finally she heard a voice whisper, 'It's over; they're gone.' She stood up and automatically brushed the dust from her skirt. No one, she thought, had been hurt. But after walking for a few minutes, they saw the first fatalities: two men and a woman. Their bodies had been torn to shreds, but by chance their three faces were untouched. Such gloomy, ordinary faces, with a dim, fixed, stunned expression as if they were trying in vain to understand what was happening to them; they weren't made, my God, to die in battle, they weren't made for death. In all her life that woman had probably never said anything but ordinary things, like 'The leeks are getting bigger' or 'Who's the dirty pig who got my floor all muddy?'

But what do I know? Jeanne asked herself. Perhaps there was a wealth of intelligence and tenderness behind their low brows, beneath their dishevelled, lifeless hair. What are we in people's eyes, Maurice and I, other than two miserable employees? It's true in a way, but in another way, we are precious and unique. I know that too. 'What a horrible waste,' she thought again. She leaned against Maurice's shoulder, trembling, her cheeks wet with tears.

'Let's go,' he said, gently pulling her away.

Both of them were thinking the same thing: 'Why?' They would never make it to Tours. Did the bank even exist any more? Was Monsieur Corbin buried beneath the rubble with his files? With his valuables? With his dancer? And his wife's jewellery! But that would be too good to be true, Jeanne thought with sudden ferociousness. Nevertheless, she and Maurice hobbled along, continuing on their way. All they could do was to keep walking and place themselves in the hands of God.

12

The little group made up of the Michauds and their companions was picked up on Friday night. A military truck stopped for them and they travelled through the night, lying among the crates, until they arrived at a town whose name they never discovered. The railway line was intact, they were told. They could go direct to Tours. Jeanne went into the first house she saw on the outskirts of the town and asked permission to wash. The kitchen was already full of refugees rinsing their clothes in the sink, but they took Jeanne to the water pump in the garden. Maurice had brought a little mirror on a small chain; he hung it from the branch of a tree and shaved. Afterwards they felt better, ready to face the long wait by the door of the barracks where soup was being given out, and an even longer wait at the third-class ticket window at the train station. They had eaten and were crossing the square in front of the station when the bombs exploded. Enemy planes had been flying above the town for the past three days and air-raid warnings had been constant. The town had to make do with an old fire siren to sound the alarm; through the din of the cars, the screaming children, the noise of the terrified crowd, you could barely hear its faint, ridiculous sound. The people arriving off trains would ask, 'Is it an air raid?' and be told, 'No, it's over,' only for the faint bell to be heard again five minutes later. There was laughter. Shops were open, little girls played hopscotch on the pavement and dogs ran through the dust near the old cathedral. The Italian and German planes were ignored as they glided calmly overhead. People were used to them.

Suddenly, one broke loose and swooped down at the crowd. 'He's going to crash,' Jeanne thought, then, 'No, he's going to fire, he's firing, we're finished . . .' Instinctively, she covered her mouth to stifle a scream. The bombs had fallen on the train station and, a bit further along, on the railway tracks. The glass roof shattered and exploded outwards, wounding and killing the people in the square. Panic-stricken, some of the women threw down their babies as if they were cumbersome packages and ran. Others grabbed their children and held them so tightly they seemed to want to force them back into the womb, as if that were the only truly safe place. A wounded woman was writhing around at Jeanne's feet: it was the one with the costume jewellery. Her throat and fingers were sparkling and blood was pouring from her shattered skull. Her warm blood oozed on to Jeanne's dress, on to her shoes and stockings.

But Jeanne was saved from thinking about the dead by the wounded, who were calling for help from beneath the piles of shattered stone and broken glass. She joined Maurice and some other men who were trying to clear away the rubble. But it was too difficult for her. She couldn't do it. Then she remembered the children who were wandering piteously about the square, looking for their mothers. She called them over, took them by the hand and led them to the cathedral, where she assembled them in the front portico. Then she returned to the crowd. When she saw a frantic woman, screaming, running back and forth, she would call out in a calm, loud voice, so calm and loud that she herself was amazed, 'The children are by the church door. Go and get them, over there. Could everyone who has lost their children please go and get them at the church.'

The women rushed towards the cathedral. Sometimes they wept, sometimes they burst out laughing, sometimes they let out a sort of wild cry, a choking noise, like no other sound. The children were much calmer. Their tears dried quickly. Their mothers carried them away, holding them tightly. Not one of them thought to thank Jeanne. She went back into the square where she learned the town had not suffered much damage. A hospital convoy had been hit just as it was pulling into the station, but the line to Tours was still intact. The train was getting ready right now and would leave in a quarter of an hour. Immediately the dead and injured were forgotten; people rushed towards the station clutching their suitcases and hatboxes like life jackets. The Michauds spotted the first stretchers transporting the wounded soldiers. Because of the crush it was impossible to get close enough to see their faces. They were being piled into trucks and cars, both military and civilian, requisitioned in haste. Jeanne saw an officer going towards a truck full of children, supervised by a priest. She heard him say, 'I'm terribly sorry, Father, but I must take this truck. We have to get our wounded to Blois.'

The priest motioned to the children who started to climb out.

'I'm terribly sorry, Father,' the officer repeated. 'A school, is it?'

'An orphanage.'

'I'll send the truck back to you if I can get any petrol.'

The children – teenagers between fourteen and eighteen – each carrying a little suitcase, got out and formed a small group round the priest.

Maurice turned towards his wife. 'Are you coming?'

'Yes. Wait a minute.'

'What is it?'

She was trying to catch sight of the stretchers moving one after the other through the crowd. But there were too many people: she couldn't see anything.

Next to her another woman was also standing on tiptoe. Her lips were moving but she made no sound: she was praying or repeating someone's name. She looked at Jeanne. 'You always think you see yours, don't you?' she said.

Jeanne sighed faintly. There was no reason at all why it should be her son rather than another woman's who appeared, suddenly, there in front of her eyes, her son, her own, her beloved. Perhaps he was in some peaceful spot? The most terrible battles leave some places untouched, protected, despite being surrounded by fire.

'Do you know where that train was coming from?' she asked the woman next to her.

'No.'

'Are there many dead?'

'They say there are two carriages full of casualties.'

Jeanne gave in and let Maurice pull her away. With great difficulty they made their way to the railway station. In places, they had to step over stone slabs and piles of broken glass. They finally made it to platform 3, where the train for Tours was getting ready to depart, a small local train from the provinces, peaceful and black, puffing out its smoke.

13

It was two days since Jean-Marie had been wounded: he was in the train that was bombed. He wasn't hit, but the carriage caught fire. In his attempt to get out of his seat and make it to the door, his wound reopened. When he was picked up and hoisted into the truck, he was only semi-conscious. He lay motionless on his stretcher; his head had fallen side-ways so that, at each jolt, it banged hard against an empty crate. Three vehicles full of soldiers were moving slowly down a road that had been machine-gunned and was hardly passable. Above the convoy the enemy planes flew back and forth. Jean-Marie came out of his delirium for a moment and thought, 'This is how birds must feel when the hawks circle above them . . .'

In his confusion he could picture his nanny's farm, where he used to spend the Easter holidays as a child. The farmyard was bright with sun: the chickens pecked at grain and hopped friskily about in the ash pile; then his nanny's large bony hand would snatch one of them, tie its feet together and five minutes later . . . that stream of blood and that little gurgling sound. Grotesque. Death. 'And me too; I've been snatched and carried away,' he thought, '. . . snatched and carried away . . . and tomorrow, thin and naked, tossed into a grave, I'll be as ugly as that chicken . . .'

His forehead banged against the crate with such force that he let out a faint protest: he didn't have the strength to cry out any more, but it caught the attention of the soldier on the next stretcher, wounded in the leg, but not too badly. 'Hey, Michaud? What's wrong? Michaud, are you OK?'

'Give me something to drink and get my head in a better position and get this fly away from my eyes,' Jean-Marie wanted to say, but he only sighed. 'No.' And he closed his eyes.

'They're starting again,' groaned his friend.

At that very moment more bombs fell around the convoy. A small bridge was destroyed: the road to Blois was cut off; they would have to retreat, clear a passage through the crowd of refugees, or go through Vendôme, but they wouldn't make it there until nightfall.

Poor lads, thought the Major, looking at Michaud, the worst off. He gave him an injection. They started moving again. The two trucks carrying the minor casualties crawled towards Vendôme; the one carrying Jean-Marie took a path through the fields to shorten the journey by a few kilometres. The truck soon stopped, out of petrol. The Major went to see if he could find a house in which to lodge his men. They were away from the mass exodus here; the river of cars was moving along the road down below. From the top of the hill, in the periwinkle-blue twilight of this peaceful, tender June night, the Major could see a black swarm from which arose a troubling sound – distinct from the sound of car horns, cries and shouts – a muted, sinister murmur that pierced the soul.

The Major saw a row of farms. They were inhabited, but only by women and children. The men were at the front. It was into one of these farms that Jean-Marie was taken. The neighbouring houses took in the other soldiers. The Major found a woman's bicycle and said he was going to the nearest town to get help, petrol, trucks, whatever he could find . . . 'If he has to die,' he thought, as he said goodbye to Michaud who was still lying on the stretcher in the farm's large kitchen while the women prepared and warmed up a bed, 'if he can't go on, he's better off between two clean sheets than on the road . . .'

He cycled towards Vendôme. It took him the whole night and, when he was about to enter the town, he fell into the hands of the Germans who took him prisoner. However, realising that he wasn't coming back, the women had already rushed to the village to warn the doctor and nurses at the hospital. But the hospital was full of the victims of the last bombing, so the soldiers remained in the hamlet. The women complained: with the men gone, they had enough work to do in the fields and looking after the animals without having to take care of these wounded men who'd been dropped on them!

Jean-Marie, burning with fever, painfully opened his eyes and saw an old woman with a long, sallow nose at the foot of his bed, knitting and sighing as she watched him: 'If I could just be sure that my old man, wherever he is, the poor bloke, was being looked after like this one who means nothing to me . . .' Through his confused dream he could hear the clicking of the steel knitting needles. The ball of wool was bouncing on his blanket;

in his delirium he thought it had pointed ears and a tail, and he stretched out his hand to stroke it. Now and again the woman's adopted daughter would stand close to him; she was young, with a fresh, rosy face, slightly heavy features and lively brown eyes. One day she brought him a bunch of cherries and put them next to him on the pillow. He was not allowed to eat them, but he pressed them against his burning cheeks and felt content and almost happy.

14

Corte and Florence had left Orléans and were driving towards Bordeaux. Things were complicated, however, by the fact that they didn't know exactly where they were going. First they had headed towards Brittany, but then decided to go south, to the Midi. And now Gabriel was saying that he wanted to leave France altogether.

'We'll never get out alive,' said Florence.

What she resented, more than the weariness and fear, was her anger – a blind, maddening rage that rose up from inside to suffocate her. She felt that Gabriel had broken the tacit agreement that bound them together. After all, for a man and woman in their position, and at their age, love was a contract. She had given herself to him because she hoped he would take care of her – not just materially but emotionally. Until now she had been dutifully repaid: he had given her wealth and prestige. But suddenly he seemed to her a weak and despicable creature.

'And would you care to tell me just what we would do abroad? What we would live on? All your money is here, since you were foolish enough to have the whole lot sent back from London, not that I've ever understood why!'

'Because I thought England was more under threat than us. I had faith in my country, in my country's army. Surely you're not going to reproach me for that? Besides, what are you so worried about? You know I'm famous everywhere – thank God!'

He stopped speaking suddenly, pressed his face against the window and jerked his head back, annoyed.

'What is it now?' mumbled Florence, raising her eyes to heaven.

'Those people . . .' He pointed to the car that had just overtaken them. Florence looked at the people inside. It was the group they had spent the night parked next to in the town square in Orléans. She recognised them right away – the dented car, the man in the cap, the woman with the child on her lap and the one with the birdcage whose head was wrapped in bandages.

'Oh, stop looking at them!' said Florence wearily.

Corte had been leaning on a small travel case decorated in gold and ivory. Now he struck it forcefully with his hand several times. 'If events as painful as defeat and mass exodus cannot be dignified with some sort of nobility, some grandeur, then they shouldn't happen at all! I will not accept that these shopkeepers, these caretakers, these filthy people with their whining, their malicious gossip, their vulgarity, should be allowed to debase this atmosphere of tragedy. Just look at them! Look at them! There they are again. They're honking at me, for goodness sake! . . . Henri, drive faster, won't you!' he shouted to the driver. 'Can't you shake off this riff-raff?'

Henri didn't even reply. The car moved forward three metres, then stopped, caught up in the unimaginable confusion of vehicles, bicycles and pedestrians. Once again Gabriel saw the woman with the bandaged head only a short distance away. She had thick, dark eyebrows, long, white, closely set teeth and hairs dotted about her upper lip. Her bandages were bloodstained, her black hair matted on the cotton wool and cloth. Gabriel shuddered in disgust and turned away, but the woman was actually smiling at him and trying to make conversation.

'Hey! It's not moving very fast, is it?' she said politely through the lowered window. 'But it's still a good thing we came this way. You should see the damage the bombing's done on the other side! They've destroyed all the châteaux of the Loire, Monsieur . . .'

She finally noticed Gabriel's icy stare and went silent.

'You see,' he muttered to Florence, 'I can't get away from them!'

'Stop looking at them.'

'As if it's that easy! What a nightmare! Oh, the ugliness, the vulgarity, the horrible crudeness of these people!'

They were getting close to Tours. Gabriel had been yawning for some time: he was hungry. He'd hardly eaten anything since Orléans. Just like Byron, Corte used to say, he was a man of frugal habits, content with vegetables, fruit and mineral water; but once or twice a week he needed a large, filling meal. He felt that need now. He remained motionless, silent, eyes closed, his handsome pale face ravaged by an expression of suffering like at those moments when he conceived the first neat, pure sentences of his books (he liked them as light and rustling as cicadas at first, then passionate and sonorous; he talked about his 'violins' – 'Let's make my violins sing,' he would say). But other worries took hold of him tonight. He pictured with extraordinary intensity the sandwiches Florence had offered him in Orléans: they had seemed rather unappetising then, a bit soggy because of the heat. There had been some small sweet rolls with foie gras, black bread garnished with cucumber and lettuce, which would be deliciously cool and refreshing. He yawned again. Opening the case, he found a dirty napkin and a jar of gherkins.

'What are you looking for?' asked Florence.

'A sandwich.'

'There aren't any left.'

'What do you mean? There were three of them in here a while ago.'

'The mayonnaise was runny, they were ruined, I threw them away. We can have dinner in Tours . . . I hope,' she added.

They could see the outskirts of Tours in the distance but the cars weren't moving; a barricade had been set up at one of the crossroads. Everyone had to wait their turn. A whole hour went by like this. Gabriel was growing paler. It wasn't sandwiches he was dreaming of now, but light, warming soup, or the buttery pâtés he'd once had in Tours. (He had been coming back from Biarritz with a woman.) It was odd, he couldn't remember her name any more, or her face; the only thing that stuck in his memory were the smooth, rich little pâtés, each with a slice of truffle tucked away inside. Then he started thinking about meat: a great red slab of rare beef, with a curl of butter melting slowly over its tender flesh. What a delight . . . Yes, that was what he needed . . . roast beef . . . sirloin . . . fillet . . . a pork cutlet or mutton chop at a pinch. He sighed deeply.

It was a light, golden evening, with no trace of wind or heat – the end of a divine day. A soft shadow spread over the fields and pathways, like the shadow cast by the wing of a bird. From the nearby woods the faint perfume of strawberries wafted up now and then through the petrol fumes and smoke. The cars inched towards a bridge. Women were calmly washing their clothes in the river. The horror and strangeness of recent events were softened by these images of peace. Far away, a watermill turned its wheel.

'There must be fish here,' Gabriel mused. Two years before, in Austria, he had eaten fresh trout near a small river as clear and rapid as this one. Their flesh, beneath the bluish, pearly skin, had been as pink as a small child's. And those steamed potatoes . . . so simple, traditional, with a bit of fresh butter and chopped parsley . . . He looked hopefully at the walls of the town. Finally, finally, they were there. But as soon as he put his head out of the window he saw the long line of refugees waiting in the street. A soup kitchen was giving out food to the hungry, they were told, but there was nothing to eat anywhere else.

A well-dressed woman, holding a child by the hand, turned towards Gabriel and Florence. 'We've been here for four hours,' she said. 'My child won't stop screaming. It's awful . . .'

'Awful,' Florence repeated.

Behind them the woman with the bandaged head appeared. 'There's no point in waiting. They're closing. There's nothing left.' She made a small dismissive gesture with her hand. 'Nothing, nothing. Not even a crust of bread. My friend who's with me, who just gave birth three weeks ago, hasn't had anything to eat since yesterday and she's breastfeeding her kid. And they tell you to have children, dammit. Children, sure! Don't make me laugh!'

A murmur of despair ran through the long queue.

'Nothing, they have nothing left, nothing. They're saying "Come back tomorrow." They're saying the Germans are getting closer, that the regiment is leaving tonight.'

'Did you go into the town to see if there's anything there?'

'You must be joking! Everyone's leaving, it's like a ghost town. Some people are already hoarding, I'm sure.'

'Awful,' Florence groaned again.

In her distress she was talking to the occupants of the battered car. The woman with the child on her lap was as pale as death.

The other one shook her head gloomily. 'That's nothing. They're all rich, they are, it's the workers that suffer the most.'

'What are we going to do?' said Florence, turning towards Gabriel with a gesture of despair. He motioned to her to move away from the crowd and began striding along. The town was full of closed shutters and locked doors; there wasn't a single lamp shining or a soul to be seen at the windows. But, the moon had just risen and by its light it was easy to find one's way.

'You understand,' he whispered, 'it's farcical, all this . . . It is impossible not to find something to eat if we pay. Believe me, there's this panic-stricken herd and then there are the sly devils who have hidden food away in a safe place. We've just got to find them.' He stopped. 'We're in Paray-le-Monial, aren't we? See, here's what I've been looking for. I had dinner in this restaurant two years ago. The owner will remember me, you'll see.' He banged on the padlocked door and called out in a commanding voice, 'Open up, open up, my good man! It's a friend!'

And the miracle happened. They heard footsteps; a key turned in the lock, an anxious face appeared.

'Look here, you know who I am, don't you? I'm Corte, Gabriel Corte. I'm famished, my friend . . . Yes, yes, I know there's nothing, but for me . . . if you look carefully . . . Don't you have anything left? Ah! Yes! You remember me now!'

'I'm sorry, Sir, I can't let you in,' whispered the owner. 'I'd be mobbed! Go down to the corner and wait for me. I'll meet you there. I'd really like to help you, Monsieur Corte, but we're so low on provisions, so desperate. But maybe if I look carefully . . .'

'Yes, that's it, look carefully . . .'

'But you wouldn't tell anyone, would you? You can't imagine what's been going on here today. It's been madness, my wife is sick about it. They devour everything and leave without paying!'

'I'm counting on you, my friend,' said Gabriel, slipping some money into his hand.

Five minutes later he and Florence went back to the car, carrying a mysterious basket wrapped in a linen napkin.

'I have no idea what's inside,' muttered Gabriel in the same detached, dreamy tone he used when speaking to women, to women he desired but still hadn't conquered. 'No, no idea at all . . . but I think I can smell foie gras.'

Just at that moment a shadowy figure passed between Gabriel and Florence and grabbed the basket they were holding, separating them with a blow. Florence, panic-stricken, grasped her neck with both hands, shouting, 'My necklace, my necklace!' But her necklace was still there, as well as the jewellery box they were carrying. The thieves had only taken their food. She made her way back safe and sound to Gabriel, who was dabbing at his painful jaw and nose, and muttering over and over again, 'It's a jungle, we're trapped in a jungle . . .'

15

'You shouldn't have done it,' the woman holding the newborn baby in her arms sighed.

A bit of colour gradually returned to her cheeks. The old battered Citroën had managed quite well to manoeuvre its way out of the crowd and its occupants were resting on the mossy ground in a little wood. The moon, round and flawless, was gleaming, but even without the moon the vast fire burning in the distance would have lit up the landscape: groups of people were lying here and there, scattered beneath the pine trees; cars stood motionless; next to the young woman and the man in the cap lay the open basket of food, half empty, and the gold foil from an uncorked bottle of champagne.

'You shouldn't have, Jules. I don't like it, it's upsetting to have to do a thing like that.'

The man was small and scrawny, with a big forehead and enormous eyes, a weak mouth and a little weasely chin. 'What do you want?' he protested. You want us to starve to death?'

'Leave him alone, Aline, he's right, for goodness sake!' said the woman with the bandaged head. 'What do you want us to do? Those two, they don't deserve to live, they don't, I'm telling you!'

They stopped talking. She had been a servant until she'd married a worker from the Renault car factory. They'd managed to keep him in Paris during the first few months of the war, but he'd gone in February and now he was fighting God knows where. He'd already fought in the other war and he was the oldest of four children, but none of that had made any difference. Privileges, exemptions, connections, all that was for the middle classes. Deep in her heart were layer upon layer of hatred, over-lapping yet distinct: the countrywoman's hatred, who instinctively detests city people, the servant's hatred, weary and bitter at having lived in other people's houses, the worker's hatred. For the past few months she had replaced her husband at the factory. She couldn't get used to doing a man's work; it had strengthened her arms but hardened her soul.

'You really got them, Jules,' she said to her brother. 'I'm telling you, I didn't think you had it in you!'

'When I saw Aline about to faint, and those bastards with all their wine, foie gras and everything, I don't know what came over me.'

Aline, who seemed shyer and softer, ventured, 'We could have just asked them for some, don't you think, Hortense?'

'What, are you crazy?' her husband exclaimed. 'For goodness sake! No, you don't know their type. They'd rather see us die like dogs, worse! You're crazy . . .'

'I know those two, I do,' said Hortense. 'They're the worst, they are. I saw him once at that old bag the Countess Barral du Jeu's; he writes books and plays. A madman, according to the driver, and thick as two short planks.'

Hortense put away the rest of the food as she spoke. Her large red hands were extraordinarily nimble and agile. Then she picked up the baby and undressed him. 'Poor little thing, what a journey! Oh, he'll have learned about life early, he will. Maybe that's better. Sometimes I don't regret having had a hard life: knowing how to use your hands, there are some who can't even say that. You remember, Jules, when Ma died, I was just about thirteen. I went to the wash-house no matter what the weather, breaking the ice in winter and carrying bundles of laundry on my back . . . I used to cry into my raw hands. But then, that taught me to stand on my own two feet and not to be afraid.'

'You really can cope, for sure,' said Aline with admiration.

Once the baby was changed, washed and dried, Aline unbuttoned her blouse and held her little one to her breast; the others watched her, smiling.

'At least he'll have something to eat, poor little chap, won't he!'

The champagne was going to their heads; they felt vaguely, sweetly intoxicated. They watched the flames in the distance in a deep stupor. Now and again they would forget why they were in this strange place, why they had left their little flat near the Gare de Lyon, rushed along the roads, crossed the forest at Fontainebleau, robbed Corte. Everything was becoming dark and cloudy, as in a dream. They'd hung the cage from a low branch and now they fed the birds. Hortense had remembered to bring a packet of seeds for them when they left. She took a few pieces of sugar from her pocket and put them into a cup of boiling hot coffee: the thermos had survived the car accident. She drank it noisily, bringing her thick lips to the cup, one hand placed on her enormous bosom to protect it from coffee stains. Suddenly, a rumour spread from group to group: 'The Germans marched into Paris this morning.'

Hortense dropped her half-full cup; her round face had gone even redder. She bowed her head and began crying. 'Now that hurts . . . that hurts here,' she said, touching her heart.

A few hot tears ran down her face, the tears of a hard woman who seldom pities either herself or anyone else. A feeling of anger, sadness and shame swept through her, so violently that she felt a physical pain, piercing and sharp, near her heart. Finally she said, 'You know I love my husband . . . Poor Louis, it's just the two of us and he works, doesn't drink, doesn't fool around, you know, we love each other, he's all I've got, but even if they told me, "You'll never see him again, he's just died, but we won . . ." well, I'd rather have that, oh, I'm telling you, I'm not kidding, I'd rather have that!'

'I know,' said Aline, trying in vain to find better words, 'I know, it's upsetting.'

Jules said nothing, thinking of his partially paralysed arm, which had allowed him to escape military service and the war. 'I've been very lucky,' he said to himself, but at the same time there was something upsetting him, he didn't know what, maybe remorse. 'Well, that's the way it is, that's the way it is, nothing we can do about it,' he said gloomily.

They started talking about Corte again. They thought with pleasure of the excellent dinner they had eaten instead of him. All the same, they now judged him less harshly. Hortense, who at the Countess Barral du Jeu's house had seen writers, academics and even, one day, the Countess de Noailles, made them laugh till they cried with her stories about them.

'It's not that they're so bad,' said Aline, 'They just don't know about life.'

16

The Péricands couldn't get lodgings in the town but they did find a large room in a neighbouring village, in a house inhabited by two elderly spinsters which was opposite the church. The children were put to bed still in their clothes, utterly exhausted. Jacqueline asked in a tearful voice if she could have the cat's basket next to her. She was obsessed by the idea he might escape, that he would be lost, forgotten, and would die of hunger on the road. She put her hand through the basket's wicker bars, which made a kind of window for the cat allowing a glimpse of a blazing green eye and long whiskers bristling with anger. Only then did she calm down. Emmanuel was frightened by this strange, enormous room and the two old ladies running about like headless chickens. 'Have you ever seen anything like it?' they groaned. 'How could you not feel sorry for them . . . poor unfortunate dears . . . dear Jesus . . .' Bernard lay there watching them without batting an eye, a dazed, serious expression on his face as he sucked on a piece of sugar he'd kept hidden in his pocket for three days; the heat had melted it, so it was lumped together with a bit of lead from a pencil, a faded stamp and a piece of string. The other bed in the room was occupied by the elder Monsieur Péricand. Madame Péricand, Hubert and the servants would spend the night on chairs in the dining room.

Through the open windows you could see a little garden in the moonlight. A brilliant peaceful light glistened on the clusters of sweet-scented white lilacs and on the path's silvery stones where a cat stepped softly. The dining room was crowded with refugees and villagers listening to the radio together. The women were crying. The men, silent, lowered their heads. It wasn't exactly despair they were feeling; it was more like a refusal to understand, the stupor you feel when you're dreaming, when the veil of sleep is about to lift, when you can feel the dawn light, when your whole body reaches out towards it, when you think, 'It was just a nightmare, I'm going to wake up now.' They stood there, motionless, avoiding each other's eyes. When Hubert switched off the radio, the men left without saying a word. Only the group of women remained in the room. You could hear them sighing, lamenting the misfortunes of their country, which, for them, bore the features of cherished husbands and sons still at the front. Their pain was more physical than the men's, simpler as well and more open. They consoled themselves with recriminations: 'Well . . . I don't know why we bothered! . . . To end up here . . . It's shameful, it is . . . we've been betrayed, Madame, betrayed I say . . . we've been sold out and now it's the poor men who are suffering . . .'

Hubert listened to them, clenching his fists, rage in his heart. What was he doing here? Bunch of old chatterboxes, he thought. If only he were two years older! Suddenly his young and innocent mind – younger, until now, than his years – was overtaken by the passions and torment of a grown man: patriotic anguish, a burning feeling of shame, pain, anger and the desire to make a sacrifice. Finally, and for the first time in his life, he thought, he felt linked to a truly serious cause. It wasn't enough to cry or shout traitor, he was a man; he might not be legally old enough to fight but he knew he was stronger, more robust, more able, more cunning than these old men of thirty-five and forty who had been sent to war, and *he* was free. He wasn't held back by family ties, by love! 'Oh, I want to go,' he murmured, 'I want to go!'

He rushed towards his mother, grabbed her hand, took her aside. 'Mummy, let me have some food and my red jumper from your bag and . . . give me a kiss,' he said. 'I'm leaving.' He couldn't breathe. Tears were streaming down his face.

His mother looked at him and understood. 'Come on now, darling, you're mad . . .'

'Mother, I'm leaving. I can't stay here . . . I'll die, I'll kill myself if I have to stay here and be useless, twiddling my thumbs while . . . and don't you realise the Germans will come and force all the boys to fight, make them fight for them. I couldn't! Let me go.'

He had gradually raised his voice and was shouting now; he couldn't control himself. He was surrounded by a circle of trembling, terrified old women: another young boy, scarcely older than him, the nephew of the two spinsters, rosy and fair, with curly hair and big innocent blue eyes, had joined him and repeated in a slight southern accent (his parents were civil servants – he'd been born in Tarascon), 'Of course we have to go, and tonight! Look, not very far from here, in the Sainte woods, there are troops . . . all we have to do is get on our bikes and join them . . .'

'René,' moaned his aunts, holding on to him, 'René, my darling, think of your mother!'

'Let go of me, Auntie, this is not a matter for women,' he replied, pushing them away, and his lovely face flushed with pleasure: he was proud of what he'd said.

He looked at Hubert, who had dried his tears and was standing next to the window, serious and determined. He went up to him and whispered in his ear, 'Are we going, then?'

'Yes, we're going,' Hubert whispered back. He thought for a minute and added, 'Meet on the road leading out of the village, at midnight.'

They shook hands in secret. Around them the women were all talking at once, begging them to give up their plan, to take pity on their parents, to hold on to their lives, such precious lives, to think of the future. At that moment they heard Jacqueline's piercing screams from upstairs. 'Mummy, Mummy, come quickly! Albert's run away!'

'Albert, is that your other son? Oh, my God!' exclaimed the spinsters.

'No, no, Albert's the cat,' said Madame Péricand who thought she was going mad.

Meanwhile, the sound of deep muffled explosions reverberated through the air: guns were firing in the distance, they were surrounded by danger. Madame Péricand collapsed into a chair. 'Hubert, just listen to me! In the absence of your father I am in charge. You are a child, barely seventeen, your duty is to save yourself for the future . . .'

'For the next war?'

'For the next war,' Madame Péricand repeated automatically. 'In the meantime, you must simply be quiet and do as I say. You are not going anywhere! If you had any feelings at all such a cruel, stupid idea would not even have crossed your mind! Don't you think I'm miserable enough? Don't you realise we've lost? That the Germans are coming and you'd be killed or taken prisoner before going a hundred metres? No! Not a word! I'm not even going to discuss it; you'll leave here over my dead body!'

'Mummy, Mummy,' Jacqueline kept shouting. 'I want Albert! Find Albert for me! The Germans will take him! He'll be bombed, stolen, killed! Albert! Albert! Albert!'

'Jacqueline, be quiet, you'll wake up your brothers!'

Everyone was shouting at once. Hubert, lips trembling, broke away from the frenzied group of gesticulating old women. Did they understand nothing at all? Life was like Shakespeare, noble and tragic, and they wanted to debase it. The world was crumbling, was nothing more than rubble and ruins, yet they remained the same. Women were inferior creatures; they didn't know the meaning of heroism, glory, faith, the spirit of sacrifice. All they did was to bring everything they touched down to their level. God! Just to see a man, to shake the hand of a man! Even father, he thought, but most of all his beloved brother, the good, the great Philippe. He longed for his brother so much that, once again, tears came to his eyes. The incessant noise of gunfire filled him with anxiety and excitement; he started trembling all over, shaking his head from side to side like a frightened horse. But he wasn't afraid. Not at all! He wasn't afraid! He welcomed, he embraced, the idea of death. It would be a beautiful death for this lost cause. It would be better than crouching in trenches as they did in '14. Now they fought in the open air, beneath the beautiful June sun or in the brilliant moonlight.

His mother had gone upstairs to Jacqueline, but she'd taken precautions: when he tried to get into the garden he found the door locked. He banged on it, shook it.

'Leave the door alone, Monsieur!' protested the two old ladies who were already in bed. 'It's late. We're tired, we want to go to sleep. Let us sleep.'

'Go to bed, my little one,' one of them said.

Angrily he shrugged his shoulders. '*My little one* . . . old hag!'

His mother came back downstairs. 'Jacqueline was hysterical,' she said. 'Fortunately I had a flask of orange flower water in my bag. Don't bite your nails. Hubert, you're getting on my nerves. Come on, settle down in this armchair and go to sleep.'

'I'm not tired.'

'I don't care, go to sleep,' she said in a strict, impatient tone of voice, as if she were talking to Emmanuel.

His soul full of indignation, he flung himself into an old cretonne armchair, which creaked under his weight.

Madame Péricand raised her eyes to heaven. 'You are so clumsy, darling. You'll break the seat. Do stay still.'

'Yes, Mother,' he said submissively.

'Did you remember to get your raincoat from the car?'

'No, Mother.'

'You never remember anything!'

'But I won't need it. It's nice out.'

'It could rain tomorrow.'

She took her knitting out of her bag. Her needles clicked. When Hubert was little, she would sit near him knitting during his piano lessons. He closed his eyes and pretended to be asleep. A while later she nodded off. He jumped out of the open window, ran to the shed where his bicycle had been put away and, silently opening the gate, slipped away. Everyone was asleep now. The gunfire had stopped. Cats wailed from the rooftops. A splendid church, with sky-blue windows, rose up in the middle of a dusty old avenue where refugees had parked. The people who hadn't been able to find accommodation were sleeping inside their cars or on the grass. Anguish oozed from their pale faces, tense and fearful, even in their sleep. They slept so soundly, though, nothing would wake them before daybreak. That was obvious. They could pass from sleep to death without even realising it.

Hubert walked among them feeling shock and pity. He wasn't tired. His overexcited state of mind gave him strength and kept him going. He thought with sadness and remorse of the family he had abandoned. But this very sadness and remorse increased his elation. He wasn't going into it with his eyes closed; he was sacrificing not just his own life, but the life of everyone in his family to his country. He marched towards his destiny like a young god bearing offerings. At least, that was how he saw himself. He left the village, got to the cherry tree and threw himself to the ground beneath its branches. A lovely sweet feeling suddenly made his heart beat faster: he thought of the new friend who would share his dangerous exploits and glory. He barely knew him, the boy with the blond hair, but he felt bound to him with extraordinary violence and tenderness. He had heard that, while crossing a bridge in the north, a German regiment had had to walk over the bodies of their dead comrades and that they had started singing: 'Once I had a comrade . . .' He understood that feeling of pure, almost savage love. Unconsciously, he was trying to replace Philippe, whom he loved so much and who had separated himself from his younger brother with such implacable gentleness; Philippe was too strict, too saintly, Hubert thought, and with no feelings, no passion for anyone but Christ.

For the past two years Hubert had felt very lonely and, at school, had almost made a point of befriending only bullies or snobs. Also, he was attracted, almost without realising it, to physical beauty – and René had the face of an angel. He waited for him, starting at every sound. It was nearly midnight. A horse went by without a rider. Strange sights like this occasionally reminded him of the war, but otherwise everything was quiet. He pulled a long weed out of the ground and chewed it, then examined the contents of one of his pockets: a bit of bread, an apple, some nuts, gingerbread crumbs, a pocket knife, a ball of string, his little red notebook. On the first page he wrote: 'If I am killed, could you please notify my father, Monsieur Péricand, 18 Boulevard Delessert in Paris, or my mother . . .' He added the address in Nîmes. He remembered he hadn't said his prayers that night. He knelt down in the grass and prayed, adding a special Creed for his family. He felt at peace with man and God. While he was praying, the bells sounded midnight. Now he had to be ready to go.

The moon lit up the road. It was empty. He waited patiently for half an hour, then became overwhelmed with anxiety. Hiding his bicycle in the ditch, he walked towards the village hoping to meet René, but there was no sign of him. Back under the cherry tree, he waited some more, examining the contents of his other pocket: some crumpled-up cigarettes, a bit of money. He smoked a cigarette without pleasure. He still wasn't used to the taste of tobacco. His hands were shaking nervously. He pulled flowers out of the ground and flicked them away. It was past one o'clock. Was it possible that René . . . ? No, no . . . you don't break a promise like that . . . He'd been prevented from coming, locked in by his aunts perhaps, but he, Hubert, hadn't let his mother's precautions prevent him from getting away. Mother. She would soon wake up and then what would she do? They would look everywhere for him. He couldn't stay here, so close to the village But what if René came? . . . He would wait for him until daybreak, then leave.

The first rays of sun were beginning to light up the road when Hubert finally set off. Pushing his bicycle, he cautiously climbed the hill to the Sainte woods, preparing what he would say to the soldiers. He heard voices, laughter, a horse neighing. Someone shouted. Hubert stopped, out of breath: they were speaking German. He jumped behind a tree, saw a greenish uniform a few feet away and, abandoning his bicycle, shot off like a hare. At the bottom of the hill he took the wrong path, kept on running and reached the village, but didn't recognise it. Then he went down to the main road and ended up in the middle of all the refugees' cars. They were driving insanely fast, insanely. He saw one (a big grey open touring car) that had just knocked a small van into the ditch and driven off without slowing down even for a moment. The further he walked, the faster the flood of cars was moving, like in some mad film, he thought. He saw a truck full of soldiers. He waved at them desperately. Without stopping, someone stretched out his hand and hoisted him up amid the camouflaged guns and boxes of tarpaulins.

'I wanted to warn you,' said Hubert, panting. 'I saw Germans in the woods nearby.'

'They're everywhere, my boy,' the soldier replied.

'Can I go with you?' Hubert asked shyly. 'I want . . .' (his voice breaking with emotion), 'I want to fight.'

The soldier looked at him and remained silent. Nothing these men heard or saw seemed to be able to surprise or move them any more. Hubert learned that they had picked up a pregnant woman along the way, as well as a child wounded in the bombing who'd been either abandoned or lost and a dog with a broken leg. He also learned they intended to hold the enemy back and prevent them, if possible, from crossing the bridge.

'I'm with them,' Hubert thought. 'That's it, I'm in it now.'

The surging wave of refugees surrounded the truck, preventing them from moving forward. Sometimes it was impossible for the soldiers to move at all. They would fold their arms and wait until someone let them pass. Hubert was sitting at the back of the truck, his legs dangling outside. He was filled with an extraordinary sense of turmoil, a confusion of ideas and emotions, but what he felt most was utter scorn for humanity as a whole. The feeling was almost physical. A few months earlier, his friends had given him some drink for the first time in his life. He thought of the taste now: the horrible taste of bitter ashes that bad wine leaves in your mouth. He had been such a good little boy. He had seen the world as simple and beautiful, men as worthy of respect. Men . . . a herd of cowardly wild animals. That René who had urged him to run off, and then stayed tucked up under his quilt, while France was dying . . . Those people who refused to give the refugees a bed, a glass of water, who charged a fortune for an egg, who stuffed their cars full of luggage, packages, food, even furniture, but who told a woman dying of exhaustion, children who had walked from Paris, 'You can't come with us . . . you can see very well there's no room . . .' Leather suitcases and painted women in a truck full of officers: such egotism, cowardice, such vicious, useless cruelty made him sick.

And the most horrible thing was that he couldn't ignore the sacrifices, the heroism, the kindness of some. Philippe, for example, was a saint; these soldiers who'd had nothing to eat or drink (the supply officer had left that morning but hadn't returned in time) going to do battle for a hopeless cause, they were heroes. There was courage, self-sacrifice, love among these men, but that was frightening too: even goodness was predestined according to Philippe. Whenever Philippe spoke, he seemed both enlightened and passionate at the same time, as if lit up by a very pure flame. But Hubert had serious doubts about religion and Philippe was far away. The outside world was incoherent and hideous, painted in the colours of hell, a hell Jesus never could enter, Hubert thought, 'because they would tear him to pieces'.

Machine-guns fired on the convoy. Death was gliding across the sky and suddenly plunged down from the heavens, wings outstretched, steel beak firing on this long line of trembling black insects crawling along the road. Everyone threw themselves to the ground; women lay on top of their children to protect them. When the firing stopped, deep furrows were left in the crowd, like wheat after a storm when the fallen stems form close, deep trenches. Only when it had been quiet for a few moments could you hear the cries and moans: people calling to one another, moans that went ignored, cries shouted out in vain . . .

The refugees got back into the cars they'd left beside the road and started off again, but some of the cars remained abandoned, their doors open, baggage still tied to the roof, a wheel in the ditch where the driver had rushed to take shelter. He would never return. In the car, amid the abandoned packages, there was sometimes a dog howling, pulling on his lead, or a cat miaowing frantically, locked in its basket.

17

The instincts of a former age were still at work in Gabriel Corte: when someone hurt him, rather than defend himself, his first reaction was to complain. Dragging Florence behind him, he strode impatiently through Paray-le-Monial looking for the mayor, the police, a councillor, a deputy, any government official at all who could get him back his dinner. But it was extraordinary . . . the streets were empty, the houses silent. At a cross-roads he came across a small group of women who seemed to be wandering about aimlessly.

'We have no idea, we don't come from here,' they replied to his questions. 'We're refugees, like you,' one of them added.

They could smell smoke, very faintly, carried by the soft June wind.

After a while he began to wonder where their car was. Florence thought they'd left it near the railway station. Gabriel remembered seeing a bridge they could look for; the moon, magnificent and peaceful, lit their way, but all the streets in this small old town looked the same. Everywhere there were gables, ancient stone walls, lopsided balconies, dark cul-de-sacs.

'Like a bad opera set,' Corte groaned.

It even smelled of backstage: sad and dusty, with the faint lingering odour of urine. Sweat was running down his face in the heat. He could hear Florence calling from behind, 'Wait for me! Will you stop a minute, you coward, you bastard! Where are you, Gabriel? Where are you? Gabriel, I can't see you. You pig!' Her cries of rage rebounded off the old walls and their echo struck him like bullets: 'Pig, you old bastard, coward!'

She finally caught up with him near the railway station. She leapt at him, hitting, scratching, spitting in his face while he shrieked and tried to fight her off. No one could ever have imagined that the low, weary voice of Gabriel Corte concealed such resonant, shrill sounds, so feminine and wild. They were both being driven mad by hunger, fear and exhaustion.

As soon as they saw that the Avenue de la Gare was deserted, they realised the order had been given to evacuate the town. Everyone else was far away, on the moonlit bridge. Only a few exhausted soldiers remained, sitting on the pavement in small groups. One of them, a very young pale boy with thick glasses, hauled himself up to separate Florence and Corte.

'Come on, Monsieur . . . Now, now, Madame, you should be ashamed of yourselves!'

'But where are the cars?' Corte shouted.

'Gone. They were ordered to leave.'

'But, but . . . by whom? Why? What about our luggage? My manuscripts! I am Gabriel Corte!'

'Good God, you'll find your manuscripts. And I can tell you that other people have lost a lot more.'

'Philistine!'

'Of course, Monsieur, but . . .'

'Who gave this stupid order?'

'Well, Monsieur . . . there have been a lot of orders which were just as stupid, I'll admit. Don't worry, you'll find your car and your papers. But in the meantime, you can't stay here. The Germans will be here any minute. We've been ordered to blow up the station.'

'Where will we go?' Florence groaned.

'Go back to the town.'

'But where can we stay?'

'There are plenty of rooms. Everyone's run off,' said one of the soldiers who had come up to them and was standing a few steps away from Corte.

The moon gave off a soft blue light. The man had a harsh, heavy face; two vertical lines cut down his thick cheeks. He put his hand on Gabriel's shoulder and effortlessly spun him round. 'Off you go. We've had enough of you, got it?'

For a second Gabriel thought he might jump at the soldier, but the pressure of that hard hand on his shoulder made him flinch and take two steps backwards. 'We've been on the road since Monday . . . and we're hungry . . .'

'We're hungry,' Florence echoed, sighing.

'Wait until morning. If we're still here we'll give you some soup.'

The soldier with the thick glasses said again in his soft, weary voice, 'You can't stay here, Monsieur . . . Go on, off you go.' He took Corte by the hand and gave him a little push, just as you would send the children out of the drawing room when it was time for bed.

They went back across the town square, side by side now and dragging their weary legs; their anger had subsided and with it the nervous energy that had kept them going. They were so demoralised that they didn't have the strength to start looking for another restaurant. They knocked at doors that never opened and eventually collapsed on a bench near a church. Florence, wincing with pain, took off her shoes.

Night passed. Nothing happened. The railway station was still standing. Now and again, they could hear soldiers walking in the streets nearby. Some men passed by the bench once or twice without even glancing at Florence and Corte, huddled together in the silent shadows, leaning their heavy heads together. They could smell the stench of meat: a bomb had hit the abattoir on the outskirts of the town and it was on fire. They dozed off. When they woke up, they saw soldiers going by with tin dishes. Florence cried out in hunger and the soldiers gave her a bowl of soup and a bit of bread. Daylight returned and with it Gabriel recovered some dignity: he wouldn't dream of fighting with his mistress over some soup and a crust of bread!

Florence drank slowly. Then she stopped and walked towards Gabriel. 'You have the rest,' she said to her lover.

'No, no, there's barely enough for you,' he protested. She handed him the tin bowl of warm liquid that smelled of cabbage. Trembling, he gripped it with both hands and, placing his mouth at the edge of the bowl, wolfed it down in big gulps, barely stopping to catch his breath. When he had finished, he gave a happy sigh.

'Better?' a soldier asked.

They recognised the man who'd chased them away from the railway station the night before, but the dawn light softened his fierce centurion's face. Gabriel remembered he had some cigarettes in his pocket and offered them to him. The two men smoked for a while without speaking, while Florence tried in vain to get her shoes back on.

'If I were you,' the soldier finally said, 'I'd hurry up and get out of here 'cause the Germans are definitely going to show up. It's a miracle they aren't here yet. Still, they don't have to hurry,' he added bitterly, 'they've got it sewn up from here to Bayonne . . .'

'Do you think we have any chance?' Florence asked shyly.

The soldier didn't answer and suddenly left. They left too, hobbling along, heading straight for the outskirts. Gradually, refugees began to emerge from the seemingly deserted town, weighed down with baggage. In the same way that animals separated in a storm find their herd when the storm has passed, they came together in small groups and walked towards the bridge; it was guarded by soldiers who let them pass. Gabriel and Florence followed. Above, the sky shimmered a pure azure blue: no clouds, no planes. Below, a beautiful glistening river flowed by. In front of them, they could see the road leading south and some very young trees with new green leaves. Suddenly the trees seemed to be moving towards them. German trucks and guns, covered with camouflage, were heading straight at them. Corte saw people ahead raising their arms and running back. At that moment the French soldiers opened fire. When the German machine-guns fired back, the refugees were caught in the crossfire. They ran in all directions. Some simply whirled round on the spot as if they'd gone mad; one woman climbed over the parapet and threw herself into the river.

Florence dug her nails into Corte's arm and screamed, 'Turn back, hurry!'

'But they'll blow up the bridge,' Corte shouted.

Taking her hand, he propelled her forward and suddenly a thought shot through him, as strange, burning and sharp as lightning: they were running towards death. He pulled her close and, pushing her head down, covered it with his coat as you cover the eyes of a condemned man. Then, stumbling, panting, half carrying her, he ran the short distance to the other side of the river. Even though his heart was pounding in his chest, he wasn't actually afraid. He had a passionate, urgent desire to save Florence. He had faith in something invisible, in a guiding hand reaching out to him, to *him*, weak, miserable, insignificant, so insignificant that destiny would spare him, as a wisp of straw sometimes survives a storm. They made it across the bridge, narrowly missing the advancing Germans with their machine-guns and green uniforms. The road was clear, death was behind them and suddenly they saw it – yes, they were right, they recognised it – right there, at the edge of a little country lane, their car and their loyal servants waiting for them. Florence could only groan, 'Julie, thank God. Julie!'

To Corte, the voices of the driver and maid sounded like the low, strange noises you hear through a fog just before you faint. Florence was crying. Slowly, incredulously, painfully, Corte realised that he had his car back, his manuscripts back, his life back. He would no longer be an ordinary man, suffering, starving, both courageous and cowardly at the same time, but instead a privileged creature, protected from all evil. He would be – Gabriel Corte!

18

At last Hubert arrived at the Allier river with the men he'd met on the road. It was noon on Monday 17 June. Volunteers had joined the soldiers along the way. There were policemen, members of the home guard, a few Senegalese, and soldiers whose defeated companies were trying in vain to regroup and who clung on to any little island of resistance with hopeless courage. There were also young boys like Hubert Péricand who'd become separated from their fleeing families or run away in the night 'to join the troops'. These magical words had spread from village to village, from one farm to the next. 'We're going to join the troops, dodge the Germans, regroup by the Loire,' said hordes of sixteen-year-olds. These children carried sacks over their shoulders (the remainder of yesterday's afternoon tea hastily wrapped up in a shirt and jumper by a tearful mother); their faces were round and rosy, their fingers stained with ink, their voices breaking. Three of them were accompanied by their fathers, veterans of '14, whose age, former injuries and family situation had prevented them from joining up in September.

At the bottom of the steps that led down from a stone bridge sat the Commander in Chief of the battalion. Hubert counted nearly 200 men on the road and river bank. In his naïvety he believed that this powerful army would now confront the enemy. He saw explosives stacked up on the stone bridge; what he didn't know was that there was no fuse to light them. Silently the soldiers went about their business or slept on the ground. They hadn't eaten anything since the day before. Towards evening, bottles of beer were handed out. Hubert wasn't hungry but the frothy, bitter beer made him feel happy. It helped him to keep up his courage. No one actually seemed to need him. He went from one person to the other, shyly offering to help; no one answered him, no one even looked at him. He saw two soldiers dragging some straw and bundles of firewood to the bridge; another was pushing a barrel of tar. Hubert grabbed an enormous bundle of wood but so clumsily that splinters ripped his hands and he let out a little cry of pain. Throwing it on to the bridge, he heaved a sigh of relief that no one appeared to have noticed, only to hear one of the men call out, 'What the hell are you doing here? Can't you see you're just in the way?'

Wounded to the core, Hubert moved aside. He stood motionless on the road to Saint-Pourçain, facing the river, and watched the incomprehensible actions of the soldiers: the straw and the wood had been doused in tar and placed on the bridge next to a fifty-litre drum of petrol; by using a seventy-five-millimetre gun to detonate the explosives, they were counting on this barricade to hold back the enemy troops.

And so the rest of the day went by, then the night and the entire next morning. The hours of boredom felt strange and incoherent, like a fever. Still nothing to eat, nothing to drink. Even the young boys from the countryside lost their fresh complexions. Pale with hunger, blackened by dust, hair dishevelled, eyes burning, a sad and stubborn expression on their faces, they seemed suddenly older.

It was two o'clock when the first Germans came into sight on the other side of the river. Their motor convoy had come through Paray-le-Monial that very morning. Dumbfounded, Hubert watched them head towards the bridge at incredible speed, like a wild, warlike streak of lightning searing through the peaceful countryside. It only lasted a second: a gunshot set off the barrels of explosive forming the barricade. Debris from the bridge, the vehicles and their drivers all fell into the river. Hubert saw soldiers running ahead.

'This is it! We're attacking,' he thought. He got goose bumps and his throat went dry, like when he was a child and heard the first strains of military music in the street. He hurled himself towards the straw and wood barricade just as it was being set on fire. The black smoke from the tar filled his nose and mouth. Behind this protective wall, machine-guns were holding back the German tanks. Choking, coughing, sneezing, Hubert crawled a few steps backwards. He was in despair. He had no weapon. All he could do was stand there. They were fighting and he just stood there, arms folded, inert, useless. He felt a little better when he saw that all around him they were taking the enemy's attack without fighting back. He considered this a complex tactical manoeuvre until he realised that the men had almost no ammunition. 'Nevertheless,' he thought, 'if we've been left here it's because we're needed, we're useful, we're defending the bulk of the French army, for all we know.' At every moment he expected to see more troops appearing on the road to Saint-Pourçain. 'We're here, lads,' they'd shout, 'don't worry! We'll beat them!' – or some other warlike cry. But no one came.

Nearby he saw a man, his head covered in blood, stumble like a drunkard into a thicket; he sat there between the branches in a bizarre and uncomfortable position, his knees folded under him, his chin resting on his chest. He heard an officer shouting angrily, 'No doctors, no nurses, no ambulances! What are we supposed to do?'

'There's a beat-up ambulance in the garden of the toll-house,' someone replied.

'What am I supposed to do with that, for God's sake?' the officer repeated. 'Forget it.'

The shells had set fire to a part of the town. In the splendid June light, the flames took on a transparent pink colour; a plume of smoke drifted up to the sky, flecked with gold by the sunlight, tinged with sulphur and ash.

'Well, they're off,' a soldier said to Hubert, pointing to the machine-gunners who were abandoning their post on the bridge.

'But why?' Hubert shouted, dismayed. 'Aren't they going to keep fighting?'

'With what?'

'This is a disaster,' thought Hubert with a sigh. 'This is defeat! I am here, watching an enormous defeat, worse than Waterloo. We are all lost, I'll never see Mother or any of my family again. I'm going to die.' He felt doomed, numb to everything around him, in a terrible state of exhaustion and despair. He didn't hear the order to retreat. He saw men running through the machine-gun fire. Rushing forward, he climbed over a wall into a garden where a baby's pram still stood in the shade. The battle wasn't over. Without tanks, without weapons, without ammunition, they were still trying to defend a few square metres of ground, a bridgehead, while from all directions the German conquerors were sweeping through France.

Hubert was suddenly gripped by a feeling of hopeless courage, almost madness. He realised that he was running away when his duty was to go back towards the fighting, towards the automatic rifles he could still hear obstinately returning the German fire, to die with them. Once again, risking his life at every moment, he crossed the small garden, trampling on children's toys. Where were the people who lived in this little house? Had they fled? He climbed over the wire fence under a hail of bullets and, still alive, fell back on to the road and began crawling towards the river again, his hands and knees bleeding. He would never make it, never. He was halfway there when everything fell silent. He realised that it was night and that he must have fainted from exhaustion. The extraordinary sudden silence had brought him round. He sat up. His mind was blank and his head throbbed. A magnificent moon lit up the road, but he was sitting in a line of shade cast by a tree trunk. Villars was still burning, all the guns were silent.

Afraid he might encounter more Germans, Hubert left the road and entered a small wood. Now and again he stopped, wondering where he was. There was no doubt whatsoever that the motor convoys that had taken only five days to invade half of France would reach the borders of Italy, Switzerland, Spain by tomorrow. He wouldn't be able to escape them. He had forgotten that he wasn't wearing a uniform, that nothing showed he'd been fighting. He was sure he'd be taken prisoner. He kept running, following the same instincts that had taken him to the battle-ground and that now led him far from the fires, the destroyed bridges, the dreams in which, for the first time in his life, he had come face to face with death. He spent the night frantically trying to work out which route the Germans might take. He could picture the towns falling, one after the other, the defeated soldiers, the discarded weapons, the trucks abandoned on the road for lack of petrol, the tanks, the big guns (whose toy models he had so admired) and all the treasure fallen into enemy hands! He was shaking, crying as he crawled on his hands and knees through the moonlit fields, but still he wouldn't believe they'd been defeated: a healthy young boy always refuses to believe in death. The soldiers would meet up again a bit further away, they'd regroup, do battle once more and he'd be with them. And he'd be . . . with them . . .

'But what have *I* done?' he thought all of a sudden. 'I haven't fired a single shot!' He felt so ashamed of himself that he started crying again, bitter, painful tears. 'It's not my fault, I didn't have any weapons, just my own two hands.' Suddenly he pictured himself trying in vain to drag the bundle of wood to the river. No, he hadn't even been able to do that, he who'd wanted to rush the bridge, lead the soldiers, throw himself on the enemy tanks and die shouting '*Vive la France!*' He was wild with exhaustion and despair, yet nevertheless some oddly mature ideas passed through his mind: he thought about the disaster, what had caused it, the future, death. Then he wondered about himself, what would become of him and, little by little, he came back to reality. 'Mother is going to be furious!' he muttered and his pale, tense face, which seemed to have aged and grown thin in only two days, lit up for a second as he grinned in an innocent childlike way.

He found a track between two fields, which led deeper into the countryside. Here there were no signs of war. Streams flowed, a nightingale sang, a bell chimed the hours, there were flowers in all the hedges, young green leaves on the trees. He washed his hands and face in a stream, drank some water from his cupped hands and felt better. He desperately tried to find some fruit on the trees. He knew very well it was the wrong time of year, but the young believe in miracles. At the end of the track he was back on the main road. There was a sign: Cressange, 22 kilometres. He stopped in confusion, then saw a farm. After hesitating for a long time, he finally brought himself to knock on the shutter. He heard footsteps inside the house. They asked who he was. When he said he was lost and hungry, they let him in. Three French soldiers were asleep inside. He recognised them. They had defended the bridge at Moulins. Now they were stretched out on benches, snoring, their filthy haggard faces thrown back as if they were dead. A woman watched over them, knitting; a cat chased her ball of wool as it rolled along the floor. The scene was at once so familiar and so strange after everything Hubert had seen during the past week that his legs gave way under him and he had to sit down. On the table he saw the soldiers' helmets; they had covered them with leaves to stop the moonlight reflecting off them.

One of the men woke up and pushed himself up on to his elbow. 'Did you see any, lad?' he asked in a low hoarse voice.

Hubert realised he meant the Germans. 'No,' he said quickly, 'no, not one since Moulins.'

'Seems like they don't even want prisoners any more,' the soldier said. 'Too many. They just take their guns and tell them to bugger off.'

'Seems like it,' said the woman.

They fell silent. Hubert ate what they'd given him: a bowl of soup and some cheese. 'What are you going to do now?' he asked the soldier.

His friend had opened his eyes. They debated. One wanted to go to Cressange.

'What for?' the other one replied, sounding devastated. 'They're everywhere, everywhere . . .' He looked around him with the sad, frightened eyes of a stunned bird.

He seemed convinced there were Germans all around, ready to capture him. Now and again he let out a sort of clipped, bitter laugh. 'Good God, to have fought in '14 and then see this . . .'

The woman kept on knitting calmly. She was very old and had on a white fluted bonnet. '*I* saw '70. Now then . . .' she muttered.

Hubert listened to them in horror. They hardly seemed real to him, more like groaning ghosts conjured up from the pages of his *History of France*. My God! The present with all its tragedy was more important than the glories of the past and its stench of blood. Hubert drank a cup of hot black coffee, despite the grounds. Then, thanking the woman and saying goodbye to the soldiers, he set off, determined to make it to Cressange by morning. From there he could get in touch with his family to let them know he was all right. At eight in the morning he found himself in front of a hotel in a small village a few kilometres from Cressange; he could smell the delicious aroma of coffee and fresh bread coming from inside. Suddenly Hubert felt he couldn't go on, that his legs wouldn't carry him. He walked into the hotel where he found a large room full of refugees. No one could tell him if there were any beds. The owner had gone to see if she could find some food for this horde of hungry people; she'd be back soon. He went back out into the street.

Up on the first floor a woman sat at a window putting on make-up. Her lipstick clattered to the ground at Hubert's feet and he quickly picked it up. Leaning out to look for it, the woman saw him and smiled. 'How can I get it back?' she asked. And she dangled her bare arm, her white hand, out of the window.

Hubert was dazzled by the sunlight glinting off her polished nails. Her milky-white skin, her red hair were almost painful to him, like a blinding light. 'I . . . I could bring it to you, Madame,' he stammered, lowering his eyes.

'Oh, yes please, if you wouldn't mind,' she said and smiled again.

He went back into the building, through the breakfast room and up a small, dark staircase. Through an open door he saw a pink room. In fact, the pink was the effect of sunlight filtering through cheap red curtains and filling the room with a warm, vibrant light the colour of rose bushes.

The woman, who was polishing her nails, showed him in and took the lipstick. 'Oh, he's going to faint!' she said, looking at him. Hubert felt her take his hand and help him walk a few steps to a chair; she slipped a pillow under his head. His heart was pounding, but he hadn't lost consciousness. Everything was whirling around as if he were seasick, and great waves of hot and cold ran through him, one after the other.

He felt intimidated but rather proud of himself. When she asked him, 'Are you tired? Hungry? What's wrong, my poor darling?' he exaggerated the trembling in his voice: 'It's nothing,' he replied, 'it's just . . . I walked here from Moulins where we were defending the bridge.'

She looked at him, surprised. 'But how old are you?'

'Eighteen,' he lied.

'Are you a soldier?'

'No, I was travelling with my family. I left them. I joined the troops.'

'That's wonderful!' she said.

Even though she'd spoken with the tone of admiration he'd hoped for, he blushed when she looked at him; he didn't know why. Close up, she didn't seem young. You could see tiny wrinkles on her lightly powdered face. She was very slim, very elegant, with magnificent legs.

'What's your name?' she asked.

'Hubert Péricand.'

'Isn't there a Péricand who's the curator at the Beaux-Arts?'

'He's my father, Madame.'

While they were talking, she had stood up and poured him some coffee. She had just finished breakfast and the tray with the half-full coffee pot, cream jug and toast was still on the table.

'It's not very hot,' she said, 'but you should have some anyway, it will do you good.'

He obeyed.

'It's such madness downstairs with all those refugees; I could ring for service all day long and still no one would come! You come from Paris, of course?'

'Yes, and you as well, Madame?'

'Yes. I got caught in the bombing at Tours. Now I'm thinking about going to Bordeaux. Though I imagine the Opéra in Bordeaux has been evacuated.'

'Are you an actress, Madame?' Hubert asked respectfully.

'A dancer. Arlette Corail.'

Hubert had only ever seen dancers on stage at the Châtelet Theatre. Instinctively he glanced with curiosity and longing at her long ankles and muscular calves, sheathed in silk stockings. He was extremely flustered. A lock of his blond hair fell into his eyes.

The woman gently pushed it back with her hand. 'And where will you be going now?'

'I don't know,' Hubert admitted. 'My family was staying in a small village about thirty kilometres from here. I'd go back and find them, but the Germans must be there by now.'

'We expect them here too, any time now.'

'Here?'

He started and leapt up as if to run away.

She held him back, laughing. 'Now what do you think they would do with you? A young boy like you . . .'

'All the same, I did fight,' he protested, his feelings hurt.

'Yes, of course you did, but no one's going to tell them *that*, are they?' She was thinking, frowning slightly. 'Listen. This is what you're going to do. I'll go downstairs and ask for a room for you. They know me here. It's a very small hotel but marvellous food and I've spent a few weekends here. They can give you their son's room – he's away at the front. Rest for a day or two and then contact your parents.'

'I don't know how to thank you,' he murmured.

She went out. When she came back a few moments later he was asleep. She wanted to lift his head, put her arms round his broad shoulders, feel his chest gently rising and falling. She watched him closely, smoothed back the lock of wild golden hair that had fallen on to his forehead, then looked at him again with a dreamy, hungry look, like a cat staring at a little bird. 'He's not at all bad, this boy . . .' she sighed.

19

The entire village was waiting for the Germans. Faced with the idea of seeing their conquerors for the first time, some people felt desperate shame, others anguish, but many felt only apprehensive curiosity, as when some astonishing new theatrical event is announced. The civil servants, police, postmen had all been ordered to leave the day before. The mayor was staying. He was a placid old farmer with gout; nothing flustered him. With or without a leader, things in the village went on much the same. At noon, in the noisy dining room where Arlette Corail was finishing lunch, some travellers brought news of the armistice. The women burst into tears. It seemed that the situation was rather confused. In certain places the army was still resisting and civilians had joined them. However, everyone agreed that the army had failed and there was nothing more to be done; they had no choice but to give up. The room was filled with chatter. It was stiflingly hot.

Arlette pushed away her plate and went out into the hotel's small garden. She had some cigarettes, a deckchair, a book. She'd left Paris a week earlier so panic-stricken she'd felt close to madness; now, despite having met with real danger, she was herself again: perfectly calm and collected. What's more, she was convinced that, from now on, she could survive any situation, that she was gifted with a real genius for obtaining maximum pleasure and comfort regardless of the circumstances. Her flexibility, lucidity, detachment were qualities that had been of enormous use to her in her career and relationships, but until now she hadn't realised they would be just as useful in a crisis.

When she thought of how she had begged Corbin's help she smiled scornfully. They had arrived in Tours just in time to be bombed; Corbin's suitcase with his personal effects and the bank's documents had been buried in the rubble, while she had emerged from the disaster without having lost a single handkerchief, a single box of make-up, a single pair of shoes. She had seen Corbin's face distorted with terror and thought how much pleasure she would get from reminding him of it, often. Then she remembered his drooping, corpse-like jaw; she'd wanted to give him a chin strap to hold it closed. Pathetic! Leaving him in Tours amid the terrible confusion and chaos, she'd taken the car, managed to find some petrol and left. She'd spent two days in this village, where she'd had good food and lodgings, while a pathetic crowd of people camped in barns and in the village square. She had even allowed herself the luxury of being charitable by leaving her room for that lovely boy, that young Péricand . . . Péricand? They were an upper-middle-class family, dull, respectable, very rich, with excellent connections in the government, among diplomats and wealthy industrialists, thanks to their relatives from Lyon . . . the Maltêtes . . . She sighed with annoyance, realising she would now have to rethink everything. How irritating, too, that she'd recently gone to so much trouble to seduce Gérard Salomon-Worms, the Count de Furières's brother-in-law. A quite useless conquest that had cost her a great deal of time and effort.

Frowning slightly, Arlette studied her fingernails. The ten little sparkling mirrors seemed to put her in a pensive mood. Her lovers knew that when she contemplated her hands in this reflective, malicious way, it meant she was about to express her opinion on things like politics, art, literature and fashion, and that, in general, her opinions were insightful and just. For a few seconds, in this little garden in bloom, while bumble-bees gathered pollen from a bush with scarlet bell-shaped flowers, the dancer imagined the future. She came to the conclusion that for her nothing would change. Her wealth consisted of jewellery – which could only increase in value – and property (she'd made some good invest-ments in the Midi, before the war). Yet they were mere trimmings. Her principal assets were her legs, her figure, her scheming mind – things vulnerable only to time. But there was the rub . . . She immediately thought of her age and, taking a mirror from her handbag in the way that you touch a good-luck charm to ward off evil spirits, looked care-fully at her face. An unpleasant thought occurred to her: she used nothing but American make-up. It had been difficult to get hold of any for a few weeks now. That put her in a bad mood. So what! Things might change on the surface but underneath everything would be the same. There would be new rich men, just as there always were after great disasters –

men prepared to pay dearly for their pleasures because their money had come easily and so would love. But please, dear God, let all this chaos end quickly! Please let us get back to a normal way of life, whatever it might be; these wars, revolutions, great historical upheavals might be exciting to men, but to women . . . Women felt nothing but boredom. She was positive that every woman would agree with her: they were tired of crying, bored to death by all these noble words and noble feelings! As for men . . . it was hard to know, difficult to say . . . In some ways those simple souls were incomprehensible, whereas for at least fifty years women had been concerned only with the commonplace, the ordinary . . . She looked up and saw the owner of the little hotel leaning out of the window, looking at something. 'What is it, Madame Goulot?' she asked.

'Mademoiselle,' the woman replied in a solemn, trembling voice, 'it's them . . . they're coming . . .'

'The Germans?'

'Yes.'

The dancer was about to get up to go to the gate so she could see down the road, but she was afraid to in case someone took her deckchair and her spot in the shade, so she stayed where she was.

It wasn't the Germans who were coming but *one* German: the first. From behind closed doors, through half-closed shutters, from attic windows, the entire village watched him arrive. He stopped his motorcycle in the deserted village square. He had on a green uniform, gloves and a helmet with a visor. When he raised his head, you could see a rosy, thin, almost childlike face. 'But he's so young!' murmured the women. Without actually realising it, they were expecting some vision from the Apocalypse, some terrifying, foreign monster. Since he looked around expectantly, the newsagent, who had fought in '14 and wore his Croix de Guerre and military medals on the inside of his old grey jacket, came out of his shop and walked towards the enemy. For a moment, the two men just stood there, face to face, without saying a word. Then the German took out a cigarette and asked for a light in bad French. The newsagent replied in bad German; he had been among the occupying forces in Mainz in '18. There was such total silence (the whole village was holding its breath) that you could hear each and every word. The German asked for directions.

The Frenchman replied, then became bolder: 'Has the armistice been signed?'

The German threw open his arms. 'We don't know yet. We hope so,' he said.

And the humanity of his words, his gesture, everything proved they were not dealing with some bloodthirsty monster but with a simple soldier like any other, and suddenly the ice was broken between the town and the enemy, between the country folk and the invader.

'He doesn't seem so bad,' the women whispered.

He smiled and then, raising his hand to his helmet, made an unconfident, half-finished gesture: not quite a military salute but not a civilian greeting either. He glanced curiously at the closed windows for a moment, started up his motorcycle and disappeared. One after the other, doors opened and the entire village spilled out into the square until the newsagent was surrounded. Standing motionless, his hands in his pockets, he was frowning and staring into the distance. Contradictory expressions appeared on his face: relief it was all over, sadness and anger that it had all ended this way, memories of the past, fear of the future; and all these feelings were mirrored in the faces around him. The women dried tears from their eyes; the men stood silent, looking obstinate and hostile. The children, distracted from their games for a moment, turned back to their marbles and hopscotch. The sky was shining with the kind of brilliant, silvery light you sometimes find in the middle of a truly beautiful day; an almost imperceptible iridescent mist hovered in the air and all the fresh colours of June were intensified, looked richer and softer, as if reflected through a prism.

The hours passed by peacefully. There were fewer cars on the road. Bicycles still sped along as if caught up in the angry wind that had been blowing in from the north-east for over a week now, dragging with them their miserable human cargo. A little while later there was a surprising sight: cars appeared – travelling in the opposite direction from a week ago. People were going back to Paris. When they saw that, the villagers finally believed it was all over. They went home. Once again you could hear the women rattling the dishes as they washed them in their kitchens, the faint footsteps of an old woman going to feed her rabbits, even a little girl singing as she drew water from a pump. Dogs rolled around, playing in the dust.

It was an exquisite evening with clear skies and blue shadows; the last rays of the setting sun caressed the roses, while the church bells called the faithful to prayer. But then a noise rose up from the road, a noise unlike any they'd heard these past few days, a low, steady rumbling that seemed to move slowly closer, heavy and relentless. Trucks were heading towards the village. This time it really was the Germans. The trucks stopped in the village square and men got out; others pulled up behind them, then more and still more. In a few seconds the whole of the old, dusty square, from the church to the municipal hall, became a dark, still mass of grey vehicles with a few faded branches clinging to them, the remains of their camouflage.

There were so many! Silently, cautiously, people came out on to their doorsteps again. They tried in vain to count the flood of soldiers. Germans were coming from all directions. They filled the squares and streets – more and more of them, endlessly. The villagers hadn't heard the sound of footsteps in the street, young voices, laughter, since September. They were stunned by the noise emerging from this wave of green uniforms, by the scent of these healthy men, their young flesh, and especially by the sound of this foreign language. Germans poured into the houses, the shops, the cafés. Their boots clanked over the red tiles of the kitchens. They asked for food, drink. They stroked the children as they went by. They threw open their arms, they sang, they laughed with the women. Their obvious happiness, their delight at being conquerors, their feverish bliss – a bliss combined with a touch of wonder, as if they themselves could hardly believe what had happened – all this contained such drama, such excitement, that the defeated villagers forgot their sadness and bitterness for a few seconds. They just stood and watched, speechless.

In the little hotel, below the room where Hubert was still sleeping, the main room echoed with songs and shouting. The Germans had immediately demanded champagne (*Sekt! Nahrung!*) and corks flew from their hands. Some of them were playing billiards, others went into the kitchen carrying piles of raw pink pork cutlets which they threw on to the fire; the meat sizzled and let off thick smoke as it cooked. The soldiers brought bottles of beer up from the cellar, impatiently pushing aside the waitress who wanted to help them; a young man with a rosy complexion and a mass of golden hair was cracking eggs open on the edge of the stove; in the garden, someone else was picking the first strawberries of summer. Two half-naked young boys were dipping their heads in buckets of cold water drawn from the well. They ate their fill, gorged themselves with all the good things the gardens provided; they had cheated death, they were young, alive, they were conquerors! Their excitement spilled out in urgent, rapid chatter; they spoke bad French to anyone who would listen to them, pointing to their boots, saying over and over again, 'We walking, walking, comrades falling and we always walking . . .' The clinking of weapons, belts, helmets filled the room.

Hubert could hear it in his dream and, confusing it with his memories of the day before, imagined once more the battle on the Moulins bridge. He tossed about, sighing and moaning as if in pain, fighting off some invisible person. When he finally woke up, he was in a strange bedroom. He'd slept all day. He could see the full moon shining through the open window. Hubert started, rubbed his eyes and looked at the dancer who had come in while he was asleep. He muttered his thanks and apologies.

'You must be hungry,' she said. It was true, he was famished. 'You know, perhaps it would be better if you had dinner here with me? It's unbearable downstairs, there are soldiers everywhere.'

'Soldiers!' he said, rushing towards the door. 'What are they saying? Are things looking any better? Where are the Germans?'

'The Germans? But they're here. It's the German soldiers who are downstairs.'

He leapt away from her in surprise, as fearful as a hunted animal. 'The Germans? No, you're joking?' He tried in vain to find some other words and then repeated in a low, shaky voice, 'You're joking . . . ?'

She opened the door; the smell of thick, acrid smoke rose up from the room downstairs, along with the unmistakable sound of a group of victorious soldiers: shouting, laughter, singing, their noisy boots, the clanging of heavy guns thrown on to the marble tables, the crashing of helmets against metal belt buckles, and the joyous roar from a proud, happy crowd, intoxicated by their victory, 'like the winning team at a rugby match', Hubert thought. He found it almost impossible not to shout out insults or collapse in tears. Rushing to the window, he looked outside. The street was starting to empty, but four men were walking abreast, rapping on the doors of the houses as they passed, shouting, 'Lights out!' One after the other, lights were submissively switched off. All that remained was the moonlight which cast a dull blue glow as it shimmered off the helmets and grey gun barrels. Hubert was shaking; he grabbed the curtain with both hands, pressed it against his mouth and burst into tears.

'Come on, now,' the woman said, stroking his shoulder and feeling mildly sorry for him. 'There's nothing we can do about it, is there? What can we do? All the tears in the world won't change anything. There are better times ahead. We have to live to see the better times, first and foremost we have to live . . . to go on . . . But you acted very bravely . . . If everyone had been as brave as you . . . and you're so young! Almost a child . . .'

He shook his head.

'No?' she said, lowering her voice. 'Are you a man, then?'

She fell silent. Her fingers were trembling slightly and she dug her nails into the boy's arm as if she were grabbing hold of some fresh prey and kneading it before biting into it to satisfy her hunger. 'Don't cry,' she said very quietly, her voice faltering. 'Only children cry. You're a man. When a man is unhappy he knows what he needs . . .'

She waited for a response but he said nothing and lowered his eyes. His mouth was closed and sad, but his nose wrinkled and his nostrils quivered slightly. So she said in a very quiet voice, 'Love . . .'

20

In the room where the Péricand children were sleeping Albert the cat had made his bed. First he'd climbed on to Jacqueline's small floral quilt and started to paw at it, gnawing at the cotton fabric that smelled of glue and fruit, but Nanny had come in and chased him away. Three times in a row, as soon as she'd turned away, he'd returned with a silent, graceful leap, but finally he'd had to admit defeat and so had curled up at the back of an armchair under Jacqueline's dressing gown. Sleep filled the room. The children were resting peacefully and Nanny had fallen asleep while saying her rosary. The cat, absolutely still, stared intently with one green eye at the rosary gleaming in the moonlight; the other eye remained closed. His body was hidden by the pink flannel dressing gown. Little by little, extremely quietly, one leg emerged, then the other; he stretched them out and felt them tremble slightly, all the way from his shoulder joint – that steel spring hidden beneath a soft, warm fur coat – right down to his hard, transparent claws. He sprang forward, jumped on to Nanny's bed and stared at her for a long time without moving; only the ends of his delicate whiskers quivered. He stretched one paw forward and started playing with the rosary beads; they hardly moved at first, but then he began to enjoy the smooth, cool feel of these perfect, tiny balls rolling between his claws; he swiped at them harder and the rosary fell to the floor. The cat took fright and disappeared under an armchair.

A while later Emmanuel woke up and started crying. The windows and shutters were both open. The moon lit up the rooftops in the village; the tiles glistened like the scales on a fish. The garden was fragrant, peaceful, and the silvery light seemed to shimmer like clear water, gently rising and falling over the fruit trees.

The cat poked his nose through the fringes of the armchair and studied the scene with a dreamy expression. He was a very young cat who had only ever lived in the city, where the scent of such June nights was far away. Occasionally he had caught a whiff of something warm and intoxicating, but nothing like here where the smell rose up to his whiskers and took hold of him, making his head spin. Eyes half closed, he could feel waves of powerful, sweet perfume running through him: the pungent smell of the last lilacs, the sap running through the trees, the cool, dark earth, the animals, birds, moles, mice, all the prey, the musky scent of fur, of skin, the smell of blood . . . His mouth gaping with longing, he jumped on to the window sill and walked slowly along the drainpipe. This was where a strong hand had grabbed him the night before and thrown him back to Jacqueline who was crying in bed. But he would not allow himself to be caught tonight.

He eyed the distance from the drainpipe to the ground. It was an easy jump, but he appeared to want to flatter himself by exaggerating the difficulty of the leap. He balanced his hindquarters, looking fierce and confident, swept his long black tail across the drainpipe and, ears pulled back, leapt forward, landing on the freshly tilled earth. He hesitated for a moment, then buried his muzzle in the ground. Now he was in the very black of night, at the heart of it, at the darkest point. He needed to sniff the earth: here, between the roots and the pebbles, were smells untainted by the scent of humans, smells that had yet to waft into the air and vanish. They were warm, secretive, eloquent. Alive. Each and every scent meant there was some small living creature, hiding, happy, edible . . . June bugs, field mice, crickets and that small toad whose voice seemed full of crystallised tears . . . The cat's long ears – pink triangles tinged with silver, pointed and delicately curly inside like the flower on bindweed – suddenly shot up. He was listening to faint noises in the shadows, so delicate, so mysterious but, to him alone, so clear: the rustling of wisps of straw in nests where birds watch over their young, the flutter of feathers, the sound of pecking on bark, the beating of insect wings, the patter of mice gently scratching the ground, even the faint bursting of seeds opening. Golden eyes flashed by in the darkness. There were sparrows sleeping under leaves, fat blackbirds, nightingales; the male nightingales were already awake, singing to each other in the forest and along the river banks.

There were other sounds as well: the steady thud of explosions, rising and bursting forth like flowers and, when the noise stopped, the rattling of every window-pane in the village, the banging of shutters being opened and closed, anxious words flying from window to window. At first, the cat had started every time he heard an explosion, his tail stiff, his fur bristling, his whiskers tense with fear. But he had got used to the way the rumble came closer and closer, no doubt imagining it was thunder. He leapt about in the flower beds, pulled the petals off a rose with his claws (the rose was in full bloom; the slightest breeze could destroy it; its white petals would fall to the ground, like soft, sweet-smelling rain). Suddenly, as quick as a squirrel, the cat darted up a tree, ripping the bark with his claws. Terrified birds flew off. At the end of a branch he began a savage, arrogant dance, taunting in his bold, warlike way, the sky, the earth, the animals, the moon. Now and again he opened his deep, narrow mouth and let out a piercing miaow, a sharp, provocative call to all the cats nearby.

The birds in the henhouse and the dovecote all woke up and hid their heads beneath their wings, catching the scent of fate and death; a small white hen tentatively climbed on to a metal drinking trough, knocked it over and rushed away, making terrified screeching noises. But the cat had jumped on to the ground now. He stood motionless . . . waiting. His round golden eyes shone in the darkness. There was the sound of leaves rustling and he came back carrying a small dead bird in his mouth, his tongue slowly lapping at its wound. Eyes closed, he savoured the warm blood. He had plunged his claws into the bird's heart and clenched and unclenched his talons, digging deeper and deeper into the tender flesh that covered its delicate bones with slow and rhythmical movements until its heart stopped beating. He ate the bird slowly, then licked himself clean, polishing the tip of his beautiful bushy tail, which was moist and shiny from the damp night air. He was feeling benevolent now: when a shrew darted between his legs he let it go; he was content merely to swipe at a mole's head, leaving it only half dead, a trail of blood on its muzzle. He studied the mole with a scornful trembling of his nostrils but didn't touch it. A different kind of hunger had arisen within him; he arched his back, raised his head and miaowed again, a call that ended in a harsh, imperious cry. An old red pussycat suddenly appeared on the roof of the henhouse, basking in the moonlight.

The short June night was fading. The stars grew paler, the air smelled of milk and moist grass; now, half-hidden behind the forest, only the pink tip of the moon could be seen, growing dimmer and dimmer in the mist.

Tired, triumphant and covered in dew, the cat gnawed on a sprig of grass, then slipped back into Jacqueline's room, on to her bed, looking for that warm spot near her thin feet. He was purring like a kettle on the boil.

A few seconds later, the arsenal exploded.

21

The arsenal exploded and the horrible echo of the explosion had only just stopped (the air all around them shook; all the doors and windows were vibrating and the small wall at the cemetery crumbled) when a long flame shot up, whistling, from the bell tower. The noise of the incendiary bomb had merged with the explosion of the arsenal. In a second, the entire village was in flames. There was hay in the barns, straw in the lofts. Everything caught fire. Roofs caved in, floors cracked in half; the refugees rushed into the streets while the villagers ran to open the cowsheds and stables to save the animals. The horses were neighing, rearing, terrified by the intensity of the noise and fire; they refused to come out and beat their heads and hoofs against the burning walls. A cow rushed by, bellowing in pain and terror as it frantically tried to shake a bale of burning hay from its horns; pieces of glowing straw flew everywhere. In the garden, the blossoming trees were bathed in a red as blood light. Normally, the firemen would have come and people would have calmed down, once the initial fear had passed. But this disaster, happening after so many others, was more than they could bear. Also, they knew the firemen had received orders to leave with all their equipment three days before. They felt hopeless. 'If only the men were here,' cried the women, 'the men!' But the men were far away and the children were running, screaming, rushing about, causing even greater confusion.

The refugees were howling in terror. Among them were the Péricands, half-dressed, faces dirty, hair dishevelled. It was the same as when the bombs had fallen on the road: everyone was shouting at once, calling to each other, and the voices all merged into one – the village was reduced to a roar. 'Jean!', 'Suzanne!', 'Mummy!', 'Grandma!' No one replied. A few youngsters who had managed to get their bicycles out of the burning sheds pushed them violently through the crowd. Yet, oddly enough, everyone believed that they were remaining calm, that they were behaving exactly as they should. Madame Péricand was holding Emmanuel in her arms, Jacqueline and Bernard were clutching her skirt (Jacqueline had even managed to get the cat back into his basket when her mother had pulled her out of bed and she now gripped it tightly to her). 'The most precious things have been saved!' Madame Péricand said to herself over and over again, 'Thank you God!' Her jewellery and money were sewn into a suede pouch pinned inside her blouse and she could feel it against her chest as she ran. She'd had the presence of mind to grab her fur coat and the small overnight case full of the family silver, which she'd kept beside her bed. She had her children, her three children! Sometimes a thought shot through her, as sharp and rapid as lightning, of her two older sons, in danger, far away: Philippe and that mad Hubert. She'd been desperate when Hubert ran away, yet rather proud of him. His behaviour had been irrational, wild, but manly. For them, Philippe and Hubert, she could do nothing, but her three little ones! She had saved her three little ones! She was sure she'd had a premonition the night before; she'd put them to bed half-dressed. Jacqueline didn't have a dress on but a jacket covered her naked shoulders; she wouldn't be cold; it was better than wearing just a blouse; the baby was wrapped up in a blanket; Bernard even had his beret on. She herself had no stockings, just red slippers on her bare feet, but gritting her teeth, arms tight round the baby, who wasn't crying but whose eyes were rolling wildly with fear, she made her way through the panic-stricken crowd, without the slightest idea where she was going. The sky above seemed filled with countless planes (there were two) flying back and forth with their evil buzzing, like hornets.

'Please don't let them bomb us any more! Please don't let them bomb us any more! Please . . .' These words went round and round endlessly in her bowed head. Out loud she said, 'Don't let go of my hand, Jacqueline! Bernard, stop crying! You're behaving like a girl! There, there, baby, don't worry, Mummy's here!' She said these words mechanically, while silently continuing to pray: 'Please don't let them bomb us any more! Let them bomb anyone else, dear God, but not us! I have three children! I have to save them! Please don't let them bomb us any more!'

They finally made it out of the narrow village street; she was in the open countryside; the fire was behind her; the flames fanned out across the sky. Scarcely an hour had passed since dawn, when the bomb had struck the bell tower. They were passed by car upon car fleeing Paris,

Dijon, Normandy, the Lorraine region, France itself. The people inside them were numb. Sometimes they raised their heads to look at the fire in the distance, but their faces were indifferent. They had seen so many things . . .

Nanny was walking behind Madame Péricand. She seemed mute with terror; her lips were moving but she made no sound. She was holding her fluted bonnet with its cotton ties, newly ironed. Madame Péricand looked at her indignantly. 'Really, Nanny, couldn't you have found something more useful to bring? Honestly!' The old woman made an extraordinary effort to speak. She went red in the face, her eyes filled with tears. 'Good Lord,' thought Madame Péricand, 'now *she's* going mad! Whatever will I do?'

But the harsh voice of her mistress had miraculously returned the gift of speech to Nanny . . . She replied in her usual tone of voice, simultaneously respectful and bitter: 'Madame didn't think I would leave it behind? It's valuable!' This bonnet was a bone of contention between them: Nanny hated the hats she was forced to wear – 'so suitable', Madame Péricand thought, 'so appropriate for a servant', for she felt that each social class should wear some sign indicative of their station to avoid any misconceptions, just as shops displayed price tags. 'You can tell it's not her who does the washing and ironing, nasty old bag!' Nanny would say as she worked. Her hands trembling, she put the lace butterfly of a bonnet on over the enormous nightcap she was already wearing.

Madame Péricand looked at her, thought there was something odd about her but couldn't say exactly what it was. Everything seemed incredible. The world was a horrible dream. She dropped down on to the verge, put Emmanuel back into Nanny's arms and said as vehemently as possible, 'Now we have to get out of here' and remained on the ground, waiting for some miracle. There was none, but a donkey pulling a cart passed by. When she saw the driver slow down at the sight of her and her children, Madame Péricand's intuition took over – the intuition innate to the wealthy who can always tell when and where something can be bought.

'Stop!' Madame Péricand shouted. 'Where's the nearest railway station?'
'Saint-Georges.'
'How long would it take you to get there with your donkey?'
'Well, about four hours.'
'Are the trains still running?'

'I've heard they are.'

'Good. I'm getting in. Come on, Bernard, Nanny, bring the baby.'

'But Madame, I wasn't going that way and what with going and coming back, that'll be at least eight hours.'

'You'll be well paid,' said Madame Péricand.

She climbed into the carriage, calculating that if the trains were running normally, she would be in Nîmes the next morning. Nîmes . . . her mother's dear old house, her bedroom, a bath; she nearly fainted at the thought. Would there be enough room for her on the train? 'With three children,' she said to herself, 'I'm sure to manage it.' Because of her position as the mother of a large family, Madame Péricand was usually treated like royalty and came first wherever she was . . . nor was she the kind of woman who allowed anyone to forget what was rightfully hers. She crossed her arms and studied the countryside victoriously.

'But, Madame, what about the car?' Nanny moaned.

'It'll be reduced to ashes by now,' replied Madame Péricand.

'What about the trunks, the children's things?'

The trunks had been loaded on to the servants' van. Only three suitcases were left by the time disaster struck, three suitcases full of linen . . .

'I'll just have to do without them.' Madame Péricand sighed, looking up at the sky, picturing once more, as in a wonderful dream, the deep wardrobes in Nîmes with their treasured cambric and linen.

Nanny, who had lost her big trunk with the metal bands and an imitation pigskin handbag, began to cry. Madame Péricand tried in vain to make her see how ungrateful she was being towards Providence. 'Remember that you are alive, my dear Nanny, nothing else matters!' The donkey trotted on. The farmer took small side roads thick with refugees. At eleven o'clock they arrived at Saint-Georges and Madame Péricand managed to get on a train heading in the direction of Nîmes. Everyone around her was saying the armistice had been signed. Impossible, some said. Nevertheless, there was no more gunfire, no bombs were falling. 'Could this nightmare finally be over?' thought Madame Péricand. She looked again at everything she had brought, 'everything she had saved': her children, her overnight case. She placed her hand over the jewellery and money sewn into her blouse. Yes, during this terrible time she had acted with determination, courage and composure. She hadn't lost her head! She hadn't lost . . . She hadn't . . . Suddenly she cried out in a choked voice.

She clutched her throat and fell backwards, letting out a low moan as if she were suffocating.

'My God, Madame! Madame, what's the matter?' exclaimed Nanny.

'Nanny, my dear Nanny,' Madame Péricand finally groaned in a barely audible voice, 'We forgot . . .'

'What? What did we forget?'

'We forgot my father-in-law,' said Madame Péricand, dissolving into tears.

22

Charles Langelet had driven all night long from Paris to Montargis and so had shared in the general misfortune. Nevertheless, he demonstrated great strength of character. In the hostelry where he stopped for lunch, the groups of refugees around him were complaining about the horrors they had encountered on the journey. They looked to him for confirmation, saying, 'Isn't that so, Monsieur? You saw it too, didn't you? No one can accuse us of exaggerating!' but he merely replied, drily, '*I* didn't see anything.'

'What? No bombs?' asked the surprised owner.

'No, Madame.'

'No fires?'

'Not even a traffic accident.'

'Well, lucky you,' the woman said after thinking for a moment and shrugging her shoulders doubtfully, as if to say, 'He's peculiar!'

Langelet took a bite of the omelette he'd just been served, pushed it away mumbling 'inedible', asked for his bill and left. He got a kind of perverse pleasure from depriving these good souls of the satisfaction they hoped to attain by questioning him, for *they* – vulgar, vile creatures that they were – imagined they were feeling compassion for all mankind, while in reality they were merely thrilled by base, melodramatic curiosity. 'It's unbelievable how much vulgarity there is!' Charles Langelet thought sadly. He was always pained and scandalised when he encountered the real world full of unfortunate people who had never seen a cathedral, a statue, a painting. What was more, the *happy few*, among whom he flattered himself he belonged, displayed the same spinelessness, the same stupidity in the face of misfortune as these common types. Lord! Just think of what these people would make of this 'exodus', '*their* exodus' later on. He could just hear them: '*I* wasn't afraid of the Germans, not me,' an old bag would whine, 'I went straight up to them and said, "This house belongs to the mother of a French officer" – and they didn't say a word.' And another woman would say, 'Bullets were flying all around me, but it's funny, I wasn't scared, not a bit.' It was understood that everyone would embellish their tales with terrifying scenes.

As for Charles, he would simply reply, 'That's odd. Everything seemed quite normal to me. There were a lot of people on the road, but that's all.' He imagined their surprise and smiled, feeling smug. He needed to feel smug. When he thought about his apartment in Paris, his heart broke. Now and again he turned round towards the back of the car to look lovingly at the crates containing his porcelain, his greatest treasures. There was a Capodimonte group he was worried about: he wondered if he'd put enough wood shavings and tissue paper round it. There wasn't much tissue paper left by the time he'd finished wrapping everything. It was a centrepiece for a table: young women dancing with cupids and fawns. He sighed. In his mind, he thought of himself as a Roman fleeing the lava and ash of Pompeii, abandoning his slaves, his house, his gold, but taking with him, in the folds of his tunic, some terracotta figurine, a perfectly shaped vase, or a bowl modelled on a beautiful breast.

He felt simultaneously comforted and bitter at being so different from other people. He looked out at them with his pale eyes. The wave of cars was still moving and all the anxious, sombre faces were the same. What a sad breed! What were they thinking about? What they would eat, what they would drink? *He* was thinking about the cathedral in Rouen, the châteaux of the Loire, the Louvre. A single one of those venerable stones was worth more than a thousand human lives. He was approaching Gien. A black spot appeared in the sky. In a flash he realised that the stream of refugees near the level crossing would be a sitting target for an enemy plane so he pulled off on to a side road. Fifteen minutes later, there was a crash only a few metres away from him. Other cars also trying to avoid the main road collided with each other when a terrified driver took a wrong turn. They rebounded off each other into the fields, shedding luggage, mattresses, birdcages, injured women. Charlie heard confused sounds but didn't turn round. He headed at full speed towards a thick wood. There he stopped his car, waited a moment, then set off again through the countryside. The main highway was clearly becoming too dangerous.

He stopped thinking about the dangers the Rouen cathedral might face for a moment to imagine very precisely what was threatening him, Charles Langelet. He didn't want to dwell on it, but the most unpleasant images filled his mind. His large, delicate, slim hands clenched the steering wheel, trembling slightly. There were few cars and houses where he was, and he had no idea were he was going. He had always had a bad sense of direction. He wasn't used to travelling without a chauffeur. For a while he got lost in the outskirts of Gien, becoming ever more agitated for fear he might run out of petrol. He sighed and shook his head. He had predicted what would happen: he, Charles Langelet, was not made for this uncouth existence. The thousand little pitfalls of daily life were too much for him. The car stopped: out of petrol. He made a small gracious gesture to himself, as one bows before the inevitable. There was nothing to be done, he would have to spend the night in the woods.

'You wouldn't possibly have a can of petrol you could let me have?' he asked a passing driver.

The man said no and Charlie smiled, depressed and bitter. 'Well, that's the human race for you! Egotistical and mean. In times of misfortune, no one will share with his brother, not a crust of bread, not a bottle of beer, not a pathetic little can of petrol.'

The driver turned round and shouted at him, 'There's some about ten kilometres from here, in . . .'

The name of the hamlet was lost as he drove off but Charlie had already started to walk towards the trees. He thought he could make out one or two houses.

'But what about the car? I can't leave the car!' Charlie said to himself in despair. 'Let's try to start it again.' Nothing happened. He was covered with dust as thick as chalk.

A car was slowly making its way towards him. It was jammed with young people, some even clinging to the running board and the roof, like flies. They seemed drunk. 'What a bunch of louts,' Langelet thought, shuddering. Nevertheless, he spoke to them in his most pleasant voice. 'You gentlemen wouldn't happen to have a drop of petrol? I'm stuck.'

They stopped with a horrible screeching of overworked brakes, looked at Charlie and sniggered. 'What's it worth?' one of them finally said.

Charlie knew very well he should have replied, 'However much you want!' but he was mean and, moreover, he was afraid these tramps would be tempted to rob him if they thought he was too rich. Truth be told, he was terrified of being duped. 'I'd pay a reasonable price,' he replied haughtily.

'There ain't none,' said the driver of the jerky, creaking car, and drove off along the sandy road through the forest while Langelet, beside himself, waved his arms about and shouted at him.

'Wait a minute, wait! Stop! At least tell me how much you want!'

They didn't even reply. He was alone. But not for long, for night was falling and refugees were gradually coming into the forest. They hadn't been able to find rooms in a hotel; even the private houses were completely full, so they had decided to spend the night in the woods. Soon it was just like a July campsite in Elisabethville, Langelet thought, feeling sick to his stomach. Children were squealing, the mossy ground was littered with discarded newspaper, dirty clothes and empty tins of food. Some of the women were crying, others were shouting or laughing. Horrible filthy children came up to Charles, who chased them away by rolling his eyes at them angrily but without raising his voice, for he didn't want any trouble from their parents. 'They're the dregs of the dregs, from Belleville,' he mumbled, horrified. 'How did I end up here?' Had chance brought him together with the inhabitants of one of the worst neighbourhoods in Paris, or had Charlie's vivid, anxious imagination got the better of him? All the men looked like bandits, the women like con artists.

Soon it was completely dark, and beneath the thick trees, the translucent shadows of a June night were transformed into black shade interspersed with silver glades, drenched in moonlight. Every sound echoed, distinct and sinister: the planes flying across the sky, the night birds, the distant explosions – either gunfire or tyres bursting, you couldn't be sure. Once or twice a prowler stared at Charles maliciously. He heard things that made him shudder. People weren't thinking straight . . . They kept talking about rich people who'd run away to save their skins and their money, jamming up the roads, while poor people had only their own two legs and had to walk 'till they dropped down exhausted. 'Well, *they're* not those poor people; they've got cars,' Charlie thought, outraged, 'and stolen no doubt!'

He was extremely relieved when a little car pulled up next to him with a young man and woman who were clearly a better class of people than the other refugees. The young man's arm was slightly deformed; he held it in front of him ostentatiously, as if it carried a sign, in big letters, which read 'Unfit for military service'. The woman was young, pretty, and very fair. They shared some sandwiches and soon fell asleep in the front of the car, leaning against each other, cheek to cheek. Charlie tried to sleep as well, but fatigue, overexcitement, fear kept him awake. An hour later the young man in the car opened his eyes, gently disentangled himself from the young woman and lit a cigarette. He saw that Langelet was also awake.

'This is so bad!' he said quietly, leaning towards him.

'Yes, it's very bad.'

'Well, the night will go by fast. I hope to make it to Beaugency tomorrow by taking the side roads because the main road down there is impossible.'

'Really? And it seems there's been some heavy bombing too. Well, you're lucky,' Charlie said. 'I haven't got a drop of petrol left.' He paused. 'If I could impose on you to watch my car for a while' (he really does seem like an honest person, he thought), 'I could go to the next village where I heard I could get some.'

The young man shook his head. 'Unfortunately, Monsieur, there's none left. I bought the last cans . . . and at an outrageous price.' He pointed to the petrol cans tied to the back of the car. 'I have just enough to get to the Loire and cross the bridges before they're blown up.'

'What? They're going to blow up all the bridges?'

'That's what everyone's saying. They're going to fight along the Loire.'

'So you think there's no petrol at all?'

'Oh, I'm sure of it! I would have been glad to let you have some but I only have just enough for myself. I have to get my fiancée to safety at her parents' house. They live in Bergerac. Once we've crossed the Loire, it will be easy to find petrol, I hope.'

'Oh, so she's your fiancée?' Charlie said while thinking of other things.

'Yes. We were supposed to get married on 14 June. Everything was arranged, the invitations were sent, the rings bought, the dress was supposed to be delivered tomorrow morning.' He drifted off into deep thought.

'It's just a delay,' Charles Langelet said politely.

'Who knows where we'll be tomorrow, Monsieur? Obviously, I shouldn't complain. At my age I should have been in the army but with my arm . . . yes, an accident at school . . . but I think that in this war civilians are facing more dangers than the soldiers. They say that certain towns . . .' he lowered his voice '. . . are in ashes and piled high with bodies and there are mass graves. And I've heard some horrifying stories. You know that they've let everyone out of the prisons and insane asylums? Yes, they have, Monsieur. Our leaders have lost their minds. Prisoners are running loose without wardens. I heard that the director of one of these prisons was murdered by the inmates he was ordered to evacuate; it happened right near here. I've seen it with my own eyes: private houses turned upside down, pillaged. And they attack people who are travelling, they steal from people in cars . . .'

'Oh! They steal from . . .'

'We'll never know everything that happened during the exodus. Now they're saying, "You should have stayed at home!" That's nice of them. So we could get massacred in our own homes by the artillery and planes. I'd rented a small house in Montfort-l'Amaury to have a lovely month after our wedding, before going back to my in-laws. It was destroyed on 3 June, Monsieur,' he said indignantly.

He talked a lot and feverishly; he looked exhausted. He touched his fiancée's cheek tenderly as she slept. 'I just want to save Solange!'

'You're both very young, aren't you?'

'I'm twenty-two and Solange is twenty.'

'She's not very comfortable like that,' Charles Langelet said suddenly, sweetly, in a voice even he himself didn't recognise, as sweet as sugar, while his heart beat harder and faster. 'Why don't you both go and stretch out on the grass, over there?'

'What about the car?'

'Oh, I'll watch the car! Don't worry,' Charlie said, trying not to laugh.

The young man still hesitated. 'I want to leave as early as possible. And I sleep so soundly . . .'

'But I'll wake you up. What time do you want to leave? Look, it's nearly midnight,' he said, consulting his watch. 'I'll call you at four o'clock.'

'Oh, Monsieur! You are too kind!'

'Not at all. When I was twenty-two, I was also in love . . .'

The young man made a confused gesture. 'We were supposed to get married on 14 June,' he repeated, sighing.

'Yes, of course, of course . . . we're living through terrible times . . . but I assure you, it's ridiculous to stay cramped in your car. Your fiancée is all bent up. Do you have a blanket?'

'My fiancée has a big travelling coat.'

'It's so nice on the grass. If I didn't have to worry about my rheumatism . . . Oh, you're so lucky to be a young man of twenty!'

The fiancé corrected him: 'Twenty-two.'

'You will see better times, you will always find a way out, you will, while a poor old gentleman like me . . .' He lowered his eyes, like a cat when it purrs. Then he stretched out his hand towards a moonlit clearing just visible between the trees. 'It must be so nice over there . . . you could forget everything.' He waited, then whispered in a falsely nonchalant tone of voice, 'Can you hear that nightingale?'

The bird had been singing for some time, perched high on a branch, indifferent to the noise, the refugees complaining, the large fires they had lit on the grass to chase away the damp. The bird sang and other nightingales in the countryside answered his song. The young man listened to the bird, tilting his head, and he put his arm round his sleeping fiancée. A few moments later he whispered something in her ear. She opened her eyes. He whispered to her again, closer, urging her. Charlie turned away. Nevertheless, he could hear certain words: 'Since this gentleman said he'd watch the car . . .' And: 'You don't love me, Solange, no, you don't . . . And yet you . . .'

Charlie yawned loudly, obviously, and, addressing no one in particular with the exaggerated ease of a bad actor, said, 'I think I'll go to sleep now . . .'

Solange stopped hesitating. She giggled nervously, pushing her fiancé away only to give in and kiss him, saying, 'If Mummy could see us now! Oh, Bob, you're terrible . . . you won't hold it against me afterwards, will you, Bob?'

She walked away with her fiancé's arm around her. Charlie saw them beneath the trees, holding each other and exchanging little kisses. Then they disappeared from sight.

He waited. The half-hour that followed seemed the longest of his life. But he was determined. He felt both anguish and extraordinary pleasure at the same time. His heart beat so violently, so painfully that he muttered, 'This heart of mine . . . can't take it!'

But he knew he had never felt such exquisite pleasure. A cat who sleeps on velvet cushions and is fed on chicken breasts and suddenly finds himself in the middle of the countryside, on the dry branch of a tree wet with dew, sinking his teeth into a trembling, bleeding bird, must feel the same terror, the same cruel joy, he thought, for he was too intelligent not to understand what was happening to him. Quietly, ever so quietly, taking great care not to make any noise with the doors, he climbed into the car next to his, untied the petrol cans (he also took some oil), cut his hands getting the cap off his tank, poured in the petrol and, taking advantage of a moment when several other cars started their motors, drove off.

Once out of the forest, he turned round, smiled up at the trees, silvery green beneath the moon, and thought, 'They will indeed have been married on 14 June after all . . .'

23

The uproar in the streets woke the elder Monsieur Péricand. He opened one pale eye, just one, in confusion and reproach. 'What on earth are they shouting about?' he thought. He had forgotten the journey, the Germans, the war. He thought he was at his son's home in Boulevard Delessert, even though he was staring at a strange room; he didn't understand a thing. He was at an age when the past was more real than the present; he pictured the green cover on his bed in Paris. He stretched his shaking fingers towards the bedside table where, every morning, some attentive person would put out a tray with porridge and his special biscuits. There was no tray, no bowl, not even a table. It was then that he heard the fire roaring in the neighbouring houses, smelled the smoke and guessed what was happening. He opened his mouth, gasped silently, like a fish out of water, and fainted.

Yet the house hadn't burned to the ground. Only a part of the roof had been destroyed. After a great deal of panic and chaos, the flames died down. Amid the wreckage, the fire smouldered and sizzled quietly, but the house was intact and towards evening they discovered the elder Monsieur Péricand, alone in his bed. He was muttering, confused. He calmly let them take him to the nursing home.

'He'll be better off there. I've got no time to take care of him. Imagine the idea,' said the owner, 'what with the refugees, the Germans about to march in and the fire and all . . .'

But she said nothing about what was worrying her most: her husband and two sons, gone, all three called up and missing . . . All three away in that vaguely defined, ever-changing, terrifyingly imminent place called 'the war' . . .

The nursing home was very clean, very well looked after by the Sisters of the Sacred Sacrament. They put Monsieur Péricand in a bed next to a window; he would be able to see the tall green June trees outside and the fifteen old people around him, silent and calm in their white sheets. But he saw nothing. He thought he was still at home. Now and again he seemed to talk to his weak purplish hands, folded on top of the grey blanket. He would utter a few harsh, broken words to them, then slowly shake his head and, out of breath, close his eyes. The flames hadn't touched him, he hadn't been wounded, but he had a very high fever. The doctor was in the next village, tending to the victims of the bombing. Late that evening he was finally able to examine Monsieur Péricand. He didn't say much: he was staggering with exhaustion, he had cared for sixty wounded and hadn't slept in forty-eight hours. He gave him an injection and promised to come back the next day. To the Sisters there was no question: they had enough experience with the dying to recognise death by a sigh, a whimper, drops of cold sweat, motionless fingers. They sent someone to get the priest who had been with the doctor in town and hadn't slept either. He gave Monsieur Péricand the last rites and the old man seemed to come round. As he left, the priest told the Sisters that the poor old gentleman had made his peace with God and would die a very Christian death.

One of the Sisters was small and thin, with deep blue mischievous eyes that sparkled with courage from beneath her white wimple; the other was sweet and shy, with red cheeks and a terrible toothache, which caused her to bring her hand to her painful gums now and again, in the middle of saying her rosary, smiling humbly as if she were ashamed that the cross she had to bear was so light during these terrible times. It was to her that Monsieur Péricand suddenly said (it was just after midnight and the commotion of the day had died down; now all you could hear were the cats howling in the convent garden), 'Daughter, I'm not well . . . Go and get the notary.'

He thought she was his daughter-in-law. In his delirium, he was very surprised that she had put on a wimple to nurse him, but nevertheless it could only be her. He repeated quietly, patiently, 'Monsieur Nogaret . . . notary . . . last Will . . .'

'What should we do?' said Sister Marie of the Sacred Sacrament to Sister Marie of the Chérubins.

The two white wimples tilted towards each other, almost meeting above Monsieur Péricand in his bed.

'The notary won't come out at this hour, my poor dear . . . Go to sleep . . . There'll be time enough tomorrow.'

'No . . . no time . . .' the quiet voice said. 'Monsieur Nogaret will come
. . . telephone him, please.'

Once again the nuns conferred and one of them disappeared, then came
back carrying some hot herbal tea. He tried to take a few sips but spat it
out immediately; it ran down his white beard. Suddenly he became
extremely agitated; he was groaning, shouting orders: 'Tell him to hurry
. . . he promised . . . as soon as I called . . . please . . . hurry, Jeanne!' (He
no longer thought he was talking to his daughter-in-law but to his wife,
who had been dead for forty years.)

A particularly sharp pain from her bad tooth prevented Sister Marie of
the Sacred Sacrament from protesting. She nodded – 'Yes, all right' – but
remained where she was, dabbing her cheek with her handkerchief.

Her friend stood up decisively. 'We have to get the notary, Sister.'

She was passionate, with a natural fighting spirit and her forced in-
activity was frustrating. She had wanted to go to the town with the doctor
and priest but couldn't leave the fifteen old people at the nursing home
(she didn't have much faith in the leadership qualities of Sister Marie of
the Sacred Sacrament). When the fire had started she had trembled
beneath her wimple. Nevertheless, she had managed to roll the fifteen
beds out of the room and prepare ladders, ropes and buckets of water.
The fire had not reached the nursing home, which was two kilometres
away from the bombed church, but she had waited, flinching at the
screams from the frightened crowd, the smell of smoke, the sight of
flames – fixed to her post and ready for anything. But nothing happened.
The disaster victims were treated at the hospital; there was nothing to
do but make soup for the fifteen old people. Until the sudden arrival of
Monsieur Péricand galvanised her once more. 'We have to go.'

'Do you think so, Sister?'

'He might have some important last wishes to set down.'

'But what if Maître Charboeuf isn't at home?'

Sister Marie of the Chérubins shrugged her shoulders. 'At half past
midnight?'

'He won't want to come.'

'That will be the day!' the young nun said indignantly. 'It's his duty to
come. I'll pull him out of bed myself if I have to.'

She went out, but hesitated on the doorstep. The religious community
– which consisted of four nuns, two of whom had gone into retreat at the

convent of Paray-le-Monial at the beginning of June and still hadn't been able to return – owned a single bicycle. Up until now, none of the Sisters had dared use it, afraid of causing a scandal in the village. Sister Marie of the Chérubins herself had said, 'We must wait until the Good Lord Himself provides an emergency. For example, a sick person is dying and we have to get the doctor and the priest. Every second is precious, I jump on my bicycle, no one would dare say a word! And the next time I do it they won't even notice . . .' They hadn't yet had an emergency, but Sister Marie of the Chérubins was longing to ride that bicycle! Five years ago, before she became a nun, she'd had so many happy outings with her sisters, so many races, so many picnics. She threw back her black veil, said to herself, 'It's now or never' and, her heart pounding with joy, grabbed the handle-bars.

Within a few minutes she was in the village. She had some difficulty waking Maître Charboeuf, who was a sound sleeper, and even more trouble persuading him he had to come to the nursing home right away. Maître Charboeuf, whom the local girls called 'Big Baby' because of his chubby pink cheeks and full lips, had an easygoing nature and a wife who terrified him. He got dressed, sighing, and headed for the nursing home. He found Monsieur Péricand wide awake, very red and burning with fever.

'Here's the notary,' the nun said.

'Sit down, sit down,' said the old man, 'There's no time to lose.'

The notary asked the nursing home's gardener and three sons to act as witnesses. Seeing that Monsieur Péricand was in a hurry, he took some paper out of his pocket and prepared to start writing.

'I'm ready, Monsieur. If you would, please first tell me your surname, Christian names and title.'

'You're not Nogaret?'

Péricand came back to his senses. He glanced at the nursing home's walls, at the plaster statue of St Joseph opposite his bed, at the two amazing roses Sister Marie of the Chérubins had picked from the window box and put into a slim blue vase. He tried to work out where he was and why he was alone, but gave up. He was dying, there it was, and he wished to have a proper death. This final act, this death, this Will, how many times had he imagined them, the final brilliant performance of a Péricand-Maltête on this earth. For ten years he had been nothing more than a pitiful old man who needed someone else to dress him and wipe his nose, and now suddenly he could reclaim his rightful place! To punish, reward, disappoint, delight, distribute his worldly goods according to his own wishes. To control everyone. To influence everyone. To come first. (Afterwards, there would be a ceremony in which he would indeed come first, in a black coffin, on a raised platform, with flowers, but he would be there only symbolically or as a winged spirit, while here, once more, he was alive . . .)

'What is your name?' he asked quietly.

'Maître Charboeuf,' the notary said unassumingly.

'All right, it doesn't matter. Let's get on with it.'

He began dictating slowly, with difficulty, as if he were reading sentences written for himself and visible only to him.

'Before Maître Charboeuf . . . notary at . . . and in the presence of . . .' mumbled the notary, 'Monsieur Péricand in person . . .'

Monsieur Péricand made a feeble attempt at saying his name louder, to emphasise its importance, but had to pause for breath, making it impossible for him to enunciate the prestigious syllables individually. His purple hands fluttered for a moment over the sheets, like puppets: he thought he was writing thick black marks on white paper, as he had in the past, when he signed cards, bonds, sales documents, contracts: Péricand . . . Pé – ri – cand, Louis-Auguste.

'Residing at?'

'18 Boulevard Delessert, Paris.'

'In ill health, but sound of mind, he comes before the notary and witnesses,' said Charboeuf, glancing up at the sick man and looking doubtful.

He was overwhelmed by this dying man. He was fairly experienced; his clients were mainly local farmers, but all rich men make their wills the same way. This was a rich man, there was no doubt about it. Even though he was wearing one of the nursing home's coarse nightshirts, it was clear he was someone important. To be of service like this to him on his deathbed – Maître Charboeuf felt honoured. 'Do you wish, Monsieur, to name your son as sole beneficiary?'

'Yes, I bequeath all my worldly goods and possessions to Adrien Péricand, with instructions for him to deposit immediately and without delay five million to the charitable institution I founded, known as the

Penitent Children of the 16th Arrondissement. This institution is instructed to commission an excellent artist to paint a life-size portrait of me on my deathbed, or to sculpt a bust that is a good likeness of me, and to place it in the entrance hall of the aforementioned establishment. To my dearly beloved sister Adèle-Emilienne-Louise, to compensate her for the feud caused by the inheritance left me by our venerable mother, Henriette Maltête, I do bequeath as hers and hers alone the property I own in Dunkerque bought in 1912 with all its existing buildings and that portion of the docks which also belongs to me. I entrust my son with the responsibility of carrying out this wish. I desire that my château in Bléoville, in the Vorhange region in Calvados, be turned into a home for former soldiers severely wounded in the war, preferably for those who have been paralysed or have suffered mental breakdowns. I desire that a simple plaque be displayed on the wall inscribed with the words "Péricand-Maltête Charitable Institution, in memory of his two sons killed in Champagne". When the war is over . . .'

'I think . . . I think it *is* over,' Maître Charboeuf shyly interjected.

But he didn't realise that Monsieur Péricand was thinking about the last war, the one that had taken two sons from him and tripled his fortune. He was back in September 1918, just after their victory, when he had nearly died of a bout of pneumonia and when, in the presence of his family gathered at his bedside (all the relatives from the north and south had rushed to be there when they heard the news), he had performed what turned out to be a rehearsal of his death: he had dictated his last wishes then and they had remained intact within him until now, when he could give them life.

'When the war is over, I wish a monument to be built to honour the dead for which I bequeath the sum of three thousand francs to be taken from my estate and to be erected on the town square in Bléoville. At the top, in large gold letters, the names of my two oldest sons, then a space, then . . .' he closed his eyes, exhausted, '. . . then all the other names in small letters . . .'

He was silent for such a long time that the notary looked anxiously at the Sisters. Was he . . . ? Was it all over already? But Sister Marie of the Chérubins calmly shook her head. He wasn't dead yet. He was thinking. In his motionless body, his memory was travelling through immense spans of time and space: 'Almost all of my fortune is tied up in American stocks and bonds, which I was advised would be a good investment. I don't believe it any more.' He shook his beard mournfully. 'I don't believe it any more. I wish my son to convert them immediately into French francs. There is also some gold, but it's not worth keeping. It should be sold. A copy of my portrait should also be placed in the château in Bléoville in the downstairs ballroom. I bequeath to my faithful valet an annual income of one thousand francs for the rest of his life. As for my future great-grandchildren, I wish their parents to name the boys Louis-Auguste and the girls Louise-Augustine after me.'

'Is that everything?' Maître Charboeuf asked.

He bowed his long beard, indicating yes, that was everything. For a few moments that seemed brief to the notary, the witnesses and the Sisters, but to him were as long as a century, as long as delirium, as long as a dream, Monsieur Péricand-Maltête moved back in time to recall the life he had been given on this earth: the family dinners, the Boulevard Delessert, naps in the drawing room, Albert the cat on his lap; the last time he saw his older brother when they had parted vowing never to have anything more to do with each other (and he had secretly bought back the shares in that deal). Jeanne, his wife in Bléoville, hunched up with rheumatism, lying on a cane chaise longue in the garden, holding a paper fan (she died a week later), and Jeanne, in Bléoville, thirty-five years earlier, just after their wedding, when some bees had come in through the open window and were gathering pollen from the lilies in her bridal bouquet and the garland of orange blossom thrown at the foot of the bed. Jeanne had rushed into his arms, laughing, so he could protect her . . .

Then he was certain he could feel death approaching. He made a startled little gesture (as if he was trying to get through a door that was too narrow for him, saying, 'No, please, after you') and a look of surprise appeared on his face. 'Is this what it is?' he seemed to say. 'So this is death, then?' The surprise on his face faded and he looked stern, solemn.

Maître Charboeuf wrote very quickly, '. . . When the Testator was handed the pen to affix his signature to this Last Will and Testament, he tried to lift his head, but could not, and immediately breathed his last, in the presence of the notary and the witnesses, who nevertheless, after reading the document, signed their names to render the document legal.'

24

Jean-Marie, meanwhile, was starting to come round. He had drifted in and out of sleep for four days, semi-conscious and feverish. It was only today he felt a bit stronger. A doctor had been able to come the night before to change the dressing; his temperature had dropped. From where he was lying on the bed, he could see a large, dark kitchen, the white hat on an old woman who was sitting in the corner, beautifully shiny pots on the wall and a calendar depicting a chubby-cheeked French soldier hugging two young women from Alsace, a souvenir of the previous war. It was strange to see how the memories of the last war were still so alive in this house. Four pictures of men in uniform had pride of place: a small tricolour ribbon and a crêpe rosetta were pinned up in a corner; and next to him, to keep him from getting bored during the long hours of his convalescence, was a collection of the 1914–18 editions of *L'Illustration* bound in green and black.

He kept overhearing the same phrases in the conversations around him: 'Verdun, Charleroi, the Marne . . .', 'During the other war . . .', 'When I was part of the occupying forces in Mulhouse . . .' They hardly spoke about the present war, their defeat. It was something they couldn't quite believe yet. Something that would only become a living, horrible reality a few months later, perhaps a few years later, perhaps not until these little boys with dirty faces that Jean-Marie could see peering over the wooden gate in front of the door grew into men. Wearing torn straw hats, their cheeks rosy or dark-skinned, holding long green sticks, frightened, curious, they stood on tip-toes to make themselves tall enough to see the wounded soldier inside, and when Jean-Marie moved they disappeared, like frogs jumping into the water. Sometimes the open gate let in a chicken, a ferocious old dog, an enormous turkey. Jean-Marie only saw his hosts at mealtimes. During the day, the old woman in the white hat tended to him. In the evening, two young women would sit with him. One was called Cécile, the other Madeleine. For a long time he thought they were sisters. But no. Cécile was the farmer's daughter and Madeleine was a foster-child. Both of them were attractive, not beautiful but fresh-faced. Cécile had a round red face and lively brown eyes; Madeleine was more delicate, a blonde with bright cheeks, smooth as satin and pink as apple blossom.

From the young women he learned what had happened that week. As they spoke about it, in their slightly harsh accent, all those terribly serious events lost their tragic element. 'It's really sad,' they would say and, 'It's not very nice to see things like that' . . . 'Oh, Monsieur! It's really upsetting!' He wondered if all the people here spoke like them, or whether it was something much deeper, rooted in the very souls of these girls, in their youth, some instinct that told them that wars end and invaders leave, that even when distorted, even when mutilated, life goes on. His own mother, knitting while the soup was cooking, would sigh and say, '1914? That's the year your father and I got married. We were miserable by the end of it, but very happy at the beginning.' Even that bleak year was sweetened, bathed in the reflection of their love.

In the same way, he thought, the summer of 1940 would remain in the memories of these young women as the summer they were twenty, in spite of everything. He didn't want to think; thinking was worse than physical pain, but everything flooded back, everything went round and round in his head endlessly: being called back from leave on 15 May, those four days in Angers, no trains running any more, soldiers lying on wooden boards, being bitten by insects, then the air raids, the bombings, the battle of Rethel, the retreat, the battle of the Somme, another retreat, days when they had fled from city to city, without officers, without orders, without weapons, and finally the train compartment in flames. He tossed and turned, groaning. He didn't know if the fighting was real, or if it was all a confusing dream born of his thirst and high fever. Come on, it wasn't possible . . . There are some things that just aren't possible . . . Hadn't someone said something about Sédan? That was in 1870. He could picture it still: it was at the top of the page, in the history book with the reddish cloth cover. It was . . . He quietly pronounced the words: 'Sédan, the defeat at Sédan . . . the disastrous battle of Sédan decided the outcome of the war . . .' On the wall above him the image on the calendar, the smiling rosy-cheeked soldier with the two women from Alsace who were showing off their white stockings . . . Yes, all that was a dream, the past and he . . . he started trembling and said, 'Thank you, it's nothing, thank you, please don't trouble yourself . . .' while they slipped a hot-water bottle under his heavy, stiff legs.

'You seem better tonight.'

'I feel better,' he replied.

He asked for a mirror and smiled when he saw the black beard on his chin.

'I'll have to shave tomorrow . . .'

'If you're strong enough. Who do you want to look handsome for?'

'For you.'

They laughed and moved closer. They were curious to know where he came from, where he'd been wounded. Now and again, feeling guilty, they would stop talking. 'Oh, but you mustn't let us chatter on . . . you'll get tired . . . then we'll start arguing, we will . . . It's Michaud, your name? . . . Jean-Marie?'

'Yes.'

'Are you from Paris? What do you do? Are you a worker? Of course not! I can tell by your hands. You work in business or maybe in the government?'

'Just a student.'

'Oh! You study? Why?'

'My goodness,' he said after thinking a moment, 'I wonder why myself sometimes!'

It was funny . . . he and his friends had worked, sat and passed exams, earned diplomas, all the time knowing it was pointless, it wouldn't do them any good because there would be a war . . . Their future had been mapped out in advance, their careers were made in heaven, just like they used to say that 'marriages were made in heaven'. He had been conceived while his father was home on leave in 1915. He was born out of the war and (he had always known it) war would be his fate. There was nothing morbid in this idea; he shared it with many boys his age; it was simply logical and reasonable. But, he said to himself, the worst is over now, and that changes everything. Once again there is a future. The war is over – terrible, shameful, but over. And . . . there is hope . . .

'I wanted to write books,' he said shyly, expressing to these country girls, these strangers, a wish buried deep in his heart that had barely taken shape in his mind.

Then he wanted to know the name of the place, the farm where he was.

'It's far from everywhere,' said Cécile, 'the middle of nowhere. Oh, it's not usually much fun, I can tell you. The more we look after the animals, the more like them we become, right, Madeleine?'

'Have you been here a long time, Mademoiselle Madeleine?'

'I was three weeks old. Cécile's mother brought the two of us up together. We're sisters, 'cause we nursed from the same mother.'

'I can see you get along well together.'

'We don't always think alike,' said Cécile. 'She'd like to become a nun!'

'Sometimes . . .' said Madeleine, smiling.

She had a pretty smile, unhurried and a little shy.

'I wonder where she came from,' Jean-Marie thought. Her hands were red but they were graceful, like her ankles and legs. A foster-child . . . He felt a little curious and a bit sorry for her. He was grateful to her for the hazy daydreams she inspired in him. They were a diversion, they prevented him from thinking about himself, about the war. It was just a shame he felt so weak. It was difficult to laugh, to joke with them . . . and that must be what they were hoping for. In the countryside, it was commonplace for young girls and boys to tease each other . . . It was their custom, it was what they did. They would be disappointed and upset if he didn't laugh with them.

He made an effort to smile.

'A boy will come along who will make you change your mind, Mademoiselle Madeleine, then you won't want to be a nun any more!'

'It's true, it comes over me sometimes, it does . . .'

'When?'

'Oh, I don't know . . . on sad days . . .'

'As for boys, well, there aren't many around here,' said Cécile. 'I told you we're in the middle of nowhere. The few there are get taken by the war. So then what? Oh, it's really bad luck being a girl!'

'Everyone,' said Madeleine, 'has some bad luck.' She had sat down next to the wounded young man, but suddenly she got up. 'Cécile, did you forget! The floor's not been washed.'

'It's your turn.'

'Oh, really! You've got some nerve! It's *your* turn!'

They argued for a few minutes, then did the job together. They were amazingly skilful and lively. Soon the cool water made the red flagstones shine. The smell of grass, milk and wild mint drifted in from the doorway. Jean-Marie rested his cheek on his hand. It was strange, the contrast between this absolute serenity and the turmoil within him, for the unbearable din of the last six days had remained in his ears and it only took a moment of silence for it all to rise up again: the sound of twisting metal, the dull, slow beating of an iron hammer on an enormous anvil . . . He winced and started sweating all over . . . train compartments being machine-gunned, the crash of collapsing beams drowning out people's screams.

'Even so,' he said out loud, 'I just have to put that out of my mind, don't I?'

'What's that? Do you need something?'

He didn't reply. Suddenly he didn't recognise Cécile and Madeleine. They shook their heads, dismayed.

'It's his fever getting worse.'

'And you made him talk too much!'

'Are you having me on! He didn't say a word. We were the ones talking the whole time!'

'It wore him out.'

Madeleine leaned down over him. He saw her pink cheek right next to his, caught its scent of strawberries and kissed it. She stood back blushing and laughing, fixing some locks of hair that had fallen down.

'All right, all right now, you scared me . . . You're not as sick as all that!'

'Who on earth is this girl?' he thought. He had kissed her as if he were bringing a glass of cool water to his lips. He was on fire. His throat, the inside of his mouth seemed to crack from the heat, dried out by the intensity of the flames. This bright, soft skin quenched his thirst. At the same time he felt totally lucid, with the kind of lucidity that comes from sleeplessness and fever. He had forgotten the names of these young girls and his own. The mental effort it took to understand his present condition, in this place he didn't recognise, was too difficult for him. He wore himself out trying, but in the meantime his soul drifted light and serene, like a fish in the water, like a bird blown along by the wind. He didn't see himself, Jean-Marie, but someone else, a nameless soldier, defeated, but refusing to give up hope, a wounded young man who did not want to die, a desperate man who refused to despair. 'Even so, we have to make it through . . . we have to get away, from this blood, from this mud dragging us down . . . We're not just going to lie down and die . . . Are we, well, are we? That would be too ridiculous. We have to hang on . . . hang on . . . hang on . . .' he muttered, and when he came to, eyes wide open, clinging to his bolster, sitting up in bed, he gazed at the night with its full moon, the silent, sweet-smelling night, the sparkling night, so gentle after the heat of the day and which, for once, the farmhouse welcomed through its open doors and windows so it could refresh and bring peace to the suffering man.

25

When Father Péricand found himself forced to continue the journey on foot, the boys following after him, each carrying a blanket and haversack and dragging their feet in the dust, he had decided to head away from the Loire, an area fraught with danger, towards the woods; but soldiers had already set up camp there and, since planes were bound to spot them from the air, the danger seemed just as great amid the trees as on the river banks. And so, leaving the main road, he took a path covered with stones, virtually a footpath, trusting his instinct to lead him to some isolated house, just as when, in the mountains, he led his group of skiers towards a refuge hidden by the fog or snowstorm. It was a beautiful June day, so brilliant and hot that the boys felt intoxicated. Silent until now and well-behaved, too well-behaved, they began jostling each other, shouting, and Father Péricand could hear laughter and snatches of whispered songs. He listened more closely and, hearing an obscene refrain mumbled behind him, as if through half-closed lips, he suggested they all sing a song together. He struck up, energetically enunciating the words, but only a few voices joined in. After some moments everyone fell silent. He too walked on without speaking, wondering what this sudden freedom might awaken within these poor children, what disturbing desires? What dreams? One of the younger ones stopped suddenly and cried, 'A lizard, oh! A lizard! Look!' In the sunshine, between two rocks, agile tails appeared, disappeared; they could see their delicate flat heads; their throats pulsating in and out to a rapid, frightened beat. The boys watched, entranced. Some of them even knelt down on the path. The priest waited a few moments, then waved to them to move on. The children meekly got up, but at that very moment pebbles flew out of their hands with such dexterity, such surprising speed, that two of the lizards – the most beautiful, the biggest, their skin a delicate blue-grey colour – were killed on the spot.

'Why did you do that?' the priest exclaimed, upset.

No one replied.

'Well, why? What a spineless act!'

'But they're like snakes, they bite,' said a boy with a long pointed nose and a pale, dazed expression.

'Don't be ridiculous! Lizards are harmless.'

'Oh! We didn't know, Father,' he replied in a sly voice, with a feigned innocence that didn't fool the priest.

But he knew it was neither the time nor the place to insist; he just nodded briefly as if he were satisfied with the answer and added, 'Well, now you know.'

He organised them into lines to follow him. Until now he had let them walk as they liked, but he suddenly thought that some of them might try to run away. They obeyed him so perfectly, so mechanically – no doubt used to hearing the whistle blow, to standing in line, to being docile, to enforced silence – that it broke his heart. He glanced at their faces, which had suddenly became glum and lifeless – as closed as a house when the door is locked, the life within withdrawn, absent or dead.

'We'd better hurry up if we want to find shelter tonight,' he said. 'As soon as I know where we'll be sleeping and after we eat (you'll be getting hungry soon!) we can make a campfire and you can stay outdoors as long as you like.'

He walked among them, talked to them about his young boys from the Auvergne, about skiing, mountain climbing, trying to interest them, to get closer to them. All in vain. They didn't even seem to be listening; he realised that anything he said to them – encouragement, reprimands, information – would never sink in, for their souls were shut off, walled up, secret and silent.

'If only I could look after them for longer,' he thought to himself. But in his heart he knew he didn't really want to. He only wanted one thing: to be rid of them as soon as possible, to be relieved of his responsibility and this feeling of unease he felt weighing down on him. The duty of love which, until now, he had felt was almost simple, so great was the Grace of God within him, now seemed almost impossible to feel. 'Even though', he thought humbly, 'it would mean that, for the first time perhaps, I would really have to try, it would be a true sacrifice. How weak I am!'

He called over one of the younger boys who was always lagging behind. 'Are you tired? Do your shoes hurt?'

Yes, he had guessed correctly: the lad's shoes were too tight and hurting him. He took his hand to help him, talking to him quietly and, since the boy was slouching – his shoulders stooped, his back round – the priest gently placed two fingers round his neck and pulled him up straight. The young boy didn't resist. In fact, with a distant, indifferent look on his face, he leaned his neck against the hand that held it, and this light, insistent pressure, this strange, ambiguous caress (or rather this expectation of a caress) made the priest blush. He took the child by the chin and tried to look into his eyes, but his eyelids were lowered and he couldn't see into them.

He walked faster, trying to collect himself with an internal dialogue, as he always did at sad moments. It wasn't exactly what you'd call a prayer. Often it wasn't even a collection of words recognisable as human speech. It was a kind of intangible meditation from which he emerged bathed in joy and peace. But both abandoned him today. The pity he felt was corrupted by a stirring of anxiety and bitterness. It was only too clear that these poor wretches were lacking Grace: His Grace. He wanted to be able to shower them with Grace, inundate their barren hearts with love and faith. It would take but a sigh from our Crucified Lord, the flutter of a wing from one of His angels to bring about the miracle, but nevertheless he, Philippe Péricand, had been chosen by God to soften them, to unlock their souls, to prepare them to receive God. He suffered because he was incapable of bringing it about. He had been spared the moments of doubt and the sudden hardening of the soul that take hold of some believers, abandoning them, not in the hands of the princes of this world, but in a terrible darkness halfway between Satan and God.

His temptation was different: it was a kind of impatience to be holy, the desire to gather liberated souls around him, a ripple of urgency which, once he had opened someone's heart to God, propelled him towards other conquests, leaving him forever frustrated, dissatisfied, disappointed with himself. It wasn't enough! No, Lord Jesus, it wasn't enough! The old heathen who had confessed, taken Communion in his final hour, the sinful woman who had renounced vice, the pagan who had wanted to be baptised. Not enough, no, not enough! He recognised something similar in the way a greedy man hoards his gold. And yet, no, it wasn't exactly like that. It reminded him of certain moments he'd spent at the river when he was a child: the quiver of joy every time he caught a fish (yet now he didn't understand how he could have liked such a cruel game, and even found it difficult to eat fish; vegetables, dairy products, fresh bread, chestnuts and that country soup so thick the spoon stands straight up in it all by itself, these were all he needed to sustain him). But as a child he had been fanatical about fishing and he remembered his anguish when the sun began to set on the water, when he had hardly caught any fish and he knew the day was nearly over. He had been criticised for his excessive scruples. He himself feared they might not come from God but from an Other . . . Yet never had he felt that anguish as he did today, on this journey, beneath this sky where lethal planes sparkled, among these children whose physical bodies were the only thing he could hope to save . . .

They had been walking for some time when they saw the first houses of a village. It was very small, intact, empty: its inhabitants had fled. However, before leaving, they had firmly secured the doors and windows; they had taken their dogs with them, carried the rabbits and chickens. Only a few cats were left behind, sleeping in the sunshine on garden paths or walking along the low roofs, looking replete and tranquil. It was the time of year when all the roses were in bloom, so above every doorway beautiful flowers opened their petals, generously, happily, inviting the wasps and bumblebees to drink from deep inside their hearts. This village abandoned by its people, where no footsteps, no voices could be heard and where all the sounds of the countryside were absent – the creaking of wheelbarrows, the cooing of pigeons, the clucking from the poultry yards – this village had become the kingdom of the birds, the bees and the hornets. Philippe thought he had never heard so many vibrant, joyous songs nor seen so many swarms all around him. Hay, strawberries, blackcurrants, the little sweet-smelling flowers in the borders, each flower bed, each lawn, each blade of grass gave off a soft buzzing sound, like a spinning wheel. All these small plots had been tended with loving care; all of them had an archway covered with roses, a tunnel where you could still see the last lilacs of the season, two iron chairs, a bench in the sunshine. The redcurrants were enormous, transparent and golden.

'What a wonderful dessert they will make for us tonight,' said Philippe. 'The birds will have to share with us – we won't be harming anyone by picking this fruit. Now, you all have plenty of food in your backpacks, so we won't go hungry. But don't expect to be sleeping in a bed tonight. I don't suppose sleeping under the stars for one night would frighten you, would it? You have good blankets. Let's see, what do we need? A meadow, a natural spring. The barns and stables don't appeal to you, I bet! Me neither . . . It's so beautiful out. Come on, eat some fruit to keep you going and follow me, we'll try to find a good spot.'

He waited a quarter of an hour while the children gorged themselves on strawberries; he watched them carefully to make sure they didn't step on the flowers and vegetables but he didn't have to intervene, they were really very good. He didn't blow the whistle this time, he just spoke loudly. 'Come on, now, leave some for tonight. Follow me. If you don't dawdle you won't have to line up.'

Once again they obeyed. They looked at the trees, the sky, the flowers, without Philippe being able to guess what they were actually thinking . . . What they really liked, he thought, what really touched their hearts, was not the natural world, but this intoxicating scent of fresh air and freedom they were breathing in, so new to them.

'Do any of you know the countryside?' Philippe asked.

'No, Father, no, Sir, no,' they all said, one after the other.

Philippe had already noticed that he would only get a response from them after a few moments' silence, as if they were making up a story, a lie, or as if they didn't exactly understand what they were meant to do . . . Always the same feeling of dealing with people who were . . . not quite human . . . he thought. Out loud he said, 'Come on, let's get moving.'

When they left the village, they saw a large, overgrown private park, a beautifully deep, clear lake and a house up on a hill.

The château, without a doubt, thought Philippe. He rang the bell at the gate in the hope of finding someone at home, but the caretaker's cottage was locked up and no one answered.

'There's a meadow over there that looks perfect for us,' said Philippe, pointing towards the banks of the lake. 'We must make the best of it, boys! We'll cause less damage there than in these beautiful little gardens; we'll be better off than on the road and, if there's a storm, we could take shelter in those little changing huts . . .'

The park had only a wire fence round it; they got over it easily.

'Don't forget', Philippe said, laughing, 'that even though I'm breaking a rule, I still insist you treat this property with the utmost respect; I don't want to see a single branch broken, papers left on the lawn, or any empty tins. Understand? If you behave then I'll let you go swimming in the lake tomorrow.'

The grass was so high it came up to their knees and they crushed flowers underfoot. Philippe showed them the flowers associated with the Virgin, stars with six white petals, and St Joseph's flowers, pale lilac, almost pink.

'Can we pick them, Sir?'

'Yes. You can pick as many of those as you like. They just need a bit of sun and rain to grow back again. Now *those* must have taken a lot of time and effort,' he said, pointing to the flower beds planted all around the château.

One of the boys next to him raised his small square face towards the large shuttered windows. 'There must be some great stuff in there!'

He had spoken quietly but with such muted envy that the priest was troubled. When he didn't reply, the boy persisted: 'Don't you think, Father, there must be some stuff in there?'

'We ain't never seen a place like that,' said another.

'Of course, there must be some very beautiful things inside, furniture, paintings, statues . . . but many of these houses are just ruins and you would probably be disappointed if you expected to see amazing things,' Philippe replied cheerfully. 'But I suppose you are most interested in the food. I should tell you that the people from around here seem to have planned ahead and taken everything away with them. And since we wouldn't have the right to help ourselves to anything that didn't belong to us in any case, it's better not to think about it and just make do with what we have. Now, I'm going to put you into three groups: the first will find some dead wood, the second will get some water, the third will lay out the food.'

They followed his orders, working quickly and efficiently. They lit a big fire at the edge of the lake; they ate, they drank, they picked some wild strawberries. Philippe wanted to organise some games but the children seemed gloomy and restrained, there was no shouting, no laughter. The lake no longer shone in the sunlight, just faintly glimmered, and they could hear frogs croaking on the banks. In the light of the fire the boys sat motionless, wrapped up in their blankets.

'Do you want to go to sleep?'

No one answered.

'You aren't cold, are you?'

Silence again.

They can't all be asleep, thought the priest. He got up and walked between the rows. Sometimes he bent down, covered someone up who was thinner, frailer than the others, with limp hair, ears that stuck out. Their eyes were closed. They were pretending to be asleep or perhaps sleep really had overcome them. Philippe went back to read his Bible next to the fire. Now and again he raised his eyes to look at the reflections in the water. These moments of silent meditation took away all his cares, made up for all his pain. Once again, love entered his heart like rain falling on dry ground, first drop by drop, fighting to carve a path through the pebbles, then in a long cascade straight to his heart.

These poor children! One of them was dreaming and letting out a long plaintive moan. The priest raised his hand in the darkness, blessed them, murmured a prayer. 'Pater amat vos,' he whispered. He liked to say this to his catechism students when he was urging them to repent, to be submissive, to pray. 'The Father loves you.' How could he have believed they were lacking divine Grace, these poor wretches? Might he not perhaps be less loved than them, treated with less indulgence, less divine affection than the most insignificant, the most lowly of them? Oh Lord Jesus, forgive me! It was a moment of pride, a trap set by a demon! What am I? Less than nothing, dust beneath your dear feet, Lord! Yes, without a doubt, I whom you have loved, whom you have protected since I was a child, whom you have led towards you – you have the right to ask anything of me. But these children . . . some will be saved . . . the others . . . The Saints will redeem them . . . Yes, all is well, all is goodness, all is Grace. Lord Jesus, forgive me my sorrow!

The water gently rippled, the night was peaceful and solemn. This presence without whom he could not live, this Breath, this watchful Eye was upon him in the darkness. A child sleeping in the dark, pressed against his mother's heart, has no need of light to recognise her cherished features, her hands, her rings! He even laughed softly with pleasure. 'Jesus, you are here, with me once again. Please remain by my side, my cherished Friend!' A long pink flame shot up from a black log. It was late; the moon was rising, but he wasn't tired. He took a blanket, stretched out on the grass.

There he remained, eyes wide open, a flower brushing lightly against his cheek. There wasn't a single sound in this little corner of the world.

He heard nothing, saw nothing, but felt by a kind of sixth sense two boys silently rushing towards the château. It happened so quickly that at first he thought he was dreaming. He didn't want to call out for fear of waking the other sleeping boys. He got up, brushed the grass and flowers off his cassock and headed for the château. The thick lawn hid the sound of his footsteps. He remembered now he had noticed one of the shutters had been badly secured and was slightly ajar. Yes, he was right! The moon lit up the front of the house. One of the boys was pushing the shutter, forcing it open. Before Philippe could shout at them to stop, a stone shattered the window and there was a rain of glass. The boys, as lithe as cats, leapt inside.

'Oh, you little brats! Just wait till I sort you out!' Philippe said to himself.

Hoisting up his cassock, he followed them through the window, and found himself in a drawing room with furniture covered by dustsheets and a large, cold parquet floor. He groped about in the dark for a few moments before finding the light switch. When he turned the lights on he saw no one. He hesitated, looked around (the boys were hiding or had run off): the sofas, the piano, the winged bergère chairs covered by billowing sheets, the flowered chintz curtains at the windows – all made good hiding places. Seeing some fabric move, he walked towards a bay window and yanked back the curtains. One of the boys was there. He was among the oldest, almost an adult with a blackish face, rather beautiful eyes, a low forehead and a strong jaw.

'What are you doing here?' said the priest.

He heard a noise behind him and turned round; another boy was in the room, standing right behind him; he too was about seventeen or eighteen. He had thin, contemptuous lips and his yellowish face looked wild, as if he were possessed. Philippe was on his guard but they were too fast for him. In a flash they attacked; one tripped him and knocked him down, the other grabbed his throat. But he managed to fight them off, silently, successfully. Catching hold of one of them by the collar, he tightened his grip so much that the boy was forced to let go. As the boy pulled away, something fell out of his pocket and rolled along the ground: it was some silver.

'Congratulations, you've moved fast,' said Philippe, half choking, sitting on the floor, thinking to himself, 'The main thing is not to make a big thing of it, just get them out of here and they'll follow me like little puppies. Then we'll sort it out tomorrow.'

'That's enough, now! Enough of this nonsense . . . get going.'

He had barely finished speaking when once again they threw themselves on him, silently, desperately, savagely; one of them bit him, drew blood.

'They're going to kill me,' Philippe thought in amazement. They hung on to him like wolves. He didn't want to hurt them, but he was forced to defend himself; they punched him, kicked him, he fought them off and they came back at him even more violently than before. They no longer looked human, they were demented, animals . . . Philippe would have proven the stronger in spite of everything but they hit him on the head with a pedestal table with bronze legs; he fell down and as he fell he heard one of the boys run to the window and whistle. He saw nothing else: not the twenty-eight teenagers suddenly waking up, running across the lawn, climbing through the window; not the rush towards the delicate furniture that was being ripped apart and thrown out on to the grass. They were frenzied, they danced around the priest as he lay sprawled on the floor, they sang and shouted. One of the youngest, with a girlish face, jumped with both feet on to a sofa whose old springs creaked under the weight. The older ones had discovered a liquor cabinet. They dragged it into the drawing room, kicking it to move it along; when they opened it, they saw it was empty but they didn't need liquor to be drunk: the carnage was enough for them. They felt a terrifying kind of joy. Dragging Philippe by the feet, they threw him out of the window, so he fell heavily on to the lawn. At the edge of the lake, they swung him like a bundle . . . 'Heave-ho! Kill him!' they shouted in their harsh, high-pitched voices, some of which still sounded childlike.

When Philippe fell into the water he was still alive. Out of a sense of self-preservation, or a final burst of courage, he managed to remain at the edge of the lake; he clutched the branch of a tree with both hands and tried hard to keep his head above water. His battered face was red, swollen and grotesque. They were throwing stones at him. He held on at first, clinging with all his might to the branch that was swaying, cracking, giving way. He tried to get to the other shore but he was being bombarded.

Finally he raised both arms, put them in front of his face, and the boys saw him sink straight down, in his black cassock. He hadn't drowned: he'd got trapped in the mud. And that was how he died, in water up to his waist, head thrown back, one eye gouged out by a stone.

26

At the Cathedral of Notre-Dame in Nîmes, a Mass was celebrated every year for the members of the Péricand-Maltête family who had passed on. Since only Madame Péricand's mother lived in Nîmes, this service was usually a brief affair in one of the side chapels, attended by the elderly lady herself – half-blind and obese, whose heavy breathing drowned out the priest's voice – and a cook who had worked for the household for thirty years. Madame Péricand had been born a Craquant, related to the Marseilles branch of the Craquant family who had made their money in olive oil. This ancestry seemed extremely respectable to her, of course (and her dowry had been two million, at its pre-war value), but it paled in comparison with that of her new relations. Her mother, the elder Madame Craquant, agreed with this view of things and, having gone to live alone in Nîmes, she observed all the Péricand rituals with great fidelity, praying for the dead and sending letters of congratulations to the living on the occasion of marriages and baptisms, just as the colonial English raised solitary glasses on the day London was celebrating the Queen's birthday.

This Mass for the deceased was particularly agreeable to Madame Craquant because she would stop at a tearoom on her way home from the cathedral and have a cup of hot chocolate and two croissants. As she was extremely fat, her doctor made her follow a strict diet, but her early morning rise and the lengthy and, to her, very tiring walk from the great carved door of the cathedral to her pew allowed her to devour these fortifying foods without remorse. Sometimes when her cook, of whom she lived in fear, had her back turned and was standing rigid and silent near the door of the tearoom – their two prayer books in her hand, Madame Craquant's black shawl over her arm – she would even draw a platter of little cakes towards her and, with affected nonchalance, pop a cream-filled choux bun into her mouth, or a cherry tart, or both.

Outside, her carriage, drawn by two old horses and driven by a coachman almost as fat as Madame Craquant herself, waited, flies buzzing around in the heat.

This year, everything was at sixes and sevens. The Péricands, who had fled to Nîmes after the events of June, had just learned of the deaths of the old Monsieur Péricand-Maltête and Philippe. News of the first had been conveyed by the Sisters in the nursing home where the old gentleman had had, according to Sister Marie of the Sacred Sacrament's letter, 'a good death, very comforting, very Christian'. She had even been so kind as to describe in the most minute detail the contents of his Last Will and Testament, which would be written up as soon as possible.

Madame Péricand read and reread the final sentence of the letter and sighed, a look of anxiety spreading across her face, only to be replaced, a moment later, with the expression of contrition a good Christian feels when she learns that someone she loves has gone to find peace with the Good Lord. 'Your grandfather is with Jesus, children,' she said.

Two hours later, the second blow to strike the family was revealed, but in less detail. The mayor of a little village in the Loiret informed them that Father Philippe Péricand had been killed in an accident and sent them papers that confirmed his identity beyond a doubt. As for the thirty wards in his care, they had disappeared. Since half of France was looking for the other half, this surprised no one. There was mention of a truck which had fallen in the river, not far from where Philippe had met his death, and his relations remained convinced that this had something to do with him and his unfortunate orphans. To cap it all, Madame Péricand was told that Hubert had been killed at the Battle of Moulins. This time the catastrophe was complete. The intensity of her sorrow caused her to cry out in proud despair.

'I gave birth to a saint and a hero,' she said. 'Our sons are making sacrifices for other people's sons.' And she looked darkly at her cousin Craquant whose only child had managed to get a peaceful little post in the home guard in Toulouse. 'Dear Odette, my heart is breaking. You know that I lived only for my children, that I was a mother, nothing but a mother' (Madame Craquant, who had been a trifle frivolous in her youth, lowered her head), 'but I swear to you, the pride I feel makes me forget my bereavement.'

She drew herself up and, already imagining the black veil fluttering around her, showed her cousin to the door with pride and dignity.

'You are a true Catholic.' Odette sighed humbly.

'Just a good Frenchwoman,' Madame Péricand replied drily, turning her back.

This conversation had lessened her sorrow slightly. She had always respected Philippe and in some way understood he was not of this world. She knew that, if he had renounced his dream of being a missionary, it was out of humility and that he had chosen to serve God in the way that was the most difficult for him: by subjecting himself to the most commonplace duties. She was certain her son was with Jesus. (When she said the same thing about her father-in-law, it was with a secret doubt for which she reproached herself, but there it was . . .) But Philippe . . . 'I can see him as if I were there,' she thought. Yes, she could be proud of Philippe and the radiance of his soul reflected back on to her.

Whereas when she thought of Hubert she felt a strange turmoil. Hubert, who failed miserably at school, who bit his nails, Hubert with his ink-stained fingers, his lovely chubby face, his wide young mouth, for Hubert to die a hero was . . . inconceivable . . . When she talked to her sympathetic friends about how Hubert had left ('I tried to stop him, but I saw how impossible it was. He was a child, but a courageous child, and he has given his life for the honour of France. As Rostand said, "It is even more beautiful because it is pointless".'), she found that she was rewriting the past. She actually believed she had said all these proud words, that she had sent her son off to war.

Nîmes, which had looked upon her until now rather bitterly, felt a respect for this sorrowful mother that was almost affectionate.

'The whole town will be there today,' old Madame Craquant sighed with melancholy satisfaction.

It was 31 July. Their Mass for the Dead was due to be celebrated at ten o'clock, with three names tragically added.

'Oh, Mother, what does it matter?' replied Madame Péricand, and it was impossible to tell if she was referring to the uselessness of such consolation or to the very poor opinion she had of her fellow citizens.

The town gleamed beneath the blazing sun. In the poor districts, a dry and insidious wind rattled the bead curtains in doorways. The flies bit; you could smell a storm coming. Nîmes, normally sleepy at this time of year, was crowded with people. The refugees who had poured in were still there, unable to leave because of petrol shortages and the temporary closure of the border along the Loire. The streets and town squares had been transformed into parking lots. There was not a spare room anywhere.

People had been sleeping in the streets; the ultimate luxury was a bale of hay to use as a bed. The citizens of Nîmes were proud of themselves for having done their duty, and more, towards the refugees. They had welcomed them with open arms, pressed them against their bosoms. There was not a single family who had not offered hospitality to these poor people. It was just a shame that this state of affairs was dragging on so unreasonably long. There was also the matter of provisions, and you can't forget either, said the townspeople, that all these poor refugees, exhausted by their journey, would be susceptible to the most terrible epidemics. There were veiled hints in the press and more open, brutal demands from other quarters, urging the refugees to leave as soon as possible. But as yet, circumstances had prevented anyone from going anywhere.

Madame Craquant, who had her entire family living with her and was therefore able, head held high, to refuse to donate even a pair of sheets, rather enjoyed all this hustle and bustle, which she witnessed through her half-closed Venetian blinds. She was having her breakfast, along with the Péricand children, before going to church. Madame Péricand watched them eat. She did not touch her own food even though, thanks to the stock of supplies accumulated in her mother's enormous cupboards since war had been declared, it was more appetising than the usual rations.

Madame Craquant was troubled by her daughter's cold stare. A snow-white napkin covering her vast chest, she was polishing off her third piece of buttered toast when she felt a touch of indigestion. She put the toast down and looked at her daughter timidly. 'I don't know why I'm eating, Charlotte,' she said, 'it's not going down well.'

'You'll have to force yourself, Mother,' replied Madame Péricand ironically, her voice as cold as ice. And she pushed the full jug of hot chocolate towards the old lady.

'All right then. Pour me another half-cup, Charlotte, but not more than half a cup now!'

'You know it's your third?'

But Madame Craquant seemed suddenly struck deaf. 'Yes, yes,' she said vaguely, nodding her head. 'You're right, Charlotte, we must fortify ourselves before the sad ceremony.' And she drank up the frothy chocolate with a sigh.

Meanwhile, the doorbell rang and one of the servants brought in a package for Madame Péricand. It contained photographs of Philippe and Hubert: she had sent them to be framed. She looked at them for a long time, then got up, put them down on the sideboard, stood back to see how they looked, went into her bedroom, and came back carrying two black rosettas and two red, white and blue ribbons. As she draped them over the picture frames, they heard Nanny sobbing in the doorway, Emmanuel in her arms. Jacqueline and Bernard also started crying.

Madame Péricand took the children by the hand, gently pulled them from their chairs and walked them over to the sideboard. 'Just look at your two big brothers, my darlings! Ask the Good Lord to bless you so you might be like them. Try to be as good, as studious and obedient as they were. They were such good sons,' said Madame Péricand, her voice choking with pain, 'and I wouldn't be at all surprised if God has rewarded them by recognising them as martyrs. You musn't cry. They are with the Good Lord; they are looking down on us, protecting us. They will be waiting for us in heaven, and in the meantime, here on earth, we must be proud of them, both as Christians and as citizens of France.'

Everyone was crying now; even Madame Craquant had stopped drinking her hot chocolate and was looking for her handkerchief, her hands trembling. The photograph of Philippe was amazingly lifelike. It really captured his pure, intense expression, and he seemed to contemplate his family with that smile of his that was sweet, kind and loving.

'And when you say your prayers, you mustn't forget,' Madame Péricand concluded, 'those unfortunate children who died with him.'

'But maybe they aren't all dead?'

'It's possible,' Madame Péricand said vaguely, 'very possible. Those poor children . . . On the other hand,' she added, 'that charitable institution really is a great responsibility,' and her thoughts ran back to her father-in-law's Will.

Madame Craquant dried her eyes. 'Little Hubert . . . he was so sweet, so funny. I remember one day when you were visiting, I'd fallen asleep in the sitting room after lunch, and that naughty boy goes and takes down the flypaper from the chandelier and quietly lowers it on to my head. I woke up and screamed . . . You certainly punished him that day, Charlotte.'

'I don't remember,' said Charlotte drily. 'Now, come on, Mother, finish your hot chocolate; we have to hurry. The carriage is downstairs. It's nearly ten o'clock.'

They went into the street, the grandmother first, puffing and leaning on her cane, then Madame Péricand, swathed in black crêpe, followed by her two children in black, Emmanuel in white, and a few of the servants, all in full mourning attire. The carriage was waiting. The driver was getting down from his seat to open the door when, suddenly, Emmanuel pointed a little finger towards the crowd. 'Hubert! Look, it's Hubert!'

Turning automatically to look, Nanny blanched and let out a strangled cry: 'Jesus, Blessed Virgin Mary!'

A sort of hoarse howl came from the mouth of Madame Péricand; she threw back her black veil, took a few steps towards Hubert, then slipped on the pavement and collapsed into the arms of the driver, who had rushed forward just in time to catch her.

It really was Hubert, a lock of hair in his eyes, skin as pink and golden as a nectarine, with no bags, no bicycle, no wounds, walking towards them with a huge grin on his face. 'Hello, Mother, hello, Grandmother. How is everyone?'

'Is it you? Is it you? You're alive!' said Madame Craquant, laughing and crying at the same time. 'Oh, my darling Hubert, I knew you couldn't really be dead! Dear God, you're too mischievous for that!'

Madame Péricand came round. 'Hubert? Is it really you?' she stammered weakly.

Hubert was both pleased and embarrassed by this welcome. He took a few steps towards his mother and leaned over so she could kiss his cheeks (which she did, not knowing exactly what she was doing). Then he stood in front of her, shifting from one foot to the other just as he did when he failed Latin translation at school.

'Hubert,' she sighed, and threw her arms round his neck, hanging on to him, showering him with kisses and tears. An emotional little crowd had gathered around them.

Hubert, who had no idea what to do, patted Madame Péricand's back, as if something had gone down the wrong way. 'Weren't you expecting me?'

She shook her head.

'Were you going out?'

'My poor boy! We were going to the cathedral to say a Mass for your soul!'

Hubert was taken aback. 'You're joking!'

'But where have you been? What have you been doing these past two months? We were told you'd been killed in Moulins.'

'Well, you can see *that* wasn't true since I'm right here.'

'But you did go and fight? Hubert, don't lie to me! Did you really have to go and do that, you little idiot. And what about your bicycle? Where's your bicycle?'

'Lost.'

'Of course! This boy will be the death of me! Well, come on, speak, tell us, where were you?'

'I was trying to find you.'

'You would have been better off not leaving us in the first place,' said Madame Péricand harshly. Then, her voice breaking with emotion: 'Your father will be so happy when he hears.'

She burst into tears and started kissing him again. It was getting late now. But, even though she wiped her eyes, the tears kept falling. 'Go on, then, go inside and get washed! Are you hungry?'

'No, I had a good lunch, thanks.'

'Get a clean handkerchief, change your tie, wash your hands, make yourself decent, for goodness sake! Hurry up, and meet us at the cathedral.'

'What? You're still going? Since I'm alive, wouldn't it be better to go and stuff ourselves at a restaurant instead?'

'Hubert!'

'What? Is it because I said "stuff ourselves"?'

'No, but . . .'

It would be terrible to tell him, like this, in the middle of the street, she thought. She took his hand and pulled him inside the carriage. 'My darling, there have been two great tragedies. First Grandpa, poor Grandpa died, and Philippe . . .'

He took the shock in an odd way. Two months earlier he would have burst into tears, big fat salty tears rolling down his pink cheeks. Now he went very pale and his face took on an expression she had never seen before: manly, almost harsh. 'I don't much mind about Grandpa,' he said after a long silence. 'As for Philippe . . .'

'Hubert, are you mad?'

'No, I don't much mind and neither do you. He was old and ill. What would he have done in all this chaos?'

'Well, really!' Madame Craquant protested.

But he ignored her and continued talking to his mother. 'As for Philippe . . . But first, are you really sure? It couldn't be like what happened with me?'

'We are sure, I'm afraid . . .'

'Philippe . . .' His voice trembled and broke. 'He wasn't of this world. Other people talk about heaven all the time but they only think about this world . . . Philippe, he came from God and he must be very happy now.' He hid his face in his hands and remained motionless for a long time. Then they heard the cathedral bells ringing.

Madame Péricand touched her son's arm. 'Shall we go?'

He nodded. They all got into the carriage, the servants following in another, and made their way to the cathedral. Hubert walked between his mother and grandmother. They remained on either side of him as he knelt on his prayer cushion. He had been recognised; he could hear whispering, muffled cries. Madame Craquant had not been wrong: the whole town was there. Everyone had a good view of the survivor who had come to give thanks to God for his deliverance on the very day his family had gathered to pray for their dead. On the whole, everyone was happy: the fact that a good lad like Hubert had managed to avoid German bullets flattered their sense of justice and their craving for miracles. All the mothers who had had no news since May (and there were so many of them!) felt hope beat within their breast. And it was impossible to feel resentful about it, as they might have been tempted to do – 'Some people have all the luck' – when, sadly, poor Philippe (an excellent priest, absolutely everyone said so) had died.

And so, despite the solemnity of the surroundings, many women smiled at Hubert. He didn't see them. His mother's words had thrust him into a state of profound shock from which he still hadn't emerged. Philippe's death was tearing him apart. He had returned to that terrible state of mind he felt when France was falling, before the desperate and vain battle of Moulins. 'If we were all the same,' he thought, looking over the congregation, 'if we were all pigs and dogs, then it might be understandable. But saints like Philippe, why are they sent here? If it's to save us, to make up for our sins, it's like offering a pearl in exchange for a bag of stones.'

The people around him, his family, his friends, aroused a feeling of shame and rage within him. He had seen them on the road, them and people like them: he recalled the cars full of officers running away with their beautiful yellow trunks and their painted women, civil servants abandoning their posts, panic-stricken politicians dropping files of secret papers along the road, young girls, who had diligently wept the day the armistice was signed, being comforted in the arms of the Germans. 'And to think that no one will know, that there will be such a conspiracy of lies that all this will be transformed into yet another glorious page in the history of France. We'll do everything we can to find acts of devotion and heroism for the official records. Good God! To see what I've seen! Closed doors where you knock in vain to get a glass of water and refugees who pillaged houses; everywhere, everywhere you look, chaos, cowardice, vanity and ignorance! What a wonderful race we are!'

Meanwhile, he was absently following the service, his heart so heavy and hard that it caused him physical pain. Several times he sighed gruffly, which worried his mother. She turned towards him, her eyes shining with tears through her black veil. 'Are you in pain?' she whispered.

'No, Mother,' he replied, looking at her so coldly that he reproached himself for it, but he couldn't help it.

He judged his family with bitterness and a painful harshness. His grievances whirled around in his mind in the form of brief, violent images, without him being able to express them clearly: his father calling the Republic 'this decaying regime . . .' but that same evening, twenty-four places set for dinner at their apartment, with their most beautiful tablecloths, wonderful foie gras and expensive wines, all in honour of a former minister who might be re-elected and might therefore be useful to Monsieur Péricand (God, his mother's tight little mouth saying, 'Oh, my dear Minister . . .'); their cars full to bursting with fine linen and silver caught up among the refugees, and his mother, pointing to women and children forced to walk with just a few bits of clothing wrapped up in a piece of cloth, saying, 'Do you see how good our Lord Jesus is? Just think, *we* could be those unfortunate wretches!' Hypocrites, frauds!

And what about him? What was he doing here? His heart full of disgust and hatred, he was just pretending to pray for Philippe. But Philippe was . . . My God! Philippe, my beloved brother! He whispered these words and, as if they had some divine power to console, his painful heart relented.

Warm tears flooded down his cheeks. Thoughts of kindness, forgiveness, ran through him. They did not come from within him but from beyond, as if some friend had leaned down to whisper in his ear, 'A family that produced Philippe can't be all bad. You're being too harsh. You've only seen things from the outside, you can't look into their souls. Evil is visible, it burns, it smugly displays itself for all to see. There is only One who can count the sacrifices, who can measure all the blood and tears.'

He looked at the marble plaque engraved with the names of those who had died in the war . . . the last war. Among them were some Craquants and Péricands – uncles, cousins he'd never known, children barely older than him, killed at the Somme, Flanders, Verdun, killed twice since they had died in vain. Little by little, out of this chaos of contradictory feelings, was born a strange, bitter feeling of peace. He had gained valuable experience, knowledge; no longer in an abstract, bookish way, but in his heart, which had beat so wildly, in his hands which had been torn to shreds trying to defend the bridge at Moulins, in his lips which had kissed a woman while the Germans celebrated their victory. Danger, courage, fear, love: now he knew the real meaning of these words . . . Yes, even love . . . He felt better now, stronger, and very confident. He would never see the world through anyone else's eyes again. But more than that, anything he might love and believe from now on would come from himself, and no one else. Slowly, he put his hands together, lowered his head and, finally, prayed.

The Mass was over. Outside the cathedral he was surrounded by people wanting to kiss him and congratulate his mother.

'And he still has those lovely cheeks,' the women all said, 'after all he's been through . . . He's hardly lost any weight, he hasn't changed at all. Dear little Hubert . . .'

27

Gabriel Corte and Florence arrived at the Grand Hotel at seven o'clock in the morning. Collapsing with exhaustion, they looked around fearfully, as if they expected, once through the revolving doors, to plunge back into the nightmare of an incoherent world, with refugees sleeping on the cream carpets of the writing room, a hotel manager who didn't recognise them and refused to give them a room, no hot water for a bath and bombs falling in the lobby. But, thank God, this Queen of French spas had remained intact and the feverish, noisy activity at the lake was simply the way it always was. All the staff were in place. Despite the manager's insistence that they were short of everything, the coffee was delicious, the cocktails were mixed with crushed ice and the taps poured out as much water as you liked, cold and boiling hot. At first everyone had been worried: the unfriendly attitude of England made them fear that the blockade would remain in place, thus depriving them of fresh supplies of whisky, but they had a large quantity in stock. They could wait.

As soon as they set foot on the marble floor of the lobby, Gabriel and Florence felt they had been reborn. Everything was calm. You could barely hear the distant whirring of the great lifts. Through the open bay windows, misty, shimmering rainbows created by the hotel's water sprinklers hovered over the lawns. They were recognised and surrounded. The manager of the Grand Hotel, where they had stayed every year for twenty years, raised his arms to heaven and told them it was all over; they had glimpsed the bottom of the abyss, but now they had to try to restore some sense of duty and nobility in the people. Then he confided in them that they were expecting members of the government to arrive at any moment (their suites had been reserved the previous day), and that the ambassador of Bolivia was having to sleep on a billiard table. However for him, Gabriel Corte, he would always manage to find something (more or less the same words he had used as a newly promoted deputy manager of the Normandy Hotel in Deauville at the height of the racing season).

Corte wearily passed his hand over his painful forehead. 'My good man, you could put a mattress in the lavatory if you had to!'

All around him, everything was taking place in an appropriately discreet manner. There were no more women giving birth in a ditch, no more lost children, no more bridges blown up with such ill-calculated amounts of dynamite that they demolished the houses nearby. Here, windows were politely closed to keep out draughts, doors were opened for him, he felt plush carpets beneath his feet.

'Do you have all your luggage? You didn't lose anything? What luck! People have been arriving without pyjamas, without even a toothbrush. There was one unfortunate gentleman who arrived with no clothes on. He was wounded in an explosion and made the entire journey from Tours completely naked, with only a blanket round him.'

'Well, I nearly lost my manuscripts,' said Corte.

'Good gracious, how awful! But you found them intact? All the same, what you must have been through! What you must have been through! Excuse me, Monsieur, excuse me, Madame, right this way. Here is the suite I have given you; it's on the fourth floor, I do apologise; you will excuse me, won't you?'

'Oh,' muttered Corte, 'nothing matters at the moment.'

'I do understand,' said the manager, lowering his head and looking saddened. 'Such a tragedy . . . I was born in Switzerland but I am French at heart. I do understand.'

And he stood motionless for a few moments, his head down like a mourner at a funeral who wants to rush to the exit, but feels obliged to pay his respects to the family. He had put on this expression so often in the past few days that his kindly, chubby face had been transformed. He had always walked and spoken softly, as befitted his profession. Now he exaggerated his natural tendencies even further, crossing the room utterly silently, as if he were in a funeral parlour, and when he said to Corte, 'Shall I have breakfast sent up?' it was in a discreet and mournful tone of voice, as if he were looking at the body of a cherished relative and asking, 'May I kiss him one last time?'

'Breakfast?' Corte sighed, returning with difficulty to reality and the trivial problems of everyday life. 'I haven't eaten in twenty-four hours,' he added with a faint smile.

That had been true the day before, but not this morning: at six o'clock he had eaten a hearty meal. Nevertheless, he wasn't lying: he had eaten absent-mindedly because of his extreme exhaustion and the concern he felt at the tragedy taking place in France. He *felt* as though he hadn't eaten.

'Oh, but you must force yourself, Monsieur! I don't like seeing you like this, Monsieur Corte. You mustn't give in. You owe it to mankind.'

Corte nodded in resignation; he didn't dispute his obligation to mankind, but at the moment he couldn't be expected to have more courage than the most humble citizen. 'My good man,' he said, turning away to hide his tears, 'it is not just France who is dying, it is Art as well.'

'Not as long as you are here, Monsieur Corte,' the manager replied warmly, as he had a great number of times since the Fall of France. Corte was, in the list of celebrities, the fourteenth to arrive from Paris since the sad events began and the fifth writer to seek refuge at the luxury hotel.

Corte smiled weakly and asked him to make sure the coffee was very hot.

'Boiling hot,' the manager assured him, then gave the necessary orders over the telephone and left.

Florence had gone into her room, locked the door and anxiously looked at herself in the mirror. Her face, normally so soft, so well made-up, so rested, was covered in a shiny coat of sweat; it no longer absorbed the powder and foundation, but turned them into thick lumps, like curdled mayonnaise. Her nose was pinched, her eyes sunken, her mouth pale and limp. She turned away from the mirror in horror.

'I could be fifty,' she said to her maid.

This was quite literally true, but she said it with such disbelief and terror that Julie took it as she should: that is to say figuratively, as a metaphor for expressing extreme old age.

'After everything that's happened it's understandable . . . Madame should take a little nap.'

'It's impossible . . . As soon as I close my eyes I hear the bombs, I see the bridge again, the dead bodies . . .'

'Madame will forget.'

'Never! Could *you* forget?'

'It's different for me.'

'Why?'

'Madame has so many other things to think about!' said Julie. 'Shall I lay out Madame's green dress?'

'My green dress? With the way I look?'

Florence, who had slumped down into her chair with her eyes closed, suddenly rallied, summoning all her meagre strength like the head of an army who, despite needing rest and acknowledging the inefficiency of his subordinates, pulls himself together and, still weak with exhaustion, leads his troops on to the battlefield. 'Listen, this is what you are going to do. First, while you are running the bath, prepare me a face mask, number 3, the American one. Then telephone the hairdresser and ask if Luigi is still there. Tell him to come and give me a manicure in three quarters of an hour. Then get my little grey suit ready, with the pink linen blouse.'

'The one with the collar like this?' Julie asked, drawing a low-cut shape in the air.

Florence hesitated. 'Yes . . . no . . . yes . . . that one, and the new little hat with the cornflowers. Oh, Julie, I really never thought I would get to wear that little hat. Well . . . you're right, I mustn't think about it any more, I'd go mad . . . I wonder if they have any more of that ochre powder, the last one . . .'

'We'll have to find out . . . Madame would be wise to buy several boxes. It came from England.'

'You don't have to tell me! You know, Julie, we don't really understand what is going on. These events will have an unimaginable impact, believe me, unimaginable . . . People's lives will be changed for generations. We'll be hungry this winter. Just get out my grey leather handbag with the gold clasp, that's all . . . I wonder what Paris is like,' said Florence walking into the bathroom. But the noise of the running water Julie had just turned on drowned out her words.

Meanwhile, less frivolous thoughts were passing through Corte's mind. He too was lying in the bath. At first he had been filled with such joy, such profound natural peace, that he was reminded of the delights of childhood: his happiness when eating an iced meringue full of cream; dipping his feet in a cool stream; pressing a new toy to his heart. He felt no desire, no regret, no anguish. His head was clear and calm; his body floated in a warm, liquid element that caressed him, gently tickled his skin, washed away the dust, the sweat, insinuated itself between his toes and slid beneath his back like a mother lifting her sleeping child. The bathroom smelled of tar soap, hair lotion, eau de Cologne, lavender water. He smiled, stretched out his arms, cracked the knuckles on his long, pale fingers, savoured the divine, simple pleasure of being safe from the bombs and taking a cool bath on a very hot day. He couldn't pinpoint the exact moment when bitterness cut through him like a sharp knife through a piece of fruit. Perhaps it was when he happened to glance at the suitcase full of manuscripts on the chair, or when the soap fell into the water and he had to fish it out, the strain to his muscles disrupting his state of euphoria. Whenever it was, at a certain point he frowned and his face, which had been clearer, smoother than usual, almost rejuvenated, became sombre and anxious once again.

What would become of him? What would become of Gabriel Corte? What was happening to the world? What would be the general mood in future? Either people would think only about being able to survive and there would be no place for Art, or they would become obsessed by a new ideal, as after every crisis before. A new ideal? 'A new fashion, more like,' he thought with cynicism and weariness. But he, Corte, was too old to adapt to new tastes. He had already changed his style in 1920. A third time would be impossible. It exhausted him just to think about what was to come, what kind of world was about to be born. Who could predict the shape it would take as it emerged from the harsh matrix of this war, as from a bronze mould. It would be magnificent or misshapen (or both), this universe now showing its first signs of life. It was terrible to look at himself, to see himself . . . and to understand nothing. For he understood nothing. He thought of his book, his manuscript sitting on a chair, rescued from the fire, from the bombs. He felt intensely despondent. The passions he described, his feelings, his scruples, this history of a generation, his generation – they were all old, useless, obsolete. 'Obsolete!' he repeated in despair. And a second time the soap, slippery as a fish, disappeared into the water. He swore, sat up, angrily rang the bell; his servant came in.

'Rub me down,' Gabriel Corte sighed, his voice shaking.

Once his legs had been massaged with the glove and the eau de Cologne applied, Corte felt better. Standing naked in the bathroom he began to shave while the servant laid out his clothes: a linen shirt, a lightweight tweed suit, a blue tie.

'Are there any people we know?' asked Corte.

'I don't know, Monsieur. I haven't seen many people, though I've been told a lot of cars arrived last night and then left straightaway for Spain. Monsieur Jules Blanc was here. He went to Portugal.'

'Jules Blanc?'

Corte paused, his soapy razor poised in mid-air. Jules Blanc, gone to Portugal, on the run! This piece of news was a bad blow. Like everyone who makes sure they get the most comfort and pleasure from life, Gabriel Corte had a politician in his pocket. In exchange for excellent dinners, wonderful parties, Florence's little attentions, in exchange for a few well-placed and timely newspaper articles, he had had from Jules Blanc (member with portfolio in nearly every Cabinet, twice Prime Minister, four times Minister of War) thousands of the small favours that make life easier. It was thanks to Jules Blanc that he had been commissioned to present his *Great Lovers* series on the radio last winter. It was Jules Blanc who had given him responsibility for the patriotic addresses and moral exhortations broadcast on the radio, and it was Jules Blanc who had insisted that the head of an important daily newspaper pay 130,000 francs instead of the 80,000 previously agreed for Corte's novel. Finally, he had promised that Corte would be made a Commander of the Legion of Honour. Jules Blanc was a small but necessary cog in the machinery of his career, for genius cannot simply float in the clouds, it must also operate down on earth.

On learning of his friend's fall (Blanc must have been involved in some pretty dishonest business to have taken this desperate measure, since it was he who always liked to say that, in politics, defeat prepares you for victory), Corte felt alone and abandoned at the edge of an abyss. Once again, he was struck with dreadful force by the existence of a new world, unknown to him, a world where everyone would become miraculously chaste, selfless and full of noble ideals. Already, that tendency to imitate which is an integral part of the survival instinct for plants, animals and people, made him declare: 'Ah, so he's left? The day of these hedonists, these political wheeler-dealers is over . . .' After a moment's silence he added, 'Poor France . . .'

Slowly he put on his blue socks. Naked, except for his black silk suspenders and socks, his skin a shiny white with yellowish tinges, he did some arm and chest exercises, then looked at himself approvingly in the mirror. 'Now that is definitely better,' he said, as if he expected the words to make his servant very happy. Then he finished dressing.

He went down to the bar just after noon. There was a certain panic going on in the lobby and it was clear that distant disasters were sending tremors through the rest of the universe. People had left their luggage piled untidily on the stage that was normally used as a dance floor; shouting was coming from the kitchens; pale, dishevelled women were wandering around the corridors looking for a room; the lifts weren't working; and an old man was crying, standing in front of a porter who refused to give him a bed.

'You must understand, Monsieur, it's not that I don't want to, but it's impossible, simply impossible. We're full to bursting, Monsieur.'

'Just a tiny little corner room, that's all,' begged the poor man. 'I told my wife I would meet her here. We got separated in the bombing in Etampes. She'll think I'm dead. I'm seventy years old, Monsieur, and she's sixty-eight. We've never been apart before.' He took out his wallet, hands trembling. 'I'll give you a thousand francs.' And on this ordinary Frenchman's honest, modest face you could see his shame at having to offer a bribe for the first time in his life, and his fear at having to spend all his money.

But the porter refused to take it. 'I'm telling you, Monsieur, it's impossible. Try in town.'

'In town? But I've just come from there! I've been knocking at doors since five o'clock this morning. They treat me like a dog! I'm not just anyone. I'm a physics teacher at the Saint-Omer sixth form college. I've been decorated for services to education.'

But he finally realised the porter had stopped listening a long time ago and had turned his back on him. Picking up a little hatbox he'd dropped on the ground, which clearly contained all his belongings, he left without saying a word.

The porter was now fighting off four Spanish women with black hair and heavy make-up. One of them was clutching his arm. 'Once in a lifetime, all right, it happens, but twice is too much,' she exclaimed in bad French, her voice hoarse and loud. 'To have lived through the war in Spain, escaped to France and then end up in this mess, it's too much!'

'But Madame, there's really nothing I can do!'

'You can give me a room!'

'That's impossible, Madame, impossible.'

The Spaniard tried to think of some scathing reply, an insult, but her mind was blank. For a moment she was choked with anger, then she exlaimed, 'Well, you're not what I call a man!'

'Me?' shouted the porter, suddenly losing all his professional passivity and jumping up and down in outrage. 'And what about you? Have you quite finished insulting me? Just remember you're a foreigner – so shut up or I'll call the police.' Regaining a little of his dignity, he held open the door and pushed out the four women who were still shouting insults in Castilian.

'What hard days, Monsieur, and nights,' he said to Corte. 'The world has gone mad, Monsieur!'

Corte walked into a long, cool room; it was silent and dark, and the bar was quiet. All the commotion stopped at this doorway. The closed shutters on the large windows protected him from the heat of the raging sun; the aroma of quality leather, excellent cigars and vintage brandy hung in the air. The Italian barman, an old friend of Corte's, welcomed him impeccably, expressing his joy at seeing him again and his sympathy at France's misfortunes. He did this with such dignity and tact, mindful of his inferior status with regard to Corte and aware that the terrible events demanded respect, that Corte felt immediately comforted. 'I'm pleased to see you as well, my good man,' he said gratefully.

'Did Monsieur have difficulty leaving Paris?'

'Ah!' was all Corte said. He raised his eyes to heaven. Joseph, the barman, made a discreet little gesture with his hand as if to prevent Corte from confiding in him, refusing to be the one to bring back such fresh, painful memories, and in the same way a doctor might say to a patient who is having a fit, 'Drink this first, then you can tell me all about it', he murmured, 'Shall I fix you a martini?'

With the chilled glass and two small dishes of olives and crisps in front of him, Corte took in the familiar surroundings with the weak smile of a convalescent. He then looked at the men who had just joined him in the room. Well, well! They were all there: the academic and the former minister, the important industrialist, the editor, the head of a newspaper, the MP, the playwright and the writer who, under the pseudonym 'General X', wrote articles for an important Parisian magazine in which he summarised military events for the masses in great technical detail and with the utmost optimism, while always managing to remain vague: 'The next military theatre of operations will be in northern Europe or the Balkans or the

Ruhr or all three simultaneously, or else at some point on the globe impossible to predict'. Yes, they were all here and in perfect health. For a brief moment Corte was stunned. He couldn't have said why, but for the past twenty-four hours he had thought the old world was crumbling and he was the only man left amid the rubble. It was an inexpressible relief to see once again all his famous friends, even his enemies. Today, any disagreements seemed unimportant. They were all on the same side, they were all together! They were living proof that nothing was changing. Contrary to belief, they weren't witnessing some extraordinary cataclysm, the end of the world, but rather a series of purely human events, limited in time and space, which, all in all, affected only the lives of people they didn't know.

Their conversation was pessimistic, almost despairing, but their voices light-hearted. Some of them had done very well for themselves; they were at that age when one looks at young people and thinks, 'Let them make their own way!' Others were compiling a hasty mental inventory of all the pages they'd written, all the speeches they'd given, which might help them win favour with the new government (and since they had all more or less lamented the fact that France had lost her greatness, lost her daring and was no longer producing children, none of them was very worried). The politicians were rather more anxious, for some of them were in a difficult position and were pondering a change of alliance. The playwright and Corte discussed their own work, without a thought for the rest of the world.

28

The Michauds never made it to Tours. A bomb destroyed the railway line, the train stopped and the refugees found themselves once more on the road, mingling with the German troops. They were ordered to go back the way they had come.

The Michauds found Paris half empty. They had been away for two weeks and expected to find it different, as one does after a long trip. Instead, they walked home through the untouched streets and couldn't believe their eyes: everything was in its place. The blazing sun shone down on the houses, all with their shutters closed, exactly as on the day they had left; a sudden heatwave had shrivelled all the leaves on the plane trees, but no one had swept them up and the refugees waded through them with weary legs. There didn't seem to be a food shop open. Now and again, this barren landscape threw up a surprise: it looked like a city wiped out by the plague, but just as you were about to scream, 'Everybody's either dead or gone', you'd find yourself face to face with a nicely dressed lady wearing make-up or, in the Michauds' case, a woman getting a perm at a hairdresser's nestled between a boarded-up butcher's shop and bakery. It was Madame Michaud's hairdresser. She called to him. He, his assistant, his wife and the client all ran to the door and exclaimed, 'Were you on the roads?'

Madame Michaud pointed to her bare legs, her torn dress, her face covered with sweat and dust. 'As you can see! What's happened to our apartment?'

'Well, everything is fine. I was walking past your windows just today,' said the hairdresser's wife. 'Nothing's been touched.'

'What about my son? Jean-Marie? Has anyone seen him?'

'How could you expect anyone to have seen him, my poor darling?' said Maurice who had joined her. 'You're not being logical.'

'And what about you, always so calm? You'll be the death of me,' she replied angrily. 'Maybe the concierge . . .' and she turned to go.

'Don't get upset, Madame Michaud. There's nothing for you. I asked as I was passing. There's no post any more.'

Jeanne tried to hide her cruel disappointment with a smile. 'All right, all we can do is wait,' she said, but her lips were trembling. She sat down without thinking and murmured, 'What should we do now?'

'If I were you,' said the hairdresser, a fat little man with a round, sweet face, 'I'd start by having your hair washed; it will clear your mind; we could also freshen Monsieur Michaud up a bit, and while I'm doing that my wife can make you something to eat.'

So it was agreed. He was massaging Jeanne's head with lavender oil when his son ran in to announce that the armistice had been signed. She was too exhausted and downcast to take in the importance of the news – just as a person who has shed so many tears at the bedside of someone who is dying has none left for the actual moment of death. But Maurice, remembering 1914, the battles, his wounds, his suffering, felt a wave of bitterness wash over his heart. But there was nothing more to say so he remained silent.

They were in Madame Josse's salon for more than an hour, then left to go home. People were saying that there were relatively few casualties among French soldiers, but that the prisoners numbered nearly two million. Could Jean-Marie perhaps be a prisoner? They daren't hope for anything more. They reached their house. Despite all Madame Josse's assurances, they couldn't really believe that it was still standing and not reduced to ashes like the burning buildings they had walked past last week in the Place du Martroi, in Orléans. But they could see the door, the concierge's lodge, the letter box (empty!), the key waiting for them and the concierge herself. The risen Lazarus must have experienced the same feeling of astonishment and quiet pride on seeing his sisters and the soup cooking on the fire: 'In spite of everything, we've come back, we're home,' they thought.

'But what's the point if my son . . .' was Jeanne's second thought.

She looked at Maurice who smiled weakly at her, then said out loud to the concierge, 'Hello, Madame Nonnain.'

The concierge was elderly and half deaf. The Michauds cut short their stories of the exodus as much as possible. Madame Nonnain had gone as far as the Porte d'Italie with her daughter, who was a laundress. She had then had an argument with her son-in-law and come back home. 'They have no idea what's happened to me; they probably think I'm dead,' she said with some satisfaction. 'They probably think they're going to get hold of my savings now. Not that she's a bad sort,' she added referring to her daughter, 'she's just canny.'

The Michauds said they were tired and went up to their apartment. The lift was broken. 'Well, that's the last straw,' Jeanne moaned, laughing in spite of herself.

While her husband slowly climbed the stairs, she rushed on ahead, recovering the speed and stamina she'd had as a young girl. My God, to think she had sometimes cursed this dark staircase, their basic apartment with no cupboards, no bathroom (they'd had to get a bathtub put in the kitchen) and radiators that regularly broke down in dead of winter! The cosy world in which she had lived for fifteen years and whose walls contained such sweet, such warm memories, had been returned to her. Peering over the banister, she saw Maurice much further down. She was alone. She leaned forward to kiss the door, then got out her key and opened it. It was her apartment, her refuge. Here were Jean-Marie's room, the kitchen, the sitting room and the sofa on which, in the evening, after getting home from the bank, she would stretch out her tired legs.

Remembering the bank suddenly made her shudder. She hadn't thought about it in a week. When Maurice came in, he saw she was worried and that her joy at being home had vanished. 'What's the matter?' he asked. 'Is it Jean-Marie?'

'No, the bank.'

'My God, we did everything humanly possible and more to get to Tours. They couldn't possibly hold it against us.'

'They won't hold it against us,' she said, 'if they want to keep us. But I've only worked there on an interim basis since the war, and as for you, my poor darling, you've never been able to get along with them, so if they want to get rid of us, now's the time.'

'The thought had crossed my mind.'

As always, when he agreed wholeheartedly and didn't argue with her, she suddenly changed her mind. 'Nevertheless, they'd have to be the worst bastards . . .'

'They *are* the worst bastards,' Maurice said gently, 'you know that, don't you? We've had our share of worries. We're together, we're at home. Let's not think about anything else . . .'

They didn't mention Jean-Marie. They couldn't even say his name without crying and they didn't want to cry. They had always had a burning desire to be happy. Perhaps because they loved each other so much, they had learned to live one day at a time, deliberately not thinking about tomorrow.

They weren't hungry. They opened a jar of jam, a box of biscuits and, with infinite care, Jeanne made them some coffee: there was only a quarter of a pound left of the pure mocha coffee they usually saved for special occasions.

'But what more special occasion could there be?' said Maurice.

'None like this, I hope,' his wife replied. 'Still, we can't pretend we'll be able to replace it easily if the war drags on.'

'You make it seem almost sinful,' said Maurice, breathing in the wonderful aroma wafting up from the coffee pot.

After their light meal, they sat down by the open window. They both had a book open on their laps but they weren't reading. They finally fell asleep, side by side, holding hands.

They spent several days rather peacefully. Since there was no post, they knew they couldn't get any news, good or bad. All they could do was wait.

At the beginning of July, Monsieur de Furières returned to Paris. It was said, after the armistice of 1919, that the Count de Furières had had a 'good war': he had faced danger heroically for a few months, then married a very rich young woman while on leave. After that he cared a little less for the idea of getting himself killed, which was understandable. Nevertheless, he refused to take advantage of his wife's excellent connections. If he no longer sought out danger, he didn't run away from it either. He finished the war without once being wounded, pleased with himself for his commendable behaviour in battle, his inner confidence and his military decoration. In 1939 he held an excellent place in society: his wife was a Salomon-Worms, his sister had married the Marquis de Maigle; he was a member of the Jockey Club; his receptions and hunting parties were famous; he had two charming daughters, the eldest of whom had recently become engaged. He had considerably less money than in 1920 but was now better equipped than before to do without it or to get hold of some when necessary. He had accepted the position of Director of the Corbin Bank.

Corbin was quite simply an uncouth individual who had begun his career in a lowly and almost vile manner. (It was said he had been a bellboy in an establishment offering loans on the Rue Trudaine.) But Corbin was also extremely adept when it came to banking and, in the end, he and the Count got along rather well. They were both very intelligent and understood how useful they were to each other; understanding this created a sort of friendship based on cordial contempt, just like certain liqueurs, which are sharp and bitter on their own but have a pleasant taste when mixed together. 'He's a degenerate, like all aristocrats,' Corbin would mutter. 'The poor man eats with his fingers,' Furières would say with a sigh. By dangling the prospect of the Jockey Club in front of Corbin's eyes, the Count got whatever he wanted from him.

All in all, Furières had organised his life most comfortably. When the second great war of the century broke out, he felt almost like a child who has worked hard at school, done nothing wrong and is thoroughly enjoying himself when someone tells him he must once again be dragged away from his pleasures. 'Once, all right, but twice, that's just too much!' he was tempted to cry out. 'Pick on someone else, dammit!' How could this be happening? He had already done his duty. He had given five years of his youth and now they wanted to steal his precious middle years – those beautiful years when a man finally understands what he is about to lose and is eager to make the most of it. 'No, it's going too far,' he remarked despondently to Corbin when he said goodbye to him the day everyone was mobilised. 'I'm doomed. I'll never get out alive again.'

He was an officer in the Reserves; he had to go. He could have fixed it . . . but his desire for continued self-respect held him back – a very strong inner desire that allowed him a severe, ironic attitude towards the rest of the world. He left. His chauffeur, who was in the same situation as him, said, 'If you have to go, you go. But if they think it'll be like '14, they've got it all wrong.' (The word 'they' in his mind meant some mythical council whose purpose and passion was to send other people to their deaths.) 'If they think we'll do *that* again' (flicking his nail on his tooth), '*that* on top of what is strictly necessary, well, I'm telling you, they've got another think coming.'

The Count de Furières would certainly not have expressed his own thoughts in this way, but they were nevertheless very similar to his chauffeur's and simply reflected the state of mind of many former soldiers. A large number of men went off to war this way, feeling muted bitterness or hopeless rebellion against fate, which twice in their lifetimes had played this horrible trick on them.

During the June debacle almost the entire regiment of de Furières fell into enemy hands. He himself had the chance to escape and he took it. In '14 he would have preferred to be killed rather than survive the disaster. In '40 he preferred to live. He returned to his wife, who was already mourning his death, to his charming daughters, the eldest of whom had just got married (to a young inspector of Public Finances), and to the de Furières château. The chauffeur wasn't as lucky: he was taken to Stalag VII A and became prisoner number 55,481.

Upon his return, the Count got in touch with Corbin, who had remained in the Free Zone, and they both set about trying to bring the bank's scattered sections back together. The Accounting Department was in Cahors, the executives in Bayonne, the secretaries had headed for Toulouse but had got lost somewhere between Nice and Perpignan. No one seemed to know where the bank's papers had ended up.

'It's chaos, a mess, unspeakable mayhem,' Corbin said to de Furières the morning of their first meeting.

He had crossed the demarcation line during the night and welcomed de Furières into an apartment empty of servants. They had all fled during the exodus, and he suspected them of having taken some brand-new suitcases and his morning coat, which aroused within him even more patriotic fury.

'You know me, don't you? I'm not usually emotional, but I nearly cried, my dear man, nearly cried like a baby when I saw the first German at the border. Very correct he was, none of this casual French demeanour, you know, as if to say "we're pals". No, really very correct, a brief salute, confident stance, but without being stiff, very correct . . . Well, what do you think? Aren't our officers just the worst!'

'Excuse me,' said Furières curtly, 'but I don't see how you can reproach our officers. What do you expect them to do with no weapons and a load of hopeless troops who only want you to p*** off and leave them in peace. First give us some real men.'

'Oh, but *they* say "there was no one in charge",' said Corbin, delighted to offend Furières, 'and just between us, old boy, I saw some pathetic sights . . .'

'Without the civilians, without everyone panicking, that wave of refugees blocking up the roads, we would have had a chance.'

'Well, you're right there! The panic was terrible. People are extraordinary. For years we've heard nothing but "it's all-out war, all-out war" – you would have thought they'd have expected it. But no! Immediately there's panic, chaos, exodus, and why? I'm asking you, why? It's insane! *I* only left because the banks were ordered to go. Otherwise, you know . . .'

'Was it terrible in Tours?'

'Absolutely terrible . . . but again for the same reason: the flood of refugees. I couldn't find a room outside Tours so I had to sleep in the city and, naturally, we were bombed, forced out by the fires,' said Corbin, thinking indignantly of the little château in the countryside where they had turned him away because some Belgian refugees were staying there. *They* hadn't been hit, not them, while he, Corbin, had nearly been buried under the rubble in Tours. 'And the chaos,' he repeated, 'everyone thinking only of himself! Such egotism . . . It makes you wonder about mankind . . . As for your staff, they were the worst of all. Not one of them was able to meet me in Tours. They all lost contact with each other. I'd told all our departments to stay together. Do you think they cared? Some are in the Midi, some are up north. You can't count on anyone. These are the circumstances in which you can judge a man, his drive, his energy, his guts. A bunch of drips, I'm telling you, a bunch of drips! Only interested in saving their own skin, without a thought for the bank or me. Well, some of them are going to get the sack, I can assure you of that. Besides, I don't imagine we're going to have much business.'

The conversation turned to more technical matters, which gave them a pleasant feeling of their own importance, barely diminished, despite recent events.

'A German group,' Corbin said, 'is going to buy out Eastern Steelworks. We're not in too bad a position there. Though it's true that the business with the Rouen Docks . . .'

They became depressed. Furières said goodbye. Corbin wanted to walk him out, but when he tried to turn on the lights in the drawing room where the shutters were closed, there was no electricity. He started swearing.

'This man is so vulgar,' the Count thought. 'Give them a call,' he advised. 'They won't take long to fix it. The telephone's working.'

'You just can't imagine how chaotic everything is here,' Corbin said, choking with rage. 'The servants have all taken off – all of them, I'm telling you – and I wouldn't be at all surprised if they made off with some of the silver! My wife isn't here. I'm lost in all this mess, I'm . . .'

'Is Madame Corbin in the Free Zone?'

'Yes,' Corbin grumbled.

He and his wife had had a painful row: in the chaos of the hurried departure, or perhaps out of malice, the chambermaid had put a small framed picture belonging to Monsieur Corbin in Madame Corbin's bag; it contained a photograph of Arlette, stark naked. The nudity itself might not have offended his wife – she was a person with a great deal of common sense – but the dancer was wearing a magnificent necklace. 'But it's not real, I promise you!' Monsieur Corbin had said with venom. His wife refused to believe him. As for Arlette, there was no sign of her. He had heard she was in Bordeaux and was often seen in the company of German officers. Thinking of this only made Monsieur Corbin's mood worse. He pushed his buzzer with all his might.

'All I have left is a typist I met in Nice. Stupid as they come but rather pretty. Oh, there you are,' he said suddenly to the young brunette who came into the room. 'The electricity's been cut off, see what you can do about it. Telephone them and give them a good talking to. Well, get on with it – and then bring me the post.'

'The post hasn't been brought up?'

'No, it's with the concierge. Chop chop. Go and get it. Do you think I'm paying you to do nothing?'

'I'm leaving,' said Furières. 'You frighten me.'

Corbin caught a glimpse of the Count's slightly scornful smile; his anger increased. 'Poseur, crook,' he thought. Out loud he replied, 'What do you want me to do? They're driving me crazy.'

The post contained a letter from the Michauds. They had gone to the bank's head office in Paris but no one could tell them anything definite. They had written to Nice and the letter had just been forwarded to Corbin. The Michauds were asking for instructions and some money.

Corbin's vague bad temper finally found something to latch on to. 'Ha! That's a good one!' he exclaimed. 'They've got some nerve! You run around bending over backwards for people, nearly get killed on the roads of France. Meanwhile Monsieur and Madame Michaud have a nice holiday in Paris and then have the cheek to demand money. You're going to write to them,' he said to the terrified typist. 'Take this down':

> Monsieur Maurice Michaud   Paris, 25 July 1940
> 23 rue Rousselet
> Paris VIIe

> Monsieur
> On 11 June we gave both you and Madame Michaud the order to take up your duties in the city to which the bank had been evacuated, that is to say Tours. You will not be unaware that during these crucial moments, every employee of the bank, and you in particular since you hold a position of trust, is like a soldier. You know what it means to abandon your post in times such as these. The result of your failings was the complete disintegration of the departments entrusted to you – the Secretarial and Accounting Services. This is not the only thing for which we hold you responsible. As we already informed you on 31 December last year when, despite my goodwill towards you, it was not considered possible to award you the increased bonus of three thousand francs that you requested, it has been pointed out that your department's efficiency is minimal in comparison with that of your predecessor's. Under the circumstances, while regretting you have waited such a long time to get in touch with the management, we consider your failure to contact us as a resignation, both by you and Madame Michaud. This resignation, which derives entirely from you and was without any notice, means we are not required to pay you any compensation whatsoever. Nevertheless, taking account of your long employment at the bank as well as the current situation, we are making an exception and, purely as a gesture of goodwill, we are allocating you compensation equivalent to two months' salary. Please find enclosed, therefore, a cheque drawn on the Bank of France in Paris, made payable to you in the sum of . . . francs. Would you please notify us of its safe arrival.
> Yours sincerely,
> Corbin

Corbin's letter plunged the Michauds into despair. They had only five thousand francs in savings, as Jean-Marie's studies had been expensive. This and their two months' salary came to barely fifteen thousand francs and they owed money to the taxman. It was almost impossible to find work now; jobs were rare and badly paid. They had lived a solitary life; they had no relatives, no one to ask for help. They were exhausted by the journey and depressed by their anguish over their son. When Jean-Marie was little and she had faced difficulties, Madame Michaud had often thought, 'If only he were old enough to manage by himself, nothing would really matter.' She had known she was strong and in good health, she felt courageous, she feared nothing for herself, nor for her husband, who thought the same way.

Jean-Marie was a man now. Wherever he might be, if he were still alive, he didn't need her. Yet this thought offered little consolation. First of all, she couldn't imagine that her child could do without her. And at the same time she realised that now *she* needed him. All her courage abandoned her; she recognised Maurice's frailty: she felt alone, old, ill. How would they find work? What would they live on when their fifteen thousand francs ran out? She had a few small pieces of jewellery; she cherished them. She had always said, 'They're not worth anything', but now she couldn't bring herself to believe that the charming little pearl brooch, the modest ruby ring, gifts from Maurice when they were young, which she loved so much, might not perhaps be sold for a good price. She offered them to the jeweller in her neighbourhood, then to a larger establishment on the Rue de la Paix, but both turned her away: the brooch and the ring were pretty but they were only interested in the stones and they were so small it wasn't worth buying them. Madame Michaud was secretly happy at the thought she could keep them, but facts were facts: it had been their only option.

By the end of July their savings were almost gone. They had considered going to see Corbin to explain that they had done their very best to get to Tours and that if he insisted on letting them go, he at least owed them the normal compensation. But they both had enough experience of him to know they didn't stand a chance. They didn't have the money to take him to court and Corbin was not easy to intimidate. They also found it wholly repugnant to think of approaching this man whom they loathed and mistrusted.

'I just can't do it, Jeanne. Please don't ask me to, I just can't,' Maurice said in his soft, low voice. 'I think if I found myself standing in front of him I'd spit in his face and that wouldn't help matters.'

'No,' said Jeanne, smiling in spite of herself, 'but we're in a terrible situation, my poor darling. It's as if we're heading towards a deep hole, watching it get closer and closer with each step without being able to escape. It's unbearable.'

'But we have to bear it,' he replied calmly.

He'd used the same tone of voice with her when he'd been wounded in '16 and she'd been called to his bedside at the hospital: 'I think my chances of pulling through are about four in ten.' He had then stopped a moment to think and added conscientiously, 'Three and a half, to be exact.'

She placed a tender hand on his forehead and thought despairingly, 'Oh, if only Jean-Marie were here, he would look after us, he would save us, I know he would. He's young, he's strong . . .' Deep inside, she felt a strange intermingling of her need to protect as a mother and her need to be protected as a woman. 'Where is he, my darling boy? Is he still alive? Is he in pain? My God, he can't be dead, it just isn't possible!' And her blood ran cold as she realised how very possible it actually was. The tears she had courageously held back for so long welled up in her eyes.

'But why are we always the ones who have to suffer?' she cried out in indignation. 'Us and people like us? Ordinary people, the lower middle classes. If war is declared or the franc devalues, if there's unemployment or a revolution, or any sort of crisis, the others manage to get through all right. We're always the ones who are trampled! Why? What did we do? We're paying for everybody else's mistakes. Of course they're not afraid of *us*. The workers fight back, the rich are powerful. *We're* just sheep to the slaughter. I want to know why! What's happening? I don't understand. You're a man, *you* should understand,' she said angrily to Maurice, no longer knowing whom to blame for the disaster they were facing. 'Who's wrong? Who's right? Why Corbin? Why Jean-Marie? Why us?'

'What do you want to understand? There's nothing to understand,' he said, forcing himself to stay calm. 'Certain laws govern the world and they're neither for nor against us. When a storm strikes, you don't blame anyone: you know the thunder is the result of two opposite electrical

forces, the clouds don't know who you are. You can't reproach them. And
it would be ridiculous if you did, they wouldn't understand.'

'But it's not the same thing. What we're going through is down to
people and people alone.'

'It only seems like that, Jeanne. It all seems caused by this man or that,
by one circumstance or another, but it's like in nature: after the calm comes
the storm; it starts out slowly, reaches its peak, then it's over and other
periods of calm, some longer, some shorter, come along. It's just been
our bad luck to be born in a century full of storms, that's all. They'll die
down.'

'Yes,' she said, although she didn't really follow this abstract argument,
'but what about Corbin? Corbin's hardly a force of nature, is he?'

'He's a harmful specimen, like scorpions, snakes, poison mushrooms.
Actually, we're a little bit to blame. We've always known what Corbin
was like. Why did we carry on working for him? You wouldn't eat bad
mushrooms and you have to be careful with bad people. There have been
several times when we could have found other jobs, with a bit of courage
and determination. And remember, when we were young I was offered
that job as a teacher in São Paulo, but you didn't want me to go.'

'All right, that's ancient history,' she said, shrugging her shoulders.

'No, I just meant . . .'

'Yes, you just meant we shouldn't hold it against anyone. But you said
yourself if you ran into Corbin you'd spit in his face.'

They continued arguing, not because they hoped or even wished to win
the other over, but because talking helped them forget their painful
problems.

'Who could we speak to?' Jeanne finally exclaimed.

'You mean you still don't understand that nobody cares about anybody?'

She looked at him. 'You're strange, Maurice. You've seen people at their
most cynical, their most disillusioned, and at the same time you're not
unhappy, I mean, not really unhappy inside! Am I wrong?'

'No.'

'So what makes it all right, then?'

'My certainty that deep down I'm a free man,' he said, after thinking
for a moment. 'It's a constant, precious possession, and whether I keep it
or lose it is up to me and no one else. I desperately want the insanity we're
living through to end. I desperately want what has begun to finish. In a

word, I desperately want this tragedy to be over and for us to try to survive it, that's all. What's important is to live: *Primum vivere*. One day at a time. To survive, to wait, to hope.'

She listened to him without saying a word. Suddenly, she got up and grabbed her hat from the mantelpiece. He looked at her in astonishment. 'And what *I* say,' she replied, 'is "Heaven helps those who help themselves." Which is why I'm going to speak to Furières. He's always been nice to me and he'll help us, even if it's only to annoy Corbin.'

Jeanne was right. Furières spoke to her and promised that she and her husband would each receive compensation totalling six months' salary, which brought their capital up to about sixty thousand francs.

'You see, I managed and heaven helped me,' Jeanne said to her husband when she got home.

'And I did the hoping,' he replied, smiling. 'We were both right.'

They were very happy with the outcome but sensed that now their money worries were off their minds, at least for the immediate future, they would be completely overwhelmed by their anguish over their son.

29

It was autumn when Charlie Langelet returned home. The porcelain hadn't been damaged by the journey. He unpacked the large crates himself, trembling with joy when he felt, beneath the straw and tissue paper, the cool smoothness of a pink glass vase or a Sèvres statuette. He still couldn't believe he was really home, reunited with all his wonderful possessions. He would raise his eyes now and again to look through his windows (which still had their strips of coloured paper) at the delightful curve of the Seine.

At noon, the concierge came up to clean; he hadn't yet hired any servants. Important events – whether serious, happy or unfortunate – do not change a man's soul, they merely bring it into relief, just as a strong gust of wind reveals the true shape of a tree when it blows off all its leaves. Such events highlight what is hidden in the shadows; they nudge the spirit towards a place where it can flourish. Charlie had always been careful with money, a penny-pincher. When he got back after the exodus, he felt truly miserly. It gave him real pleasure to save money whenever possible and he was aware of this for, to top it all off, he had become cynical. Before, he would never have considered moving into a disorganised house full of dust; he would have recoiled at the idea of going to a restaurant the very day he returned. Now, however, he had been through so much that nothing frightened him. When the concierge told him that anyway she couldn't finish the cleaning today, that Monsieur didn't realise how much work there was to do, Charlie replied sweetly but firmly, 'You'll manage somehow, Madame Logre. You'll just have to work a bit faster, that's all.'

'Fast and good don't always go together, Monsieur!'

'This time they will. The good old days are over,' Charlie said sternly, then added, 'I'll be back at six o'clock. I trust that everything will be ready.'

And after an imperious glance at the concierge, who was furious but said nothing, and a final loving look at his porcelains, he left. As he went down the stairs he calculated what he was saving: he wouldn't have to pay for Madame Logre's lunch any more; she could work for him two hours a day for a while; once the heavy work was done, it wouldn't take much to keep the apartment in order, and he could take his time to find some servants, a couple probably. Until now he had always had a couple, a valet and a cook.

He went and had lunch by the river, in a little restaurant he knew. He didn't find the food too bad, all things considered (he never ate much anyway), and the wine he drank was excellent. The owner whispered in his ear that there was still a bit of real coffee left. Charlie lit a cigar and felt that life was good. That is to say, no, not good as such, one mustn't forget the defeat of France and all the suffering, all the humiliation that resulted from it, but for him, Charlie, it was good because he took life as it came, without moaning about the past or fearing the future.

He flicked the ash from his cigar. His money was in America and since his funds were frozen, fortunately, he would have to pay less tax or perhaps even none at all. The franc would remain low for a long time. His fortune, as soon as he could get hold of it, would automatically be worth ten times what it was now. As for his day-to-day expenses, he'd made sure to put something aside a long time ago. It was forbidden to buy or sell gold, and it was already fetching outrageous prices on the black market. He thought with amazement of the wave of panic that had swept through him when he had wanted to leave France to go and live in Portugal or South America. Some of his friends had gone, but he was neither Jewish nor a Mason, thank God, he thought with a scornful smile. He had never been involved in politics and didn't see why he wouldn't be left alone, a poor man like him, very quiet, very harmless, who never hurt anybody and who loved nothing in this world but his porcelain collection. He thought, on a more serious note, that this was the secret of his happiness amid so much upheaval. He loved nothing, at least nothing that time could distort, that death could carry away; he'd been right not to have married, not to have had children . . . My God, everyone else had been taken in. He'd been the only clever one.

But coming back to that mad idea of emigrating: it had been born of a strange and almost insane belief that, in the space of a few days, the world was going to change into something horrific, a living hell. But look

. . . Everything was the same! He thought of the Bible and the description of the world before the Flood. How did it go? Oh yes: people built houses, got married, ate and drank . . . Well, the Bible was incomplete. It should have said, 'The Flood waters subsided and people began once more to build their houses, to marry, to eat and drink . . .' In fact, people weren't really very important. It was works of art, museums, collections that should be saved. What was terrible about the Spanish War was that artistic masterpieces had been left to be destroyed; but here the most important works had been saved, except for some of the châteaux near the Loire, of course. Now *that* was unforgivable. But the wine he'd drunk was so good, he felt inclined to be optimistic. After all, there were some very beautiful ruins. In Chinon, for example, what could be more admirable than the great hall with no roof and those walls – walls that had seen Joan of Arc pass, and where now birds nested and a wild cherry tree grew in a little corner.

After lunch, he wanted to stroll through the streets, but he found them depressing. There were hardly any cars, it was extraordinarily silent, and great red flags with swastikas were flying everywhere. In front of a cheese shop, some women were waiting to be served. This was the first war he'd seen. Everyone was gloomy. Charlie hastened towards the Métro, the only transport working. He would visit a bar where he was often a regular at lunchtime or in the evening. What havens of peace bars like this were! They were extremely expensive, and their clientele consisted of wealthy men, past middle age, who hadn't been affected by either the mobilisation or the war. Charlie was alone for a while, but at about six thirty all the old regulars arrived, safe and sound and in tip-top form, accompanied by charming and beautifully made-up ladies, who called out from beneath their adorable little hats, 'But it's him, it's Charlie, isn't it? . . . Well, now, not too worn out, are you? Come back to Paris?'

'Paris is dreadful, don't you think?'

And almost immediately, as if they were meeting again after the most peaceful, the most ordinary of summers, they began the kind of conversation Charlie called 'Fragile – Don't Touch' conversation: lively and light-hearted small-talk, ranging over any number of subjects but dwelling on none in particular. Among other things, he learned that certain young men had been killed or taken prisoner.

'Oh, it can't be! Just imagine . . . I hadn't the slightest idea, it's awful! Those poor boys!' he said.

The husband of one of the ladies was a prisoner in Germany.

'He writes to me regularly. He isn't too bad, but it's the boredom, you see . . . I hope to be able to get him out soon.'

The more he talked and the more he heard, Charlie found his spirits rising and he recovered the good mood that had been momentarily dampened by the sight of the Paris streets. But what succeeded in cheering him up completely was the hat worn by a woman who had just come in. All the women were well dressed but with a certain pretence of simplicity, as if to say, 'We couldn't really dress up, just imagine! First of all, we have no money and, second, it wouldn't be quite right . . . I'll get some more wear out of my old dresses . . .' But this woman showed off her hat in a daring, courageous and brazenly happy way. It was a new little hat, hardly bigger than a cocktail napkin, made of two sable skins, with a russet veil over her golden hair. As soon as he saw it, Charlie felt totally reassured.

It was getting late. Since Charlie wanted to stop at home before going out to dinner, it was time he went . . . but he didn't want to leave his friends.

'Why don't we all have dinner together?' someone suggested.

'That's an excellent idea,' Charlie said warmly. And he proposed the little restaurant where he'd had such a good lunch, for he was like a cat by nature, quickly becoming attached to places where he'd been well treated. 'I'll have to take the Métro again! It's such a ghastly place, it's making my life miserable,' he said.

'I was able to get some petrol and a pass, but I can't offer to drive you back because I promised to wait for Nadine,' said the woman in the new hat.

'How did you do that? It's amazing you could manage that!'

'Ah well, there it is,' she said, smiling.

'Listen, then, let's meet in about an hour, an hour and a quarter.'

'Do you want me to come and collect you?'

'No, thanks, you're very kind; it's only two minutes from my place.'

'Be careful, it's pitch black out. They're very strict about that.'

'She was right, it's really dark,' Charlie thought as he emerged from the warm, bright club into the unlit street. It was also raining. Autumn evenings like this were one of the things he used to like so much about

Paris, but now you could see fires burning in the distance, and everything was as black and sinister as the inside of a well. Fortunately, the entrance to the Métro was nearby.

At home, Charlie found Madame Logre sweeping the floor in a preoccupied, gloomy sort of way. At least the drawing room was finished. Charlie had the urge to put his favourite Sèvres statuette on the shiny Chippendale table – a *Venus at the Looking Glass*. He took it out of the packing case, removed the tissue paper it was wrapped in, looked at it lovingly and was taking it over to the table when the doorbell rang.

'Go and see who it is, Madame Logre.'

Madame Logre went out and then came back, saying, 'Monsieur, I told the concierge at number six that Monsieur needed someone and she's sent this woman who's looking for work.'

Seeing Charlie hesitate, she added, 'She's a very nice person who used to be a chambermaid for the Countess Barral du Jeu. She got married and didn't want to work any more, but her husband is a prisoner of war and she needs to earn a living. Monsieur could just see her and then decide!'

'All right, bring her in,' said Langelet, putting the statuette on a table.

The woman made a good impression on him. She seemed modest and calm, obviously wishing to please but without being subservient. He could see at once she had been well trained and had worked in fine homes. She was a big woman. Mentally, Charlie reproached her for this – he liked his maids to be thin and a bit austere – but she looked about thirty-five or forty, the perfect age for a servant, when they've stopped working too quickly but are still fit and strong enough to provide good service. She had a broad face, vast shoulders and her clothing was simple but appropriate (the dress, coat and hat definitely hand-me-downs from a former employer).

'What's your name?' Charlie asked, favourably impressed.

'Hortense Gaillard, Monsieur.'

'All right. And you're looking for work?'

'Well, you see, Monsieur, I left the Countess Barral du Jeu two years ago to get married. I didn't think I'd have to go back into service, but my husband was conscripted and then taken prisoner, and Monsieur will understand that I have to earn a living. My brother is unemployed and I'm looking after him, his sick wife and a small child.'

'I understand. I was thinking of hiring a couple . . .'

'I know, Monsieur, but maybe I could do instead? I was the head chambermaid for the Countess, but before that I worked for the Countess's mother as a cook. I could do the cooking and the cleaning.'

'Yes, that's possible,' Charlie murmured, thinking that such a combination would be very advantageous financially.

Naturally, there was also the matter of serving meals. He did sometimes have dinner guests, but then he wasn't expecting too many this winter.

'Do you know how to iron men's clothing? I'm very particular about that, you understand.'

'I was the one who ironed the Count's shirts.'

'And what about your cooking? I often eat out. I require simple but carefully prepared food.'

'Would Monsieur like to see my references?'

She reached into an imitation pigskin handbag and handed them to him. He read them one after the other; they spoke of her in the warmest terms: hard-working, extremely well trained, scrupulously honest, very good at cooking and even making pastries.

'Even pastries? Very good. I think, Hortense, that we can come to an arrangement. Were you with the Countess Barral du Jeu for long?'

'Five years, Monsieur.'

'And is the good lady in Paris? I prefer personal recommendations, you understand.'

'I understand completely, Monsieur. Yes, the Countess is in Paris. Would Monsieur like her phone number? It's Auteuil 3814.'

'Thank you. Write it down, would you, Madame Logre? And what about wages? How much were you hoping to earn?'

Hortense asked for six hundred francs. He offered four hundred and fifty. Hortense thought for a moment. Her shrewd little dark eyes had seen into the soul of this arrogant, well-fed man. And work was scarce.

'I couldn't do it for less than five hundred and fifty,' she said firmly. 'Monsieur must understand. I had some savings, but they were all used up during that horrible journey.'

'You left Paris?'

'During the exodus, yes, Monsieur. Bombed and everything, quite apart from nearly starving to death on the road. Monsieur doesn't know how bad it was.'

'But I do know, I do,' Charlie said, sighing. 'I too was on the road.

Such sad events! We'll say five hundred and fifty, then. But listen now, I'm agreeing because I think you will earn it. I insist on absolute honesty.'

'Oh, Monsieur!' said Hortense in a discreetly scandalised tone of voice, as if the thought alone would have wounded her to the core, and Charlie was quick to smile at her reassuringly, to make her see he was only saying it as a formality, that he didn't doubt her absolute integrity for a moment and that moreover the very idea of such dishonesty was so unbearable to him that he wouldn't give it another thought.

'I hope you are good at what you do and careful. I have a collection that is very important to me. I don't allow anyone to dust the most precious pieces, but this display cabinet over here, for example, I would trust you with.'

As he seemed to be inviting her to have a look, Hortense glanced at the half-unpacked cases. 'Monsieur has some very beautiful things. Before going into service for the Countess's mother I worked for an American, Mr Mortimer Shaw. He collected ivory pieces.'

'Mortimer Shaw? What a coincidence, I know him well! He's an eminent antiques dealer.'

'He's retired, Monsieur.'

'And were you with him long?'

'Four years. They were the only two jobs I had.'

Charlie stood up and saw Hortense to the door, saying encouragingly, 'Come back tomorrow for a definite decision, will you? If the verbal references are as good as your written ones, which I don't doubt for a moment, then you're hired. Could you start right away?'

'On Monday, if Monsieur would like.'

After Hortense had gone, Charlie hurried to change his collar and cuffs and wash his hands. He had had a lot to drink at the bar. He felt extraordinarily light-headed and pleased with himself. He didn't wait for the lift, an ancient, slow piece of equipment, but sped down the stairs like a young man. He was going to meet his lovely friends, a charming woman. He was delighted to be able to introduce them to the little restaurant he'd discovered.

'I wonder if they've got any of that Corton wine left,' he thought. The great courtyard door with its wooden panels engraved with Sirens and Tritons (a marvel, classified a work of art by the Council for Historic Monuments of Paris) opened and closed behind him with a faint creak.

Once outside, Charlie was immediately plunged into impenetrable darkness but, feeling as happy and free as a twenty-year-old, he crossed the road without a care and headed for the quayside. He'd forgotten his torch, 'but I know every step of the way in my neighbourhood,' he said to himself. 'All I have to do is follow the Seine and cross the Pont Marie. There won't be many cars.' And at the very moment he was mentally saying these words, a car passed two feet in front of him, going extremely fast, its headlights (painted blue in accordance with regulations) giving off only the faintest light. Startled, he jumped backwards, slipped, felt himself lose his balance, flailed his arms about and, finding nothing to grab on to, fell into the road.

The car swerved and a woman's voice screamed in terror, 'Watch out!' It was too late.

'I've had it. I'm going to be run over! To have made it through so much danger to end up like this, it's too . . . it's too ridiculous . . . Someone's playing a trick on me . . . Someone, somewhere is playing this horrible, bad trick on me . . .'

Just as a bird, terrified by a gunshot, flies out of its nest and disappears, so this final conscious thought went through Charlie's mind and vanished at the same moment as his life. He took a terrible blow to the head. The car's fender had shattered his skull. Blood and brains spurted out with such force that a few drops landed on the woman who was driving – a pretty woman, wearing a hat, hardly bigger than a cocktail napkin, made of two sable skins sewn together and a russet veil over her golden hair. It was Arlette Corail, back from Bordeaux the week before. She looked down at the body. 'What rotten luck,' she mumbled, devastated, 'but really, what rotten luck!'

She was a cautious woman and had her torch with her. She examined the man's face, at least what was left of it, and recognised Charles Langelet. 'Oh, the poor guy! . . . I was going fast, all right, but he couldn't have been paying attention, the silly fool! What am I going to do now?'

Nevertheless, she remembered that her insurance, licence, pass, were all in order, and she knew someone influential who would fix everything for her. Somewhat reassured but her heart still pounding, she sat down for a moment on the car's running board, lit a cigarette, fixed her make-up with trembling hands, then went to get help.

Madame Logre had finally finished cleaning the study and library. She

177

went into the drawing room to get the vacuum cleaner. As she pulled out the plug, the handle of the vacuum cleaner knocked against the table where the *Venus at the Looking Glass* was displayed. Madame Logre screamed: the statuette had fallen on to the floor. The head of Venus was smashed to bits.

Madame Logre wiped her forehead with her apron, hesitated a moment, then, leaving the statuette where it was, put the vacuum cleaner away. After that, in a manner that was surprising for such a stout woman, she rushed silently and nimbly out of the apartment. 'Right, I'll just say the door flew open and a gust of wind knocked the statue over. It's his fault too! Why leave it at the edge of the table? And anyway,' she said angrily, 'I don't care what he says. He can go to hell for all I care!'

30

If anyone had told Jean-Marie that he would one day find himself in a remote village far from his regiment, with no money, no way to communicate with his family, not knowing whether they were safe and sound in Paris or, like so many others, buried in a shell hole somewhere beside a road, and above all, if anyone had told him that, after France had been defeated, he would still be alive and would sometimes even be happy, he wouldn't have believed it. Yet that was what had happened. The very magnitude of the disaster, the fact that they had passed the point of no return, in itself provided some consolation, just as certain deadly poisons provide their own antidote: all his suffering was irreversible. He couldn't change the fact that the Maginot Line had been circumvented, or broken through (no one knew for sure), that two million soldiers had been taken prisoner, that France had been defeated. He couldn't make the post, the telegraphs or the telephones work, couldn't get hold of any petrol or a car to go to the railway station twenty-one kilometres away, and there weren't any trains anyway as the tracks had been destroyed. He couldn't walk to Paris for he had been seriously wounded and was only now just starting to get out of bed. He couldn't pay his hosts, for he had no money and no way of getting any. It was too much for him; all he could do was calmly stay where he was and wait.

This feeling of absolute dependence on other people brought about a kind of peace within him. He didn't even have his own clothes: his uniform had been torn and burned in places so he wore a khaki shirt and spare pair of trousers belonging to one of the farmhands. Meanwhile, he had managed to get himself demobilised by secretly crossing the demarcation line and giving a false address; so he no longer ran the risk of being taken prisoner. He was still living on the farm, but since he had recovered, he had moved from the bed in the kitchen to a little room above the hayloft. Through its round window he could see lovely, peaceful fields, fertile land

and woods. At night he could hear mice scurrying above his head and the cooing of doves in the dovecote.

Living constantly in fear of death like this was only bearable if you took one day at a time, if you said to yourself each evening, 'Another twenty-four hours when nothing really bad has happened, thank God! Let's see what tomorrow brings.' Everyone around Jean-Marie felt this way, or at least acted as if they did. They tended the animals, the hay, made butter . . . No one ever mentioned tomorrow. They made provision for the years to come, planting trees that would bear fruit in five or six seasons, fattening up the pigs they could eat two years later, but they did nothing about the immediate future. If Jean-Marie asked if it would be fine the next day (the usual question a Parisian on holiday would ask), they would say, 'Well, we don't know . . . How should we know?' If he asked, 'Will there be any fruit?' they'd reply, 'Maybe a little . . .' looking sceptically at the small, hard green pears trained up the trellis. 'We can't really tell . . . we don't know . . . we'll see when the time comes . . .' An almost hereditary instinct about the tricks of fate – the April frosts, the hail that ravaged the fields just before harvest, the drought in July that shrivelled up the kitchen garden – inspired wisdom and caution within them, but at the same time gave them some-thing to do every day. 'They're not exactly likeable but you have to admire them,' thought Jean-Marie, who had barely had any contact with the countryside: for five generations the Michauds had lived in the city.

The people of this hamlet were welcoming and amiable; the men were smooth talkers, the women coquettish. Once you got to know them, you discovered they were determined, tough, sometimes even surprisingly mali-cious, perhaps a result of some obscure atavistic memory of hate and fear that had been passed through the blood line from one generation to the next. Yet at the same time they were generous. The farmer's wife, who wouldn't have given an egg to a neighbour and held out for every penny she could get when selling her poultry, listened in dismal silence, together with the rest of her family, when Jean-Marie told them that he wanted to leave the farm because he had no money, that he didn't want them to have to support him and that he would try to make it to Paris on foot. 'It isn't right to talk like that, Monsieur, ' she declared with a strange kind of dignity, 'You're upsetting us . . .'

'But what else can I do?' said Jean-Marie, sitting next to her with his head in his hands, still feeling very weak.

'You can't do anything. You have to wait.'

'Yes, of course, the post will be working again soon,' the young man murmured, 'and if my parents are actually in Paris . . .'

'We'll see when the time comes . . .' said the farmer's wife.

Nowhere else would it have been as easy to forget the outside world. Without letters and newspapers, the only link with the rest of the universe was the radio, but the farmers had heard the Germans were confiscating the sets, so they hid them in lofts and old wardrobes, or buried them in the fields along with the hunting rifles they were supposed to have handed over. The village was in the Occupied Zone, very close to the demarcation line, but the German troops weren't stationed there; in fact, they had only passed through the village and never climbed the hill to the hamlet, which was two kilometres away along rough, rocky paths. Food was beginning to run out in the cities and certain other areas; here, there was even more food than usual, for there was no way of transporting their produce away from the village. Never in his life had Jean-Marie eaten so much butter, chicken, cream, or so many peaches. He recovered quickly. He even started putting on weight, the farmer's wife said, and in her kindness towards Jean-Marie there was a strange desire to make a deal with the Good Lord – to save one life for Him in exchange for the other life He held in His hands: just as she offered grain to the chickens in exchange for their eggs, so she tried to offer Jean-Marie's survival in return for her own son's life. Jean-Marie understood this very well, but it didn't change in the slightest his gratitude towards this elderly woman who had nursed him. He did his best to help out, doing odd jobs around the farm, working in the garden.

Though the women sometimes asked him questions about the war, *this* war, the men never did. They were all former soldiers (there weren't any young men). Their memories remained stuck in '14. They had had time to filter the past, to decant it, to get rid of the dregs, the poison, to make it bearable for their souls; but recent events remained confusing and laced with venom. Besides, deep in their hearts they blamed it all on the youngsters, who weren't as strong as them, weren't as patient and who'd been spoiled at school. And since Jean-Marie was young, they tactfully avoided judging him – him and his contemporaries.

This was how everything conspired to comfort and soothe the soldier, so he could rebuild his strength and courage. He was alone almost every day; it was the season when there was the most work to do in the fields. The men left home before dawn. The women looked after the animals and the washing. Jean-Marie had offered to help but they'd sent him packing. So he would go outside, crossing the courtyard where the turkeys were squawking, and walk down to a little meadow surrounded by a fence where two horses grazed. There was a golden brown mare and her two little coffee-coloured foals with their short, rough, dark manes. They would come and rub their muzzles against their mother's legs as she nibbled the grass and shook her tail impatiently to chase away the flies. Every now and again, one of the foals would turn towards the place near the fence where Jean-Marie was lying on the grass, look at him with his dark, moist eyes and whinny happily. Jean-Marie never grew tired of watching them. He wanted to write a story about these charming little horses, a story that would evoke this day in July, this land, this farm, these people, the war – and himself.

He wrote with a chewed-up pencil stub, in a little notebook which he hid against his heart. He felt he had to hurry: something inside him was making him anxious, was knocking on an invisible door. By writing, he opened that door, he gave life to something that wished to be born. Then suddenly, he would become discouraged, feel disheartened, weary. He was mad. What was he doing writing these stupid stories, letting himself be pampered by the farmer's wife, while his friends were in prison, his despairing parents thought he was dead, when the future was so uncertain, the past so bleak? But while he was thinking these thoughts, he saw one of the foals run joyously towards him, then roll around in the grass, kicking its hooves in the air and looking at him with mischievous and tender eyes. He tried to work out how to describe that look, all the time feeling impatiently curious and oddly anxious. He couldn't find the words but he knew what the little horse must feel, how good the crisp, cool grass must taste, how annoying the flies were, the sense of pride and freedom when he raised his muzzle and ran and kicked. He quickly wrote down a few awkward, unfinished lines. They were no good, he hadn't captured the essence, but it would come; he closed the notebook and finally sat still, hands open in his lap, eyes closed, tired and happy.

When he got back at dinnertime, he immediately saw that something important had happened while he was out. One of the farmhands had gone into the village to get some bread; now there he was with four round golden loaves on the handlebars of his bicycle and a group of women crowding round him. One of the girls saw Jean-Marie and shouted, 'Hey, Monsieur Michaud! This'll make you happy, there's post again.'

'Really?' said Jean-Marie to the old man. 'Are you sure?'

'Positive. I saw the Post Office open and people reading letters.'

'Then I'm going upstairs to write my family a letter and take it to the village. Will you lend me your bicycle?'

In the village, he not only posted his letter but bought the newspapers which had just arrived. How strange everything was! He was like a cast-away who had made it back to his homeland, civilisation, society. In the little village square, people were reading letters from the evening delivery. Some of the women were crying; many prisoners had sent their news, but had also given the names of friends who'd been killed. At the farm, they'd asked him to find out if anyone knew where Benoît was.

'Oh, so you're the soldier living there, are you?' the women asked. 'Well, we have no idea, but now the letters are coming, we'll soon find out where our men are!'

One of them, an older woman who'd put on a little pointed black hat with a rose at the front to come down to the village, was crying as she spoke. 'Some of us will find out too soon. I wish I'd never got this damned piece of paper. My boy was a sailor on the *Bretagne* and they say he went missing when the English torpedoed the ship. It's just too much!'

'Don't you give up hope. Missing doesn't mean dead. Maybe he's a prisoner in England!'

But to all these attempts at consoling her, she just shook her head and the artificial flower on its brass stem quivered as she trembled. 'No, no, it's all over, my poor boy! It's just too much . . .'

Jean-Marie headed back to the hamlet. At the side of the road he found Cécile and Madeleine who'd come to meet him; they both asked at the same time: 'You hear anything about my brother?', 'You hear anything about Benoît?'

'No, but that doesn't mean anything. Can you imagine how many letters must be backed up waiting to be delivered?'

As for their mother, she said nothing. She just shielded her eyes with her yellowish, dry hand and looked at him; he shook his head. The soup was on the table, the men were coming home, they ate. After dinner, when the dishes were dried and the kitchen swept, Madeleine went into the garden to pick some peas. Jean-Marie followed her. He knew he would soon be leaving the farm and everything seemed even more beautiful and peaceful to him.

It had been stiflingly hot for several days; you could hardly breathe until the sun began to set. But this was the time when the garden was at its most beautiful. The heat had withered the daisies and the white carnations bordering the kitchen garden, but around the well the rose bushes were in full bloom; a scent of sugar, musk and honey wafted up from the clusters of small red roses next to the beehives. The full moon was the colour of amber, shining so brightly that the sky was bathed in a soft green light, as far as the eye could see.

'What a beautiful summer we've had,' said Madeleine. She'd taken her basket and was walking towards the stakes of green peas. 'Only a week of bad weather at the beginning of the month and since then, not a drop of rain, not even a cloud, though if it carries on like this we won't have any more vegetables . . . and it's hard to work in this heat; but I don't care, it's still nice – as if the heavens have taken pity on us poor people. You can help if you want to, but you don't have to,' she added.

'What's Cécile doing?'

'Cécile, she's sewing. She's making herself a pretty dress to wear to Mass on Sunday.'

Her skilful, strong fingers reached between the cool green leaves of the peas, broke the stems in half, threw the peas into her basket; she looked down as she worked. 'So you're going to leave us, then?'

'I have to. I'll be glad to see my parents again and I've got to find some work, but . . .'

They both went quiet.

'Of course, you couldn't stay here your whole life,' she said, looking down even more. 'Everybody knows that's how it is, you meet people, you say goodbye . . .'

'You say goodbye,' he repeated quietly.

'Well, you're much better now. You've got a bit of colour . . .'

'Thanks to how well you took care of me.'

Her hand stopped still under a leaf. 'Have you been happy with us?'

'You know I have.'

'Well, then you better make sure you keep in touch. You should write . . .' she said, and he saw her eyes full of tears, close to him. She quickly turned away.

'Of course, I'll write to you, I promise,' said Jean-Marie and gently touched the young girl's hand.

'Everybody says that . . . After you've gone, we'll have time to think about you here, my God . . . Now it's still the busy season, we're working all day long . . . but when autumn comes, and winter, we'll have nothing to do but look after the animals, and the rest of the time we'll just stay indoors and watch the rain fall, then the snow. Sometimes I wonder if I shouldn't look for work in town . . .'

'No, Madeleine, don't do that, promise me. You'll be much happier here.'

'You think so?' she murmured, her voice low and strange.

And suddenly picking up the basket, she moved slightly away from him so he couldn't see her through the leaves. He picked some peas, lost in thought.

'Do you really think I could ever forget you?' he said finally. 'Do you think I have so many happy memories that I could forget this? Just imagine! The war, the horror, the war.'

'But what about before that? You weren't in the war for ever, were you? So before, were there . . .'

'What?'

She didn't reply.

'You mean were there women, girls?'

'Of course that's what I mean!'

'Nothing very interesting, my dear Madeleine.'

'But you're going away,' she said and finally, without the strength to hold back her tears, she let them fall down her full cheeks and said in a voice choking with emotion, 'I can't stand the thought of you leaving, I can't. I know I shouldn't say it, you'll make fun of me and Cécile will even more . . . but I don't care . . . I can't bear it . . .'

'Madeleine . . .'

She stood up straight, their eyes met. He walked towards her and, gently putting his arm round her waist, drew her close; when he started to kiss her, she sighed and pushed him away. 'No, that's not what I want . . . that would be too easy . . .'

'What do you want, then, Madeleine?' he said. 'That I promise never to forget you? Whether you believe me or not, that's the truth. I will never forget you,' and he took her hand and kissed it; she blushed with happiness.

'Madeleine, is it true you want to become a nun?'

'It's true. Well, I wanted to before, but now . . . it's not that I don't love our Good Lord any more, I just think it's not for me.'

'Of course it's not! You're meant to love and be happy.'

'Happy? I don't know, but I think I'm meant to have a husband and children, and if Benoît hasn't been killed, then . . .'

'Benoît? I didn't know . . .'

'Yes, we talked about it . . . I didn't want to. I had this idea of becoming a nun. But if he comes back . . . he's a good man . . .'

'I didn't know . . .' he said again.

How secretive these country people were! Discreet, wary, everything securely locked up . . . like their big wardrobes. He'd lived with them for two months and had never even suspected there was anything between Madeleine and the son of the house, and now that he thought about it, he realised they hardly ever talked about this Benoît . . . They never talked about anything. But that didn't mean they weren't thinking about it.

The farmer's wife called Madeleine. They went back.

Several days passed; there was no news of Benoît but Jean-Marie soon got a letter and some money from his parents. He was never alone with Madeleine again. He realised they were being watched. He said goodbye to the whole family at the door. It was raining that morning, the first rain in many long weeks; a chilly wind blew in from the hills. When he was out of sight, the farmer's wife went back inside. The two young girls lingered at the door, listening to the sound of the cart on the road.

'Well, it's not such a bad thing,' exclaimed Cécile, as if she had made an effort not to say anything for a long time and now let a rush of words tumble out. 'Maybe we'll get a little work out of you now . . . You've had your head in the clouds recently, I've had to do everything . . .'

'You've got no right to criticise me,' Madeleine replied angrily. 'All you did was sew and look at yourself in the mirror . . . I'm the one who got the cows in yesterday and it wasn't even my turn.'

'Well, I don't know anything about that. It was Mother who told you to do it.'

'Even if Mother told me to do it, I know who gave her the idea.'

'Think what you like!'

'Hypocrite.'

'Hussy! And you want to be a nun . . .'

'As if *you* didn't run around after him. But he couldn't have cared less!'

'So, and what about you? He's gone and you'll never see him again.'

Their eyes burning with rage, they looked at each other for a moment, then suddenly a surprised, soft expression came over Madeleine's face.

'Oh, Cécile! We used to be like sisters . . . We never fought like this before . . . It isn't worth it, come on. We can't have him, either of us!' She put her arm round Cécile, who started crying. 'It'll pass, come on, it'll pass . . . Dry your eyes. Mother will see you've been crying.'

'Oh, Mother . . . she knows everything but says nothing.'

They let go of each other; one went over to the stables and the other went inside the house. It was Monday, washing day, and they hardly had the chance to say two words to each other, but from their expressions, their smiles, it was clear they had made up. The wind blew the smoke from the laundry boiler towards the barn. It was one of those dark, stormy days in the middle of August when you can smell the first breath of autumn in the air.

Madeleine didn't have time to think as she washed, wrung out and rinsed the clothes, and so she managed to put aside her pain. When she looked up, she saw the grey sky, the trees battered by the storm. 'You'd think summer was over . . .' she said.

'Not before time. Filthy summer,' her mother replied resentfully.

Madeleine looked at her, surprised, then remembered the war, the mass exodus, Benoît gone, the universal misery, the war still going on far away and so many people who had died. She went back to work in silence.

That evening, she had just shut the chickens away and was hurrying across the yard in the rain when she saw a man on the road walking quickly towards her. Her heart began pounding; she thought Jean-Marie had come back. A kind of wild joy shot through her. She rushed towards him, then let out a cry: 'Benoît?'

'Yes, it's me all right,' he said.

'But how . . . Oh, your mother will be so happy . . . Did you escape, Benoît? We were afraid you were taken prisoner.'

He laughed to himself. He was a large young man with a broad, brown face and daring eyes.

'I was, but not for long!'

'You escaped?'

'Yes.'

'But how?'

'Well, with my friends.'

And suddenly she became a shy country girl once more, with that ability – lost with Jean-Marie – to love and suffer in silence. She didn't ask him anything, she just walked alongside him without saying a word.

'And how's everything here?' he asked.

'Fine.'

'Nothing new?'

'No, nothing,' she said.

And leaping up the first three of the steps into the kitchen, she went inside the house and called out, 'Mother, come quick, it's Benoît! Benoît's come home!'

31

The preceding winter – the first of the war – had been long and hard. But what of the winter of 1940–1? The end of November saw the beginning of the cold and snow. It fell on the houses destroyed by the bombs, on the bridges they were trying to rebuild, on the Paris streets where there were no cars or buses, where women in fur coats and wool hoods hurried by, where other women shivered and huddled in doorways. It fell on the railway tracks and on the telegraph wires, which were sometimes dragged to the ground by the weight and snapped; on the green uniforms of the German soldiers standing at the entrance to their barracks and on the red flags with their swastikas draped over the monuments. In freezing apartments, it cast a mournful, deathly pallor that made everything feel even colder and more inhospitable. In the poorer families, the old people and children stayed in bed for weeks: it was the only place they could be warm.

That winter, Gabriel Corte's terrace was covered in a thick layer of snow; he and Florence put the champagne out there to chill. Corte would write sitting next to the fire, which still didn't quite manage to replace the lost heat of the radiators. His nose was blue; he could have cried from the cold. With one hand he held a piping hot-water bottle against his chest, with the other he wrote.

At Christmas the cold became even fiercer; only in the Métro could you warm up a little. And still the relentless snow fell – softly, cruelly – on the trees along the Boulevard Delessert where the Péricands had come back to live (for they belonged to the French upper middle class who would prefer to see their children with no bread, no meat, no air rather than no education, and under no circumstances would they interrupt Hubert's studies, already so damaged by the terrible events of the past summer, nor Bernard's, who was nearly nine and had forgotten everything he'd learned before the exodus and was forced by his mother to recite 'The earth is a sphere which sits on absolutely nothing' as if he were seven instead of eight – what a disaster!)

Snowflakes gathered on Madame Péricand's black mourning veil as she marched proudly past the long queues of customers in front of the shop, stopping at the entrance to wave like a flag the priority ration card given to large families.

In the snow, Jeanne and Maurice Michaud waited their turn, leaning against one another like weary horses during a short pause in their journey.

The snow covered Charlie Langelet's grave at the Père-Lachaise cemetery, the piles of wrecked cars near the Gien bridge – and all the shelled, burned-out, abandoned vehicles left along the roads in June, tilted over on one wheel or on their side, or ripped open, or nothing more than a twisted mass of steel. The countryside was white, endless, silent. Only after several days did the snow melt; the country folk were delighted. 'It's good to see the earth again,' they said. But the next day it snowed again and the crows screeched in the skies. 'There's a lot of snow this year,' the young people murmured, thinking of the battlefields, the towns that had been bombed. But the older people replied, 'No more than usual!' In the countryside nothing changed, everyone just waited. They waited for the war to end, for the blockade to be lifted, for the prisoners to come home, for the end of winter.

'There won't be any spring this year,' the women sighed as February passed, then the beginning of March and still it got no warmer. The snow had disappeared, but the earth was grey and as hard as iron. The potatoes froze. The animals had nothing to eat. They should have been put out to pasture by now, but there wasn't a single blade of grass in sight. In the Sabaries' hamlet, the old people shut themselves away behind their great wooden doors, which they nailed shut at night. The family huddled round the stove, knitting for the prisoners, without saying a word. Madeleine and Cécile were making little nightshirts and nappies out of old sheets: Madeleine had married Benoît in September and was expecting a baby. When a harsh gust of wind shook the door, the old women would say, 'Ah, dear God, it's just too much!'

At the neighbouring farm a baby was crying. He'd been born just before Christmas and his father was a prisoner of war. His mother already had three other children. She was a tall, thin countrywoman, modest, reserved, who never complained. When people asked her, 'How are you going to manage, Louise, with no man at home, with all the work, no one to help you and four children?' her eyes would be sad and cold, but she would smile faintly and reply, 'I have no choice . . .' In the evening, when the children were asleep, she would go round to the Sabaries and sit down with her knitting, next to the door so she could hear if her children called her through the silent darkness. When no one was looking she would secretly watch Madeleine with her young husband, without envy, without malice, but in silent sorrow; then she would quickly look back down at her work. After a quarter of an hour she would get up, put on her shoes and say quietly, 'Well, I'd better get going. Goodnight, goodbye everyone' and go home. It was a March evening. She couldn't sleep. It was the same almost every night when she tried to fall asleep in the cold, empty bed. She had thought about having her eldest child sleep with her, but a kind of superstitious fear prevented her: that place had to be saved for her absent husband.

On this particular night, a violent wind was blowing as a storm from the Morvan mountains swept over the village. 'There'll be more snow tomorrow!' everyone said. In her large, silent house that creaked like a ship adrift at sea, the woman couldn't bear it any more and, for the very first time, burst into tears. She hadn't cried when her husband had left in '39, nor when he'd said goodbye after his few days home on leave, nor when she'd found out he'd been taken prisoner, nor when she'd given birth all alone. But she just couldn't bear it any more: so much work to do . . . the baby was so big and wore her out with his feeding and crying . . . the cow hardly gave any milk because it was so cold . . . the chickens had nothing to eat and weren't laying any eggs . . . in the wash-house she had to break the ice . . . It was all too much. She just couldn't do it any more – it was making her ill. She had lost the will to live . . . What was the point of living? She would never see her husband again. They missed each other so much; at that moment he was probably dying in Germany. It was so cold in that big bed.

She reached for the warming stone, which a few hours ago had been burning hot but was now icy cold, took it out from under the sheets and set it gently down on the floor. As her hand touched the freezing tiles, she felt an even icier chill run straight through her heart. She was sobbing violently. What could anyone say to ease her pain? 'You're not the only one . . .' She knew that only too well but other people seemed to be lucky . . . Madeleine Sabarie, for example . . . She didn't wish her harm . . . It was just too much! Life was too painful. Her thin body was frozen. It did her no good to huddle under the eiderdown, she felt the cold seeping right down to her bones. 'It will pass, he'll come home and the war will be over!' people would say. No. She didn't believe it any more. No. It would go on and on and on . . . Even spring didn't seem to want to come . . . Had there ever been such terrible weather in March? March was nearly over and the ground was still frozen, frozen to the core, like her. Such harsh winds! Just listen to them! They would surely blow the tiles off the roof.

She sat up in bed and listened for a moment. A look of mild surprise suddenly passed across her sad, tear-stained face. The wind had stopped. Just as it had come out of nowhere, so it had now disappeared without a trace. It had broken branches off the trees, whipped the rooftops in its blind rage, carried away the last of the snow on the hill, and now, out of the dark sky devastated by the storm, the first rain of spring began to fall, still cold, but torrential and urgent, carving its way down to the smallest roots of the trees, down to the very heart of the deep, black earth.

TWO

Dolce

1

Occupation

In the Angellier household they were locking away all the important papers along with the family silver and the books: the Germans were coming to Bussy. For the third time since the defeat of France, the village was to be occupied. It was Easter Sunday, High Mass. A cold rain was falling. At the entrance to the church, the branches of a small peach tree, pink with blossom, swayed mournfully. The Germans marched in rows of eight; they wore their field dress and metal helmets. Their faces maintained the impenetrable and impersonal expression of professional soldiers, but their eyes glanced furtively, inquisitively, at the grey façades of the town that was to be their home. There was no one at the windows. As they passed the church, they could hear the sound of the harmonium and the murmur of prayers; but a frightened member of the congregation shut the door. The stomping of German boots reigned supreme. The first detachment swung past and was followed by an officer on horseback; his beautiful dappled mare seemed furious at being forced to go so slowly; as she placed each hoof on the ground with reluctant care, she trembled, neighed and shook her proud head. Great grey armoured tanks pounded the cobblestone streets. Then came the cannons on their rolling platforms, a soldier positioned high above each one to keep watch. The column of soldiers was so long that throughout the priest's sermon a kind of constant thunder resounded through the church's vaults. The women sighed in the shadows.

After the metallic rumbling subsided, the motorcycles arrived, flanking the Commandant's car. Behind him, at a respectful distance, came trucks packed to the brim with large round loaves of black bread. They made the church windows rattle. The regiment's mascot – a thin, silent Alsatian dog, trained for combat – ran beside the cavalrymen who brought up the rear. Perhaps because they were so far away from the Commandant that he couldn't see them, or for some other reason incomprehensible to the locals, these soldiers were more informal, friendlier than the others. They talked and laughed among themselves. The Lieutenant in charge smiled when he saw the lone pink peach tree lashed by the bitter wind; he snapped off a branch. Since he saw nothing but closed windows all around him, he assumed he was alone. Far from it. Behind each shutter was an old woman, eyes as piercing as a knife, watching the conquering soldier's every move. Deep within hidden rooms, voices groaned.

'Could you ever have imagined such a thing . . .'

'He's destroying our fruit trees, for heaven's sake!'

'Seems this lot's the worst,' a toothless mouth whispered. 'I heard they did a lot of damage before coming here. Just our luck.'

'I bet they'll take our sheets,' said one housewife. 'Just imagine, sheets I got from my mother! Only the best for them . . .'

The Lieutenant shouted an order. The men seemed very young. They had rosy complexions and golden hair. They rode magnificent, well-fed horses with wide, shiny rumps, which they tied up in the square, around the War Memorial. The soldiers broke ranks and started to make themselves at home. The village was filled with the sound of boots, foreign voices, the rattling of spurs and weapons. In the better houses, they hid away the good linen.

The Angellier women – the mother and wife of Gaston Angellier, prisoner of war in Germany – were finishing their packing. The elder Madame Angellier, a thin, pale person, frail and austere, quietly read out loud the title of each book in the library and religiously stroked its cover, before putting it away. 'My son's books,' she murmured, 'to see them in the hands of a German! . . . I'd rather burn them.'

'But what if they ask for the key to the library,' groaned the fat cook.

'They'll have to ask *me* for it,' said Madame Angellier and, standing very tall, she lightly tapped the pocket sewn inside her black wool dress; the bunch of keys she always kept with her jingled. 'They won't be asking twice,' she concluded darkly.

She instructed her daughter-in-law, Lucile Angellier, to remove the decorative ornaments from the mantelpiece. Lucile wanted to leave an ashtray out. At first the elder Madame Angellier objected.

'But they'll drop ash all over the carpets,' Lucile pointed out. Pursing her lips, Madame Angellier gave in.

This older woman had such a transparent, pale face that she seemed to have not a drop of blood beneath her skin; her hair was pure white, her mouth like the blade of a knife, her lips almost purple. An old-fashioned high collar made of mauve cotton, held rigid by stays, covered but didn't hide her sharp, bony neck which pulsated with emotion like a lizard. When she heard a German soldier's footsteps or voice near the window, she would tremble from the tips of her small pointy little boots to the top of her impressively coiffed head. 'Hurry up, hurry up, they're coming,' she'd say.

They left only the bare essentials in the room: not one flower, not one cushion, not one painting. In the large linen cupboard, beneath a pile of sheets, they buried the family picture album, to prevent the sacrilegious enemy from seeing Great-Aunt Adelaide at her First Communion and Uncle Jules, aged six months, naked on a cushion. They packed away everything – right down to the mantelpiece ornaments: two porcelain Louis-Philippe vases decorated with parrots holding a garland of roses in their beaks (a wedding gift from a relative who came to visit less and less frequently but whom they didn't dare offend by getting rid of the present) and the two vases about which Gaston had said, 'If the maid breaks them while sweeping, I'll give her a rise.' Yes, even them. They had been given by French hands, looked at by French eyes, touched by the feather dusters of France – they would not be defiled by contact with Germans. And the crucifix! In the corner of the room, above the sofa . . . Madame Angellier took it down herself, slipped it beneath her lace shawl and held it to her breast. 'I think that's everything,' she said at last.

She took a mental inventory: the furniture from the main reception room had been removed, the curtains taken down, the provisions crammed into the shed where the gardener kept his tools (oh, the large hams smoked in ash, the jars of clarified butter, the salted butter, the fine, pure pork fat, the thick streaky sausages!). All her possessions, all her treasures . . . The wine had been lying buried in the cellar since the day the English army had left Dunkerque. The piano was locked; Gaston's hunting rifle was in an impregnable hiding place. Everything was in order. There was nothing to do but wait for the conquerors. Pale and silent, with a delicate, trembling hand, she half closed the shutters, as you would in a room where someone had died, and went out, followed by Lucile.

Lucile was a young woman – beautiful, blonde, with dark eyes, but a quiet, modest demeanour and 'a faraway expression', for which Madame

Angellier reproached her. She'd been acceptable because of her family connections and dowry (she was the daughter of an important landowner in the area). However, Lucile's father had gone on to make some bad investments, lost his fortune and mortgaged his land; the marriage was, therefore, not the most successful; she hadn't had any children, after all.

The two women went into the dining room where the table was set. It was just after twelve o'clock, but only according to the clocks on the church and the municipal hall, which they were obliged to set to German time; every French home set their clocks back by sixty minutes as a point of honour; every Frenchwoman would scornfully say, 'At our house, we don't live by German time.' This practice left great voids at various points of the day when there was nothing to do. Now, for example, a deadly gap loomed between the end of Mass and the beginning of Sunday lunch. They didn't read. If Madame Angellier saw Lucile with a book in her hands, she would look at her, surprised, and say reproachfully, 'What's this? Are you reading?' She had a soft, refined voice, as faint as the echo of a harp: 'Don't you have anything else to do?' No one was working: it was Easter Sunday.

They didn't speak. Between these two women, every topic of conversation was a thorn bush they only approached with caution: if they reached out a hand, they risked getting hurt. Every word Madame Angellier heard brought back the memory of some loss, some family story, some former pain Lucile knew nothing about. She would reply with reluctance, then stop to look at her daughter-in-law in sad surprise, as if she were thinking, 'How strange that her husband is a German prisoner of war and yet she can still breathe, move, speak, laugh . . .' She could barely admit that the problem between them was Gaston. Lucile's tone was never what it should be. Sometimes she seemed too sad: was she talking about someone who was dead? Surely her duty as a Frenchwoman, as a wife, was to bear separation courageously, as she, Madame Angellier, had done between 1914 and 1918, just after – or not so long after – her own marriage. But whenever Lucile murmured words of consolation, of hope, her thoughts were similarly bitter: 'Ah, you can tell she never really loved him; I've always suspected it. Now I can tell, I'm sure of it . . . That tone is unmistakable. She's cold and indifferent. *She* wants for nothing, while my son, my poor child . . .' She imagined the prisoner-of-war camp, the barbed wire, the guards, the sentries. Tears would well up in her eyes and she would say in a broken voice, 'We mustn't speak of him . . .' Then she would take a clean handkerchief from her bag, always there in case anyone made her think of Gaston or the misfortunes of France, and delicately dab at her eyes with the same gesture she would use to remove a drop of ink with some blotting paper.

And so, silent and still, next to the cold fireplace, the two women stood and waited.

2

The Germans had moved into their lodgings and were getting to know the village. The officers walked about alone or in pairs, heads held high, boots striking the paving stones. The ordinary soldiers stayed in groups; they had nothing to do, so they paced up and down the only street or gathered in the square near the old crucifix. When one of them stopped, all the others did too, forming a long line of green uniforms that made it impossible for the villagers to get by. Faced with this obstacle, they simply pulled their caps even further down over their eyes, turned away and used the small winding lanes to return to the fields.

The local policeman, under the surveillance of two non-commissioned officers, was putting up posters on the walls and main buildings. These posters were of various types. Some depicted a smiling German soldier with fair hair and perfect teeth giving out jam sandwiches to a group of French children gathered around him under the caption, 'Abandoned citizens, trust in the soldiers of the Third Reich!' Other posters used drawings or caricatures to illustrate world domination by the English and the detestable tyranny of the Jews. But most of them began with the word *Verboten* – Forbidden. It was forbidden to walk down the street between nine o'clock in the evening and five o'clock in the morning; forbidden to keep any firearms; forbidden to 'aid, abet or shelter' escaped prisoners, English soldiers, or citizens of countries which were enemies of Germany; forbidden to listen to foreign radio stations; forbidden to refuse German currency. And beneath each poster was the same warning in black lettering, underlined twice: ON PAIN OF DEATH.

Meanwhile, Mass was over and the shops were opening for business. In the spring of 1941, there was still no shortage of goods in the provinces: people had secreted away such hoards of fabric, shoes and provisions that they were now rather inclined to sell them. The Germans were not difficult and were prepared to be palmed off with junk: women's corsets from the last war, ankle boots from 1900, linen decorated with little flags and embroidered Eiffel Towers (originally intended for the English) – they'd buy anything. They inspired in the inhabitants of the occupied countries fear, respect, aversion and the amusing desire to fleece them, to take advantage of them, to get hold of their money.

'It's our money anyway . . . they stole it from us,' thought the grocer as he gave a soldier from the invading army his most charming smile and a pound of wormy prunes at double the price they were worth.

The soldier examined the goods sceptically. It was obvious he suspected fraud but, intimidated by the grocer's impenetrable expression, he said nothing. The regiment had previously been stationed in a small town in the north that had been destroyed and pillaged; there had been no supplies for a long time. But in this rich province of central France, the soldier once more found things to covet. His eyes lit up with desire in front of displays full of reminders of comfortable civilian life: pine furniture, ready-to-wear suits, children's toys, little pink dresses. Their expressions serious and dreamy, the troops marched from one shop to the other, jingling the money in their pockets. Behind the soldiers' backs, or above their heads, the French sent little signals to each other from their open windows – they raised their eyes to heaven, shook their heads, smiled, made faint grimaces of scorn or defiance, an entire language of gestures to show that they needed God's help during such terrible times (but that even God . . . !), that they intended to remain free, free in spirit in any case (if not in actions then at least in words), that these Germans weren't really very clever since they believed favours were done for them willingly, whereas the French knew they were obliged to because, after all, the Germans were the masters. 'Our masters,' said the women who looked at the enemy with a mixture of desire and hatred. (The enemy? Of course. But they were also men, and young . . .) The French took special pleasure in cheating them. 'They think we like them, but *we* know we just want to get passes, petrol, permits,' thought those women who had already met the occupying forces in Paris or the larger provincial cities, while the naïve country girls shyly lowered their eyes when the Germans looked at them.

On entering the cafés, the soldiers took off their belts and threw them on the marble tables before sitting down. At the Hôtel des Voyageurs, the non-commissioned officers reserved the main room for their mess. It was the kind of long, dark room you find in country hotels. Above the mirror at the back, two red flags with swastikas were draped over the cupids and burning torches that adorned the old gilt frame. In spite of the season, the stove was still lit; some of the men had dragged their chairs up to it and basked in its warmth, looking blissfully happy and drowsy. The large purple and black stove sometimes belched out acrid smoke, but the Germans didn't care. They moved even closer; they dried their clothes and boots; they looked pensively around, a look that was simultaneously bored and vaguely anxious, and seemed to say, 'We've seen so many things . . . Let's see what happens here . . .'

These were the older, wiser ones. The younger ones made eyes at the serving girl who, ten times a minute, lifted open the cellar door, descended into the underground darkness and emerged back into daylight carrying twelve beers in one hand and a box full of sparkling wine in the other ('*Sekt!*' shouted the Germans. 'French champagne, please, Mam'zelle! *Sekt!*').

The serving girl – plump, round and rosy-cheeked – moved quickly between the tables. The soldiers smiled at her. She felt torn between the desire to smile back at them, because they were young, and the fear of getting a bad reputation, because they were the enemy – so she frowned and tightly pursed her lips, without, however, quite managing to erase the two dimples on her cheeks which showed her secret pleasure. My God, there were so many men! So many men for her alone . . . In the other establishments the serving girls were the owners' daughters and their parents kept an eye on them, while she . . . Whenever they looked at her they made kissing noises. Restrained by a residue of modesty, she pretended not to hear them calling. 'All right, all right, I'm coming! You're in a big hurry!' she muttered to no one in particular. When they talked to her in their language she retorted proudly, 'You think I understand your gobbledegook?'

But as an ever-increasing wave of green uniforms swept in through the open doors, she began to feel exhilarated, overwhelmed, unable to resist. Her defence against their passionate appeals grew weaker: 'Oh, do stop it now! You're like animals!'

Other soldiers played billiards. The banisters, window ledges, backs of chairs were hung with belts, pistols, helmets and rounds of ammunition.

Outside, the church bells sounded Vespers.

3

The Angellier ladies were leaving their house to go to Vespers when the German officer who was to lodge with them arrived. They met at the door. He clicked his heels, saluted. The elder Madame Angellier grew even paler and with great effort managed a silent nod of the head. Lucile raised her eyes and, for a brief moment, she and the officer looked at each other. In a split second a flurry of thoughts flashed through Lucile's mind. 'Maybe he's the one', she thought, 'who took Gaston prisoner? My God, how many Frenchmen has he killed? How many tears have been shed because of him? It's true that if the war had ended the other way, Gaston might today be entering a German house. That's how war is, it isn't this boy's fault.'

He was young, slim, with beautiful hands and wide eyes. She noticed how beautiful his hands were because he was holding the door of the house open for her. He was wearing an engraved ring with a dark, opaque stone; a ray of sunshine appeared between two clouds, causing a purple flash of light to spring off the ring; it lit up his complexion, rosy from the fresh air and as downy as a lovely piece of fruit growing on a trellis. His cheek-bones were high, strong but delicate, his mouth chiselled and proud. Lucile, in spite of herself, walked more slowly; she couldn't stop looking at his large, delicate hand, his long fingers (she imagined him holding a heavy black revolver, or a machine-gun or a grenade, any weapon that metes out death indifferently), she studied the green uniform (how many Frenchmen, on watch all night, hiding in the darkness of the undergrowth had looked out for that same uniform?) and his sparkling-clean boots.

She remembered the defeated soldiers of the French army who a year before had fled through the town, dirty, exhausted, dragging their combat boots in the dust. Oh, my God, so this is war . . . An enemy soldier never seemed to be alone – one human being like any other – but followed, crushed from all directions by innumerable ghosts, the missing and the dead. Speaking to him wasn't like speaking to a solitary man but to an invisible multitude; nothing that was said was either spoken or heard with simplicity: there was always that strange sensation of being no more than lips that spoke for so many others, others who had been silenced.

'And what about him?' the young woman wondered. 'What must he be feeling coming into a French home where the head of the house is gone, taken prisoner by him or his comrades? Does he feel sorry for us? Does he hate us? Or does he just consider our home a hotel, thinking only about the bed, wondering if it's comfortable, and the maid, if she's young?' The door had closed on the officer a long time ago; Lucile had followed her mother-in-law; entered the church and knelt at her pew; but she couldn't stop thinking about the enemy. He was alone in the house now. He had taken over Gaston's office, which had its own entrance; he would have his meals out; she wouldn't see him; but she would hear his footsteps, his voice, his laughter. He was able to laugh. . . . He had the right. She looked at her mother-in-law who sat motionless, her face in her hands, and for the first time, felt pity and a vague tenderness for this woman she disliked. Leaning towards her, she said softly, 'Let's say our rosary for Gaston, Mother.'

The old woman nodded in agreement. Lucile started to pray with sincere fervour, but soon her mind began to wander. She thought of the past that was both near and distant at the same time, undoubtedly because of the grim intrusion of the war. She pictured her husband, a heavy, bored man, interested only in money, land and local politics. She had never loved him; she had married him because her father wished it. Born and brought up in the countryside, she had little experience of the outside world, with the exception of a few brief trips to Paris to visit an elderly relative. Life in the provinces of central France is affluent and primitive; everyone keeps to himself, rules over his own domain, reaps his own wheat and counts his own money. Leisure time is filled with great feasts and hunting parties. This village, where the forbidding houses were protected by large, prison-like doors and had drawing rooms crammed full of furniture that were always shut up and freezing cold to save lighting the fire, had seemed the very picture of civilisation to Lucile. When she left her father's house deep in the woods, she had felt joyous excitement at the idea of living in the village, having a car, sometimes going out to lunch in Vichy . . . Her upbringing had been strict and puritanical, but she had not been unhappy: the garden, the housework, a library – an enormous, damp room where the books grew mouldy and where she would secretly rummage around – were all enough to amuse her. She had got married; she had been a cold, docile wife. Gaston Angellier was only twenty-five when they married, but he had had that kind of precocious maturity brought about by a sedentary provincial lifestyle, excellent rich food eaten in abundance, too much wine, and the complete absence of any strong emotions. Only a truly deceptive man can affect the habits and thoughts of an adult while the warm, rich blood of youth still runs in his veins.

During one of his business trips to Dijon, where he had been a student, Gaston Angellier ran into a former mistress – a hatmaker with whom he'd broken off; he fell in love with her again and more passionately than before; she had his child; he rented a small house for her in the suburbs and arranged his life so he could spend half his time in Dijon. Lucile knew everything but said nothing, out of shyness, scorn or indifference. Then the war . . .

And now, for a year already, Gaston had been a prisoner. Poor boy . . . He's suffering, Lucile thought, as the rosary beads slipped mechanically through her fingers. What was he missing most? His comfortable bed, his fine dinners, his mistress? She would like to give him back everything he'd lost, everything that had been taken from him. Yes, everything, even that woman . . . Realising this, realising the spontaneity and sincerity of this feeling, she also realised how very empty was her heart; it had always been empty – empty of love, empty of jealous hatred. Sometimes her husband treated her harshly. She forgave him his infidelities, but he had never forgotten his father-in-law's bad investments. She could hear the words ringing in her ears, which more than once had made her feel he'd slapped her face: 'Imagine if I'd known there wasn't any money!'

She lowered her head. But no – there was no resentment left in her. What her husband had undoubtedly been through since the defeat – the recent battles, flight, capture by the Germans, forced marches, cold, hunger, death all around him, and now being thrown into a prisoner-of-war camp – all that wiped out everything else. 'Please just let him come home to everything he loved: his bedroom, his fur-lined slippers, strolling in the garden at dawn, fresh peaches picked from the trellis, his favourite dishes, great roaring fires, all his pleasures, even the ones I don't know about but can imagine, please give them back to him. I don't ask anything for myself. I just want to see him happy. As for me . . .'

Lost in thought, she let the rosary slip from her fingers and fall to the ground; she realised everyone was standing up, Vespers was over.

Outside, the Germans were standing around in the square. The sunlight glinting off the silver stripes on their uniforms, their light-coloured eyes, their blond hair and their metal belt buckles gave a feeling of cheerfulness, energy and new life to the dusty spot in front of the church which was enclosed within high walls (the remains of ancient ramparts). The Germans were exercising their horses. They had set up a dining area outside: planks of wood the local carpenter had meant to use to make coffins formed a table and benches. The men ate and looked at the townspeople with amused curiosity. You could tell that eleven months of occupation hadn't yet made them blasé. They regarded the French with the same cheerful surprise as in the early days: they found them odd, strange; they couldn't get used to how fast they spoke; they tried to work out whether this defeated people hated them, tolerated them or liked them . . . They smiled from afar at the young girls and the young girls walked by, proud and scornful – just like on the first day! So the Germans looked down at the crowd of kids around their knees: all the village children were there, fascinated by the uniforms, the horses, the high boots. However loudly their mothers called them, they wouldn't listen. They furtively touched the heavy material of the soldiers' jackets with their dirty fingers. The Germans beckoned to them and filled their hands with sweets and coins.

It felt like a normal, peaceful Sunday. The Germans added a strange note to the scene, but the essential remained unchanged, thought Lucile. There had been some upsetting moments; some of the women (the mothers of prisoners like Madame Angellier or widows from the other war) had hurried home, closed their windows and drawn their curtains so they wouldn't have to see the Germans. In small, dark bedrooms, they cried as they reread old letters; they kissed yellowing photographs draped with black crêpe and decorated with red, white and blue ribbons . . . But just like every Sunday, the young women gathered in the village square to chat. They weren't going to miss out on an afternoon when they didn't have to work, a holiday, just because of the Germans; they had on their new hats: it was Easter Sunday. Furtively and with inscrutable faces, the men studied the Germans; it was impossible to tell what they were thinking. One German went up to a group of them and asked for a light; they gave him one; they responded to his salute warily; he went away; the men continued talking about the price of cattle. As on every Sunday, the notary went over to the Hôtel des Voyageurs to play cards. Some families were returning from their weekly visit to the cemetery – an almost pleasurable outing in a village where there was nothing much to do: they went in a group; they picked bunches of flowers between the graves. The teaching nuns brought the children out of the church; they made their way through the soldiers; they were impassive beneath their wimples.

'Will they be here long?' murmured the tax inspector to the court clerk, pointing to the Germans.

'Three months, I've heard,' he whispered back.

The tax inspector sighed. 'That'll force prices up.' And, with a mechanical gesture, he rubbed the hand that had been lacerated by a shell explosion in 1915.

Then they changed the subject. The bells that had been ringing since the end of Vespers grew fainter; the final low chimes faded in the evening air.

To get home, the Angellier ladies took a winding lane; Lucile knew its every stone. They walked in silence, responding to greetings with a nod of the head. Madame Angellier was not liked by the villagers, but they felt sorry for Lucile – because she was young, because her husband was a prisoner of war and because she wasn't stuck-up. They sometimes went to ask her opinion about educating their children, about a new blouse, or about how to send a package to Germany. They knew there was an enemy officer lodging at their home – they had the most beautiful house in the village – and they expressed sympathy that they too had to be subjected to the law like everyone else.

'Well, you've certainly got a good one,' whispered the dressmaker as she passed them.

'Let's hope they'll be on their way soon,' said the chemist.

And a little old lady who was trotting along behind a goat with a soft white coat stood on tiptoe to whisper to Lucile, 'I've heard they're all bad and evil, and that they're causing misery to all us poor people.'

The goat gave a jump and butted a German officer's long grey cape. He stopped, laughed and wanted to stroke it. But the goat ran off; the frightened little old lady disappeared, and the Angellier ladies closed the door of their house behind them.

4

The house was the most beautiful for miles. A hundred years old, it was long, low and made of porous yellow stone that in sunlight took on the colour of golden bread. The windows that gave on to the street (those of the most elegant rooms) were carefully sealed, their shutters closed and protected against burglars by iron bars; the small window of the pantry (where they hid prohibited food in an array of different jars) lay behind thick railings whose high spikes in the shape of a fleur-de-lis impaled any cat who wandered by. The front door, painted blue, had the kind of lock you find on prisons and an enormous key that creaked dolefully in the silence. Downstairs, the rooms had a musty smell – that cold smell of an empty house – despite the constant presence of the owners. To prevent the draperies from fading and to protect the furniture, no air or light was allowed in. Through the panes of glass in the hall – the colour of broken bottles – the day seemed murky and overcast; the sideboard, the antlers on the walls, the small antique engravings discoloured by damp were drowned in the gloom.

In the dining room (the only place the stove was lit) and in Lucile's room, where she sometimes took the liberty of lighting a small fire in the evening, you could smell the smoky perfume of sweet wood, chestnut bark. The dining-room doors opened out on to the garden. It looked its saddest at this time of the year: the pear trees stretched out their arms, crucified on wires; the apple trees had been cut back, and their branches were rough, twisted and bristling with spiky twigs; there was nothing left on the vine but some bare shoots. But with just a few more days of sunshine, the early little peach tree in front of the church would not be the only one covered with flowers: every tree would blossom. While brushing her hair before going to bed, Lucile looked out of her window at the garden bathed in moonlight. On the low wall some cats were howling. Beyond was the countryside, its secret, fertile valleys thick with deep woods, and pearl-grey under the moonlight.

Lucile always felt anxious at night in her enormous empty room. Before, Gaston would sleep there; he would get undressed, grunt, bump into the furniture; he was a companion, another human being. For nearly a year, now, there had been no one. Not a single sound. Outside, everything was asleep. Without meaning to, she stopped and listened, trying to hear a sign of life in the room next door where the German officer slept. But she heard nothing. Perhaps he hadn't come back yet? Or maybe he was sitting still and silent like her? A few seconds later she heard a rustling sound, a sigh, then a low whistling, and she thought he was probably standing at the window looking out at the garden. What could he be thinking about? She tried to imagine but couldn't; in spite of herself, she couldn't credit him with having the thoughts, the desires of an ordinary human being. She couldn't believe he was simply looking out at the garden in complete innocence, admiring the shimmering fish pond where silent slippery shapes slid past: carp for tomorrow's dinner. 'He's elated,' she said to herself. 'He's recalling his battles, reliving past dangers. In a moment he'll be writing home, to his wife, in Germany – no, he can't be married, he's too young – to his mother then, or fiancée, or mistress. He'll say. "I'm living in a French house, Amalia" – she must be called Amalia, or Cunegonde or Gertrude' (she deliberately chose grotesque, harsh-sounding names). '"Our suffering hasn't been in vain, for we are the victors."'

She couldn't hear anything at all now; he wasn't moving; he was holding his breath. A toad croaked in the darkness. It was a soft, low musical note, a bubble of water bursting with a silvery sound. 'Croak, croak . . .' Lucile half closed her eyes. How peaceful it was, sad and overwhelming . . . Every so often something came to life inside her, rebelled, demanded noise, movement, people. Life, my God, life! How long would this war go on? How many years would they have to live like this, in this dismal lethargy, bowed, docile, crushed like cattle in a storm? She missed the familiar crackling of the radio: when the Germans arrived it had been hidden in the cellar because people said they confiscated or destroyed them. She smiled. 'They must find French houses rather sparsely furnished,' she thought, recalling everything Madame Angellier had crammed into wardrobes and locked away out of sight of the enemy.

At dinner time the officer's orderly had come into the dining room with a short note:

Lieutenant Bruno von Falk presents his compliments to Mesdames
Angellier and requests they kindly give the bearer of this letter the keys
to the piano and the library. The Lieutenant gives his word of honour
that he will not remove the instrument or damage the books.

Madame Angellier did not appreciate this courtesy. She raised her eyes to
heaven, moved her lips as if she were praying and acquiescing to God's
will. 'Might over right, isn't it?' she asked the soldier, who didn't understand French and so simply replied '*Jawohl*' with a wide grin, while nodding
his head several times.

'Tell Lieutenant von . . . von . . .' she mumbled scornfully, 'that he is
in charge here.'

She took the two keys he wanted from her chain and threw them on to
the table. Then she whispered to her daughter-in-law in a tragic tone of
voice, 'He'll be playing "Wacht am Rhein" . . .'

'I think they have a different national anthem now, Mother.'

But the Lieutenant didn't play anything at all. The deepest silence still
prevailed. When the ladies heard the great courtyard doors slamming like
a gong in the peaceful evening, they knew the officer had gone out and
sighed with relief.

Now, thought Lucile, he's walked away from the window. He's pacing
up and down. His boots . . . The sound of his boots . . . It would pass.
The occupation would end. There would be peace, blessed peace. The
war and the tragedy of 1940 would be no more than a memory, a page in
history, the names of battles and treaties children would recite in school,
but as for me, for as long as I live, I will never forget the low, regular
sound of those boots pacing across the floorboards. Why doesn't he go
to bed? Why doesn't he put slippers on in the evening, like a civilised
person, like a Frenchman? He's having a drink. (She could hear the
squirting of seltzer water and the faint 'jzz, jzz' of a lemon being squeezed.
'So *that*'s why we're short of lemons,' her mother-in-law would have said.
'They're taking everything from us!') Now he's turning the pages of a
book. Oh, it's horrible, thinking this way . . . She shuddered. He'd opened
the piano; she recognised the dull sound of the cover thrown backwards
and the creaking of the piano stool as it swivelled. Oh, no! Really, he's
not going to start playing in the middle of the night! True, it was only

nine o'clock. Perhaps in the rest of the universe people didn't go to bed so early . . . Yes, he was playing. She listened, her head lowered, nervously biting her lips. It wasn't quite an arpeggio; it was more like a sigh rising up from the keyboard, a flurry of notes; he touched them lightly, caressed them, finished with a rapid, light trill that sounded like a bird singing. Then everything went silent.

For a long time Lucile sat very still, brush in hand, her hair loose over her shoulders. Then she sighed, thinking vaguely, 'It's such a shame!' (A shame that the silence was so complete? A shame that the boy had stopped playing? A shame that he was here, he, the invader, the enemy, he and not someone else?) She made an annoyed little gesture with her hand, as if she were trying to push away great masses of heavy air, so heavy she couldn't breathe. A shame . . . She climbed into the large, empty bed.

5

Madeleine Sabarie was alone in the house; she was sitting in the room where Jean-Marie had lived for several weeks. Every day, she made the bed where he had slept. This irritated Cécile. 'Why bother! No one ever sleeps here, so you don't need to put clean sheets on every day, as if you were expecting someone. Are you expecting someone?'

Madeleine didn't reply and continued, every morning, to shake out the big feather mattress.

She was happy to be alone with her little boy; he was feeding, his head against her bare breast. When she changed sides, a part of his face was as moist, red and shiny as a cherry, and the shape of her nipple was imprinted on his cheek. She kissed him gently. She thought now as she had before, 'I'm glad it's a boy, men don't have it so bad.' She dozed while watching the fire: she never got enough sleep. There was so much work to do; they hardly got to bed before ten, eleven o'clock, and sometimes they got up in the middle of the night to listen to English radio. In the morning they had to be up by five o'clock to tend the animals. It was nice today, to be able to take a little nap. The meal was already cooking, the table was set, everything around her was in order. The faint light of a rainy spring day lit up the shoots in the vegetable plot and the grey sky. In the courtyard the ducks quacked in the rain, while the chickens and turkeys – a little mound of ruffled feathers – sheltered sadly under the shed. Madeleine heard the dog bark.

'Are they home already?' she wondered. Benoît had taken the family to the village.

Someone crossed the courtyard, someone who was not wearing the same kind of shoes as Benoît. And every time she heard footsteps that weren't her husband's or someone else's from the farm, every time she saw a strange shape in the distance, she would immediately panic and think: 'It's not Jean-Marie, it can't be him, I'm mad to think it might be.

First of all, he's not coming back, and then, even if he did, what would change? I'm married to Benoît. I'm not expecting anyone, quite the opposite, I pray to God that Jean-Marie never comes back because, little by little, I'll get used to my husband and then I'll be happy. But I don't know what I'm going on about, honest to God. What am I thinking? I *am* happy.' At the very moment she had these thoughts, her heart, which was less rational, would start beating so violently that it drowned out every other sound, so violently that she wouldn't hear Benoît's voice, the baby crying, the wind beneath the door; the uproar in her heart was deafening, as if a wave had washed over her. For a few seconds she would be about to faint; she would only come round when she saw the postman bringing the new seed catalogue (he'd been wearing new shoes that day) or the Viscount de Montmort, the landowner.

'Well, Madeleine, aren't you going to say hello?' Mother Sabarie would say, surprised.

'I think I woke you up,' the visitor would say, as she feebly apologised and mumbled, 'Yes, you frightened me . . .'

Woke her up? From what dream?

Now she felt that emotion within her once more, that secret panic caused by the stranger who had entered (or was coming back into) her life. She half sat up in the chair, stared at the door. Was it a man? It was a man's footsteps, that light cough, the aroma of fine cigarettes . . . A man's hand, pale, well-manicured, was on the latch, then a German uniform came into sight. As always, when it wasn't Jean-Marie, her disappointment was so intense that she sat dazed for a moment; she didn't even think of buttoning up her blouse. The German was an officer – a young man who couldn't be more than twenty, with an almost colourless face and equally fair and dazzling eyebrows, hair and small moustache. He looked at her bare bosom, smiled and saluted with an exaggerated, almost insolent politeness. Certain Germans knew how to place in their salute to the French a mere show of politeness (or perhaps it just seemed like that to the defeated French in all their bitterness, humiliation and anger). It was not the courtesy accorded to an equal, but that shown to the dead, like the Presentation of Arms after an execution.

'Can I help you, Monsieur?' Madeleine said, finally buttoning up her blouse.

'Madame, I have been billeted on the farm,' replied the young man, who spoke extremely good French. 'I apologise for the inconvenience. Would you be so kind as to show me my room?'

'We were told we'd have ordinary soldiers,' Madeleine said shyly.

'I am the lieutenant who serves as interpreter to the Commandant.'

'You'll be far away from the village and I'm afraid the room won't be good enough for an officer. It's just a farm, here, and you won't have any running water or electricity, or anything a gentleman needs.'

The young man glanced around. He looked closely at the faded red tiles on the floor, worn pink in places, the big stove standing in the middle of the room, the bed in the corner, the spinning wheel (they had brought it down from the attic where it had been since the other war: all the young women in the area were learning to spin; it was impossible to find wool in the shops any more). The German then looked carefully at the framed photographs on the walls, the certificates for agricultural prizes, the empty little niche that used to hold a statue of a saint, surrounded by a delicate frieze now half worn away; finally, his eyes fell once more upon the young farmgirl holding the baby in her arms. He smiled. 'You needn't worry about me. This will do nicely.'

His voice was strangely harsh and resonant, like metal being crushed. His steel-grey eyes, sharply etched face and the unusual shade of his pale-blond hair, which was as smooth and bright as a helmet, made this young man's appearance striking to Madeleine; there was something about his physique that was so perfect, so precise, so dazzling, she thought to herself, that he reminded her more of a machine than a human being. In spite of herself, she was fascinated by his boots and belt buckle: the leather and steel seemed to sparkle.

'I hope you have an orderly,' she said. 'No one here could make your boots shine like that.'

He laughed and said again, 'You needn't worry about me.'

Madeleine had put her son in his crib. She could see the German's reflection in the mirror above the bed. She saw the way he looked at her and smiled. She was afraid and thought, 'What will Benoît say if he starts chasing after me?' She didn't like this young man, he frightened her a bit, yet despite herself she was attracted by a certain resemblance to Jean-Marie – not to Jean-Marie as a man, but as a member of a higher social class, a gentleman. Both were carefully shaven, well brought-up, with pale hands and delicate skin. She realised the presence of this German in the house would be doubly painful for Benoît: because he was the enemy but also because he wasn't a peasant like him – because he hated whatever aroused Madeleine's interest in and curiosity about the upper classes to such an extent that for a while now, he had been snatching fashion magazines from her hands; and if she asked him to shave or change his shirt, he'd say, 'Better get used to it. You married a farmer, a country bumpkin, I got no fancy manners' with such resentment, such deep-seated jealousy that she knew who had given him these ideas, that Cécile must have been talking. Cécile wasn't the same with her as before either . . . She sighed. So many things had changed since the beginning of this damned war.

'I'll show you your room,' she said finally.

But he said no; he took a chair and sat down near the stove.

'In a minute, if that's all right with you. Let's get to know each other. What's your name?'

'Madeleine Sabarie.'

'I'm Kurt Bonnet' (he pronounced it Bonnett). 'It's a French name, as you can see. My ancestors must have been your countrymen, chased out of France under Louis XIV. There is French blood in Germany, and French words in our language.'

'Oh?' she said indifferently.

She wanted to say, 'There's German blood in France too, but in the earth and since 1914.' But she didn't dare: it was better to say nothing. It was strange: she didn't hate the Germans – she didn't hate anyone – but the sight of that uniform seemed to change her from a free and proud person into a sort of slave, full of cunning, caution and fear, skilful at cajoling the conquerors while hissing 'I hope they drop dead!' behind closed doors, as her mother-in-law did; *she* at least didn't pretend, or act nice to the conquerors, Madeleine thought. She was ashamed of herself; she frowned, put on an icy expression and moved her chair away so the German would understand she didn't want to talk to him any more and she didn't like him being there.

He, however, looked at her with pleasure. Like many young men subjected to strict discipline from childhood, he had acquired the habit of bolstering his ego with outward arrogance and stiffness. He believed that any man worthy of the name should be made of steel. And he had behaved accordingly during the war, in Poland and France, and during the occupation. But far more than any principles, he obeyed the impulsiveness of youth. (When she first saw him, Madeleine thought he was twenty. He was even younger: he had turned nineteen during the French campaign.) He behaved kindly or cruelly depending on how people and things struck him. If he took a dislike to someone, he made sure he hurt them as much as possible. During the retreat of the French army, when he was in charge of taking the pathetic herd of prisoners back to Germany, during those terrible days when he was under orders to kill anyone who was flagging, anyone who wasn't walking fast enough, he shot the ones he didn't like the look of without remorse, with pleasure even. On the other hand he would behave with infinite kindness and sympathy towards certain prisoners who seemed likeable to him, some of whom owed him their lives. He was cruel, but it was the cruelty of adolescence, cruelty that results from a lively and subtle imagination, focused entirely inward, towards his own soul. He didn't pity the suffering of others, he simply didn't see them: he saw only himself.

Mixed in with this cruelty was a slight affectation that was a product of his youth as well as a certain leaning towards sadism. For example, although he was harsh towards people, he displayed the greatest solicitude towards animals. It was at his instigation that the Headquarters at Calais had issued an order several months earlier. Bonnet had noticed that, on market days, the farmers carried their chickens feet tied and head down. 'As a gesture of humanity' it was forthwith forbidden to continue this practice. The farmers paid no attention, which only increased Bonnet's loathing of the 'barbaric and thoughtless' French, while the French were outraged to read such a decree beneath another announcing that eight men had been executed as a reprisal for an act of sabotage. In the northern city where he'd been billeted, Bonnet had only been friendly with the woman whose house he lived in because one day, when he'd been suffering from flu, she'd taken the trouble to bring him breakfast in bed. Bonnet had immediately thought of his mother, his childhood years and, tears in his eyes, thanked Lili – a former Madam in a house of prostitution. From that moment on he did everything he could for her, granting her passes of all kinds, coupons for petrol etc.; he spent the evenings with the old hag because, he would say, she was old and alone and bored; though he wasn't a rich man, he brought her expensive trinkets every time he returned from missions to Paris.

These acts of kindness were sometimes the result of musical, literary or, as on this spring morning when he walked into the Sabaries' farmhouse, artistic impressions: Bonnet was a cultured man, gifted at all the arts. The Sabaries' farm, with its slightly damp, sombre atmosphere created by the rainy day, its faded pink floor tiles, its empty little niche from which he imagined a statue of the Virgin Mary had been removed during the last revolution, its little palm branch above the cradle and the sparkling copper warming pan half in shadow, had something about it, thought Bonnet, that reminded him of a 'domestic scene' of the Flemish School. This young woman sitting on a low chair, her child in her arms, her delightful breast lustrous in the shadow, her ravishing face with its rosy complexion, her pure white chin and forehead, was herself worthy of a portrait. As he admired her, he was almost transported to a museum in Munich or Dresden, alone in front of one of those paintings that aroused within him that intellectual and sensual intoxication he preferred above all else. This woman could treat him coldly, even with hostility, it wouldn't matter; he wouldn't even notice. He would only ask of her, as he asked of everyone around him, to provide him with purely artistic acts of kindness: to retain the lighting of a masterpiece, with luminous flesh set against a background of velvety shadows.

At that very moment a large clock struck midday. Bonnet laughed, almost with pleasure. It was just such a deep, low, slightly cracked sound he had imagined coming from the antique clock with the painted casing in some Dutch Old Master, along with the smell of fresh herring prepared by the housewife and the sounds from the street beyond the window with its tarnished panes of glass; in such paintings there was always a clock like this one hanging on the wall.

He wanted to make Madeleine speak; he wanted to hear her voice again, her young, slightly lilting voice.

'Do you live here alone? Your husband must be a prisoner?'

'Oh, no,' she said quickly.

At the thought of Benoît, a German prisoner who had escaped, she was afraid again; it struck her that the German would guess and arrest him. 'I'm so stupid,' she thought, and instinctively softened: she had to be nice to the conqueror.

'Will you be here long?' she asked in a frank, humble voice. 'Everyone's saying three months.'

'We don't know ourselves,' Bonnet explained. 'That's military life for you: in war, it all depends on orders, a general's whim or chance. We were on our way to Yugoslavia, but it's all finished over there.'

'Oh? Is it?'

'It will be in a few days. In any case, it would be all over by the time we got there. And I think they'll keep us here all summer, unless they send us to Africa or England.'

'And . . . do you like it?' said Madeleine, intentionally feigning innocence, but with a little shudder of disgust she couldn't hide, as if she were asking a cannibal, 'Is it true you eat human flesh?'

'Man is made to be a warrior, just as woman is made to please the warrior,' Bonnet replied, and he smiled because he found it comical to quote Nietzsche to this pretty French farm girl. 'Your husband must think the same way, if he's young.'

Madeleine didn't reply. Actually, she had very little idea what Benoît thought, even though they'd been brought up together. Benoît was taciturn and cloaked in a triple armour of decency: masculine, provincial and French. She didn't know what he hated or what he liked, just that he was capable of both love and hatred.

'My God,' she said to herself, 'I hope he doesn't take against this German.'

She continued to listen but said little, straining all the while to hear any sounds on the road. Carts passed by, the church bells chimed for evening prayers. You could hear the bells ring out one after the other across the countryside; first the light silvery note of the little chapel on the Montmort estate, then the deep sound from the village, then the hurried little peal from Sainte-Marie that you could only hear in bad weather, when the wind blew in from the tops of the hills.

'The family will be home soon,' murmured Madeleine.

She placed a creamy earthenware jug of forget-me-nots on the table.

'You won't be eating here, will you?' she suddenly asked.

He reassured her. 'No, no, I've paid to have my meals in town. I'll only have some coffee in the morning.'

'Well, that's easy enough, Monsieur.'

It was an expression they used a lot around Bussy. She said it in an affectionate sort of way, with a smile. It didn't mean a thing, though; it was a mere politeness and didn't actually mean you would get anything. A mere politeness and, if the promise wasn't kept, there was another expression ready and waiting, this time spoken with a tinge of regret and apology: 'Ah, well, you can't always do what you want.'

But the German was delighted. 'How kind everyone is here,' he said naïvely.

'You think so, Monsieur?'

'And I hope you'll bring me my coffee in bed?'

'We only do that for sick people,' said Madeleine ironically.

He wanted to take her hands; she quickly pulled away.

'Here's my husband.'

He wasn't there yet, but he would be soon; she recognised the sound of the mare's hooves on the road. She went out into the courtyard; it was raining. Through the gates came the old horse and trap, unused since the other war but now a replacement for the broken-down car. Benoît held the reins. The women were sitting under wet umbrellas.

Madeleine ran towards her husband and put her arm round his neck. 'There's a Boche,' she whispered in his ear.

'Is he going to be living with us?'

'Yes.'

'Damn!'

'So what?' said Cécile. 'They're not so bad if you know how to handle them, and they pay well.'

Benoît unharnessed the mare and took her to the stable. Cécile, intimidated by the German but conscious of having an advantage because she was wearing her best Sunday dress, a hat and silk stockings, proudly walked into the room.

6

The regiment was passing beneath Lucile's windows. The soldiers were singing; they had excellent voices, but the French were bemused by this serious choir whose sad and menacing music sounded more religious than warlike.

'That how they pray?' the women asked.

The troops were returning from manoeuvres; it was so early in the morning that the whole village was still asleep. A few women woke with a start. They leaned out of the windows and laughed. It was such a fresh, gentle morning! The roosters crowed huskily after the cold night. The peaceful sky was tinged with pink and silver. Its innocent light played on the happy faces of the men as they marched past (how could you not be happy on such a glorious spring day?). The women watched them for a long time: these tall, well-built men with their hard faces and melodious voices. They were beginning to recognise some of the soldiers. They were no longer the anonymous crowd of the early days, the flood of green uniforms indistinguishable from each other, just as no wave in the sea is unique but merges with the swells before and after it. These soldiers had names now: 'Here comes that short blond who lives with the shoemaker and whose friends call him Willy,' the townspeople would say. 'That one over there, he's the redhead who orders omelettes with eight eggs and drinks eighteen glasses of brandy one after the other without getting drunk or being sick. That little young one who stands so straight, he's the interpreter. He calls the shots at Headquarters. And there's the Angelliers' German.'

Just as farmers used to be given the names of the places where they lived, to such an extent that the postman who was a descendant of former tenant farmers on the Montmort estate was called Auguste de Montmort to this very day, so the Germans more or less inherited the social status of their landlords. They were called the Durands' Fritz, the La Forges' Ewald, the Angelliers' Bruno.

Bruno rode at the head of his cavalry detachment. The well-fed, fiery animals pranced and eyed the onlookers with pride and impatience; they were the envy of the villagers.

'Mama, did you see?' the children shouted.

The Lieutenant's horse had a golden-brown coat, as glossy as satin. Both horse and rider were aware of the cheers, the women's cries of pleasure. The handsome animal arched its neck, violently shook its bit. The officer smiled faintly and sometimes made a little affectionate smacking sound with his lips, which controlled the horse better than the whip. When a young girl, at a window, exclaimed, 'He's a good rider, that Boche, he is,' he raised his gloved hand to his helmet and solemnly saluted.

Behind the young girl you could hear nervous whispering.

'You know very well they don't like being called that. Are you crazy?'

'Oh, so what! So I forgot,' the young girl retorted, red as a cherry.

The detachment broke ranks at the village square. In a great clanking of boots and spurs, the men went back to their billets. The sun was shining and it was hot now, almost like summer. The soldiers got washed in the courtyards; their naked torsos were red, burned by being outdoors so much, and covered with sweat. One soldier had hooked a mirror on to the branch of a tree and was shaving. Another plunged his head and bare arms into a large tub of cool water. A third called out to a young woman, 'Beautiful day, Madame!'

'Well now, so you speak French?'

'A little.'

They looked at each other; smiled at each other. The women went over to the wells and sent down their buckets on long creaking chains. Once retrieved and full of shimmering, icy water that reflected the dark blue of the sky, these buckets always attracted a soldier, who would hurry over to take the heavy burden. Some of the soldiers did it to prove that, even though they were German, they were polite; others did it out of natural kindness; some because the beautiful day and a kind of physical invigoration (brought on by the fresh air, healthy tiredness and the prospect of a well-earned rest) put them in a state of exaltation, of inner strength — a state where men who would gladly act maliciously towards the strong feel even more kindly towards the weak (the same state, doubtless, that in spring causes male animals to fight each other yet graze, play and gambol in the dust in front of the females). A soldier walked a young woman home, solemnly carrying two bottles of white wine she had just pulled out of the well. He was a very young man with light-blue eyes, a turned-up nose, large strong arms.

'They're nice,' he said, looking at the woman's legs, 'they're nice, Madame . . .'

'Shh . . . My husband . . .'

'Ah, husband, *böse* . . . bad,' he exclaimed, pretending to be very frightened.

The husband was listening behind the closed door and, since he trusted his wife, instead of getting angry he felt rather proud. 'Well, our women *are* beautiful,' he thought. And the small glass of white wine he had every morning seemed to taste better.

Some soldiers went into the shoemaker's. He was a disabled war veteran who had his workbench in the shop; the deep, natural aroma of fresh wood hung in the air; the freshly cut blocks of pine still shed tears of sap. The shelves were crammed with hand-carved clogs decorated with all manner of patterns – chimera, snakes, bulls' heads. There was a pair in the shape of a pig's snout.

One of the Germans looked at them appreciatively. 'Magnificent work,' he said.

The morose, taciturn shoemaker didn't reply, but his wife, who was setting the table, was so curious she couldn't help but ask, 'What did you do in Germany?'

At first the soldier didn't understand; then he said he'd been a locksmith. The shoemaker's wife thought for a moment, then whispered in her husband's ear, 'We should show him that broken key to the dresser, maybe he could fix it . . .'

'Forget it,' her husband said, frowning.

'You? Lunch?' the soldier continued. He pointed to the white bread on a plate decorated with flowers: 'French bread . . . light . . . not in stomach . . . nothing . . .'

What he meant was that the bread didn't seem nourishing, wouldn't fill you up, but the French couldn't believe anyone would be crazy enough not to recognise the excellence of their food, especially their golden round loaves, their crown-shaped breads. There were rumours they would soon have to be made with a mixture of bran and poor-quality flour. But no one believed it. They took the German's words as a compliment and were flattered. Even the sour expression on the shoemaker's face softened. He sat down at the table with his family. The Germans sat on wooden stools, at a distance.

'And do you like this village?' the shoemaker's wife continued.

She was naturally sociable and suffered from her husband's long silences.

'Oh, yes, beautiful . . .'

'And what about where you come from? Is it like here?' she asked another soldier.

The soldier's face began quivering; you could tell he was desperately trying to find the words to describe his own land, the fields of hop and deep forests. But he couldn't find the words; he just spread out his arms. 'Big . . . good earth . . .' He hesitated and sighed. 'Far . . .'

'Do you have a family?'

He nodded yes.

'You don't need to talk to them,' the shoemaker said to his wife.

The woman felt ashamed. She continued working in silence, pouring the coffee, cutting the children's sandwiches. They could hear joyful sounds coming from outside. It was the cheerful din of laughter, weapons rattling, soldiers' voices and footsteps. No one quite knew why, but they felt light-hearted. Maybe it was because of the beautiful weather. The sky, so blue, seemed gently to bow down towards the horizon and caress the earth. The hens were squatting in the dust: every so often they made sleepy squawking sounds and fluffed themselves up. Bits of straw, feathers, invisible grains of pollen floated in the air. It was nesting season.

There had been no men in the village for so long that even these soldiers, the invaders, seemed in their rightful place. The invaders felt it too; they stretched out in the sunshine. The mothers of prisoners or soldiers killed in the war looked at them and begged God to curse them, but the young women just looked at them.

7

In one of the classrooms of the independent school, the ladies of the village and some of the fat farmers' wives from the surrounding countryside had gathered together for the monthly 'Packages for Prisoners' meeting. The village had taken responsibility for local children of prisoners of war who had been on welfare before the war. The Charity's President was the Viscountess de Montmort. She was a shy, ugly young woman who got flustered whenever she had to speak in public. On each occasion she stuttered; her hands would sweat; her legs trembled; in short, she was just as prone to stage fright as any member of the aristocracy. But she felt it was an obligation, that it was her personal responsibility, her vocation, to enlighten the peasants and middle classes, to show them the way, to plant the seed of righteousness within them.

'You see, Amaury,' she explained to her husband, 'I cannot believe there is any essential difference between them and me. Even though they disappoint me (if you only knew how crude and petty they can be!), nevertheless I persist in trying to find some spark within them. Yes,' she added, looking up at him with tears in her eyes – she cried easily – 'yes, our Lord would not have died for such souls if there had been nothing inside them . . . But their ignorance, my dear, they are steeped in such ignorance that it is truly frightening. So at the beginning of each meeting, I give them a little talk to help them understand why they are being punished and (go ahead and laugh Amaury) I have sometimes seen a glimmer of understanding on their chubby faces. I do regret,' the Viscountess thoughtfully concluded, 'I do regret not having followed my vocation: I would have enjoyed preaching in an isolated region, working alongside some missionary in a savannah or virgin forest. Well, best not to think about it. Our mission is here where the Good Lord has sent us.'

She was standing on a small platform; the classroom had quickly been cleared of its desks; a dozen or so pupils deemed the most worthy had been allowed to come and hear the Viscountess speak. They were scraping their shoes on the floor and looking vacantly into space with their large, dull eyes, 'like cows,' the Viscountess thought, feeling rather annoyed.

She decided to speak directly to them. 'My dear girls,' she said, 'you have been the victims of our country's misfortunes at such a tender age . . .'

One of the girls was listening so attentively that she fell off her wooden stool; the eleven other girls tried to stifle their riotous laughter in their aprons.

The Viscountess frowned and continued more loudly. 'You play your childish games. You seem carefree, but your hearts are full of sadness. What fervent prayers you must offer to Almighty God, day and night, begging Him to take pity on our dear suffering France!'

She paused and nodded curtly to the teacher who had just come in: she was a woman who did not attend Mass and who had buried her husband in a civil ceremony; according to her pupils she hadn't even been baptised, which seemed not so much scandalous as unbelievable, like saying someone had been born with the tail of a fish. As this person's conduct was irreproachable, the Viscountess hated her all the more: 'because', she explained to the Viscount, 'if she drank or had lovers, you could understand her lack of religion, but just imagine, Amaury, the confusion that can be caused in people's minds when they see virtue practised by people who are not religious.'

The presence of this teacher was so odious to the Viscountess that her voice took on the same burning passion that seeing the enemy stirs in our hearts, and it was with true eloquence that she continued, 'But our prayers, our tears are not enough. I say this not only to you; I say it to your mothers. We must be charitable. But what do I see? No one is charitable; no one puts other people first. I am not asking you for money; alas, money doesn't mean very much any more,' the Viscountess said with a sigh, remembering she had spent 850 francs on the shoes she was wearing (fortunately, the Viscount was the local Mayor and she had coupons for shoes whenever she pleased). 'No, it isn't money, it's food I want to send in these packages to our prisoners of war, food we have in such abundance in this region. Each one of you is thinking of your own relatives, your husband, son, brother, father who is a prisoner, and nothing is too much for them; you send them butter, chocolate, sugar, tobacco, but what about the men who have no families? Oh, ladies, think of it, just imagine the state of these poor wretches who never receive any packages, never receive any letters! Come now, what could you do for them? I'll collect all the donations, I'll sort them all out; I'll send them to the Red Cross to distribute them to the different Stalags. What do you say, ladies?'

They said nothing; the farmers' wives looked at the village ladies, who pursed their lips and stared back at them.

'Come along now, I'll start,' said the Viscountess sweetly. 'I have an idea: we could send a letter written by one of the children here in the next package. A letter that in simple, touching words would reveal their hearts and express their sorrowful, patriotic feelings. Just think,' the Viscountess continued in an impassioned voice, 'just think of the joy a poor abandoned soldier will feel when he reads those words, when he can almost touch, in a way, the very soul of his country; their words will remind him of the men, the women, the children, the trees, the houses of his dear little home, and as the poet said, loving our home makes us love our country even more. But most of all, my children, let your hearts speak. Do not aim for stylistic effect: forget your letter-writing skills and speak from the heart. Ah, the heart,' said the Viscountess, half closing her eyes, 'nothing beautiful, nothing great is accomplished without heart. You could put a little flower from the fields in your letter, a daisy or a primrose . . . I don't think that would be breaking any rules. Do you like that idea?' the Viscountess asked, tilting her head slightly and smiling graciously. 'Come, now, I've talked enough. It's your turn.'

The notary's wife, a woman with hard features and a slight moustache, said sharply, 'It's not that we don't want to spoil our dear prisoners. But what can we poor villagers do? We have nothing. We don't have enormous estates like you, Viscountess, or big farms like the country folk. We can barely feed ourselves. My daughter just gave birth and can't even get any milk for her baby. Eggs cost two francs each, if you can find any.'

'Are you saying we farmers are running a black market?' asked Cécile Sabarie who was in the audience. When she got angry, her neck swelled up like a turkey and her face went purplish-red.

'I'm not saying that, but . . .'

'Ladies, ladies,' the Viscountess said softly, and she thought despondently, 'Well, there you have it, there's nothing to be done, they feel nothing, they understand nothing, they have base souls. What am I thinking? Souls? They're nothing more than stomachs with the gift of speech.'

'It's hurtful to hear you say that,' Cécile continued, 'it's hurtful to see you with your houses and having everything you want and then to hear you cry poverty. Come on, everyone knows you villagers have everything. You hear me? Everything! You think we don't know you're getting all the meat? You buy up all the coupons. Everybody knows it. You pay a hundred for each meat coupon. If you've got money, you want for nothing, that's for sure, while we poor people . . .'

'Well of course we have to have meat, Madame,' said the notary's wife haughtily, anxiously wondering if she'd been spotted coming out of the butcher's with a leg of lamb the day before (the second one that week). '*We* don't have pigs we can kill! We don't have hams in our kitchens, tubs of lard and cured sausages we'd rather see eaten by worms than give them to the miserable people in the village.'

'Ladies, ladies,' the Viscountess implored. 'Think of France, elevate your hearts. Control yourselves. Silence these hurtful remarks. Think of our situation. We are ruined, defeated . . . We have only one consolation: our dear Maréchal. And all you can talk about is eggs, milk, pigs! How important is food? Really, ladies, this is all so vulgar! We have so many other things to worry about. What is really important in the end? Helping each other a little, a little tolerance. Let us unite just as the soldiers in the last war did in the trenches, just as, I am sure, our dear prisoners of war are doing in their camps, behind their barbed-wire fences.'

It was strange. They had barely been listening to her until now. Her imploring had been like a priest's sermon you hear without understanding. But the image of a German prisoner-of-war camp, with men herded behind barbed wire, touched them. Every one of these large, heavy women had someone they loved in one of those camps; they were working for him; they were saving for him; they were putting money aside for his return, so he could say, 'You really took care of everything; you're a good wife.' Each woman pictured her absent man, just hers; each woman imagined in her own way the place he was held captive; one thought of a pine forest, another of a cold room, yet another of fortress-like walls, but each of them ended up imagining miles of barbed wire surrounding their men and isolating them from the rest of the world. The farmers' wives and villagers alike felt their eyes fill with tears.

'I'll bring you something,' one of them said.

'Me too,' said another with a sigh. 'I'll manage to find a bit of something.'

'I'll see what I can do,' promised the notary's wife.

Madame de Montmort hurried to write down their promises. Every one of the women stood up, went over to the President and whispered something in her ear, because now they were all deeply moved and touched; they truly wanted to give, not only to their sons and husbands, but to strangers, to children on Welfare. However, they didn't trust each other; they didn't want to seem richer than they were; they feared being denounced. There wasn't a single household that didn't hide its provisions; mothers and daughters spied on each other, denounced each other; housewives closed their kitchen doors at mealtimes so they wouldn't be betrayed by the smell of lard sizzling in the pot, or the piece of prohibited meat, or the cake made with illegal flour. Madame de Montmort wrote down:

Madame Bracelet, farmer's wife in Les Roaches, two sausages, a pot of honey, a jar of potted meat . . . Madame Joseph, from the Rouet estate, two potted guinea fowl, some salted butter, chocolate, coffee, sugar . . .

'I can count on you, can't I, ladies?' the Viscountess said again.

But the farmers' wives just stared at her, astonished: they never went back on their word. They said goodbye to the Viscountess, holding out their red hands that were chafed by the harsh winter, by caring for animals, by doing the washing. She shook each hand reluctantly; touching them was physically distasteful to her. But she made the effort to overcome this feeling so contrary to Christian charity and, in the spirit of mortification, forced herself to kiss the children who accompanied their mothers; they were all fat and pink, overfed and with dirty faces, like little pigs.

At last the room was empty. The teacher had taken the girls out; the farmers' wives were gone. The Viscountess sighed, not from tiredness but from disgust. How base and ugly people were! 'You have to go to so much trouble to instil a glimmer of love into these sad souls . . .' she said to herself out loud, but as her spiritual adviser had suggested, she offered up her day's tiredness and work to God.

8

'And what do the French think, Monsieur, of the outcome of the war?' Bonnet asked.

The women looked at each other, scandalised. It just wasn't done. You simply didn't talk to a German about the war – not about this one, or the other one, or about Maréchal Pétain, or about Mers-el-Kébir, or about how France had been split in two, or about the occupying forces, or about anything that mattered.

There was only one possible attitude: an affectation of cold indifference, the tone of voice Benoît used as he raised his glass, full to the brim with red wine: 'They don't give a damn, Monsieur.'

It was evening. The setting sun, clear and crisp, was a sign there would be a frost that night, but that the next day would undoubtedly be magnificent. Bonnet had spent all day in the village and was on his way to bed. But before going up, he had lingered downstairs – out of politeness, natural kindness, the desire to be well regarded or perhaps simply the wish to warm himself a moment by the fire. Dinner was almost over; Benoît was alone at the table; the women had already got up and were tidying the room, doing the dishes.

The German looked at the big useless bed with curiosity. 'No one sleeps here, do they? It isn't used for anything? How odd.'

'Sometimes it's used,' said Madeleine, thinking of Jean-Marie.

She thought no one would guess, but Benoît frowned; every allusion to what had happened that past summer pierced straight through his heart like an arrow, but it was his business, no one else's. He looked reproachfully at Cécile who had started to snigger.

'Sometimes it can be useful,' he replied with excessive politeness. 'You never know . . . If something bad happened to you, for example (not that I'd want it to). Around here, we lay out our dead on beds like this.'

Bonnet looked at him, amused, with the same scornful pity you feel when a wild animal grinds its teeth behind the bars of its cage. 'Fortunately,' he thought, 'this man will be busy working and won't be around too often . . . and the women are more approachable.' He smiled. 'In wartime, none of us wants to die in a bed.'

Madeleine, meanwhile, had gone out into the garden; she came back with some flowers to decorate the mantelpiece. They were the first lilacs of the season, as white as snow, with greenish tips. At the top of each stem the clusters of flowers were still in bud, but further down they opened out into perfumed blooms.

Bonnet lowered his pale face deep inside the bouquet. 'How divine . . . and how well you know how to arrange flowers.'

For a second they stood silently, side by side. Benoît thought that she (his wife, his Madeleine) always seemed comfortable when it came to doing lady's work – when she chose flowers, polished her nails, wore her hair differently from the other women in the area, when she spoke to strangers, held a book . . . 'People shouldn't take in foster-children, you never know where they come from,' he said to himself. Once more that painful thought . . . When he said, 'You don't know where they come from,' what he imagined, what he was afraid of, wasn't that Madeleine might come from a family of alcoholics or thieves, but from the middle classes; perhaps it was *that* which made her sigh and say, 'Oh, it's so boring in the countryside,' or 'I want to have pretty things, I do,' and it was *that* which made her feel some vague bond with strangers, with the enemy, so long as he happened to be a gentleman with fine clothes and clean hands.

He pushed his chair back angrily and went outside. It was time to get the animals in. He stayed in the warm darkness of the stables for a long time. A cow had given birth the day before. She tenderly licked her little calf with its big head, its thin trembling legs. Another cow was breathing quietly in the corner. He listened to her calm, deep breaths. From where he was, he could see the open door of the house; a shape appeared on the doorstep. Someone was worried because he hadn't come back, they were looking for him. His mother or Madeleine? His mother, no doubt . . . Just his mother, sadly . . . He wouldn't move from here until the German had gone upstairs. He'd see his light go on. Sure, electricity didn't cost *him* anything. He was right; after a few moments a light shone through the window. At the same time the shadowy figure who'd been looking for him left the doorstep and ran lightly towards him. He felt his heart soften, as if some invisible hand had suddenly lifted the burden that had weighed so heavily on his chest for so long that he felt crushed by it.

'That you, Benoît?'

'Yes, I'm over here.'

'What are you doing? I was scared.'

'Scared? Of what? You're crazy.'

'I don't know. Come in.'

'Wait. Wait a little.'

He pulled her towards him. She struggled and pretended to laugh, but he could sense, by a kind of stiffening throughout her body, that she didn't really want to laugh, that she didn't find it funny, that she didn't like being thrown down in the hay and cool straw, she didn't like it . . . No! She didn't like him . . . She got no pleasure from him.

He said very quietly, in a low voice, 'Is there nothing you like?'

'There is . . . But not here, not like this, Benoît. I'm embarrassed.'

'Why? You think the cows might see you?' he said harshly. 'Fine, go on, get out.'

She let out the despondent little moan that made him want to cry and kill her at the same time.

'The way you talk to me! Sometimes, I think you're cross with me. For what? It's Cécile who's . . .'

He put his hand over her mouth; she quickly pulled away and continued, 'She's the one who's getting you all worked up.'

'No one's getting me worked up. I don't need other people's eyes to see, do I? All I know is whenever I come near you it's always "Wait. Not now. Not tonight, the baby's worn me out." Who are you waiting for?' he roared suddenly. 'Who are you saving yourself for? Well? Well?'

'Let go of me!' she cried as he grabbed hold of her. 'Let go of me! You're hurting me.'

He pushed her away so violently that she hit her head on the low door frame. They looked at each other for a moment in silence. He picked up a rake and angrily stabbed at the hay.

'You're wrong,' Madeleine said finally, then whispered tenderly, 'Benoît . . . Poor dear Benoît . . . You're wrong to think such things. Come on, I'm your wife; if I seem cold, sometimes, it's because the baby wears me out. That's all.'

'Let's get out of here,' he said suddenly. 'Let's go up to bed.'

They went into the dark empty house. There was a little light left in the sky and at the tops of the trees. Everything else – the earth, the house, the meadows – was plunged into cool darkness. They undressed and got into bed. That night he didn't try to take her. They lay awake, motionless, listening to the German's breathing above their heads, the creaking of his bed. In the darkness, Madeleine reached for her husband's hand and squeezed it tightly. 'Benoît!'

'What?'

'Benoît, I just remembered. You have to hide your shotgun. Did you read the posters in town?'

'Yes,' he said sarcastically. '*Verboten. Verboten.* Death. That's all they know how to say, the bastards.'

'Where are you going to hide it?'

'Forget it. It's fine where it is.'

'Benoît, don't be stubborn! It's serious. You know how many people have been shot for not turning in their weapons.'

'You want me to give them my gun? Only chickens do that! I'm not scared of them. You want to know how I got away last summer? I killed two of them. They didn't know what hit them! And I'll kill some more,' he said furiously, shaking his fist in the dark at the German upstairs.

'I'm not saying you should hand it in, just hide it, bury it . . . There are plenty of good hiding places.'

'Can't.'

'Why not?'

'I've got to have it to hand. You think I'm going to let the foxes near us – or all the other stinking beasts? The château grounds are crawling with them. The Viscount, he's a real coward. He's shaking in his boots. He couldn't kill a thing. Now there's one who's handed in his gun to the Commandant, and with a nice little salute to boot: "You're very welcome, Messieurs, I'm truly honoured . . ." It's lucky me and my friends go up to his grounds at night. Otherwise the whole area would be overrun.'

'Don't they hear the gunshots?'

'Of course not! It's enormous, almost a forest.'

'Do you go there often?' said Madeleine, curious. 'I didn't know.'

'There's lots of things you don't know, my girl. We go looking for his young tomato plants and beetroot, fruit, anything he's not taking to market. The Viscount . . .' He paused for a moment, plunged in thought, then added, 'The Viscount, he's one of the worst . . .'

For generations the Sabaries had been tenants of the Montmorts. For generations they had hated each other. The Sabaries said the Montmorts were mean to the poor, haughty, shifty; the Montmorts accused their tenants of having a 'bad attitude'. They whispered these words as they shrugged their shoulders and raised their eyes to heaven; it was an expression that meant far more than even the Montmorts thought. The Sabaries' way of perceiving poverty, wealth, peace, war, freedom, property, was not in itself less logical than the Montmorts', but it was as contrary to theirs as fire is to water. Now there was even more to complain about. The way the Viscount saw it, Benoît had been a soldier in 1940 and, in the end, it was the soldiers' lack of discipline, their lack of patriotism, their 'bad attitude' that had been responsible for the defeat. Benoît, on the other hand, saw in Montmort one of those dashing officers in their tan boots who during those June days had headed towards the Spanish border in their expensive cars, with their wives and suitcases. Then had come 'Collaboration' . . .

'He licks the Germans' boots,' Benoît said darkly.

'Be careful,' said Madeleine. 'You say what you think too much. And don't be rude to that German up there . . .'

'If he starts chasing after you, I'll . . .'

'You're crazy!'

'I have eyes.'

'Are you going to be jealous of him too?' Madeleine exclaimed.

She regretted it as soon as she had said it: she shouldn't have given substance to her jealous husband's imagination. But after all, what was the use of keeping quiet about something they both knew.

'They're both the same to me,' Benoît replied.

These well-groomed, clean-cut men with their quick, witty way of talking – the girls are drawn to them, in spite of themselves, because they're flattered to be sought after by gentlemen . . . that's what he means, thought Madeleine. If only he knew! Knew she'd loved Jean-Marie from the first moment, the very first moment she saw him lying on that stretcher, exhausted, covered in mud, in his bloody uniform! Loved. Yes. Lying in the dark, deep in that secret part of her heart, she repeated to herself over and over again, 'I loved him. There it is. I still love him. I can't help it.'

At dawn, the husky crow of the cock pierced the silence and put an end to their sleepless night. They both got up. She went to make the coffee, he to tend the animals.

9

Lucile Angellier sat in the shade of the cherry trees with a book and some embroidery. It was the only corner of the garden where trees and plants were left to grow untended, for these cherry trees bore little fruit.

But it was blossom time. Against a sky of pure and relentless blue – that deep but lustrous Sèvres blue seen on certain precious pieces of porcelain – floated branches that appeared to be covered in snow. The breath of wind that moved them was still chilly on this day in May; the flowers gently resisted, curling up with a kind of trembling grace and turning their pale stamens towards the ground. The sun shone through them, revealing a pattern of interlacing, delicate blue veins, visible through the opaque petals; this added something alive to the flower's fragility, to its ethereal quality, something almost human, in the way that human can mean frailty and endurance both at the same time. The wind could ruffle these ravishing creations but it couldn't destroy them, or even crush them; they swayed there, dreamily; they seemed ready to fall but held fast to their slim strong branches – branches that had something silvery about them, like the trunk itself, which grew tall and straight, sleek and slender, tinged with greys and purples. Between the clusters of white flowers were long thin leaves; in the shade they looked a delicate green, covered in silvery down; in the sunlight they seemed pink.

The garden ran alongside a narrow road, a country lane dotted with little cottages. This was where the Germans had set up their ammunitions store. A guard marched up and down, beneath a red sign that said in large letters:

VERBOTEN

and further down, in small writing, in French:

Keep out under penalty of death

The soldiers whistled as they groomed their horses and the horses ate the green shoots of the young trees. In the gardens bordering the road, men calmly went about their work. In shirtsleeves, corduroy trousers and straw hats, they tilled, pruned, watered, sowed, planted. Sometimes a German soldier would push open the gate of one of these little gardens to ask for a match to light his pipe, or for a fresh egg, or a glass of beer. The gardener would give him what he wanted; then, leaning on his spade and lost in thought, watch him walk away before turning back to his work with a shrug of the shoulders that was no doubt a reaction to a world of thoughts, so numerous, so deep, so serious and strange that it was impossible to express them in words.

Lucile began to embroider, but soon set down her work. The cherry blossom above her head was attracting wasps and bees; they were coming and going, darting about, diving into the centre of the flowers and drinking greedily, heads down and bodies trembling with a sort of spasmodic delight, while a great golden bumblebee, seemingly mocking these agile workers, swayed in the soft breeze as if on a hammock, barely moving and filling the air with its peaceful golden hum.

From her seat, Lucile could see their German officer at the window; for a few days now he'd had the regiment's Alsatian with him. He was in Gaston Angellier's room, sitting at the Louis XIV desk; he emptied the ashes from his pipe into the blue cup that the elder Madame Angellier used for her son's herbal tea; he tapped his heel absent-mindedly against the gilt bronze mounts that supported the table. The dog had put his snout on the German's leg; he barked and pulled on his chain.

'No, Bubi,' the officer told him, in French, and loud enough for Lucile to hear (in this quiet garden, all sound hung in the air for a long time, as if carried by the gentle breeze), 'you can't go running about. You will eat all these ladies' lettuces and they will not be happy with you; they will think we are all bad-mannered, crude soldiers. You must stay where you are, Bubi, and look at the beautiful garden.'

'What a child!' Lucile thought. But she couldn't help smiling.

The officer continued, 'It's a shame, isn't it, Bubi? You would love to make holes in the garden with your nose, I'm sure. If there were a small child in the house it would be different . . . He'd call us over. We've always got along well with small children . . . But here there are only two very serious ladies, very silent and . . . we're better off staying where we are, Bubi!'

He waited another moment and when Lucile said nothing, he seemed disappointed. He leaned further out of the window, saluted her and asked with excessive politeness, 'Would it inconvenience you in any way, Madame, if I were to ask your permission to pick the strawberries in your flower beds?'

'Make yourself at home,' said Lucile with bitter irony.

The officer saluted again. 'I wouldn't take the liberty of asking you for myself, I assure you, but this dog loves strawberries. I would point out, as well, that it is a French dog. He was found in an abandoned village in Normandy, during a battle, and taken in by my comrades. You wouldn't refuse to give your strawberries to a fellow Frenchman.'

'We must be idiots,' thought Lucile. But all she said was, 'Come, both of you, and pick whatever you like.'

'Thank you, Madame,' the officer exclaimed happily and immediately jumped out of the window, the dog following behind.

The two of them came up to Lucile; the German smiled. 'I hope you don't mind me asking, Madame. Please do not think me rude. It's just that this garden, these cherry trees, it all seems like a little corner of paradise to a simple soldier.'

'Did you spend the winter in France?' Lucile asked.

'Yes. In the north, confined to the barracks and the café by the bad weather. I was billeted with a poor young woman whose husband had been taken prisoner two weeks after they got married. Whenever she saw me in the hallway she started to cry. As for me, well, it made me feel like a criminal. Though it wasn't my fault . . . and I could have told her I was married too, and separated from my wife by the war.'

'You're married?'

'Yes. Does that surprise you? Married four years. A soldier four years.'

'But you're so young!'

'I'm twenty-four, Madame.'

They fell silent. Lucile took up her embroidery. The officer knelt on the ground and began picking strawberries; he held them in the palm of his hand and let Bubi come and find them with his wet black nose.

'Do you live here alone with your mother?'

'She's my husband's mother; he's a prisoner of war. You can ask the cook for a plate for your strawberries.'

'Oh, all right . . . Thank you, Madame.'

After a moment he came back with a big blue plate and continued picking strawberries. He offered some to Lucile who took a few and then told him to have the others. He was standing in front of her, leaning against a cherry tree.

'Your house is beautiful, Madame.'

The sky had become hazy, cloaked in a light mist, and in this softer light the house took on a pinkish ochre colour, like certain eggshells; as a child, Lucile had called them 'brown eggs' and thought they tasted more delicious than the snow-white ones most of the hens laid. This memory made her smile. She looked at the house, its bluish slate roof, its sixteen windows with their shutters (carefully left only slightly ajar so the spring sunshine couldn't fade the tapestries), the great rusty clock over the entrance that no longer sounded the hour and whose glass cover mirrored the sky.

'You think it's beautiful?' she asked.

'One of Balzac's characters might live here. It must have been built by a wealthy provincial notary who retired to the countryside. I imagine him, at night, in my room, counting out his gold coins. He was a free-thinker, but his wife went to first Mass every morning, the one whose bells I hear ringing on my way back from night manoeuvres. His wife would have been blonde, with a rosy complexion and a large cashmere shawl.'

'I'll ask my mother-in-law who built this house,' said Lucile. 'My husband's parents were landowners, but in the nineteenth century there must have been notaries, lawyers and doctors, and before that farmers. I know there was a farm here a hundred and fifty year ago.'

'You'll ask? You don't know? Doesn't it interest you, Madame?'

'I don't know,' said Lucile, 'but I can tell you about the house where I was born; I can tell you when it was built and by whom. I wasn't born here. I just live here.'

'Where were you born?'

'Not far from here, but in another province. In a house in the woods . . . where the trees grow so close to the sitting room that in summer their shadows bathe everything in a green light, just like an aquarium.'

'There are forests where I live,' said the officer. 'Very big forests. People hunt all day long.' After thinking for a moment he added, 'An aquarium, yes, you're right. The sitting-room windows are dark green and cloudy, like water. There are also lakes where we hunt wild duck.'

'Will you be getting leave soon so you can go home?' asked Lucile.

Joy flashed across the officer's face. 'I'm leaving in ten days, Madame, a week from Monday. Since the beginning of the war I've only had one short leave at Christmas, less than a week. Oh, Madame, we look forward to our leave so much! We count the days. We hope. And then we get there and we realise we don't speak the same language any more.'

'Sometimes,' murmured Lucile.

'Always.'

'Are your parents still alive?'

'Yes. My mother will probably be sitting in the garden right now, like you, with a book and some embroidery.'

'And your wife?'

'My wife', he said, 'is waiting for me, or rather, she's waiting for someone who went away four years ago and who will never return . . . Absence is a very strange thing!'

'Yes,' sighed Lucile.

And she thought of Gaston Angellier. There are some women who expect to welcome back the same man, and some who expect a different man from before, she said to herself. Both are disappointed. She forced herself to picture the husband she hadn't seen for a year, and what he must be like now, suffering, consumed with longing (but for his wife or his hatmaker in Dijon?). She wasn't being fair; he must be devastated by the humiliation of the defeat, the loss of so much wealth . . . Suddenly, the sight of the German was painful to her (no, not the German himself, but his uniform, that peculiar almond-green colour verging on grey, his jacket, his shiny bright boots). She pretended she had some work to do in the house and went inside. From her room she could see him walking up and down the narrow path between the large pear trees, their arms stretched out, heavy with blossom. What a beautiful day . . . Gradually the light began to fade, making the branches of the cherry trees look bluish and airy, like powder puffs. The dog walked quietly beside the officer, now and again rubbing his nose into the young man's hand. The officer stroked him gently each time. He wasn't wearing a hat: his silvery blond hair shone in the sunlight. Lucile saw him looking at the house.

'He's intelligent and well-mannered. But I'm glad he'll be leaving soon.

It pains my poor mother-in-law to see him living in her son's room. Passionate souls are so simple,' she thought. 'She hates him and that's all there is to it. People who can love and hate openly, consistently, unreservedly, are so lucky. Meanwhile, here I am, on this beautiful day, confined to my bedroom because that gentleman wants to take a little walk. It's too ridiculous.'

She closed the window, threw herself down on the bed and continued reading. She persevered until dinner time, but she was half asleep over her book, tired from the heat and bright light. When she entered the dining room her mother-in-law was already at her usual place opposite the empty chair where Gaston always sat. She was so pale and rigid, her eyes so raw from crying, that Lucile was frightened.

'What's happened?' she asked.

'I wonder . . .' replied Madame Angellier, clasping her hands together so tightly that Lucile could see her nails turning white, 'I wonder why you ever married Gaston?'

There is nothing more consistent in people than their way of expressing anger. Madame Angellier's way was normally as devious and subtle as the hissing of a serpent; Lucile had never endured such an abrupt, harsh attack. She was less indignant than upset; suddenly she realised how much her mother-in-law must be suffering. She remembered their melancholy, affectionate and deceitful black cat who would purr, then slyly lash out with her claws. Once she even went for the cook's eyes, nearly blinding her. That was the day her litter of kittens had been drowned. After that she'd disappeared.

'What have I done?' Lucile asked quietly.

'How could you, here, in his house, outside his windows, with him gone, a prisoner, ill perhaps, abused by these brutes, how could you smile at a German, speak with such familiarity to a German? It's inconceivable!'

'He asked my permission to go into the garden to pick some strawberries. I couldn't exactly refuse. You're forgetting he's in charge here now, unfortunately . . . He's being polite, but he could take whatever he wants, go wherever he pleases and even throw us out into the street. He wears kid gloves to claim his rights as a conqueror. I can't hold that against him. I think he's right. We're not on a battlefield. We can keep all our feelings deep inside. Superficially at least, why not be polite and considerate? There's something inhuman about our situation. Why make it worse? It isn't . . . it isn't reasonable, Mother.' Lucile spoke so passionately that she surprised even herself.

'Reasonable!' exclaimed Madame Angellier. 'But my poor girl, that word alone proves you don't love your husband, that you've never loved him and you don't even miss him. Do you think that *I* try to be reasonable? I can't bear the sight of that officer. I want to rip his eyes out. I want to see him dead. It may not be fair, or humane, or Christian, but I am a mother. Being without my son is torture. I hate the people who have taken him away from me, and if you were a real wife, you wouldn't have been able to bear that German being near you. You wouldn't have been afraid of appearing uncouth, rude, or ridiculous. You would have simply got up and, with or without an excuse, walked away. My God! That uniform, those boots, that blond hair, that voice, and that look of good health and contentment, while my poor son . . .'

She stopped and began to cry.

'Come on now, Mother . . .'

But Madame Angellier became even more enraged. 'I wonder why you ever married him!' she exclaimed again. 'For his money, for his land no doubt, honestly . . .'

'That's not true. You know very well it's not true. I got married because I was a little goose, because Papa said, "He's a good man. He'll make you happy." I never imagined he'd start being unfaithful to me with a hatmaker from Dijon as soon as we got married!'

'What? . . . What on earth are you talking about?'

'I'm talking about my marriage,' Lucile said bitterly. 'At this very moment a woman in Dijon is knitting Gaston a sweater, making him sweetmeats, sending him packages and probably writing "My poor sweetheart, I'm so lonely without you tonight, in our great big bed."'

'A woman who loves him,' muttered Madame Angellier, her lips becoming as thin and sharp as a razor, and turning the colour of faded hydrangea.

'At this very moment', Lucile thought to herself, 'she would cheerfully kick me out and have the hatmaker here instead,' and with the treachery present in even the best of women, she insinuated, 'It's true he loves her . . . a lot . . . You should see his chequebook. I found it in his desk when he left.'

'He's spending money on her?' cried Madame Angellier, horrified.

'Yes; and I couldn't care less.'

There was a long silence. They could hear the familiar sounds of evening: the neighbour's radio sending out a series of piercing, plaintive, droning notes, like Arab music or the screeching of crickets (it was the BBC of London distorted by interference), the mysterious murmuring of some stream hidden in the countryside, the insistent croak of a thirsty frog praying for rain. In the room, the copper lamp that hung from the ceiling – rubbed and polished by so many generations that it had lost its pink glow and was now the pale, yellow colour of a crescent moon – shone down on the two women sitting at the table. Lucile felt sad and remorseful.

'What's wrong with me?' she thought. 'I should have just let her criticise me and said nothing. Now she'll get even more upset. She'll want to make excuses for her son, patch things up between us. God, how tedious!'

Madame Angellier didn't say a word for the rest of the meal. After dinner they went into the sitting room where the cook announced the Viscountess de Montmort. This lady, naturally, did not associate with the middle-class people of the village; she wouldn't invite them into her home any more than she would her farmworkers. When she needed a favour, however, she would come to their homes to make the request with the simplicity, ingenuousness and innocent superiority of the 'well-bred'. The villagers didn't realise that when she dropped by, dressed like a chambermaid, wearing a little red felt hat with a pheasant feather that had seen better days, she was demonstrating the profound scorn she felt towards them even more clearly than if she had stood on ceremony: after all, they didn't get dressed up to go to a neighbouring farm to ask for a glass of milk. Her deception worked. 'She's not stuck-up,' they all thought when they met her. Nevertheless, they treated her with extraordinary condescension – and they were just as unaware of it as the Viscountess was of her feigned humility.

Madame de Montfort strode into the Angelliers' sitting room; she greeted them cordially; she didn't apologise for coming so late; she picked up Lucile's book and read the title out loud: *Connaissance de l'Est* by Claudel.

'Very good indeed,' she said to Lucile with an encouraging smile, as if she were congratulating one of the schoolgirls for reading the *History of France* without being forced to. 'You like reading serious books, very good indeed.'

She knelt down to pick up the ball of wool the elder Madame Angellier had just dropped.

'You see,' the Viscountess seemed to say, 'I've been brought up to respect my elders; their background, their education, their wealth mean nothing to me; I see only their white hair.'

Meanwhile, Madame Angellier, with an icy nod of the head, barely moving her lips, invited the Viscountess to sit down. Everything inside her seemed silently to scream, 'If you think I'm going to be flattered by your visit you're mistaken. My great-great-grandfather might have been one of the Viscount de Montmort's farmers, but that's ancient history and no one even knows about it, whereas everyone knows the exact number of hectares of land your dead father-in-law sold to my late husband when he needed money; what's more, your husband managed to come back from the war, while my son is a prisoner. I am a suffering mother and you should be showing respect to me.' To the Viscountess's questions she replied quietly that she was in good health and had recently heard from her son.

'You have no hope?' asked the Viscountess, meaning 'hope that he'll soon come back home'.

Madame Angellier shook her head and raised her eyes to heaven.

'It's so sad,' said the Viscountess and added, 'We're going through such hard times.'

She said 'we' out of that sense of propriety which makes us pretend we share other people's misfortunes when we're with them (although egotism invariably distorts our best intentions so that in all innocence we say to someone dying of tuberculosis, 'I do feel for you, I do understand, I've had a cold I can't shake off for three weeks now').

'Very hard times, Madame,' murmured Madame Angellier coldly. 'We have a guest, as you know,' she added, indicating the next room and smiling bitterly. 'One of these gentlemen . . . You're putting someone up as well, no doubt?' she asked, even though she and everyone else knew that thanks to the Viscount's personal contacts there were no Germans at the château.

The Viscountess did not reply to this question, but said indignantly, 'You will never guess what they have had the nerve to request . . . Access to the lake for fishing and swimming! And I, who love the water so much, will be forced to stay away all summer.'

'Are they forbidding you to use the lake? Well, that's a bit much,' exclaimed Madame Angellier, vaguely comforted by the humiliation inflicted upon the Viscountess.

'No, no,' she insisted, 'on the contrary, they behaved quite correctly. "Please tell us when we may use the lake so we will not disturb you," they said. But can you imagine me running into one of those men in my bathing suit? You know they even *eat* half naked? They take their meals in the courtyard of the school with bare chests and legs, and wearing a kind of jockstrap! The older girls' classroom looks out over the courtyard so they have to keep the shutters closed so the children don't see . . . what they shouldn't see. And you can imagine how pleasant that must be in this heat!'

She sighed: she was in a very difficult position. At the beginning of the war she had been passionately patriotic and anti-German, not that she particularly hated the Germans (she felt the same aversion, defiance and scorn towards all foreigners), but there was something wonderfully dramatic about patriotism and hatred of the Germans, as there was in anti-Semitism or, later, devotion to Maréchal Pétain, that sent chills down her spine. In 1939 she had organised a series of easy-to-follow lectures at the school on Hitler's psychology, which she had delivered to an audience of nuns, village gentlewomen and rich farmers' wives, and in which she had depicted all Germans, without exception, as madmen, sadists and criminals. Immediately after the defeat of France she had maintained this stance, mainly because it would have taken the kind of flexibility and sharpness of mind she clearly lacked to change camp so quickly. At the time, she herself had typed and distributed several dozen copies of the famous prophecies of Sainte Odile, who predicted the extermination of the Germans at the end of 1941.

But time had passed; the year had ended; the Germans were still here and, what's more, the Viscount had been appointed town Mayor, thus becoming a public official, forced to embrace the government's views. And so, with each day that passed, the Viscount leaned more and more towards what was called the policy of collaboration. As a result, Madame de Montfort found herself forced to water down her comments on current events. Now, once more, she remembered she mustn't show any ill will towards the conqueror and so said with tolerance (and anyway, Jesus wanted us to love our enemies, didn't he?), 'I do understand they have to wear light clothing after their tiring exercises. After all, they're just like any other men.'

But Madame Angellier refused to accept this argument. 'They are dreadful creatures who hate us. They've said they won't be happy until they see all Frenchmen on their knees.'

'It's abominable,' said the Viscountess, sincerely indignant.

After all, the policy of collaboration had only been in existence for a few months, while hatred of the Germans was nearly a century old. Madame de Montmort instinctively reverted to speaking as she had in the past.

'Our poor country . . . laid bare, oppressed, ruined . . . And so many tragedies! Just look at the blacksmith's family: three sons, one killed, one a prisoner, the third missing at Mers-el-Kébir . . . And the Bérards from La Montagne,' she said, adding the family's name to that of the farm where they lived, as was the custom in that part of the world, 'since her husband was taken prisoner, the poor woman has gone mad from exhaustion and all her problems. The only people left to keep the farm going are her grandfather and a little thirteen-year-old girl. And as for the Cléments . . . the mother has died from overwork; her four children have been taken in by neighbours. Countless tragedies . . . poor France!'

Madame Angellier, her pale lips tightly closed, nodded her head in agreement and continued knitting. However, she and the Viscountess soon stopped talking about other people's disasters in order to discuss their own problems. There was a marked difference in the lively, passionate manner in which they now spoke, compared with the slow, exaggerated, polite way they had recalled their neighbours' misfortunes: it was the way a bored schoolboy would recite the death of Hippolytus seriously and respectfully, since it meant nothing at all to him, yet make his voice miraculously persuasive and impassioned when he stopped to complain to the teacher that someone had stolen his marbles.

'It's shameful, shameful,' said Madame Angellier. 'I pay twenty-seven francs for a pound of butter. Everything is sold through the black market. The townspeople have to get by, of course, but still . . .'

'Oh, don't remind me! I wonder how much food costs in Paris . . . It's fine for anyone with money, but', the Viscountess virtuously pointed out, 'there are so many poor people, after all,' and she enjoyed feeling she was a good person, demonstrating she hadn't forgotten the destitute; her pleasure was increased by knowing that thanks to her enormous fortune, she herself would never be in a position to be pitied. 'People don't think about the poor enough,' she said.

But all this was mere banter; it was time to come to the real point of her visit: she needed to get some grain for her chickens. Her poultry were famous in the region. In 1941 all wheat was requisitioned; it was, in theory, forbidden to give any to chickens. But 'forbidden' didn't necessarily mean 'impossible to get around', just 'difficult to do'; it was simply a question of discretion, opportunity and money. The Viscountess had written a little article for the local newspaper, a right-thinking publication to which the local priest was a contributor. The article was called 'Anything for the Maréchal!'. This is how it started: 'Let everyone remember! Let everyone continue to remind each other – gathered round your cottage hearths through the long evenings – any Frenchman worthy of the name will no longer give a single grain of wheat to his hens, not a single potato to his pigs; he will save his oats and rye, his barley and his rapeseed, and having gathered together all his riches, the fruits of his labour, watered with his own sweat, he will make a wreath of them, tie them up in a red, white and blue ribbon, a symbol of his patriotism, and lay them at the feet of the Venerable Elder who has restored our hope!' But of all the poultry yards where, according to the Viscountess, not a single grain of wheat should remain, her own was, naturally, the exception: it was her pride and joy, the object of her most attentive devotion; she raised rare breeds, prize-winners in the biggest agricultural competitions, both in France and abroad. The Viscountess's land was the very best in the region, but she wouldn't dream of going to her tenant farmers about such a sensitive transaction: it was unthinkable to give the working classes anything they could use against you; they would make you pay dearly for any such collusion. Madame Angellier, on the other hand . . . well, that was different. They could always come to some arrangement.

Madame Angellier sighed deeply. 'I could perhaps . . . one or two bags . . . And you, Madame, perhaps you could arrange through the Mayor to get us a bit of coal? In theory, we shouldn't, but . . .'

Lucile left them and walked over to the window. The shutters were still open. The sitting room looked out on to the square. There was a bench opposite the War Memorial, in shadow. Everything seemed to be asleep. It was a wonderful spring night; silvery stars filled the sky. In the fading light you could just make out the rooftops of the neighbouring houses: the blacksmith's, where an old man was mourning his three lost sons; the small home of the shoemaker who had been killed in the war, and whose poor wife and sixteen-year-old son did their best to carry on. If you listened closely, thought Lucile, you might hear each of these low, dark, quiet houses moaning. But . . . what was that sound? From out of the darkness came laughter, the rustling of skirts. Then a man's voice, a foreign voice asked, 'How you say that, in French? Kiss? Yes? Oh, it's nice . . .'

Further away, shadowy figures wandered past. You could just about make out a pale bodice, a ribbon in flowing hair, a shiny boot or belt buckle. The guard was still marching up and down in front of the *Lokal*, which it was forbidden to approach upon pain of death, but his comrades were enjoying their free time and the beautiful night. Two soldiers were singing amid a group of young women –

> Trink'mal noch ein Tröpfchen!
> Ach! Suzanna . . .

– and the young women softly hummed along.

During a moment of silence, Madame Angellier and the Viscountess heard the final notes of the song.

'Who could be singing at this hour?'

'They're women with German soldiers.'

'How revolting!' the Viscountess exclaimed. She made a gesture of horror and disgust. 'I'd really like to know who those shameless girls are. I'd make sure the priest knew their names.' She leaned forward and eagerly peered out into the night.

'I can't make them out. They wouldn't dare in broad daylight. Oh, ladies, this is worse than everything! Now they're corrupting Frenchwomen! Just think of it, their brothers and husbands are prisoners and they're out having a good time with the Germans! What's come over these women?' the Viscountess cried, indignant for many reasons: wounded patriotism, a sense of propriety, doubts about her influence in society (she gave lectures every Saturday night on 'How to be a true Christian woman'; she had founded a local library and she sometimes even invited the local young people to her home to watch informative, edifying films such as *A Day at Solesmes Abbey*, or *From Caterpillar to Butterfly*. And for what? So that everyone would have a horrible, debased idea of Frenchwomen?). Finally, she was angry because she had a passionate nature that was troubled by certain stirring images. Yet she knew there was no hope of the Viscount satisfying her, since he had little interest in women in general and her in particular.

'It's scandalous!' she exclaimed.

'It's sad,' said Lucile, thinking of all the girls whose youth was passing them by in vain: the men were gone, prisoners or dead. The enemy took their place. It was deplorable, but no one would even know in the future. It would be one of those things posterity would never find out, or would refuse to see out of a sense of shame.

Madame Angellier rang for the cook, who came in and closed the shutters. Everything withdrew back into the night: the songs, the murmur of kisses, the soft brightness of the stars, the footsteps of the conqueror on the pavement and the sigh of the thirsty frog praying to the heavens for rain, in vain.

10

The German and Lucile ran into each other once or twice in the dimly lit entrance hall. When she took her garden hat down from its peg on one of the antlers, she knocked against a decorative copper plate on the wall and made it jingle. The German seemed to listen for this faint sound in the silent house. He would go to the door to help Lucile, offering to carry her basket, her secateurs, her book, her embroidery, her deckchair into the garden. But she no longer spoke to him. Instead, she thanked him with a nod of the head and a forced smile; she thought she could sense Madame Angellier lying in wait behind the shutters to spy on her. The German understood and kept to himself. He went out with his regiment on manoeuvres almost every night; he never returned until four o'clock in the afternoon and then shut himself in his room with his dog. While walking through the village in the evening, Lucile sometimes saw him sitting alone in a café, reading a book, with a glass of beer in front of him. He avoided acknowledging her and would turn away, frowning. She was counting the days. 'He'll be leaving on Monday,' she said to herself. 'By the time he gets back, his regiment may have already left. Anyway, he's understood I won't speak to him any more.'

Every morning she asked the cook, 'Is the German still here, Marthe?'

'Well, yes,' the cook would say. 'He doesn't seem so bad: he asked if Madame would like to have some fruit. He'd be happy to give us some. Good grief, they want for nothing, them! They've got crates of oranges. So refreshing . . .' she added, torn between a feeling of kindness towards the officer who offered her fruit and who always behaved, as she put it, 'very nice, very kind; he doesn't scare you', and another feeling, a surge of anger when she thought of all the French people who couldn't get any fruit at all.

This last thought was undoubtedly the stronger. 'Still, they're a rotten lot, they are!' she finally said in disgust. 'I take whatever I can get from that officer, I do: his bread, his sugar, the cakes he gets from home (made with the best flour, I can tell you, Madame), and his tobacco that I send to my prisoner of war.'

'Oh, you shouldn't, Marthe!'

But the old cook just shrugged her shoulders. 'Since they take everything from us, it's the least . . .'

One evening, just as Lucile was leaving the dining room, Marthe opened the kitchen door and called out, 'Could you please come in here, Madame? There's someone who wants to see you.'

Lucile went in, afraid of being seen by Madame Angellier who didn't like anyone to go into the kitchen or the larder. Not that she seriously believed Lucile would steal the jam, despite ostentatiously inspecting the cupboards in front of her, but rather because she felt the same sense of intrusion an artist feels when interrupted in his studio, or a socialite in front of her dressing table: the kitchen was a sacred domain that belonged to her and her alone. Marthe had been with her for twenty-seven years. And for twenty-seven years, Madame Angellier had gone to great lengths to make sure Marthe never forgot she wasn't in her own home, and that at any moment she could be forced to leave her feather dusters, her pots and pans, her stove, just as the devout must remember that, according to the rituals of the Christian religion, worldly possessions are granted only temporarily and can be taken away overnight on a whim of the Creator.

Marthe closed the door behind Lucile and said reassuringly, 'Madame is at church.'

The enormous kitchen was as big as a ballroom, with two large windows that opened out on to the garden. A man was sitting at the table. Lucile saw that a magnificent pike, its silvery body trembling in its final death throes, had been thrown on to the oilcloth, between a large loaf of bread and a half-empty bottle of wine. The man raised his head; Lucile recognised Benoît Sabarie.

'Where did you get that, Benoît?'

'In Monsieur de Montmort's lake.'

'You'll get caught one of these days.'

The man didn't reply. He lifted up the enormous fish by the gills; it flicked its transparent tail, now barely breathing.

'Is it for us?' asked Marthe, who was related to the Sabaries.

'If you want.'

'Give it to me, Benoît. Do you know, Madame, that they're cutting back the meat rations again? It'll be death and the end of the world,' she added, shrugging her shoulders while hanging a large ham from the joists. 'Benoît, since Madame isn't home, tell Madame Gaston why you've come.'

'Madame,' said Benoît with difficulty, 'there's a German at our place who's chasing after my wife. The Commandant's interpreter, a nineteen-year-old kid. I can't take it any more.'

'But how can I help?'

'One of his friends is living here . . .'

'I never speak to him.'

'Don't give me that,' said Benoît, looking up.

He went over to the stove and absent-mindedly bent the poker, then straightened it again; he was extraordinarily strong.

'You were talking to him in the garden the other day, laughing with him and eating strawberries. I'm not criticising you, it's your business, but I'm begging you. Get him to talk to his friend so he sees reason and gets himself somewhere else to live.'

'This village!' Lucile thought. 'People can see through walls!'

At that very moment a storm broke. It had been brewing for several hours. There was a single, solemn thunderbolt, followed by the sound of cold rain falling in sheets. The sky darkened; all the lights went out, just as they usually did when the wind was up.

'I guess Madame will be stuck at the church now,' Marthe said smugly.

She took advantage of the fact to bring Benoît a bowl of hot coffee. Lightning flashed through the kitchen; the water streaming down the window-panes looked green in the sulphurous light. The door opened and the German officer, forced out of his room by the storm, came in to ask for a few candles.

'Is that you, Madame?' he added, recognising Lucile. 'Excuse me, I couldn't see you in the dark.'

'There aren't any candles,' Marthe said sourly. 'There are no candles in all of France since your lot got here.'

She didn't like the officer being in her kitchen. She could put up with his presence in other rooms, but here, between the stove and the pantry, it seemed scandalous and almost sacrilegious: he was violating the very heart of the house.

'At least give me a match,' the officer implored, deliberately trying to look plaintive to soften up the cook, but she just shook her head.

'There aren't any matches either.'

Lucile began to laugh. 'Don't listen to her. The matches are on the stove, behind you. And actually, there's someone here who wants to speak to you, Monsieur; he has a complaint about a German soldier.'

'Oh, really? I'm listening,' the officer said eagerly. 'We insist that the soldiers of the Reichswehr behave with perfect correctness towards the local people.'

Benoît said nothing.

It was Marthe who spoke. 'He's chasing after his wife,' she said in a tone of voice that made it difficult to tell exactly what she was feeling: virtuous indignation, or regret she was no longer young enough to be prey to such outrages.

'Ah, but you overestimate the power we German officers have, my boy. Of course I can punish him if he bothers your wife, but if she likes him . . .'

'It isn't no joke!' Benoît growled, taking a step towards the officer.

'Excuse me?'

'It isn't no joke, I'm telling you. We didn't need you dirty . . .'

Lucile let out a cry of anguish and warning. Marthe jabbed Benoît with her elbow; she guessed he was going to say the forbidden word 'Boche', punishable by imprisonment. Benoît forced himself to stop.

'We don't need you running after our women now.'

'Well, you should have thought about defending your women before, my friend,' the officer said quietly. His face had turned bright red; he looked haughty and upset.

Lucile intervened. 'Please,' she said softly, 'this man is jealous. He's suffering. Don't push him over the edge.'

'What's the name of this man?'

'Bonnet.'

'The Commandant's interpreter? I have no control over him. He has the same rank as me. It would be impossible for me to intervene.'

'Even as a friend?'

The officer shrugged his shoulders. 'Impossible. Let me explain.'

'No point explaining!' Benoît cut in, his voice calm and bitter. 'There are always rules for the poor bloke who's a private. *Verboten*, as you say in your language. But no one bothers the officers if they want to have a good time! It's the same in all the armies in the world.'

'I certainly won't speak to him,' replied the German, 'because that would be letting him in on the game and I wouldn't be doing you any favours,' and turning his back on Benoît, he walked over to the table.

'Make me some coffee, my dear Marthe, I'm leaving in an hour.'

'Manoeuvres again? That's three nights in a row,' exclaimed Marthe, who couldn't seem to manage to keep her feelings towards the enemy straight. Sometimes, when the regiment came back in the early hours of the morning, she would say with great satisfaction, 'Look how hot and tired they are . . . Oh, that makes me feel good!' But sometimes she'd forget they were German and would feel a sort of maternal pity rising up in her: 'Still, those poor boys, what a life . . .'

For some reason, this evening saw a surge of feminine tenderness. 'All right, I'll make you some coffee. Sit down over there. You'll have some as well, won't you, Madame?'

'No . . .' Lucile started to say.

Meanwhile, Benoît had disappeared; he'd climbed out of the window without making a sound.

'Please say yes,' murmured the German softly. 'I won't be bothering you much longer: I'm leaving the day after tomorrow and there's talk of sending my regiment to Africa when I get back. We'll never see each other again and I would like to think you don't hate me.'

'I don't hate you, but . . .'

'I know. Let's leave it at that. Just agree to keep me company . . .'

Marthe laid the table with the tender, complicit, scandalised smile of someone secretly giving bread and jam to naughty children who should be punished. On a clean cloth, she placed two large earthenware bowls decorated with flowers, a piping-hot pot of coffee and an old oil lamp she'd taken out of the cupboard, filled and lit. Its soft yellow flame lit up the copperware on the walls.

The officer looked at it with curiosity. 'What do you call that, Madame?'

'That's a warming pan.'

'And that?'

'A waffle iron. It's nearly a hundred years old. We don't use it any more.'

Marthe came in with some jam in an engraved glass dish and an enormous sugar bowl; with its bronze feet and carved lid, it looked like a funeral urn.

'Well, at this time the day after tomorrow', said Lucile, 'you'll be having a cup of coffee with your wife, won't you?'

'I hope so. I'll tell her about you. I'll describe the house to her.'

'Has she ever been to France?'

'No, Madame.'

Lucile was curious to know whether the enemy liked France, but a kind of modest pride prevented her from asking. They continued drinking their coffee in silence, not looking at each other.

Then the German told her about his country: the wide avenues in Berlin, what it was like in winter, the snow, the biting cold air that blew in from central Europe, the deep lakes, the pine forests and sand quarries.

Marthe was longing to join the conversation. 'Is it going to last long, the war?' she asked.

'I don't know,' the officer said, smiling and with a slight shrug of the shoulders.

'But what do you think?' Lucile then asked.

'Madame, I am a soldier. Soldiers don't think. I'm told to go somewhere and I go. Told to fight, I fight. Told to get myself killed, I die. Thinking would make fighting more difficult and death more terrible.'

'But what about enthusiasm . . .'

'Madame, forgive me, but that's a term a woman would use. A man does his duty even without enthusiasm. Perhaps that's the way you know he's a man, a real man.'

'Perhaps.'

They could hear the rain rustling in the garden, the last droplets slowly dripping off the lilacs; the fish pond murmuring languidly as it filled with water. The front door opened.

'It's Madame, hurry!' whispered Marthe, terrified. And she pushed Lucile and the officer outside. 'Go through the garden! Good Lord, she'll give me hell!'

She quickly poured the remaining coffee down the sink, hid the cups and put out the lamp. 'Do you hear me? Hurry up! Thank goodness it's dark out.'

They both went outside. The officer was laughing. Lucile was trembling a little. Hidden in the shadows, they watched Madame Angellier walk through the house behind Marthe, who carried a lamp. Then all the shutters were closed and the doors locked with iron bars.

'It's like a prison,' the German remarked on hearing the creaking of the hinges, the rusty chains and the mournful sound of the great doors being bolted. 'How will you get back in, Madame?'

'Through the side door in the kitchen. Marthe will leave it open. What about you?'

'Oh, I'll jump over the wall.'

He made it over in one nimble leap and said softly, '*Gute Nacht. Schlafen sie wohl.*'

'*Gute Nacht,*' she replied.

Her accent made the officer laugh. She stood in the shadows for a moment, listening to his laughter fade into the distance. The damp lilacs swayed in the soft wind and brushed against her hair. Feeling light-hearted and happy, she ran back into the house.

11

Every month, Madame Angellier visited her farms. She chose a Sunday so 'her people' would be at home, which exasperated the farmers. The moment they saw her, they rushed to hide away the coffee, sugar and eau-de-vie they'd been enjoying after lunch: Madame Angellier was of the old school – she considered the food her tenant farmers ate was somehow stolen from her; she complained bitterly about anyone who bought the best-quality meat from the butcher. She had her police, as she called them, all over town, and wouldn't keep tenants whose daughters bought silk stockings, perfume, make-up or books too often. Madame de Montmort ruled her estate with similar principles, but as an aristocrat she was more attached to spiritual values than the bitter, materialistic middle classes (to whom Madame Angellier belonged). She therefore concerned herself with religious issues: she tried to find out whether all the children had been baptised, whether they took Communion twice a year, whether the women went to Mass (she let the men get away with it; it was just too difficult). Of the two families who owned all the land in the region – the Montmorts and the Angelliers – the Montmorts were the most hated.

Madame Angellier set off at first light. The weather had changed after the storm the evening before: sheets of cold rain were falling. The car was unusable, for they had no petrol or travel permit, but Madame Angellier had unearthed an old gig from the shed where it had sat for thirty years; with two strong horses in harness, it could travel fairly good distances. The entire household had got up to say goodbye to the elderly lady. At the last minute (and grudgingly) she entrusted Lucile with the keys. She opened her umbrella; it started raining even harder.

'Madame should wait until tomorrow,' said the cook.

'I have no choice but to take care of things myself, given that the head of the house is a prisoner of these gentlemen,' Madame Angellier replied in loud, sarcastic tones, undoubtedly to make the two German soldiers passing by feel guilty.

She glared at them the way Chateaubriand described his father's expression: 'a burning eye seemed to shoot out and hit home like a bullet'.

But the soldiers, who didn't understand a word of French, evidently interpreted her look as a tribute to their strong physiques, their confident bearing, their perfect uniforms, for they smiled with shy good grace. Disgusted, Madame Angellier closed her eyes. The carriage left. A gust of wind rattled the doors.

A little later that morning Lucile went to see the dressmaker, a young woman who, people whispered, socialised with the Germans. She took with her a length of light material that she wished to have made into a dressing gown.

The dressmaker nodded her head: 'You're lucky to have some silk like this now. We don't have anything left.'

She said this without apparent envy, but thoughtfully, as if she recognised that the middle classes had not so much the right to come first, but a kind of natural shrewdness which meant they could get things before anyone else, just as people who live on the plains say of mountain dwellers, 'No chance he'll loose his footing, not him! He's been climbing the Alps since he was a child.' Evidently she also believed that Lucile, because of her parentage, because of some innate gift, was more skilful than she was at evading the law, bending the rules, for she smiled at her and winked. 'I can see you know how to get by,' she said. 'Well done.'

At that moment Lucile noticed a German soldier's belt on the bed. The two women looked at each other. The dressmaker's expression was sly, cautious and implacable; she looked like a cat who's afraid someone is about to take her prey from her claws and so raises her head and miaows arrogantly, as if to say, 'No? Well, really! Just whose is it, then?'

'How can you?' murmured Lucile.

The dressmaker wavered between several attitudes. Her expression was a mixture of insolence, confusion and deceit. Then suddenly she lowered her head. 'So what? German or French, friend or enemy, he's first and foremost a man and I'm a woman. He's good to me, kind, attentive . . . He's a city boy who takes care of himself, not like the boys around here; he has beautiful skin, white teeth. When he kisses, his breath smells fresh, not of alcohol. And that's good enough for me. I'm not looking for anything else. Our lives are complicated enough with all these wars and bombings. Between a man and a woman, none of that's important. I couldn't care less if the man I fancy is English or black – I'd still offer myself to him if I got the opportunity. Do I disgust you? Sure, it's all right for you, you're rich, you have luxuries I don't have . . .'

'Luxuries!' Lucile cut in, sounding bitter without meaning to, wondering what the dressmaker could imagine might be luxurious about an existence as an Angellier: visiting her estate and investing money, no doubt.

'You're educated. You see people. For us, it's nothing but slaving away at work. If it wasn't for love, we might as well just throw ourselves in the river. And when I say love, don't think it's only about you know what. Listen, the other day this German, he was at Moulins and he bought me a little imitation crocodile handbag; another time he brought me flowers, a bouquet from town, like I was a lady. It's stupid, I know, because there are flowers all over the countryside, but he cared, it made me happy. Up until now, to me men were just good for a tumble. But this one, I don't know why, I'd do anything for him, follow him anywhere. And he loves me, he does . . . Oh, I've known enough men to tell when there's one who's not lying. So, you see, when people say to me "He's German, a German, a German", I couldn't care less. They're human like us.'

'Yes, but my poor girl, when people say "a German", of course they know he's just a man, but what they mean to say, what is so terrible, is that he's killed Frenchmen, that they're holding our relatives prisoner, that they're starving us . . .'

'You think I never think about that? Sometimes, when I'm lying in bed next to him, I wonder, "Maybe it was his father who killed mine" (my dad was killed in the last war, you know . . .). I think about it for a while and then, in the end, I don't give a damn. On one side there's me and him; on the other side there's everyone else. People don't care about us: they bomb us and make us suffer, and kill us worse than if we were rabbits. And as for us, well, we don't care about them. You see, if we did what other people thought we should do we'd be worse than animals. Around town they call me a dog. Well, I'm not. Dogs travel in packs and bite people when they're told to. Me and Willy . . .'

She stopped and sighed.

'I love him,' she said finally.

'But his regiment will be leaving.'

'I know that, but Willy said he'd send for me after the war.'

'And you believe him?'

'Yes, I believe him,' she said defiantly.

'You're mad,' said Lucile. 'He'll forget you the moment he's gone. You have brothers who are prisoners. When they come home . . . Believe me, be careful. What you're doing is very dangerous. Dangerous and wrong,' she added.

'When they come home . . .'

They looked at each other in silence. There was a rich, secret scent in this stuffy room, cluttered with heavy rustic furniture, that troubled Lucile and made her feel strangely uneasy.

As she was leaving, Lucile ran into some children with dirty faces on the staircase; they were running down the steps four at a time.

'Where are you rushing like that?' Lucile asked.

'We're going to play in the Perrins' garden.'

The Perrins were a rich local family who had fled in June 1940. They had been so panic-stricken when they fled that they'd left their house unlocked, all the doors wide open, silver in the drawers, dresses in the wardrobes. The Germans had pillaged it: even the large abandoned garden had been sacked, trampled, and looked like a jungle.

'Do the Germans let you in there?'

They didn't reply and ran off, laughing.

Lucile went home in the rain. She could see the Perrins' garden. Despite the freezing rain, the village children darted back and forth between the trees in their blue and pink smocks. Every so often she glimpsed a shiny, dirty cheek gleaming in the rain like a peach. The children picked lilacs and cherry blossom and chased each other across the lawns. Perched high on top of a cedar tree, one little boy in red trousers whistled like a blackbird.

They were managing to destroy what remained of a garden that had been so well-tended in the past, so loved – a garden where the Perrins no longer came together as a family at dusk to sit in cast-iron chairs (the men in black jackets, the women in long rustling dresses) and watch the melons and strawberries ripen. A small boy in a pink smock was walking along the iron gate, holding on to the spikes to keep his balance.

'You'll fall, you little devil,' said Lucile.

He stared at her without replying. Suddenly, she envied these children who could enjoy themselves without worrying about the time, the war, misfortune. It seemed to her that among a race of slaves, they alone were free, 'truly free', she thought to herself.

Reluctantly, she walked back to the silent, morose house, whipped by the rain.

12

Lucile was surprised to see the postman coming from her house: she didn't receive many letters. On the hall table lay a card addressed to her.

> 12 rue de la Source, Paris (XVI)
>
> Madame,
> Do you remember the old couple you took in last June?
> We have thought of you often since then, Madame, and
> your kind welcome when we stopped at your home during
> that terrible journey. We would be so pleased to hear your
> news. Did your husband come home from the war safe and
> sound? As for us, we had the great joy of being reunited
> with our son.
> We send you our best wishes,
> Jeanne and Maurice Michaud

Lucile was glad for them. Such nice people . . . They were happier than she was . . . They loved each other. They had faced such danger together, and come through it together . . .

She hid the card in her desk and went into the dining room. It was a nice day, in spite of the persistent rain. There was only one place set at the table and she felt happy again that Madame Angellier wasn't home: she could read while eating. She ate lunch very quickly, then went over to the window and watched the rain falling. It was the back end of the storm, as the cook put it. The weather had changed over the last forty-eight hours, transforming a radiant spring into a cruel, vague sort of season, where the last snow merged with the first flowers. The apple trees had lost all their blossom overnight; the rose bushes were dark and frozen; the wind had smashed flowerpots full of geraniums and sweet peas.

'Everything will be ruined! There'll be no fruit,' Marthe groaned as she cleared the table. 'I'll make a fire in here,' she added. 'It's so cold it's unbearable. The German asked me to make a fire in his room, but the chimney hasn't been swept and he'll just be breathing in smoke. Too bad for him. I told him, but he didn't want to listen. He thinks it's because I don't want to do it. As if we wouldn't give them a couple of logs after everything else they've taken from us . . . Listen, he's coughing! Good Lord! What a pain to have to wait on these Boches. All right, I'm coming, I'm coming!' she said in annoyance.

Lucile heard her open the door and reply to the irritated German, 'Well, I tried to tell you! With this wind blowing, a chimney that hasn't been swept just pushes the smoke back inside.'

'Well why hasn't it been swept, *mein Gott*?' shouted the frustrated German.

'Why? Why? I don't know anything about it. I'm not the owner. You think with your war going on we can do what we like?'

'My good woman, if you really think I'm going to let myself be smoked out like a rabbit, you're very mistaken! Where are the ladies? If they can't provide a habitable bedroom, then they can let me move into the sitting room. Make a fire in there.'

'I'm sorry, Monsieur. That's not possible,' said Lucile, walking towards him. 'In our provincial houses the sitting room is a formal room where no one sleeps. The fireplace isn't real, as you can see.'

'What? That white marble monument with the carved cupids warming their hands?'

'Has never had a fire in it,' Lucile continued, smiling. 'But do come into the dining room, if you'd like; the stove is lit. It's true that your room is in a sad state,' she added, looking at the waves of smoke pouring out of it.

'Oh, Madame, I nearly choked to death . . . Being a military man is clearly fraught with danger! But I wouldn't want to impose on you for anything in the world. There are some dusty cafés in the village where they play billiards amid clouds of chalk . . . And your mother-in-law . . .'

'She's away for the day.'

'Ah! Very well then, thank you, Madame. I won't disturb you. I have important work to finish,' he said, holding up some maps.

He sat down at the table and Lucile sat in an armchair by the fire; she stretched her hands out towards the warmth, occasionally rubbing them together absent-mindedly. 'I have the mannerisms of an old woman,' she thought sadly, 'the mannerisms and the life of an old woman.'

She let her hands settle back on to her lap. When she looked up, she saw that the officer had abandoned his maps and pushed back the curtain to look at the grey sky and the crucified pear trees.

'What a sad place,' he murmured.

'Why should that matter to you?' Lucile replied. 'You're leaving tomorrow.'

'No,' he said, 'I'm not leaving.'

'Oh! But I thought . . .'

'All leave has been cancelled.'

'Really? But why?'

He shrugged his shoulders slightly. 'No one knows. Cancelled, that's all. That's life in the army.'

She felt sorry for him: he'd been looking forward to his leave so much.

'That's very annoying,' she said compassionately, 'but it's just been postponed . . .'

'For three months, six months, for ever . . . I'm most upset for my mother. She's elderly and frail. A little old lady with white hair and a straw hat; a gust of wind could knock her over . . . She's expecting me tomorrow night and all she'll get is a telegram.'

'Are you an only child?'

'I had three brothers. One was killed in Poland, another died when we invaded France a year ago. The third one is in Africa.'

'That's very sad, for your wife as well . . .'

'Oh, my wife . . . My wife will soon get over it. We got married very young; we were practically children. What's your opinion of people getting married after a two-week acquaintance on a trip round the lakes?'

'I have no idea! That doesn't happen in France.'

'But it isn't exactly like it used to be any more, is it? When you were received twice by friends of the family and the next minute you were married, as your Balzac describes?'

'Not exactly, but it's not all that different, at least in the provinces . . .'

'My mother told me not to marry Edith. But I was in love. *Ach, Liebe* . . . You must be able to grow up together, grow old together . . . But when you're separated, when there's war, when there's suffering, and you find yourself tied to a child who is still eighteen, while you' – he raised his arms, let them drop again – 'sometimes feel twelve and sometimes a hundred . . .'

'Surely you're exaggerating . . .'

'But I'm not. A soldier remains a child in certain ways and in other ways he's so old . . . He has no age. He is as old as the most ancient events on earth: Cain murdering Abel, cannibal rituals, the Stone Age . . . Let's not talk about it any more. Here I am, locked up in this tomb-like place . . . no . . . A tomb in a country cemetery, rich with flowers, birds and lovely shade, but a tomb nevertheless . . . How can you bear to live here all year long?'

'Before the war, we used to go out sometimes . . .'

'But I bet you never travelled, did you? You've never been to Italy or central Europe . . . only rarely to Paris . . . Think of everything we're missing . . . museums, theatres, concerts . . . Oh! It's really the concerts I miss most. And all I have here is a miserable instrument I dare not play because I'm afraid of offending your justifiable feelings as French people,' he said resentfully.

'But you can play as much as you like, Monsieur. Look, you're feeling sad and I'm not very happy either. Sit down at the piano and play something. We'll forget about the bad weather, separations, all our problems . . .'

'Really, you'd really like that? But I have work to do,' he said, looking at his maps. 'Oh, well . . . You bring some embroidery or a book and sit next to me. You must listen to me play. I only play well if I have an audience. I'm truly . . . how do you say it in French? A "show-off", that's it!'

'Yes. A show-off. I compliment you on your knowledge of French.'

He sat down at the piano. The stove purred softly, its heat filling the room with the sweet smell of smoke and roasted chestnuts. Great drops of rain streamed down the windows, like tears; the house was empty and silent; the cook was at Vespers.

She watched his slim white hands run across the keyboard. The wedding ring with the dark-red stone he wore made it difficult for him to play; he took it off and absent-mindedly handed it to Lucile. She held it for a moment; it was still warm from his hand. She turned it so it caught the pale-grey light filtering through the window. She could make out two

Gothic letters and a date. She thought it was a love token. But no . . .
the date was 1775 or 1795, she couldn't tell which. It was obviously a
family heirloom. Gently she put it down on the table. He must play the
piano like this every evening, she thought, with his wife at his side . . .
What was her name? Edith? How well he played! She recognised certain
pieces.

'Isn't that Bach? Mozart?' she asked shyly.

'Do you know music?'

'No, no! I don't know anything really. I used to play a little before I
got married, but I've forgotten everything. I do love music, you're very
talented, Monsieur.'

He looked at her and said seriously, 'Yes, I think I *am* talented,' with
a sadness that surprised her.

Then he played a series of light-hearted, humorous arpeggios.

'Listen to this now,' he said.

He started playing and speaking softly: 'This is the sound of peace,
this is the laughter of young women, the joyful sound of spring, the
first swallows coming back from the south . . . This is a German village,
in March, when the snow first starts to melt. Here's the sound of the
stream the snow makes as it flows through the ancient streets. And now
there is no more peace . . . Drums, trucks, soldiers marching . . . can
you hear them? Can you? Their slow, faint, relentless footsteps . . .
An entire population on the move . . . The soldiers are lost among
them . . . Now there should be a choir, a kind of religious chant, unfinished. Now, listen! It's the battle . . .' The music was solemn, intense,
terrifying.

'Oh! It's beautiful,' Lucile said softly. 'It's so beautiful!'

'The soldier is dying, and at that very moment he hears the choir again,
but now it's a divine chorus of soldiers . . . Like this, listen . . . it has to
be both sweet and deafening at once. Can you hear the heavenly trumpets? Can you hear the brass instruments resonating, bringing down the
walls? But now everything is fading away, softening, it stops, disappears
. . . The soldier is dead.'

'Did you compose that piece? Did you write it yourself?'

'Yes. I intended to be a musician. But that's all over now.'

'But why? The war . . .'

'Music is a demanding mistress. You can't abandon her for four years.

When you return to her, you find she's gone.' He saw Lucile staring at him. 'What are you thinking?' he asked.

'I'm thinking that people shouldn't be sacrificed like this. I mean none of us. Everything has been taken away. Love, family . . . It's just too much!'

'Ah! Madame, this is the principal problem of our times: what is more important, the individual or society? War is the collaborative act *par excellence*, is it not? We Germans believe in the communal spirit – the spirit one finds among bees, the spirit of the hive. It comes before everything: nectar, fragrance, love . . . But these are very serious thoughts. Listen! I'll play you a Scarlatti sonata. Do you know this one?'

'No, I don't think so, no . . .'

'The individual or society?' she thought. 'Well, Good Lord! Nothing new there, they hardly invented that idea. Our two million dead in the last war were also sacrificed to the "spirit of the hive". They died . . . and twenty-five years later . . . What trickery! What vanity! There are laws that regulate the fate of beehives and of people, that's all there is to it. The spirit of the people is undoubtedly also ruled by laws that elude us, or by whims we know nothing about. How sad the world is, so beautiful yet so absurd . . . But what is certain is that in five, ten or twenty years, this problem unique to our time, according to him, will no longer exist, it will be replaced by others . . . Yet this music, the sound of this rain on the windows, the great mournful creaking of the cedar tree in the garden outside, this moment, so tender, so strange in the middle of war, this will never change, not this. This is for ever . . .'

He suddenly stopped playing and looked at her. 'Are you crying?'

She quickly wiped the tears from her eyes.

'Please forgive me,' he said. 'Music brings out the emotions. Perhaps my music reminded you of someone . . . someone you miss?'

In spite of herself she murmured, 'No. No one . . . That's just it . . . no one . . .'

They fell silent. He closed the piano.

'After the war, Madame, I'll come back. Please say you'll let me come back. All the conflict between France and Germany will be finished . . . forgotten . . . for at least fifteen years. One evening I'll ring the doorbell. You'll open it and you won't recognise me in my civilian clothes. Then I'll say: but it's me . . . the German officer . . . do you remember? There's peace now, freedom, happiness. I'm taking you away from here. Come, let's go away together. I'll show you many different countries. I'll be a famous composer, of course, and you'll be as beautiful as you are at this very moment . . .'

'And your wife, and my husband, what will we do about them?' she said, forcing herself to laugh.

He whistled softly.

'Who knows where they'll be? Or us? But, Madame, I'm very serious. I'll be back.'

'Play something else,' Lucile said after a brief silence.

'No, enough. Too much music *ist gefährlich* . . . dangerous. Now, you must play the society lady. Invite me to have some tea.'

'There's no more tea in all of France, *mein Herr*. I can offer you some wine from Frontignan and some cakes. Would you like that?'

'Oh, yes! But please, don't call the servant. Let me help you set the table. Tell me where the tablecloths are. In this drawer? Allow me to choose one: you know we Germans are very bold. I'd like the pink one . . . no . . . the white one embroidered with little flowers. Did you embroider it?'

'But of course.'

'The rest I leave to you.'

'That's good,' she said, laughing. 'Where's your dog? I haven't seen him lately.'

'He's away on leave: he belongs to the whole regiment, to all the soldiers; one of them took him with them, Bonnet, the interpreter, the one your country friend was complaining about. They left for three days in Munich but the new orders mean they'll have to come back.'

'Speaking of Bonnet, did you talk to him?'

'Madame, my friend Bonnet is not a simple fellow. Until now, he's been having some innocent fun, but if the husband starts getting frustrated, he's capable of getting really involved. *Schadenfreude*, do you understand? He could even fall in love for real, and if the young woman isn't faithful . . .'

'There's no question of that,' said Lucile.

'She really loves that country bumpkin?'

'Without a doubt. And don't think that all the women around here are the same just because certain young girls let themselves get involved with your soldiers. Madeleine Sabarie is a good wife and a good Frenchwoman.'

'I understand,' said the officer, nodding his head.

He helped Lucile move the card table over to the window. She put out some antique crystal glasses cut with large facets, the wine carafe with the gilt silver stopper and some small painted dessert plates. They dated back to the First Empire and were decorated with military scenes: Napoleon inspecting the troops, Hussars in gold brocade setting up camp in a clearing, a parade along the Champ-de-Mars.

The German admired the strong, bright colours. 'What beautiful uniforms! How I'd love to own a jacket embroidered in gold like that Hussar!'

'Have some cakes, *mein Herr*. They're home-made.'

He looked at her and smiled.

'Madame, have you ever heard of those cyclones which rage in the South Seas? If I've understood what I've read, they form a sort of circle whose edges are made of wind and rain but whose centre is so still that a bird or even a butterfly caught in the eye of the storm wouldn't be harmed; their wings would remain unruffled, while all around them the most horrible damage was being unleashed. Look at this house! Look at us about to have our wine from Frontignan and our cakes, and think of what's going on in the rest of the world.'

'I prefer not to think about it,' Lucile replied sadly.

Nevertheless, in her soul she felt a kind of warmth she'd never felt before. Even her gestures were more delicate, more adept than usual, and she listened to her own voice as if it were a stranger's. It was lower than normal, this voice, deeper and more vibrant; she didn't recognise it. Most exquisite of all was this sense of being on an island in the middle of the hostile house, and this strange feeling of safety: no one would come in; there would be no letters, no visits, no telephone calls. Even the old clock she had forgotten to wind that morning (what *would* Madame Angellier say – 'Of course nothing gets done when I'm away'), even the old clock whose grave, melancholy tones frightened her, was silent. Once again, the storm had damaged the power station; no lights or radios were on for miles. The radio silent . . . how peaceful . . . It was impossible to give in to temptation, impossible to look for Paris, London, Berlin, Boston on the dark dial, impossible to hear those mournful, invisible, cursed voices telling of ships being sunk, planes crashing, cities destroyed, reading out the number of dead, predicting future massacres . . . Just blessed forgetfulness, nothing else . . . until nightfall, time passing slowly, someone beside her, a glass of light, fragrant wine, music, long silences. Happiness . . .

13

One month later, on a rainy afternoon like the one the German and Lucile had spent together, Marthe announced that the Angellier ladies had visitors. Three women were shown into the sitting room. They wore long black coats, mourning hats and black veils that cascaded down towards the ground, imprisoning them in a kind of impenetrable, mournful cage. The Angelliers didn't often have guests. The cook, flustered, had forgotten to take their umbrellas; they still held them, half-open, in their hands, like bell-shaped calyx flowers, catching the last few drops of rain dripping from their veils – or like the funeral urns on the tombs of heroes into which stone women weep.

Madame Angellier had some difficulty in recognising the three black shapes. Then she said, surprised, 'But it's the Perrin ladies!'

The Perrin family (proprietors of the beautiful estate pillaged by the Germans) was 'the region's finest'. Madame Angellier's feelings towards the bearers of this name were comparable to those one member of a royal family might feel towards another: calm certainty that one was among kindred spirits who held the same opinions about everything; that despite the fleeting differences which might naturally occur, despite wars or governmental misconduct, they remained united by an indissoluble bond, to such an extent that if the Spanish royal family were dethroned, the Swedish royal family would feel the repercussions. When the Perrins had lost 900,000 francs after a lawyer in Moulins had run off, the Angelliers felt the aftershock. When Madame Angellier had paid a pittance for a piece of land that had belonged to the Montmorts 'since time began', the Perrins had rejoiced. The grudging respect the Montmorts received from the middle classes bore no comparison to this sense of shared values.

Madame Angellier warmly asked Madame Perrin to sit down again (she'd started to get up when she saw her hostess coming towards her). She didn't experience the disagreeable feeling she always had when Madame de Montmort came to visit. She knew the Perrin ladies approved of everything: the mock fireplace, the musty smell, the half-closed shutters, the slip covers on the furniture, the olive-green wallpaper with silver palm leaves. Everything was as it should be; she would soon be offering her guests a pitcher of orangeade and some stale shortbread. Madame Perrin would not be shocked by the stinginess of this offering; she would simply see it as one more proof of the Angelliers' wealth, for the richer one is, the stingier as well; she would identify with her own tendency to save money and the inclination towards asceticism that lies at the heart of the French middle classes and makes their shameful secret pleasures even more bitter-sweet.

Madame Perrin told them that her son had died a hero's death in Normandy as the Germans advanced; she had received permission to visit his grave. She complained at great length about the cost of this journey and Madame Angellier sympathised with her. Maternal love and money were two completely different things. The Perrins lived in Lyon.

'The city is destitute. I've seen crows being sold for fifteen francs each. Mothers are feeding their children on crow soup. And don't think I'm talking about the working classes. No, Madame! I'm talking about people like you and me.'

Madame Angellier sighed sadly; she imagined her relatives, members of her family, sharing a crow for supper. The idea was somehow grotesque, scandalous (though if it had been just the working classes, all they would have done was say, 'Those poor creatures' and then move on).

'Well, at least you have your freedom! You don't have any Germans living with you like us. Yes, Madame, here in this house, behind that wall,' said Madame Angellier, pointing to the olive-green wallpaper with the silver palm leaves. 'An officer.'

'We know,' said Madame Perrin, slightly embarrassed. 'We heard about it from the notary's wife who came to Lyon. Actually, that's why we've come.'

They all involuntarily looked at Lucile.

'Please explain what you mean,' Madame Angellier said coldly.

'I've heard that this officer behaves absolutely correctly, is that right?'

'Yes.'

'And he's even been seen speaking to you extremely politely on several occasions?'

'He never speaks to *me*,' Madame Angellier said haughtily. 'I wouldn't stand for it. I accept that my attitude may not be very reasonable' (she stressed this last word) 'as has been pointed out to me, but I am the mother of a prisoner of war and because of that, even if I were offered all the money in the world, I wouldn't consider these gentlemen as anything but our mortal enemies. Although other people are more . . . how can I put it? . . . more flexible, more realistic, perhaps . . . my daughter-in-law in particular . . .'

'I answer him if he speaks to me, yes,' said Lucile.

'But you're so right, absolutely right!' exclaimed Madame Perrin. 'My dear girl, I'm putting all my hope in you. It's about our poor house! You've seen what a terrible state it's in . . .'

'I've only seen the garden . . . through the gates . . .'

'My dear child, do you think you could possibly arrange for us to have back certain items from inside the house to which we are particularly attached?'

'Madame, but I . . .'

'You mustn't refuse. All you have to do is speak to these gentlemen and intervene on our behalf. It might all have been burned or damaged, of course, but I can't believe the house has been so vandalised that it is impossible to recover our family portraits, correspondence or furniture, of sentimental value only to us . . .'

'Madame, you should speak to the Germans occupying your house yourself and . . .'

'Never,' said Madame Perrin, pulling herself up to her full height. 'Never will I cross the threshold of my house while the enemy is there. It is a question of dignity and sensitivity. They killed my son, my son who had just been accepted to study at the Ecole Polytechnique, in the top six. I'll be staying at the Hôtel des Voyageurs with my daughters until tomorrow. If you could arrange to have certain things returned to us, I would be eternally grateful. Here's the list. If I found myself face to face with one of these Germans, I wouldn't be able to stop myself singing the "Marseillaise" (I know myself!),' said Madame Perrin in an impassioned voice, 'and then I'd get deported to Prussia. Not that that would be a disgrace, far from it, but I have daughters. I must keep going for my family. So, I am truly begging you, my dear Lucile, to do whatever you can for me.'

'Here's the list,' said Madame Perrin's younger daughter.
She unfolded the paper and began reading:

A china bowl and water jug with our monogram, decorated with
  butterflies
A salad dryer
The white-and-gold tea service (twenty-eight pieces, the sugar bowl
  is missing its lid)
Two portraits of grandfather: (1) sitting on his nanny's lap; (2) on
  his deathbed.
The stag's antlers from the entrance hall, a memento of my Uncle
  Adolphe
Granny's plate warmer (porcelain and vermeil)
Papa's extra set of false teeth he'd left behind in the bathroom
The pink-and-black sofa from the sitting room
In the left-hand drawer of the desk (key herewith): My brother's
  first page of writing, Papa's letters to Mama while he was away
  taking the waters in Vittel in 1924 (tied with a pink ribbon), all
  our family photographs

There was a deathly silence as she read. Madame Perrin cried softly
beneath her veil.

'It's hard, so hard to watch things you care about so much being taken
away from you. I beg you, my dear Lucile, do everything you can. Be
clever, persuasive . . .'

Lucile looked at her mother-in-law.

'This . . . this officer', said Madame Angellier barely moving her lips,
'has not yet come back. You won't see him tonight, Lucile, it's too late,
but tomorrow you could speak with him and ask for his help.'

'All right. I will.'

Madame Perrin, her hands covered in black gloves, hugged Lucile.
'Thank you, thank you, my dear child. And now we must go.'

'Not before having some refreshments,' said Madame Angellier.

'Oh, but we don't want to impose on you . . .'

'Don't be ridiculous . . .'

They made quiet, courteous little noises when Marthe brought in the
pitcher of orangeade and the shortbread. Now that they felt reassured,

they began talking about the war. They feared a German victory, yet weren't altogether happy at the idea that the English might win. All in all, they preferred everyone to be defeated. They blamed their difficulties on the fact that the desire for pleasure seemed to have taken hold of everyone. Then the conversation returned to more personal matters. Madame Perrin and Madame Angellier discussed their poor health. Madame Perrin went into great detail about her last bout of rheumatism while Madame Angellier listened impatiently and, as soon as Madame Perrin paused for breath, interjected, 'It's the same with me . . .' and talked about her own bout of rheumatism.

Madame Perrin's daughters discreetly ate their shortbread. Outside, the rain kept falling.

14

By the next morning the rain had stopped and the sun shone down on the damp, joyous ground. It was early and Lucile, who hadn't slept well, was sitting on a garden bench waiting for the German to come out of the house. As soon as she saw him she went up to him and explained her request; both of them sensed the hidden presence of Madame Angellier and the cook, not to mention the neighbours, who were spying on the couple from behind closed shutters as they stood on the path.

'If you would accompany me to these ladies' house,' said the German, 'I will have all the things they've requested gathered together for you; but a number of our soldiers have been billeted in this house since the owners abandoned it and I think the damage has been considerable. Let's go and see.'

They walked through the village, side by side, barely speaking.

Lucile saw Madame Perrin's black veil fluttering from a window of the Hôtel des Voyageurs. They were watching Lucile and her companion with curiosity, complicity and a vague sense of approval. It was clear that everyone knew she was on her way to extract from the enemy the crumbs of his conquest (in the form of a set of false teeth, a china dinner service and other household items of sentimental value).

An old woman who couldn't even look at a German uniform without being terrified nevertheless came up to Lucile and whispered, 'That's it . . . Well done! At least *you*'re not afraid of them . . .'

The officer smiled. 'They think you're Judith going to murder Holofernes in his tent. I hope you don't have the same evil plan! Here we are. Please come in, Madame.'

He pushed open the heavy gate. The little bell that used to tell the Perrins they had visitors tinkled sadly. In just one year the garden had become so neglected it would have broken your heart to look at it, had it not been such a beautiful day. But it was a May morning, the day after a storm. The grass was sparkling, the damp paths overgrown with daisies, cornflowers and all sorts of other wild flowers that gleamed in the sun. The flower beds were a riot of shrubs, and fresh clusters of lilacs gently brushed against Lucile's face as she walked by. In the house they found about a dozen young soldiers and all the children from the village who spent happy days playing in the entrance hall (like the Angelliers' hall, it was dark, with a vaguely musty smell, greenish panes of glass in the windows and hunting trophies on the walls). Lucile recognised the cart maker's two little girls, sitting on the lap of a blond soldier who had a wide grin on his face. The carpenter's little boy was playing horsy on the back of another soldier. The illegitimate children of the dressmaker, all four of them, aged two to six, were lying on the floor, plaiting crowns out of forget-me-nots and the small, sweet-smelling carnations that had once lined the formal borders.

The soldiers leapt to attention the way they do in the army: chin up, eyes straight ahead, the whole body so tense you could see the veins in their necks throbbing slightly.

'Would you be so kind as to give me your list,' the officer said to Lucile. 'We can look for the things together.'

He read it and smiled.

'Let's start with the sofa. It must be in the sitting room. Over here, I assume?'

He opened the door and went into a large room full of furniture – much of it knocked over or broken. The paintings had been removed and stacked against the walls; several had been kicked in. The floor was scattered with scraps of newspaper, bits of straw (vestiges, presumably, of the mass exodus in June 1940) and cigar stubs left by the invaders. On a pedestal stood a stuffed bulldog with a broken muzzle and a crown of dead flowers.

'What a terrible sight,' said Lucile, upset.

In spite of everything there was something comical about the room and especially about the sheepish expression on the faces of the soldiers and the officer.

Seeing the look of reproach on Lucile's face, the officer said sharply, 'My parents used to have a villa on the Rhine. Your soldiers occupied it during the last war. They smashed rare, priceless musical instruments that had been in the family for two hundred years and tore up books that once belonged to Goethe.'

Lucile couldn't help but smile; he was defending himself in the same crude and indignant way a little boy does when accused of some misdeed: 'But I wasn't the one who started it, it was the others . . .'

She felt a very feminine pleasure, an almost sensual, sweet sensation at seeing this childish look on a face that was, after all, the face of an implacable enemy, a hardened warrior. 'For we can't pretend', she thought, 'that we aren't all in his hands. We're defenceless. If we still have our lives and our possessions, it's only because of his goodwill.' She was almost afraid of the feelings growing within her. It was like stroking a wild animal – an exquisitely intense sensation, a mixture of tenderness and terror.

Wanting to hold on to the feeling a little longer, she frowned. 'You should be ashamed! These empty houses were under the protection of the German army, the honour of the German army!'

As he listened to her, he lightly tapped the back of his boots with his riding crop. He turned towards his soldiers and gave them a good dressing down. Lucile realised he was ordering them to get the house back in order, to fix what had been broken, to polish the floors and the furniture. His voice, when he spoke German, especially with that commanding tone, took on a sharp, resonant quality. Hearing it gave Lucile the same pleasure that a slightly rough kiss might – the kind of kiss that ends with a little bite. She slowly brought her hands to her burning face: 'Stop it!' she said to herself. 'Stop thinking about him, you're asking for trouble.'

She took a few steps towards the door. 'I'm going home. You have the list; you can ask your soldiers to find everything.'

In a flash he was by her side. 'Please don't go away angry, I beg of you. Everything will be repaired as well as possible, I give you my word. Listen! Let's let them look for everything; they can put it all in a wheel-barrow and, under supervision from you, take it straight over to the Perrin ladies. I'll go with you to apologise. I can't do more than that. In the meantime, come into the garden. We could go for a little walk and I'll pick some beautiful flowers for you.'

'No! I'm going home.'

'You can't,' he said, taking her by the arm, 'You promised the ladies you'd bring them their things. You have to stay and make sure your orders are carried out.'

They were outside now, standing on a path bordered with lilacs in full bloom. A multitude of honeybees, bumblebees and wasps were flying all around them, diving into the flowers, drinking their honey and settling on Lucile's arms and hair; she was frightened and laughed nervously.

'We can't stay here. Everywhere I go is dangerous!'

'Let's walk on a little further.'

They came across the village children at the back of the garden. Some of them were playing in the flower beds where everything had been pulled up and trampled; others had climbed the pear trees and were breaking off the branches.

'Little beasts,' said Lucile. 'There'll be no fruit this year.'

'Yes, but the flowers are so beautiful.'

He stretched out his arms and the children threw him some small branches with clusters of delicate petals.

'Take them, Madame, the petals will be wonderful in a bowl on the table.'

'I would never dare walk through the village carrying branches from a fruit tree,' Lucile protested, laughing. 'Just wait, you little devils! The policemen will catch you.'

'Not a chance,' said a little girl in a black smock.

She was eating a jam sandwich while wrapping her dirty little legs round a tree and climbing up.

'Not a chance. The Bo . . . the Germans won't let them in.'

The lawn hadn't been mowed for two summers and was dotted with buttercups. The officer spread out his large, pale, almost almond-green cape and sat down on the grass. The children had followed them. The little girl in the black smock was picking cowslips; she made big bouquets of the fresh yellow flowers and stuck her nose deep inside them, but her dark eyes, both innocent and crafty, remained fixed on the grown-ups. She looked at Lucile curiously and somewhat critically: the look of one woman to another. 'She looks scared,' she thought. 'I wonder why she's scared. He's not mean, that officer. I know him; he gives me money, and once he got my balloon that was caught in the branches of the big cedar tree. He's really handsome. More handsome than Daddy and all the boys around here. The lady has a pretty dress.'

Surreptitiously she moved closer and touched one of the folds of the dress with her little dirty finger; it was simple, light, made of grey cotton and decorated only with a small collar and cuffs of pleated linen. She tugged on the dress rather hard and Lucile suddenly turned round. The little girl jumped back, but Lucile looked through her with wide, anxious eyes. The little girl could see that the lady had gone very pale and that her lips were trembling. For sure she was afraid of being alone here with the German. As if he would hurt her! He was talking to her so nicely. But then again, he was holding her hand so tightly that there was no way she could escape. All boys were the same, the little girl thought vaguely, whether they were big or small. They liked teasing girls and scaring them. She stretched out in the tall grass which was so high that it hid her from sight. It felt wonderful to be so tiny and invisible, with the grass tickling her neck, her legs, her eyelids . . .

The German and the lady were talking quietly. He had turned white as a sheet too. Now and again, she could hear him holding back his loud voice, as if he wanted to shout or cry but didn't dare. The little girl couldn't understand anything he said. She vaguely thought he might be talking about his wife and the lady's husband. She heard him say several times: 'If you were happy . . . I see how you live . . . I know that you're all alone, that your husband has abandoned you . . . I've asked people in the village.' Happy? Wasn't she happy, then, the lady who had such pretty dresses, a beautiful house? Anyway, the lady didn't want him to feel sorry for her, she wanted to leave. She told him to let go of her and to stop talking. My word, it wasn't she who was scared now, it was him, in spite of his big boots and proud look. He was the nervous one now. At that moment a ladybird landed on the little girl's hand. She watched it a while. She wanted to kill it, but she knew it was bad luck to kill one of God's creatures. So she just blew on it, very gently at first, to see it lift its delicate, transparent wings; then she blew with all her might, so that the little insect must have felt it was on a raft caught in a storm at sea. The ladybird flew off. 'It's on your arm, Madame,' the little girl shouted. Once again, the officer and the lady turned and looked at her but without really seeing her. Meanwhile, the officer made an impatient gesture with his hand, as if he were chasing away a fly. 'I'm staying right here,' the little girl said to herself defiantly. 'And first of all, what are they doing here? A man and a woman: they should be in the sitting room.' Mischievously, she strained to hear them. What were they talking about? 'I'll never forget you,' said the officer, his voice low and trembling. 'Never.'

A large cloud covered half the sky; all the fresh, bright colours in the garden turned grey. The lady was picking some little purple flowers and tearing them up.

'It's not possible,' she said, on the verge of tears.

'What's not possible?' the little girl wondered.

'Of course I've also thought about it . . . I admit it, I'm not talking about . . . love . . . but I would have liked to have a friend like you . . . I've never had any friends. I have no one. But it's not possible.'

'Because of other people?' said the officer scornfully.

She just looked at him proudly. 'Other people? If I myself felt innocent then . . . No! There can be nothing between us.'

'There are many things you will never be able to erase: the day we spent together when it rained, the piano, this morning, our walks in the woods . . .'

'Oh, but I shouldn't have . . .'

'But you did! It's too late . . . there's nothing you can do about it. All that was . . .'

The little girl rested her face on her folded arms and heard nothing more than a distant murmur, like the humming of a bumblebee. That big cloud bordered with burning rays of sunlight meant it would rain. What if it suddenly started raining, what would the lady and the officer do? Wouldn't it be funny to see them running in the rain, her with her straw hat and him with his beautiful green cape? But they could hide in the garden. If they followed her, she could show them a bower where no one would be able to see them. 'It's twelve o'clock now,' she thought when she heard the church bells ringing the Angelus. Are they going to go home for lunch? What do rich people eat? Fromage blanc like us? Bread? Potatoes? Sweets? What if I asked them for some sweets?' She went up to them and was going to tug at their hands to ask for some sweets – she was a bold little girl, this Rose – when she saw them suddenly jump up and stand there, shaking. Yes, the gentleman and the lady were shaking, just like when she was up in the cherry tree at school, her mouth stuffed full of cherries, and she heard the teacher shouting, 'Rose, you little thief, come down from there at once!' But they hadn't seen the teacher: it was a soldier standing to attention, who was talking very quickly in an incomprehensible language; the words coming out of his mouth sounded like water rushing over a bed of rocks.

The officer moved away from the lady, who looked pale and dishevelled. 'What is it?' she murmured. 'What is he saying?'

The officer seemed as upset as she was; he was listening without hearing. Finally, his pale face lit up with a smile.

'He says they've found everything . . . but the old gentleman's false teeth are broken because the children have been playing with them: they tried to cram them in the mouth of the stuffed bulldog.'

Both of them – the officer and the lady – gradually seemed to come out of their stupor and return to earth. They looked down at the little girl and saw her this time. The officer tugged at her ear. 'What have you little devils been up to?'

But his voice quivered and in the lady's laugh you could hear the echo of stifled sobs. She laughed like someone who had been very frightened and couldn't forget, while laughing, that she'd had a narrow escape. Little Rose was bothered and tried in vain to run off. She wanted to say, 'The false teeth . . . yes . . . well . . . we wanted to see if the bulldog would look vicious with some brand-new teeth . . .' But she was afraid the officer would get angry (seen close up, he seemed very big and scary) so she just whined, 'We didn't do anything, we didn't . . . we didn't even see any false teeth.'

Meanwhile, children were coming over from all directions. They were all talking at once with their young shrill voices.

'Stop! Stop! Be quiet!' the lady begged. 'Never mind. We're just happy to have found everything else.'

An hour later a gang of kids in dirty clothes came out of the Perrins' garden, followed by two German soldiers pushing a wheelbarrow containing a basket of china cups, a sofa with its four legs in the air (one was broken), a plush photograph album, a birdcage that the Germans mistook for the salad dryer and many other items. Bringing up the rear were Lucile and the officer. Curious women stared at them as they walked through the village. They didn't speak to each other, the women noticed; they didn't even look at each other and they were deathly pale – the officer's expression cold and impenetrable.

'She must have given him a piece of her mind,' the women whispered. 'Said it was shameful to get a house into that state. He's furious. Goodness gracious, they're not used to people standing up for themselves. She's right. We're not dogs! She's brave, that young Angellier lady, she's not afraid.' One of them, who was tending a goat (the little old woman with white hair and blue eyes who'd run into the Angellier ladies on their way back from Vespers that Easter Sunday and had said to them, 'These Germans, I've heard they're bad and evil'), even came up to Lucile and whispered to her as she passed, 'Good for you, Madame! Show them we're not afraid. Your prisoner of war would be proud of you,' she added and she began to cry, not that she had a prisoner herself to cry over – she was long past the age of having a husband or a son at war – she cried because prejudice outlives passion and because she was sentimentally patriotic.

15

Whenever the elder Madame Angellier and the German met each other, they both instinctively stepped back. On the officer's part this could have been interpreted as a sign of exaggerated courtesy, the desire not to impose his presence on the mistress of the house. He had almost the air of a thoroughbred horse leaping away from a snake it sees at its feet. Madame Angellier, on the other hand, didn't even bother to disguise the shudder that ran through her, leaving her looking stiff and terrified, as if she'd come into contact with some disgusting, dangerous animal. But the moment lasted for only an instant: a good education is precisely designed to correct the instincts of human nature. The officer would draw himself up, put on the rigid, serious expression of an automaton, then bow and click his heels together ('Oh, that Prussian salute!' Madame Angellier would groan, without thinking that this greeting was, in fact, exactly what she should have expected from a man born in eastern Germany, since it was unlikely to be an Arab kiss of the hand, or an English handshake). As for Madame Angellier, she would clasp her hands in front of her like a nun who has been sitting at someone's deathbed and gets up to greet a member of his family suspected of anticlericalism. During these encounters, various expressions would cross Madame Angellier's face: false respect ('You're in charge here!'), disapproval ('Everyone knows who you are, you heathen!), submission ('Let us offer up our hatred to the Lord') and finally a flash of fierce joy ('Just you wait, my friend, you'll be burning in hell while I'm finding peace in Jesus'), although this final thought was replaced in Madame Angellier's mind by the desire she felt every time she saw a member of the occupying forces: 'I hope he'll soon be at the bottom of the English Channel,' for everyone was expecting an attempt to invade England, if not imminently then very soon. Taking her desires for reality, Madame Angellier even came to believe the German looked like a drowned man: pallid, swollen, thrown about by the waves. It was this thought alone that allowed her to look human again, allowed the shadow of a smile to pass over her lips (like the final rays of a dying star) and allowed her to reply to the German when he asked after her health, 'Thank you for asking. I'm as well as can be expected,' mournfully stressing these final words to imply 'as well as I can be, given the disastrous situation France is in'.

Lucile walked behind Madame Angellier. She had become colder, more distracted, more rebellious than usual. She would nod silently as she walked away from the German. He too was silent. But, thinking no one could see, he would watch her for a long time as she walked away. Madame Angellier seemed to have eyes in the back of her head to catch him. Without even turning round she would mutter angrily to Lucile, 'Pay no attention to him. He's still there.' She could only breathe freely after the door had been shut behind them, then she would give her daughter-in-law a withering look and say, 'You've done something different to your hair today,' or 'You're wearing your new dress, aren't you?' concluding sarcastically, 'It's not very flattering.'

And yet, despite the waves of hatred she felt towards Lucile because she was there and her own son was not, in spite of everything she might have imagined or suspected, she never thought her daughter-in-law and the German could possibly care for each other. After all, people judge one another according to their own feelings. It is only the miser who sees others enticed by money, the lustful who see others obsessed by desire. To Madame Angellier, a German was not a man, he was the personification of cruelty, perversity and hatred. For anyone else to feel differently was preposterous, incredible. She couldn't imagine Lucile in love with a German any more than she could imagine a woman mating with some mythical creature, a unicorn, a dragon or the monster Sainte Marthe killed to free Tarascon. Nor did it seem possible that the German could be in love with Lucile. Madame Angellier refused to accord him any human feelings. She interpreted his long looks as a further attempt to insult this already defiled French home, as a way of feeling cruel pleasure at having the mother and wife of a prisoner of war at his mercy. What she called Lucile's 'insensitivity' irritated her more than anything else: 'She's trying out new hairstyles, wearing new dresses. Doesn't she realise the German will think she's doing it for him? How degrading!' She wanted to cover Lucile's face with a mask and dress her in a sack. It pained her to see

Lucile looking healthy and beautiful. She was suffering: 'And all this time, my son, my own son . . .'

It was, for Madame Angellier, a moment of intense pleasure when they ran into the German in the hall one day and saw he was very pale and wore his arm in a sling – quite ostentatiously, in Madame Angellier's opinion. She was outraged to hear Lucile quickly ask, without thinking, 'What happened to you, *mein Herr*?'

'I came off a horse. A difficult animal I was riding for the first time.'

'You don't look well,' said Lucile when she saw the German's haggard face. 'You should go and lie down.'

'No, no . . . It's only a graze and in any case . . .' He indicated the sound of the regiment going past their windows. 'Manoeuvres . . .'

'What? Again?'

'We're at war,' he said.

He smiled slightly and, after a brief salute, he left.

'What are you doing?' Madame Angellier exclaimed sharply. Lucile had pushed aside the curtain and was watching the soldiers go by. 'You have absolutely no sense of propriety. When Germans march by, the windows and shutters should be closed . . . like in '70 . . .'

'Yes, when they march into a town for the first time . . . But since they walk around our streets nearly every day, we'd be condemned to perpetual darkness if we followed tradition to the letter,' Lucile replied impatiently.

It was a stormy night; a yellowish light fell on all the soldiers. They held their heads high and moved their lips in song. Their music began softly, as if restrained, suppressed, but it would soon burst forth into a magnificent, solemn chorale.

'They've got some funny songs,' the locals said. 'You can't help listening . . . They're like prayers.'

A streak of red lightning flashed across the setting sun and seemed to pour blood over the tight-fitting helmets, the green uniforms, the officer on horseback who commanded the detachment. Even Madame Angellier was impressed.

'If only it were an omen . . .' she murmured.

Manoeuvres finished at midnight. Lucile heard the sound of the court-yard doors open and close again. She recognised the officer's footsteps in the hall. She sighed. She couldn't sleep. Another bad night. They were all the same now: miserable sleeplessness or confused nightmares. She was up by six o'clock. But that didn't help: all it did was to make the days longer, emptier.

The cook told the Angellier ladies that the officer had come home ill and had been visited by the Major who had seen he had a fever and ordered him to stay in his room. At noon, two German soldiers arrived with a meal that the injured man wouldn't eat. He was staying in his room but he wasn't staying in bed. They could hear him pacing back and forth, and the monotonous footsteps annoyed Madame Angellier so much that she retired immediately after lunch. This was not like her. Usually she would spend the afternoon in the drawing room doing her accounts or knitting. Only after four o'clock would she go up to her rooms on the second floor, where she was insulated from all noise. Finally Lucile could breathe easily. She sometimes wondered what her mother-in-law did up there, in the darkness. She closed the shutters and windows, and never put on a light, so she couldn't be reading. Besides, she never read. Maybe she kept on knitting in the dark, making great long scarves for the prisoners of war with the confidence of a blind woman who doesn't need to look at what she is doing. Or was she praying? Sleeping? She would come downstairs at seven o'clock without a single strand of hair out of place, stiff and silent in her black dress.

On this day and the ones that followed, Lucile heard her lock her bedroom door, then nothing else; the house seemed dead; only the German's steady footsteps broke the silence. But Madame Angellier didn't hear them; she was safely tucked away behind her thick walls, all sound deadened by her draperies. Hers was a large, dark, heavily furnished room. Madame Angellier would begin by closing the shutters and curtains to make it even darker. Then she would sink into a large green armchair with tapestry upholstery, fold her translucent hands in her lap and close her eyes. Sometimes a few bright, rare tears trickled down her cheeks – the reluctant tears of the very old who have finally accepted that sorrow is futile. She would wipe them away almost angrily and, sitting up straight, murmur, 'Come along now, aren't you tired? You've been running again, and right after lunch when you should be digesting your food; you're sweating. Come along, Gaston, bring your little stool. Put it here next to Mama. You can read for me. But rest for a while first. You can lay your little head on Mama's lap.' Softly, lovingly, she stroked imaginary curls.

It was neither delirium nor the first signs of madness; never had she been more totally lucid and aware of herself. It was deliberate play-acting, the only thing that brought her some solace, in the same way as morphine or wine. In the darkness and the silence, she could relive the past; she resurrected moments she herself had thought were lost for ever; treasured memories resurfaced; she would remember certain words her son had said, certain intonations in his voice, a gesture he made with his chubby little hands when he was a baby, memories that, truly, for just an instant, could take her back in time. It was no longer her imagination but reality itself, rediscovered through her enduring memories, for nothing could change the fact that these things had actually happened. Absence, even death, could not erase the past; the pink smock her son had worn, the way he cried and held out his hand to her when he'd been stung by nettles, all these things had happened and it was within her power, as long as she was still alive, to bring them back to life. All she needed was solitude, darkness, the furniture around her and these objects that her son had touched. She would vary her hallucinations to suit her mood.

Not content merely with the past, she anticipated the future; she moulded the present to her will. Though she lied and deceived herself, the lies were her own creation and she cherished them. For very brief moments she was happy. Her happiness was not hampered by the restrictions of reality. Everything was possible, everything within reach. First of all the war was over. That was the starting point of her dream, the springboard from which she could launch herself towards endless joy. The war was over . . . It was a day like any other . . . Tomorrow – why not? She would know nothing until the very last minute; she didn't read the papers any more, didn't listen to the radio. It would be like a bolt from the blue. One morning, she would go down to the kitchen and see the cook wide-eyed: 'Haven't you heard, Madame?' The surrender of the King of Belgium, the fall of Paris, the arrival of the Germans, the Armistice . . . She had learned about all these in just this way. Well, why not peace too? Why not: 'Madame, it seems it's all over! It seems no one's fighting any more, there's no more war, the prisoners are coming home!' She couldn't care less if it was the English or the Germans who had won. All she cared about was her son. White as a ghost, eyes closed, she created the scene in her mind with the same abundance of detail found in the paintings of madmen. She could see each and every line on Gaston's face, his hair, his clothing, the laces on his army boots; she could hear every inflection in his voice. She stretched out her hands and whispered, 'Well, come inside. Don't you recognise your own house?'

During these first moments, Lucile faded away and Gaston belonged to her and her alone. She would be careful not to cry and kiss him for too long. She would make him a good lunch, run his bath, tell him immediately about his affairs: 'You know, I took good care of them. You remember that piece of land you wanted, near the Étang-Neû? I bought it, it's yours. I also bought that meadow of the Montmorts' that borders on ours – the one the Viscount was adamant he wouldn't sell to us. Well, I waited for the right moment. I got what I wanted. Are you pleased? I've put your gold, your silverware, the family jewellery all in a safe place. I did everything, courageously, all by myself. If I'd had to count on your wife . . . You can see I'm your only real friend, can't you? That I'm the only one who really understands you? But go and see your wife, my boy. Go on. Just don't expect much from her. She's a cold, rebellious creature. Together, though, we'll be able to bend her to our will better than I could do alone. She eludes me with her long silences, whereas you have the right to ask her what she's thinking. You're the master of the house: you can demand to know. Go, go and see her! Take from her what's rightfully yours: her beauty, her youth . . . I've heard that in Dijon . . . You shouldn't, my dear Gaston. A mistress is expensive. But I'm sure your long absence will have made you love our old house even more . . . Oh, what wonderful, peaceful days we're going to spend together,' murmured Madame Angellier. She had stood up and was walking around the room holding an imaginary hand and leaning against a phantom shoulder. 'Come on, let's go downstairs. I've had a light meal prepared for you in the sitting room. You've lost weight, Gaston. Come, you've got to have something to eat.'

Without thinking, she opened the door, went down the staircase. Yes, this was how she would come down from her room in the evening, opening the door to surprise the children: Gaston in an armchair next to the window with his wife by his side, reading to him. It was his wife's duty, her role, to look after him, to amuse him. When he was recovering from typhoid fever, Lucile used to read the newspapers to him. Her voice was soft and pleasant. She couldn't deny that even she herself had sometimes enjoyed listening to Lucile read. A soft, low voice . . . But was it that voice she could hear now? No, she must be dreaming! She'd allowed her imagination to drift beyond the acceptable limit. She pulled herself up, took a few steps and walked into the sitting room. The armchair had been moved next to the window and sitting in it, his injured arm leaning on the armrest, smoking a pipe, his feet on the little stool where Gaston used to sit as a child, she saw the German in his green uniform – the invader, the enemy – and next to him Lucile, who was reading a book out loud.

For a moment no one said a word. They both stood up. Lucile dropped the book she was holding. The officer quickly picked it up from the floor and put it on the table.

'Madame,' he muttered, 'your daughter-in-law was kind enough to allow me to come and keep her company for a few moments.'

The old woman, very pale, nodded. 'You're in charge here.'

'And since some new books were sent to me from Paris, I took the liberty of . . .'

'You're in charge here,' Madame Angellier said again.

She turned and walked out. Lucile heard her say to the cook, 'I'll be staying in my room from now on. You will bring my meals to me upstairs.'

'Today, Madame?'

'Today, tomorrow and for as long as this gentleman is in the house.'

When she had gone upstairs and they could no longer hear her footsteps in the depths of the house, the German whispered, 'That will be heaven.'

16

The Viscountess de Montmort suffered from insomnia. She was in tune with the cosmos; all the great contemporary problems touched her soul. When she thought about the future of the white race, or Franco-German relations, or the threat posed by the Freemasons and Communism, sleep was banished. Chills ran through her body. She would get up, put on an old worm-eaten fur wrap and go out into the grounds. She despised dressing up, perhaps because she had lost hope that putting on a pretty dress could counterbalance the overall effect of her plainness (she had a long red nose, an awkward figure and bad skin), perhaps because of a natural sense of pride that made her believe others couldn't help but see her striking qualities, even beneath a battered felt hat or a knitted wool coat (spinach-green and canary-yellow) that the cook would have rejected in horror, or perhaps out of her contempt for trivial detail. 'How important is it, my dear?' she would say sweetly to her husband when he criticised her for coming down to dinner wearing two different shoes. But she quickly returned to earth when it came to overseeing the servants' work or managing their estate.

Whenever she couldn't sleep, she would walk through the grounds reciting poetry or rush to the henhouse and examine the three enormous locks that protected the door; she kept an eye on the cows (since the war had started, no one grew flowers on the lawns any more, the cattle slept there), and in the soft moonlight she would stroll through the vegetable garden and count the maize. She was being robbed. Before the war it was almost unheard of to grow maize in this rich area where poultry was fed on wheat and oats. Now, though, the requisitioning agents searched the lofts for sacks of wheat and the housewives had no grain to feed their hens. People had come to the château to ask for feed, but the Montmorts were hoarding it, mainly for themselves, but also for all their friends and acquaintances in the area. The farmers were angry. 'We'd be happy to pay,' they said. She wouldn't have charged them anything actually, but that wasn't the issue and they sensed it. They could tell they were up against a kind of brotherhood, like the Freemasons, a closing of ranks that meant that they and their money were insignificant compared to the satisfaction the Montmorts got from doing a favour for the Baron de Montrefaut or the Countess de Pignepoule. Since they weren't allowed to buy, they simply took. There were no longer any gamekeepers at the château; they'd been taken prisoner and there weren't enough men in the area to replace them. It was also impossible to find workmen or the materials to rebuild the crumbling walls. The farmers got in through the gaps, poached whatever they wanted, fished in the lake, stole hens, corn or tomato plants – just helped themselves to anything, in fact.

Monsieur de Montmort's situation was complicated. On the one hand he was the Mayor and didn't want to upset his constituents. On the other, he naturally cared about his estate. Nevertheless, he would have chosen to turn a blind eye to it all if it hadn't been for his wife, who rejected any compromise or show of weakness on principle. 'All you want is a quiet life,' she said sharply to her husband. 'Our Lord Himself said: "I have not come to bring peace but the sword."'

'You're not Jesus Christ,' Amaury replied grumpily, but it had long ago been accepted in the family that the Viscountess had the soul of an apostle and that her opinions were prophetic. What was more, Amaury was even more inclined to adopt the Viscountess's judgements since she was the one with the family fortune and she kept her purse strings tightly closed. He therefore loyally supported her and waged a bitter war against the poachers, the thieves, the teacher who didn't go to Mass and the postman, who was suspected of being a member of the 'Popular Front' even though he had ostentatiously hung a picture of Maréchal Pétain on the door of the telephone booth in the Post Office.

And so the Viscountess walked through her grounds on a beautiful June evening and recited the poetry she intended her protégées from the school to recite on Mother's Day. She would have liked to have composed a poem herself; however, her talent was really for prose (when she wrote, she felt the deluge of ideas so powerfully that she often had to put down her pen and run her hands under cold water to force back into them the blood that had rushed to her head). The obligation to make things rhyme was unbearable. Perhaps, therefore, instead of the poem to the glory of the French Mother she would so like to compose, she would write an incantation in prose: 'O Mother!' would exclaim one of the youngest pupils, dressed all in white and holding a bouquet of wild flowers in her hand. 'O Mother! Let me see your sweet face above my little bed while the storm rages outside. The sky darkens the earth, but a radiant dawn approaches. Smile, O kind Mother! See how your child is following the Maréchal who holds peace and happiness in his hands. Join me and all the children, all the mothers in France, to form a blissful circle around the venerable Wise One who restores hope in our hearts!'

Madame de Montmort spoke these words out loud and they echoed in the silent grounds. When inspiration took hold of her, she lost all control. She strode back and forth, then collapsed on to the damp moss and sat in meditation for a long time, her fur wrap pulled tight round her thin shoulders. Whenever she reflected in this way her thoughts quickly led to passionate resentment. Why, when she was so gifted, wasn't she surrounded by love or even the warmth of admiration? Why had her husband married her for her money? Why wasn't she popular? When she walked through the village the children would hide or laugh behind her back. She knew they called her 'the madwoman'. It was very hard being hated, yet look at how much she'd done for the local people! The library (how lovingly she had chosen the books, good books to elevate the soul but which left them cold; the girls wanted her to get novels by Maurice Dekobra, these young people . . .), educational films (just as unpopular as the books), a village fête every year in the grounds, with a show put on by the school-children. Yet she had not been oblivious to the harsh criticisms bandied about. They held it against her that the chairs had been set up in the garage because the bad weather had made it impossible to enjoy being outside. What did these people want? Did they expect her to invite them into the château? They'd be the ones who felt embarrassed if she did. Ah, this deplorable new way of thinking that was sweeping through France! She alone could recognise it and give it a name. The people were becoming Bolsheviks. She had thought the defeat would be a lesson to them, that they would see the errors of their ways and be forced to respect for their leaders. But no: they were worse than ever.

Sometimes she – a passionate patriot, yes she – was actually glad the enemy was there, she thought, listening to the German guards keeping watch on the road alongside the grounds. They patrolled the village and the surrounding countryside all night long, in groups of four; you could hear the sound of church bells ringing, a sweet, familiar sound that gently lulled people as they slept, and at the same time the hammering of boots, the rattling of weapons, as in a prison courtyard. Yes, the Viscountess de Montmort had reached the point where she wondered if she shouldn't thank the Good Lord for the German occupation of France. Not that she actually liked them, Lord no! She couldn't stand them, but without them . . . who knew? It was all very well for Amaury to say 'Communists? The people around here? But they're richer than you are . . .' It wasn't simply a question of money or land, it was also, especially, a question of zeal. She vaguely sensed this without being able to explain it. Perhaps they didn't really understand the idea of Communism, but it appealed to their desire for equality, a desire so powerful that even having money and land became frustrating rather than satisfying. It was an insult, as they put it, to own livestock worth a fortune, to be able to send their sons to private school, buy silk stockings for their daughters, and in spite of all that, still feel inferior to the Montmorts.

The farmers felt they were never given enough respect, especially since the Viscount was made Mayor . . . The old farmer who had been Mayor before him had been warm and friendly to everyone; he might have been greedy, vulgar, harsh and insulting to his constituents . . . he got away with it! Yet they reproached the Viscount de Montmort for being haughty. What did they expect? For him to stand up when they came into the Mayor's office? To see them to the door or something? They couldn't bear any hint of superiority, anyone wealthier or anyone who came from a better family. No matter what people said, the Germans had good qualities. They were a disciplined race, docile, thought Madame de Montmort as she listened, almost with pleasure, to the rhythmical footsteps fading away, the harsh voices shouting *Achtung* in the distance. It must be very nice to own a lot of property in Germany, whereas here . . .

She was consumed by anxiety. It was getting darker and she was about to go back into the house when she saw – or thought she saw – a shadowy figure moving along the wall. Head down, it disappeared into the vegetable garden. Finally, she was going to catch one of these thieves. She quivered with pleasure. It was typical of her not to be afraid. Amaury was always worried about confrontations, but not she. Danger aroused the huntress in her. She hid behind some trees and followed the shadowy figure, holding the pair of shoes she had found hidden in the moss at the foot of the wall (the thief was walking in his socks to make less noise). She worked her way round so that he ran straight into her as he was coming out of the vegetable garden. He jumped back and tried to run away, but she shouted at him contemptuously, 'I've got your shoes, my friend. The police will soon find out whose they are.'

The man stopped and started walking towards her; it was Benoît Sabarie. They stood staring at each other without saying a word.

'Well, that's a fine thing to do,' the Viscountess said finally, her voice trembling with hatred.

She despised him. Of all the farmers, he was the most insolent, the most stubborn; whether it was about the hay, the livestock, the fences, everything and nothing, the château and the farm waged silent, interminable guerrilla warfare against each other.

'Well!' she said indignantly, 'now I know who the thief is and I'm going to tell the Mayor immediately. You'll live to regret this!'

'Tell me, do I talk to you like that, do I? Take your plants,' said Benoît, throwing them down on the ground where they lay scattered in the moonlight. 'Didn't we offer to pay for them? Do you think we don't have enough money to buy them? But every time we ask you for a favour – not that it would cost you anything – no! You'd rather see us starve to death!'

'Thief, thief, thief!' the Viscountess kept shrieking as he talked. 'The Mayor . . .'

'I don't give a damn about the Mayor! Go and get him then. I'll say it to his face.'

'How dare you speak to me like that?'

'Because we've all had enough around here, if you want to know the truth! You have everything and you keep everything! Your wood, your fruit, your fish, your game, your hens, you wouldn't sell any of it, you wouldn't give any of it away for all the money in the world. Your husband the Mayor makes fancy speeches about helping each other and the rest of it. You must be bloody joking! Your château's crammed full of stuff, from the cellar to the attic, everyone knows that, they've seen. Are we asking for charity? No! But that's exactly what bothers you, isn't it? You'd be happy to do it as charity because you like humiliating poor people, but when it comes to doing a favour, as equals – "I'm paying for what I take" – you're off like a shot. Why wouldn't you sell me your plants?'

'That's my business and this is my house, I believe, you insolent . . .'

'That corn wasn't even for me, I swear! I'd rather die than ask people like you for anything. It was for Louise, 'cause her husband's a prisoner and I wanted to help her out. *I* help people!'

'By stealing?'

'Well, what else are we supposed to do? You're heartless and stingy with it! What else are we supposed to do?' he repeated furiously. 'And I'm not the only one to help myself here. Everything you refuse to give away without a good reason, everything you keep out of pure spite, we're going to take. And it's not over yet. Just wait until autumn! Your husband the Mayor will be hunting with the Germans . . .'

'That's not true! That's a lie! He's never gone hunting with the Germans.'

She stamped her foot angrily, wild with rage. Again that stupid slander! The Germans did invite them both to one of their hunts last winter, it was true. They had declined, but they couldn't refuse to attend the dinner in the evening. Whether they liked it or not, they had to follow the government's orders. And besides, these German officers were cultured men, after all! What separates or unites people is not their language, their laws, their customs, their principles, but the way they hold their knife and fork.

'When it's autumn,' Benoît continued, 'he'll be hunting with the Germans, but I'll be back, I will, back to your grounds and I won't care if it's rabbits or foxes I get. You can have your groundsmen, your game-keepers and your dogs chase after me as much as you want; they won't be as clever as Benoît Sabarie! They've been running after me plenty all winter without catching me!'

'I won't go and get the groundsman or the gamekeepers, I'll get the Germans. They scare you, don't they? You can show off all you like, but when you see a German uniform, you keep your head down.'

'Listen, I've seen them Boches up close, I have, in Belgium and at the Somme. I'm not like your husband. Where was *he* during the war? In an office, where he could treat everyone like shit.'

'You vulgar little man!'

'In Chalon-sur-Saône, that's where he was, your husband, from September 'til the day the Germans arrived. Then he cleared off. That's his idea of war.'

'You are . . . you are repulsive. Get out of here or I'll scream. Get out of here or I'll call them!'

'That's it, call the Boches. You must be really glad they're here, eh? They're like the police, they watch your property. You'd better pray to the Good Lord that they stay a long time because the day they leave . . .'

He left his sentence unfinished. Quickly grabbing his shoes, the evidence, from her hands, he put them on, climbed over the wall and disappeared. Almost immediately she heard the sound of German footsteps getting closer.

'Oh, I really hope they caught him. I really hope they've killed him,' the Viscountess said to herself as she ran towards the château. 'What a man! What a species! What vile people! That's what Bolshevism is, exactly that. My God, what has happened to everyone? When Papa was alive, if you caught a poacher in the woods he'd cry and beg for forgiveness. Naturally he'd be forgiven. Papa, who was goodness personified, would shout, make a scene, then give him a glass of wine in the kitchen. I saw that happen more than once when I was a child. But then the farmers were poor. Since they've got money, it's as if all their worst instincts have resurfaced. "The château's crammed full of stuff, from the cellar to the attic,"' she repeated furiously. 'Well! And what about his house? They're richer than we are. What exactly do they want? It's envy. They're being eaten up by base feelings. That Sabarie is dangerous. He bragged about how he came to hunt here. So he's kept his rifle. He's capable of anything. If he gets up to mischief, if he kills a German, the entire region will be held responsible and especially the Mayor. It's people like him that cause all our problems. It's my duty to denounce him. I'll make Amaury see reason, and . . . if I have to, I'll go to German Headquarters myself. He prowls the woods at night, in complete breach of the rules, with a weapon – he's had it!'

She rushed into the bedroom, woke Amaury up and told him what had happened. 'So this is what it's come to!' she concluded. 'They can come and challenge me, steal from me, insult me in my own home. Well, let them. Do you think the insults of a farmer are going to affect me? But he's a dangerous man. He'll stop at nothing. I'm sure that if I hadn't had the presence of mind to keep quiet, if I'd called for the Germans who were passing by on the road, he would have been capable of attacking them or even . . .'

She let out a little cry and went deathly pale.

'He had a knife. I saw the light reflected off the blade, I'm sure of it. Can you imagine what might have happened? A German murdered, at night, in our grounds? Go and prove you're not involved, Amaury. It's your duty. You must do something. That man bragged about hunting in the grounds all winter so he must have a gun at home. A gun! Even though the Germans have said over and over again that they won't stand for it. If he's still got one at home, he must definitely be planning something terrible, an attack of some kind. Do you realise what that means? In the next town a German soldier was killed and all the important people in the town (the Mayor first) were taken as hostages until they found out who had done it. And in a little village eleven kilometres from there a young boy of sixteen got drunk and threw a punch at a guard who was trying to arrest him for being out after curfew. The boy was shot, but there's worse! Nothing would have happened if he'd obeyed the rules, but they considered the Mayor responsible for his constituents and he was almost executed as well.'

'A pocket knife,' Amaury grumbled, but she wasn't listening. 'I'm beginning to think,' he said, getting dressed, his hands shaking (it was nearly eight o'clock), 'I'm beginning to think I shouldn't have agreed to be Mayor.'

'You're going to make a formal complaint at the police station, I hope?'

'At the police station? You're mad! We'll have the whole place against us. You know that to these people taking what we've refused to sell them doesn't count as stealing. They see it as a joke. They'd make our life miserable. No, I'll go to German Headquarters right now. I'll ask them to keep the matter quiet, which they will certainly do for they're discreet and they'll understand the situation. They'll look around at the Sabaries' place and will, no doubt, find a gun.'

'Are you sure they'll find something? People like that . . .'

'People like that think they're very clever, but I know where they hide things. They brag about it in the bars, after they've had a few drinks. It's either in the loft, the cellar or the pigsty. They'll arrest that Benoît, but I'll make the Germans promise not to punish him too severely. He'll get away with a few months in prison. We'll be rid of him for a while and afterwards, I bet you anything, he'll watch his step. The Germans know how to bring people into line. What's wrong with them?' exclaimed the

Viscount, who was now half dressed, his shirt-tails flapping round his bare thighs. 'What kind of people are they? Why can't they leave well alone? What are they being asked to do? To keep quiet, to leave everyone in peace. But no! They have to grumble, quibble, show off. And just how is that going to get them anywhere, I ask you? We were defeated, weren't we? All we have to do is keep a low profile. You'd think they were doing it on purpose just to annoy me. I had succeeded, after a great deal of effort, in getting along with the Germans. There's not a single one of them living in the château, remember. That was a great favour. And what about the whole region? I'm doing everything I can for it . . . I'm losing sleep over it . . . The Germans are behaving politely to everyone. They salute the women, they stroke the children. They pay cash. But, no! That's not enough! What else do they want? That they give us back Alsace and Lorraine? That they agree to our becoming a Republic with Leon Blum as President? What do they want? What?'

'Don't upset yourself, Amaury. Look at me, see how calm I am. Just do your duty without hoping for any reward other than from heaven. Believe me, God can see into our hearts.'

'I know, I know, but it's hard all the same.' The Viscount sighed bitterly.

And without stopping for breakfast (he had such a lump in his throat, he told his wife, that he couldn't have swallowed a crumb), he left and, in the utmost secrecy, requested an audience at German Headquarters.

17

The German army had ordered a requisitioning of horses. The going price for a mare was in the region of 60,000 or 70,000 francs; the Germans were paying (promising to pay) half that amount. It was nearly harvest time and the farmers bitterly asked the Mayor how they were supposed to manage.

'With our bare hands, eh? But we're warning you, if we aren't allowed to work, it's the towns that'll starve to death.'

'But my good fellows, *I* can't do anything about it,' muttered the Mayor.

In fact, the farmers knew very well that he was powerless; it was simply that they secretly held a grudge against him. '*He*'ll be all right, he'll get by, they won't touch a single one of his cursed horses.' Nothing was going right. A storm had been raging since the night before. The gardens were soaked with rain; hail had wreaked havoc in the fields.

That morning, when Bruno left the Angelliers' house to ride to the neighbouring town where the requisitioning was to take place, he looked out over a desolate landscape, lashed by the rainstorm. The great lime trees lining the wide road had been violently battered; they creaked and groaned like masts on a ship. Bruno, however, experienced a feeling of joy as he galloped along; this pure, biting, cold air reminded him of eastern Prussia. Oh, when would he again see those plains, that pale-green grass, those marshes, the extraordinary beauty of the skies in spring – the late spring of northern countries – those amber skies, pearly clouds, reeds, rushes, sparse clumps of silver birch . . . ? When would he again hunt for heron and curlew? Along the way he came across horses and their riders from all the hamlets, villages and estates in the area heading for town. 'They're good animals,' he thought, 'but badly cared for.' The French – and all civilians actually – understood nothing about horses.

He stopped for a moment to let them pass. They were zigzagging by in small groups. Bruno studied the animals closely; he was trying to work out which ones would be suitable for war. Most of them would be sent to Germany to work the fields, but some of them would have to carry heavy loads in the African desert or the hop fields of Kent. God alone knew where the wind of war would carry them. Bruno remembered how the horses had neighed in terror as Rouen burned. It was raining now. The farmers walked with their heads down, only looking up when they saw this motionless cavalryman with his green cape thrown over his shoulders. For a moment their eyes would meet. 'They're so slow,' Bruno thought, 'look how clumsy they are. They'll get there two hours late and when are we supposed to have lunch? We'll have to see to the horses first.

'Well, go on, then, get a move on,' he muttered, impatiently hitting the back of his boots with his riding crop, restraining himself so he didn't start shouting out orders as he did during manoeuvres. Some old people walked past him, children and even women; everyone from the same village stayed together. Then there would be a gap. Only the swirling wind filled the space, the silence. Taking advantage of one of these lulls, Bruno broke into a gallop and headed for the town, leaving the patient procession behind.

The farmers were silent: they had taken all the young men; they had taken the bread, the wheat, the flour and the potatoes; they had taken the petrol and the cars, and now the horses. What would they take tomorrow? Some of them had started out at midnight. They walked with their heads down, stooped over, faces impassive. Even though they'd told the Mayor they'd had enough, that they wouldn't do another thing, they knew very well the work had to be finished, the harvest taken in. They had to eat. 'It's strange to think we used to be so happy,' they thought. 'Germans . . . bunch of bastards . . . You have to be fair, though. It's war. Still, for God's sake, how long will it go on? How long?' muttered the farmers as they looked at the stormy sky.

Men and horses had passed by Lucile's window all day long. She covered her ears so she wouldn't hear them any more. She didn't want to know anything any more. She'd had enough of these warlike scenes, these depressing sights. She was deeply disturbed by them; they broke her heart; they prevented her from being happy. Happy, my God! 'So there's a war,' she said to herself, 'so there are prisoners, widows, misery, hunger, the occupation. So what? I'm not doing anything wrong. He's a most respectful friend. The books, the music, our long conversations, our walks in the Maie woods . . . What makes them shameful is the idea of the war, this universal evil. But he's no more at fault than I am. It's not our fault. Just leave us in peace . . . leave us alone!' Sometimes she even frightened and surprised herself at feeling such rebellion in her heart – against her husband, her mother-in-law, public opinion, this 'spirit of the hive' Bruno talked about. That evil, grumbling swarm serving some unknown end. She hated it.

'Let them go where they want; as for me, I'll do as I please. I want to be free. I'm not asking for superficial freedom, the freedom to travel, to leave this house (even though that would be unimaginably blissful). I'd rather feel free inside – to choose my own path, never to waver, not to follow the swarm. I hate this community spirit they go on and on about. The Germans, the French, the Gaullists, they all agree on one thing: you have to love, think, live with other people, as part of a state, a country, a political party. Oh, my God! I don't want to! I'm just a poor useless woman; I don't know anything but I want to be free! Slaves,' she continued thinking. 'We're becoming slaves; the war scatters us in all directions, takes away everything we own, snatches the bread from out of our mouths; let me at least retain the right to decide my own destiny, to laugh at it, defy it, escape it if I can. A slave? Better to be a slave than a dog who thinks he's free as he trots along behind his master.' She listened to the sound of men and horses passing by. 'They don't even realise they're slaves,' she said to herself, 'and I, I would be just like them if a sense of pity, solidarity, the "spirit of the hive" forced me to refuse to be happy.'

This friendship between herself and the German, this dark secret, an entire universe hidden in the heart of the hostile house, my God, how sweet it was. Finally she felt she was a human being, proud and free. She wouldn't allow anyone to intrude into her personal world. 'No one. It's no one's business. Let everyone else fight each other, hate each other. Even if his father and mine fought in the past. Even if he himself took my husband prisoner . . .' (an idea that obsessed her unhappy mother-in-law) 'what difference would it make? We're friends.' Friends? She walked through the dim entrance hall and went up to the mirror on the chest of drawers that was framed in black wood; she looked at her dark eyes and trembling lips and smiled. 'Friends? He loves me,' she whispered. She brought her lips to the mirror and gently kissed her reflection. 'Yes, he loves you. You don't owe anything to the husband who betrayed you, deserted you . . . But he's a prisoner of war! Your husband is a prisoner of war and you let a German get close to you, take his place? Well, yes. So what? The one who's gone, the prisoner of war, the husband, I never loved him. I hope he never comes back. I hope he dies!

'But wait . . . think . . .' she continued, leaning her forehead against the mirror. She felt as if she were talking to a part of herself she hadn't known existed until then, who'd been invisible and whom she was seeing now for the first time, a woman with brown eyes, thin, trembling lips, burning cheeks, who was her but not entirely her. 'But wait, think . . . be logical . . . listen to the voice of reason . . . you're a sensible woman . . . you're French . . . where will all this lead? He's a soldier, he's married, he'll go away; where will it lead? Will it be anything more than a moment of fleeting happiness? Not even happiness, just pleasure? Do you even know what that is?' She was fascinated by her reflection in the mirror; it both pleased her and frightened her.

She heard the cook's footsteps in the pantry near the entrance hall; she jumped back in terror and started walking aimlessly through the house. My God, what an enormous empty house! Her mother-in-law, as she had vowed, no longer left her room; her meals were taken up to her. But even though she wasn't there, Lucile could still sense her. This house was a reflection of her, the truest part of her being, just as the truest part of Lucile was the slender young woman (in love, courageous, happy, in despair) who had just been smiling at herself in the mirror with the black frame. (She had disappeared; all that was left of Lucile Angellier was a lifeless ghost, a woman who wandered aimlessly through the rooms, who leaned her face against the windows, who automatically tidied all the useless, ugly objects that decorated the mantelpiece.)

What a day! The air was heavy, the sky grey. The blossoming lime trees had been battered by gusts of cold wind. 'A room, a house of my very own,' thought Lucile, 'a perfect room, almost bare, a beautiful lamp . . . If only I could close these shutters and put on the lights to block out this awful weather. Marthe would ask if I were ill; she'd go and tell my mother-in-law, who would come and open the curtains and turn off the lights because of the cost of electricity. I can't play the piano: it would be seen as an insult to my absent husband. I'd happily go for a walk in the woods in spite of the rain, but everyone would know about it. "Lucile

Angellier's gone mad," they'd all say. That's enough to have a woman locked up around here.'

She laughed as she recalled a young girl she'd heard about whose parents had shut her up in a nursing home because she would slip away and run down to the lake whenever there was a full moon. The lake, the night . . . The lake beneath this torrential rain. Oh, anywhere far away! Somewhere else. These horses, these men, these poor resigned people, hunched over in the rain . . . She tore herself away from the window. 'I'm nothing like them,' she told herself, yet she felt bound to them by invisible chains.

She went into Bruno's bedroom. Several times she had slipped quietly into his room in the evening, her heart pounding. He would be propped up on his bed, fully dressed, reading or writing, the metallic blond of his hair glistening beneath the lamp. On an armchair in the corner of the room would be his heavy belt with the motto *Gott mit uns* engraved on the buckle, a black revolver, his cap and almond-green greatcoat; he would take the coat and put it over Lucile's legs because the nights were cold since the week before with its endless storms.

They were alone – they felt they were alone – in the great sleeping house. Not a word of their true feelings was spoken; they didn't kiss. There was simply silence. Silence followed by feverish, passionate conversations about their own countries, their families, music, books . . . They felt a strange happiness, an urgent need to reveal their hearts to each other – the urgency of lovers, which is already a gift, the very first one, the gift of the soul before the body surrenders. 'Know me, look at me. This is who I am. This is how I have lived, this is what I have loved. And you? What about you, my darling?' But up until now, not a single word of love. What was the point? Words are pointless when your voices falter, when your mouths are trembling, amid such long silences. Slowly, gently, Lucile touched the books on the table. The Gothic lettering looked so bizarre, so ugly. The Germans, the Germans . . . A Frenchman wouldn't have let me leave with no gesture of love other than kissing my hand and the hem of my dress . . .

She smiled, shrugging her shoulders slightly; she knew it was neither shyness nor coldness, but that profound, determined German patience – the patience of a wild animal waiting for its hypnotised prey to let itself be taken. 'During the war', Bruno had said, 'we spent a number of nights

lying in wait in the Moeuvre forest. Waiting is erotic . . .' She had laughed
at the word. It seemed less amusing now. What did she do now but wait?
She waited for him. She wandered through these lifeless rooms. Another
two hours, three hours. Then dinner alone. Then the sound of the key
locking her mother-in-law's door. Then Marthe crossing the garden with
a lantern to close the gate. Then more waiting, feverish and strange . . .
and finally the sound of his horse neighing on the road, the clanking of
weapons, orders given to the groom who walks away with the horse. The
sound of spurs on the doorstep. Then the night, the stormy night, with
its great gusts of wind in the lime trees and the thunder rumbling in the
distance. She would tell him. Oh, she was no hypocrite, she would tell
him in clear, simple French – that the prey he so desired was his. 'And
then what? Then what?' she murmured; a mischievous, bold, sensual smile
suddenly transformed her expression, just as the reflection of a flame illu-
minating a face can alter it. Lit up by fire, the softest features can look
demonic; they can both repel and attract. She walked quietly out of the
room.

18

Someone was knocking at the kitchen door; they knocked shyly, softly; you could hardly hear it through the driving rain. Some kids wanting to get out of the storm, thought the cook. She looked out and saw Madeleine Sabarie standing on the doorstep, holding a dripping-wet umbrella. Marthe looked at her for a moment, astonished; people from the farms hardly ever came into the village except on Sundays for High Mass.

'What's going on? Come inside, quickly. Is everything all right at home?'

'No, something terrible's happened,' Madeleine whispered, 'I need to speak to Madame right away.'

'Lord Jesus! Something terrible? Do you want to speak to Madame Angellier or Madame Lucile?'

Madeleine hesitated. 'Madame Lucile. But be quiet . . . I don't want that awful German to know I'm here.'

'The officer? He's away at the requisitioning of the horses. Sit down by the fire, you're soaking wet. I'll go and get Madame.'

Lucile was alone, finishing her dinner. She had a book open on the tablecloth in front of her. 'Poor dear!' Marthe said to herself in a moment of sudden lucidity. 'Is this the kind of life she should have? No husband for two years . . . And as for Madeleine . . . What terrible thing could have happened? Something to do with the Germans, that's for sure.'

She told Lucile that someone was asking for her.

'Madeleine Sabarie, Madame. Something terrible's happened to her . . . She doesn't want anyone to see her.'

'Show her in here. Is the German . . . Lieutenant von Falk home yet?'

'No, Madame. I'll hear his horse when he comes back. I'll warn you.'

'Yes, good. Go on now.'

Lucile waited, her heart pounding. Madeleine Sabarie entered the room, deathly pale and out of breath. The modesty and caution innate to country folk battled against her emotional turmoil. She shook Lucile's hand, mumbled 'I'm not disturbing you, am I?' and 'How are you?' as was the custom, then said very quietly, making a terrible effort to hold back her tears (because you just didn't cry in front of anyone, unless it was at someone's deathbed; the rest of the time you had to control yourself, to hide your pain – and indeed your pleasure – from others), 'Oh, Madame Lucile! What should I do? I've come to ask your advice because we're . . . we're finished. The Germans came to arrest Benoît this morning.'

'But why?' Lucile exclaimed.

'They said it was because he had a hunting rifle hidden away. Like everyone else, as you can imagine. But they didn't search anywhere else, just our place. Benoît said, "Go ahead and look." They did look and they found it. It was hidden in the hay in the cowshed. Our German, the one living with us, the interpreter, he was in the room when the men from Headquarters came back in with the gun and ordered my husband to go with them. "Wait a minute," Benoît said. "That isn't my gun. It must be someone who lives around here who hid it so they could denounce me. Give it to me and I'll prove it to you." He was talking so naturally that the men weren't suspicious. My Benoît takes the gun, pretends to be examining it and suddenly . . . Oh, Madame Lucile, the two bullets fired almost at the same time. One killed Bonnet and the other Bubi, the big Alsatian that was with him.'

'I see,' murmured Lucile, 'I see.'

'Then he jumps out of the window and runs off, the Germans right behind. But he knows the place better than them, as you can imagine. They haven't found him yet. The storm was so bad they couldn't see two steps in front of them, thank goodness. Bonnet's laid out on my bed, where they put him. If they find Benoît, they'll shoot him. He might have been shot for hiding a gun, but if that was all he'd done we could have hoped he'd get off. Now, well we know what to expect, don't we?'

'But why did he kill Bonnet?'

'He must be the one who denounced him, Madame Lucile. He lives with us. He could have found the gun. These Germans, they're all traitors. And that one . . . was chasing after me, you see . . . and my husband knew it. Maybe he wanted to punish him, maybe he said to himself, "Might as well . . . then he won't be here to play up to my wife when I'm not around." Maybe . . . And he really hated them, Madame Lucile. He was longing to kill one of them.'

'They've been looking for him all day long you say? You're absolutely sure they haven't found him yet?'

'I'm sure,' said Madeleine after a moment's silence.

'Have you seen him?'

'Yes. This is life or death, Madame Lucile. You . . . you won't say a word?'

'Oh, Madeleine . . .'

'All right, then. He's hiding at Louise's place, our neighbour whose husband is a prisoner of war.'

'They're going to turn the village upside down, they're going to look everywhere.'

'Thank goodness they were requisitioning the horses today. All the officers are away. The soldiers are waiting for orders. Tomorrow they'll start the search. But Madame Lucile, farms have plenty of hiding places. They've had escaped prisoners right there under their noses plenty of times. Louise will hide him good, but it's just, well, it's her kids: the kids play with the Germans, they aren't afraid of them, and they talk, they're too little to understand. "I know the chance I'm taking," Louise told me. "I'm doing it willingly for your husband, just like you would do it for mine, but nonetheless, it would be better to find another house where he could hide until he can get away from here." They'll be watching all the roads now, won't they. But the Germans won't be here for ever. What we need is a big house where there aren't any children.'

'Here?' Lucile said, staring at her.

'Here, yes, I thought . . .'

'You do know that a German officer lives here?'

'They're everywhere. But the officer hardly ever comes out of his room, does he? And I've heard . . . forgive me, Madame Lucile, I've heard he's in love with you and that you can do whatever you like. I'm not offending you, am I? They're men like the rest, I know, and they get bored. So if you said to him, "I don't want your soldiers upsetting everything in the house. It's ridiculous. You know very well I'm not hiding anyone. First of all, I'd be too scared to . . ." Things that women can say . . . And in this house that's so big, so empty, it would be easy to find a hiding place, some little corner. And then there's a chance he'd be saved, the only chance. You might say that if you get caught, you risk going to prison, perhaps even being killed. With these brutes it's possible. But if we French don't help each other, who will? Louise, she has kids, she does, and she wasn't scared. You're all alone.'

'I'm not afraid,' Lucile said slowly.

She thought about it. The danger for Benoît would be the same whether he was in her house or anywhere else. What about the danger for her? 'What's my life worth anyway?' she thought with unintentional despair. Really, it had no importance. She suddenly thought of those days in June 1940 (two years, only two years ago). Then, too, amid the chaos, the danger, she hadn't thought about herself. She had let herself be carried along by a fast-flowing river.

'There's my mother-in-law,' she murmured, 'but she doesn't leave her room any more. She wouldn't see anything. And there's Marthe.'

'Marthe's family, Madame. She's my husband's cousin. There's no danger there. We trust our family. But where could he hide?'

'I was thinking maybe the blue bedroom near the attic, the old playroom that has a kind of alcove . . . But then, but then, my poor Madeleine, you mustn't have any illusions. If fate is against us they'll find him here as well as anywhere, but if it's God's will, he'll escape. After all, German soldiers have been killed in France before and they've not always found the ones who did it. We must do everything we can to hide him . . . and . . . just hope, don't you think?'

'Yes, Madame, hope . . .' said Madeleine and the tears she could no longer hold back flowed slowly down her cheeks.

Lucile put her arms round Madeleine and hugged her. 'Go and get him. Go through the Maie woods. It's still raining. No one will be out. Listen to me, trust no one, German or French. I'll wait for you at the little garden door. I'll go and warn Marthe.'

'Thank you, Madame,' Madeleine stammered.

'Go quickly. Hurry.'

Madeleine opened the door without making a sound and slipped out into the deserted wet garden where tears seemed to drip from the trees. An hour later Lucile let Benoît in through the little green door that opened on to the Maie woods. The storm was over but an angry wind continued to rage.

19

From her room, Madame Angellier could hear the local policeman shouting in front of the municipal hall: 'Public Announcement by Order of German Headquarters . . .' Worried faces appeared at all the windows. 'What is it now?' everyone thought with fear and hatred. Their fear of the Germans was so great that even when German Headquarters ordered the local police to instruct the villagers to destroy rats or have their children vaccinated, they wouldn't relax until long after the final drum roll had ceased and they had asked the educated people in the village – the pharmacist, the notary or the police chief – to repeat what had just been announced.

'Is that all? Are you sure that's all? They're not taking anything else away from us?'

They gradually calmed down.

'Oh, good,' they said, 'good, that's fine then! But I wonder why it's their business . . .'

This would have made everything all right if they hadn't added, 'They're *our* rats and *our* children. What right have they got to destroy our rats and vaccinate our children? What's it to them?'

The Germans present in the square took it upon themselves to explain the orders.

'We must have everyone in good health now, French and German.'

The villagers quickly conceded, with an air of feigned submission ('Oh, they smile like slaves,' thought the elder Madame Angellier): 'Of course . . . Good idea . . . It's in everybody's best interest . . . We understand.'

And each one of them then went home, threw the rat poison in the fire and hurried to the doctor to ask him not to vaccinate their child because he was 'just getting over the mumps', or he wasn't strong enough because they didn't have enough food. Others said straight out, 'We'd rather there were one or two sick kids: maybe it'll get rid of the Fritz.' Alone in the square, the Germans looked around them benevolently and thought that, little by little, the ice was breaking between conquered and conqueror.

On this particular day, however, none of the Germans was smiling or talking to the local people. They stood very straight, a hard stare on their pale faces. The policeman had just played a final drum roll. He was a rather handsome man from the Midi, always happy to be surrounded by women; he was obviously enjoying the importance of what he was about to say. He put his drumsticks under his arm and, with the grace and skill of a magician, he began to read. His attractive, rich, masculine voice echoed in the silence:

A member of the German army has been murdered: an officer of the *Wehrmacht* was killed in a cowardly way by one Benoît Sabarie, residing at . . . in the district of Bussy.

The criminal succeeded in escaping. Any person guilty of providing him with shelter, aid or protection, or who knows his whereabouts, is required to report this information to German Headquarters within forty-eight hours, or will otherwise incur the same punishment as the murderer, that is:

IMMEDIATE EXECUTION BY FIRING SQUAD

Madame Angellier had opened the window slightly. When the policeman had gone, she leaned out and looked into the village square. People were whispering, in shock. Only the day before they had been discussing the requisitioning of the horses; this new disaster added to the previous one led to a sort of disbelief in the slow minds of the country folk: 'Benoît? Benoît did that? It isn't possible!' The secret had been well kept: the villagers were largely ignorant of what happened in the countryside, on the large, jealously guarded farms.

As for the Germans, well, they were better informed. They now understood what the commotion was about, why there had been whistles in the night, and why, the evening before, they had been forbidden to go out after eight o'clock: 'They must have been moving the body and they didn't want us to see.' In the cafés, the Germans talked quietly among themselves. They too had the impression it was all horrible, unreal. For three months they had lived alongside these Frenchmen; they had mixed with them; they had done them no harm; they had even managed, thanks to their consideration and good behaviour, to establish a humane relationship with them. Now, the act of one madman made them doubt everything. Yet it wasn't so much the crime that affected them as the solidarity, the complicity they could sense all around them (in the end, for a man to elude an entire regiment hot on his heels meant that everyone must be helping him, hiding him, feeding him; unless, of course, he was hiding in the woods – but the soldiers had spent the entire night searching them). 'So, if a Frenchman kills me tomorrow,' each soldier was thinking, '*me* they welcome in their house, *me* they smile at, who has a place at their dinner table and is allowed to sit their children on my knee . . . there won't be a single person who'll feel sorry and speak up for me, and everyone will do their best to hide the murderer!' These peaceful country folk with their impassive faces, these women who smiled at them, who had chatted to them yesterday but today walked by embarrassed, avoiding their eye, they were nothing but a group of enemies. They could hardly believe it; they were such nice people . . . Lacombe, the shoemaker, who had offered a bottle of white wine to the Germans the week before because his daughter had just received her high school diploma and he didn't know how else to express his joy; Georges, the miller, a veteran of the last war, who had said, 'Peace as soon as possible and everyone in his own country. That's all we Frenchmen want'; the young women, always eager to laugh, to sing, to share a secret kiss, were they now and for ever to be enemies?

The Frenchmen, meanwhile, were wondering, 'That Willy who asked permission to kiss my kid, saying he had one the same age in Bavaria, that Fritz who helped me take care of my sick husband, that Erwald who thinks France is such a beautiful country, and that other one I saw standing in front of the portrait of my father who was killed in 1915 . . . if tomorrow he was given the order, he'd arrest me, he'd kill me with his own hands without thinking twice? War . . . yes, everyone knows what war is like. But occupation is more terrible in a way, because people get used to each other. We tell ourselves, "They're just like us, after all," but they're not at all the same. We're two different species, irreconcilable, enemies forever.'

Madame Angellier knew them so well, these country people, that she felt she could look at their faces and read their minds. She sniggered. She hadn't been taken in, not her! She hadn't let herself be bought. For everyone in the village of Bussy had a price, just like in the rest of France. The Germans gave money to some of them (the wine merchants who charged soldiers of the *Wehrmacht* a hundred francs for a bottle of Chablis, the farmers who got five francs each for their eggs), to others (the young people, the women) they gave pleasure. The villagers were no longer bored since the Germans arrived. Finally they had someone to talk to. God, even her own daughter-in-law . . . She half closed her eyes and raised her white, translucent hand to cover her lowered eyelids, as if she were trying not to look at a naked body. Yes, the Germans thought they could buy tolerance and forgetfulness that way. And they had.

Bitterly, Madame Angellier made a mental inventory of all the important people in the town. All of them had yielded, all of them had let themselves be seduced: the Montmorts . . . they entertained the Germans in their own home; she'd heard that the Germans were organising a celebration in the Viscount's grounds, by the lake. Madame de Montmort told everyone who would listen that she was outraged, that she would close all the windows so she couldn't hear the music or see the sparklers beneath the trees. But when Lieutenant von Falk and Bonnet, the interpreter, had gone to see her about borrowing chairs, bowls and tablecloths, she'd spent nearly two hours with them. Madame Angellier had heard this from the cook who'd heard it from the groundsman. These aristocrats were part foreigner themselves, after all, if you looked closely enough. Wasn't it true that through their veins ran the foreign blood of Bavaria, Prussia (abomination!) and the Rhineland? Aristocrats intermarried without a thought for national boundaries. But, come to think of it, the upper middle classes weren't much better. People whispered the names of collaborators (and their names were broadcast loudly on English radio every night): the Maltêtes of Lyon, the Péricands of Paris, the Corbin Bank . . . and others as well . . .

Madame Angellier came to feel that she was a race apart – staunch, as implacable as a fortress. Alas, it was the only fortress that remained standing in France, but nothing could bring it down, for its bastions were made, not of stone, not of flesh, not of blood, but of those most intangible and invincible things in the world: love and hate.

She walked quickly and silently up and down the room. 'There's no point in closing my eyes,' she murmured, 'Lucile is ready to fall into the arms of that German.' There was nothing she could do about it. Men had weapons, they knew how to fight. All she could do was spy on them, watch them, listen to them . . . keep her ears open for the sound of footsteps, a sigh in the silence of the night. So that these things, at least, would be neither forgiven nor forgotten, so that when Gaston got back . . . She quivered with intense joy. God, how she despised Lucile! When everyone was finally asleep in the house, the old woman did what she called 'her rounds'. Nothing escaped her. She counted the cigarette stubs in the ashtrays that had traces of lipstick on them; she silently picked up a crumpled, perfumed handkerchief, a flower, an open book. She often heard the piano or the German's low, soft voice as he hummed, stressing some musical phrase.

The piano . . . How could anyone like music? Every note seemed to grate on her exposed nerves and made her groan. She preferred the long conversations that she could just about hear by leaning out of the window above the library window they left open on those beautiful summer evenings. She even preferred the silences that fell between them or Lucile's laughter (laughter . . . when her husband was a prisoner of war! Shameless hussy, bitch, heathen!). Anything was better than music, for music alone can abolish differences of language or culture between two people and evoke something indestructible within them. Madame Angellier sometimes walked up to the German's room. She listened to his breathing, his mild smoker's cough. She crossed the hall where the officer's large green cape hung beneath the stuffed stag's head and slipped some sprigs of heather into his pocket. People said it brought bad luck; she didn't actually believe it herself, but it was worth a try . . .

For a few days now, two to be exact, the atmosphere in the house had seemed even more ominous. The piano was silent. Madame Angellier had heard Lucile and the cook whispering to each other for a long time. (Is she now betraying me as well?) The church bells began to ring. (Ah, the funeral of the murdered officer . . .) There were the armed soldiers, the casket, the wreaths of red flowers . . . The church had been requisitioned. No Frenchman was allowed in. They could hear a choir of excellent voices singing a religious hymn; it was coming from the Chapel of the Virgin. That winter the children had broken a pane of glass during catechism class and it hadn't been replaced. The hymn rose up through this ancient little window set above the altar of the Virgin and obscured by the great branches of the lime tree in the village square. How happily the birds were singing! Now and again, their shrill voices almost drowned out the German hymn. Madame Angellier didn't know the name or age of the dead man. All German Headquarters had said was 'an officer of the *Wehrmacht*'. That was enough. He must have been young. They were all young. 'Well, it's all over for you now. What can you do? That's war.' His mother will eventually understand that, Madame Angellier murmured, nervously fiddling with her black necklace; it was made of jet and ebony, and she'd started wearing it when her husband had died.

She sat motionless until evening, as if riveted to the spot, watching everyone who crossed the street. In the evening . . . not a single sound. 'I haven't heard even the faintest creak from the third step,' thought Madame Angellier, 'the one I hear when Lucile leaves her room and goes out into the garden. The silent, oiled doors are her accomplices, but that faithful old step speaks to me. No, there's not a sound. Are they together already? Maybe they're meeting later?'

The night passed. Madame Angellier was overcome with burning curiosity. She slipped out of her bedroom and placed her ear against the officer's door. Nothing. Not a single sound. If she hadn't heard a man's voice somewhere in the house earlier that evening, she might have thought he hadn't come back yet. But nothing got past her. Any man in the house who wasn't her son was an insult to her. There was a smell of foreign tobacco; she went pale and raised her hands to her forehead, like a woman who thinks she's about to faint. Where is he, the German? Closer than usual since the smoke is coming in through the open window. Is he going through the house? Perhaps he's leaving soon and knows it, so he's choosing the furniture he'll take: his share of the spoils. Didn't the Prussians steal the grandfather clocks in 1870? Today's soldiers won't have changed that much. She imagined his sacrilegious hands rifling through the attic, the larder and the wine cellar.

Thinking about it, it was the wine cellar that worried Madame Angellier most. She never drank wine; she recalled having had a sip of champagne for Gaston's First Communion and at her wedding. But wine was somehow part of their heritage and, as such, was sacred, like everything destined to continue after we die. That Château-d'Yquem, that . . . she'd been given those wines by her husband to pass on to her son. They had buried the best bottles in the sand, but that German . . . Who could tell? Instructed by Lucile perhaps . . . Let's go and see . . . Here's the wine cellar with its door and iron locks, like a fortress. Here's the hiding place only she knows about by a cross marked on the wall. No, everything seems in order here as well. Nevertheless, Madame Angellier's heart is pounding furiously. It is clear that Lucile has just been down to the cellar; her perfume lingers in the air. Following its scent, Madame Angellier goes back upstairs, through the kitchen, the dining room and, finally, on the staircase comes face to face with Lucile carrying a plate, a glass and an empty wine bottle. So that's why she went down into the wine cellar and the larder, where Madame Angellier had thought she heard footsteps.

'A romantic little supper?' said Madame Angellier in a voice as low and stinging as a whip.

'I beg you, please be quiet. If you knew . . .'

'And with a German! Under my own roof! In your husband's house, you miserable . . .'

'Be quiet, won't you! Can't you see the German isn't back yet? He'll be here any minute. Let me go and tidy up. In the meantime, you go upstairs, open the door to the old playroom and see who's in there . . . Then, after you've seen, meet me in the dining room. I was wrong, very wrong to act without telling you; I had no right to put your life in danger . . .'

'You've hidden that farmer here . . . the one accused of the murder?'

At that very moment they heard the regiment. There was the hoarse shout of orders being given and immediately afterwards the sound of the German officer coming up the steps to the house. His walk was unmistakable. No Frenchman could produce that hammering of boots, that rattling of spurs. It was a walk that could only belong to a proud conqueror, striding over the enemy's cobblestones, joyfully trampling the defeated land.

Madame Angellier opened the door to her own room, pushed Lucile inside, followed her in and turned the key. She took the plate and glass from Lucile, rinsed them in her dressing-room washstand, carefully dried them and put away the bottle after checking the label. Table wine? Yes, well done! 'She's prepared to be shot for hiding a man who killed a German,' thought Lucile, 'but she wouldn't be happy to give him a good bottle of Burgundy. Thank goodness it was dark in the cellar and I was lucky enough to take a bottle of red wine worth only three francs.' She remained silent, waiting with intense curiosity to hear what Madame Angellier would say. She couldn't have kept the presence of a stranger hidden from her much longer: this old woman could see through walls.

Finally, Madame Angellier spoke. 'Did you think I would hand that man over to the Germans?' she asked. Her pinched nostrils were trembling; her eyes sparkled. She seemed happy, elated, almost mad, like a former actress who is once again playing the role she starred in long ago and whose nuances and gestures are second nature to her. 'Has he been here long?'

'Three days.'

'Why didn't you say anything to me?'

Lucile didn't reply.

'You're mad to have hidden him in the blue room. He should stay in here. Since all my meals are brought to me upstairs, there is no risk of anyone challenging you: you have your excuse. He can sleep on the sofa in the dressing room.'

'But think about it, Mother! If he's found in our house the risk is terrible. I can take all the blame, say that you didn't know what I was doing, which is actually the truth, but if he's in your room . . .'

Madame Angellier shrugged her shoulders. 'Tell me everything,' she said, with an eagerness in her voice that Lucile hadn't heard for a long time. 'Tell me exactly how it all happened. All I know is what the police said. Whom did he kill? Was it just one German? Did he wound any others? Was it at least a high-ranking officer . . . ?'

'She's in her element,' thought Lucile. 'She's so eager to do her duty in the call to arms . . . Mothers and women in love: both ferocious females. I'm not a mother and I'm not in love (Bruno? No. I mustn't think of Bruno now, I mustn't . . .), so I can't see things in the same way. I'm more detached, colder, calmer, more civilised, I still believe that. And also . . . I can't imagine that all three of us are really risking our lives. It seems so melodramatic, so extreme. Yet Bonnet is dead, killed by a farmer whom some would treat as a criminal and others as a hero. And what about me? I have to choose. I've already chosen . . . in spite of myself. And I thought I was free . . .'

'You can question Sabarie yourself, Mother,' she said. 'I'll bring him to you. Make sure you don't let him smoke; the Lieutenant will smell someone else's tobacco in the house. I think that's the only danger; they won't search the house; they would scarcely believe anyone would dare hide him here in the village. They'll raid the farms. But we could be denounced.'

'Frenchmen don't denounce one another,' the old woman said proudly. 'You've forgotten that, my girl, since you got friendly with the Germans.'

Lucile remembered something Lieutenant von Falk had told her in confidence: 'The very first day we arrived,' he'd said, 'there was a package of anonymous letters waiting for us at Headquarters. People were accusing each other of spreading English and Gaullist propaganda, of hoarding supplies, of being spies. If we'd taken them all seriously, everyone in the region would be in prison. I had the whole lot thrown on to the fire. People's lives aren't worth much and defeat arouses the worst in men. In Germany it was exactly the same.' But Lucile said nothing of this to her mother-in-law and left her to make up the sofa in the dressing room. She looked impassioned, light-hearted and twenty years younger. Using her own mattress, pillow and her best sheets, Madame Angellier lovingly prepared a bed for Benoît Sabarie.

20

For a long time the Germans had been making arrangements for a great celebration at the Château de Montmort. It was to take place on the night of 21 June. This was the anniversary of the regiment's arrival in Paris, but no Frenchman was to know this was the reason the date had been chosen: the commanding officers had given orders to respect French national pride. All races are aware of their own faults; they know them better than even the most malevolent foreign observer. In a friendly conversation, a young Frenchman had recently told Bruno von Falk: 'We Frenchmen have very short memories; this is both our strength and our weakness! We forgot that after 1918 we were the victors and that was our downfall; we'll forget after 1940 that we were defeated, which will perhaps be our salvation.'

'As a nation, we Germans too have a weakness that is also our greatest quality: our tactlessness, which is really a lack of imagination; we are incapable of putting ourselves in anyone else's place; we hurt people for no reason; we make others hate us, but that allows us to behave inflexibly and without faltering.'

Since the Germans mistrusted their tendency to be tactless, they were particularly careful of what they said when speaking to the locals; they were therefore accused of being hypocrites. Even when Lucile asked Bruno 'And what's this celebration in honour of?' he avoided answering honestly. In Germany they always had a party around 24 June, he said, as it was the shortest night of the year. However, since the 24th had been set aside for large-scale manoeuvres, they had brought the date forward.

Everything was ready. They were setting up tables in the castle grounds; they had asked the local people to lend them their best table linen for a few hours. With respect, infinite care and under the supervision of Bruno himself, the soldiers had made their selection from the piles of damask tablecloths that lay deep inside cupboards. The middle-class ladies, eyes raised to heaven – 'as if they were expecting to see Sainte Geneviève herself descend from on high,' Bruno thought mischievously, 'to strike down the sacrilegious Germans, guilty of daring to touch this family treasure made of fine linen, hemstitched, embroidered with birds and flowers' – these ladies stood guard and counted their towels in front of the soldiers. 'I had four dozen of them: forty-eight, Lieutenant, and now there are only forty-seven.'

'Allow me, Madame, to count them again with you. You're just upset, Madame, I'm sure we haven't lost any. Here's the last one; it fell on the floor. Allow me to pick it up and return it to you, Madame.'

'Oh, so it is, I'm sorry, Monsieur,' the lady replied with her most sour smile, 'it's just that when cupboards are turned out like this, things disappear if you're not careful.'

Nevertheless, he'd found a way to cajole them. 'Naturally, we have no right to ask you to lend us these things,' he said, saluting solemnly. 'You know we're not entitled to them . . .'

He even implied that the General shouldn't find out: 'He's so strict. He'd tell us off for behaving impertinently, but we're so bored. We want to have a wonderful party. It's a favour we're asking of you, Madame. You are perfectly free to refuse.' Magic words! Even the most sullen face lit up with a hint of a smile (like the pale and dismal light of the winter sun, thought Bruno, shining on one of your opulent, decrepit houses).

'But why shouldn't you enjoy yourselves, Monsieur? You will take good care of these tablecloths, won't you? They were part of my dowry.'

'Ah, Madame! I give you my word of honour that they will be returned to you intact, washed and ironed . . .'

'No, no! Just give them back as they are, thank you. Wash my linen! But we don't send them to the laundry, Monsieur. The maid launders them under my supervision. We use fine ashes . . .'

Then all he had to do was smile sweetly and say, 'Well, what do you know! So does my mother.'

'Oh, really? Your mother too? What a coincidence. Perhaps you could use some napkins as well?'

'Madame, I didn't like to ask.'

'I can let you have two, three, four dozen. Would you like any cutlery?'

The soldiers had come out of the houses weighed down with clean, scented linen, their pockets full of dessert knives and holding, as if it were the Holy Sacrament, an antique punchbowl or some Empire coffee pot whose handle was decorated with ornamental leaves. Everything was stored in the château kitchens until the celebration.

The young women laughed and called out to the soldiers, 'How are you going to dance with no women?'

'We'll have no choice, ladies. That's war for you.'

The musicians would play from the conservatory. At the entrance to the grounds were pillars and poles decorated with garlands of flowers that would be used to hoist the flags: the regimental flag, which had been carried during the campaigns in Poland, Belgium and France and had emerged victorious from three capital cities, and the swastika – stained, Lucile whispered, with the blood of Europe. Yes, sadly, all of Europe, Germany included: the noblest, youngest, most fervent blood, which is always the first to be shed in battle. And with whatever blood remained, the world would have to be rebuilt. That is why the aftermath of war is so difficult . . .

Every day, from Chalon-sur-Saône, Moulins, Nevers, Paris and Epernay, military trucks arrived with cases and cases of champagne. If there couldn't be women, there would at least be wine, music and fireworks down by the lake.

'We're going to come and watch,' the young Frenchwomen said. 'Forget the curfew for one night, all right? Since you'll be having fun, you could at least let us have a good time, too. We'll take the road down to the château and watch you dance.'

Laughing, the girls tried on party hats made of silvery lace, masks and paper flowers for their hair. What party had they been meant for? Everything was slightly crumpled, faded, as if it were second-hand or from some costume wardrobe in Cannes or Deauville belonging to a nightclub manager who, before September 1939, was counting on future seasons.

'How funny you'll look in all this,' the women said.

The soldiers strutted about making funny faces.

Champagne, music, dancing, a rush of pleasure . . . so they could briefly forget the war and how quickly time was passing. The only thing they worried about was the possibility of a storm that night. But the nights were so clear . . . Then, suddenly, there was this terrible disaster! A comrade murdered, unheroically, killed by some drunken cowardly farmer.

They had considered cancelling the celebration. But no! The warrior mentality reigned supreme here: the tacit acceptance that, immediately after you had died, your comrades would dispose of your shirts, your boots, and spend the whole night playing cards while you lay in the corner of some tent – if your remains had been found, that is. Yet it was also a mentality that accepted death as something natural, an ordinary soldier's destiny, and therefore refused to sacrifice a moment's pleasure because of it. Besides, the officers' main responsibility was to think of their men, to distract them from demoralising thoughts about future dangers and how very short life was. No, Bonnet had died without suffering much. He'd been given a beautiful funeral. He would not have wanted his comrades to be disappointed because of him. The celebration would take place as arranged.

Bruno gave in to the childish excitement around him. It was mad and slightly desperate – the kind of excitement that a truce brings out in soldiers, who see the possibility of a moment's relief from the day-to-day boredom. He didn't want to think about Bonnet, or about what was whispered behind the closed shutters of these grey, cold enemy houses. Like a child who's been promised to go to the circus and is then told he must stay home because some old, annoying relative is sick, Bruno wanted to say, 'But what has that got to do with it? That's your problem. What has it got to do with me?' Did it have anything to do with him, Bruno von Falk? He wasn't just a soldier of the Reich; he wasn't motivated uniquely by what was best for his regiment or his country. He was a sensitive human being. He, like everyone else, was looking for happiness, the unhampered development of his abilities. Yet (like everyone else, sadly, during these times) his justifiable desires were constantly being thwarted by certain national interests called war, public security, the necessity of maintaining the prestige of the victorious army. A bit like the children of princes whose sole reason for existence is to carry out the wishes of their father, the king. He felt this majesty, the way the greatness and power of Germany reflected on him, as he walked through the streets of Bussy, as he rode through a village on horseback, as his spurs rattled at the doorstep of a French home. But what the French would never understand was that he was neither proud nor arrogant, but sincerely humble: terrified by the magnitude of his task.

But he didn't want to think about that, not today. He preferred to enjoy the idea of the ball, or to dream about things he could never have: Lucile by his side, for example . . . Lucile who could come with him to the ball . . . 'It's madness,' he said to himself, smiling. 'Oh, I don't care. In my soul I'm free.' He imagined the dress Lucile would wear: not a modern dress, but the kind you might find in some romantic print; a white dress with layer upon layer of chiffon, billowing out like a flower, so that when he danced with her, when he held her in his arms, he could feel the frothy lace brushing against his legs. He went pale and bit his lip. She was so beautiful . . . Lucile close to him, on a night like this, in the Montmorts' grounds, with the fanfares playing and fireworks in the distance . . . Lucile who, above all, would understand and share the almost religious thrill he felt in his soul when, standing alone in the dark, he felt the distant presence of a vague and terrible multitude – the regiment, the soldiers – and even further away, the army that fought and suffered, and the victorious army that occupied the cities.

'With her', he said to himself, 'I would be inspired.' He had worked very hard. He used to live in a state of perpetual creative exaltation, mad about music, he would say, laughing. Yes, with her and a little freedom, a little peace, he could have done great things. 'It's such a shame' – he sighed – 'such a shame . . . one of these days we'll receive orders to leave and we'll be at war again. There will be other people, other countries, such extreme physical exhaustion that I'll never be able to finish my military career. And the music, still waiting to find expression. Musical phrases, delightful chords, subtle dissonances stand poised . . . wild, winged creatures frightened off by the crash of weapons. It's such a shame. Did Bonnet care about anything besides war? I have no idea. No one can ever truly know another human being. But what if . . . he . . . who died at the age of nineteen, found more fulfilment than me, who's still alive?'

He stopped in front of the Angelliers' house. He was home. In three months he had come to think of all this as his own: the iron door, the prison-like lock, the hall with its musty smell, the back garden – the garden bathed in moonlight – and the woods in the distance. It was a June evening, divinely sweet; the roses were in bloom, but even their perfume was overpowered by the smell of hay and strawberries that hovered everywhere since the day before, for it was harvest time. On the road, the Lieutenant had come across some wagons full of freshly cut hay, drawn by cattle as there were no horses left. He had silently admired the slow, regal pace of the cattle pulling their sweet-smelling goods. The farmers looked away as he went past; he had noticed . . . but . . . he felt happy again and light-hearted. He went into the kitchen and asked for something to eat. The cook served him unusually quickly and without replying to his pleasantries.

'Where is Madame?' he said finally.

'I'm here,' said Lucile.

She had come in without making a sound as he was finishing a slice of cured ham on a big piece of fresh bread.

He looked up at her. 'You're so pale,' he said softly, sounding worried.

'Pale? Not really. It's just been very hot today.'

'Where is your good mother?' he asked, smiling. 'Let's go for a walk outside. Meet me in the garden.'

A little later, as he was walking slowly down the wide path, between the fruit trees, he saw her. She came towards him, her head lowered. When she was a few steps away, she hesitated. Then, as she always did as soon as they were hidden from sight by the great lime tree, she went up to him and slipped her arm through his. They walked a while in silence.

'They've cut the hay in the meadows,' she said finally.

He closed his eyes, breathed in the aroma. The moon was the colour of honey in a milky sky where wispy clouds drifted by. It was still light out.

'It will be nice weather tomorrow, for our celebration.'

'Is it tomorrow? I thought . . .'

She didn't finish what she was saying.

'Why not?' he said, frowning.

'Nothing, I just thought . . .'

He nervously flicked at the flowers with the riding crop he was holding. 'What are people saying?'

'About what?'

'You know very well. About the crime.'

'I don't know. I haven't seen anyone.'

'And what about you? What do you think?'

'That it's terrible, of course.'

'Terrible and incomprehensible. After all, what have we, as people, done to them? It's not our fault if we upset them sometimes, we're just following orders; we're soldiers. And I know for a fact that the regiment did everything possible to behave properly, humanely, didn't they?'

'Certainly.'

'Naturally, I wouldn't say this to anyone else . . . Among soldiers it's understood that we don't show pity towards a comrade who's been killed. That would go against military thinking, which requires that we consider ourselves solely as part of a whole. Soldiers can die just so long as the regiment lives. That's why we're not postponing tomorrow's celebration,' he continued. 'But I can tell you the truth, Lucile. My heart breaks at the thought of this nineteen-year-old boy being murdered. He was a very distant relative of mine. Our families know each other. And then, there's something else I find stupid and revolting. Why did he have to shoot the dog, our mascot, our poor Bubi? If I ever find that man, I'd happily kill him with my bare hands.'

'I expect that's what he must have been saying to himself for a long time,' Lucile said softly. 'If I ever got my hands on one of those Germans, or even one of their dogs, how happy I'd be!'

They looked at each other, dismayed; the words had slipped through their lips, almost against their will.

'It's the same old story,' said Bruno, forcing himself to sound lighthearted. '*Es ist die alte Geschichte.* The conquerors don't understand why people want nothing to do with them. After 1918, you tried in vain to make us believe that we were stubborn because we couldn't forget our sunken fleet, our lost colonies, our destroyed empire. But how can you compare the resentment of a great nation with one farmer's blind outburst of hatred?'

Lucile picked a few sprigs of mignonette, smelled them, crushed them in her hands. 'Has he been caught?' she asked.

'No. Oh, he'll be long gone by now. None of these good people would dare hide him. They know only too well they'd be risking their own lives and they're fond of their lives, aren't they? Almost as fond of their lives as their money . . .'

Smiling slightly, he looked around at all the low, squat, secret houses slumbering in the dusk. She could see he was imagining them full of chatty and emotional old women, prudent and nit-picking middle-class ladies, and further away, in the countryside, farmers who were more like animals. It was almost true, partly true. Yet there remained something shadowy, mysterious, impossible to articulate, and over which, Lucile suddenly thought, remembering something she'd read at school, 'even the proudest tyrant will never rule'.

'Let's walk on a bit further,' he said.

The path was lined with lilies; their silky buds had burst open under the last rays of the sun and now the sweet-smelling flowers blossomed proudly in the night air. During the three months they had known each other, Lucile and the German had taken many walks together, but never in such splendid weather, so conducive to love. By tacit agreement they tried to forget everything except each other. 'It's nothing to do with us, it's not our fault. In the heart of every man and every woman a kind of Garden of Eden endures, where there is no war, no death, where wild animals and deer live together in peace. All we have to do is to reclaim that paradise, just close our eyes to everything else. We are a man and a woman. We love each other.'

Reason and emotion, they both believed, could make them enemies, but between them was a harmony of the senses that nothing could destroy; the silent understanding that binds a man in love and a willing woman in mutual desire. In the shade of a cherry tree heavy with fruit, near the little fountain where the frogs croaked, he had to have her. He pulled her into his arms with a violence he couldn't control, tearing at her clothes, crushing her breasts.

'No, never!' she cried out. 'Never!' Never would she be his. She was afraid of him. She no longer craved his touch. She wasn't depraved enough (or too young perhaps) to allow her fear to be transformed into desire. The love she had welcomed so willingly that she didn't believe it could be shameful, suddenly seemed to her disgraceful madness. She was lying; she was betraying him. How could you call that love? What had it been, then? Simply a moment of pleasure? But she was incapable of feeling even pleasure. What now made them enemies was neither reason nor emotion, but the secret movements of blood they had counted on to unite them and over which they were powerless. He touched her with his beautiful slim hands. She had so desired them, yet she felt nothing, nothing but the cold buckle of his uniform pressing against her chest, which froze her to the core. He was whispering to her in German. Foreigner! Foreigner! Enemy, in spite of everything. Forever he would be the enemy, with his green uniform, with his heavenly beautiful hair and his confident mouth.

Suddenly, it was he who pushed her away. 'I won't take you by force. I'm not a drunken boor . . . Just go.'

But the chiffon ties of her dress were caught on the officer's metal buttons. Slowly, his hands shaking, he freed her. She, meanwhile, was looking anxiously towards the house. The first lamps were being lit. Would Madame Angellier remember to close both sets of curtains so the fugitive's silhouette couldn't be seen through the window? People weren't careful enough on these beautiful June evenings. Secrets were revealed through open bedroom windows, where anyone could see in. People weren't careful enough . . . They could distinctly hear the English radio coming from a neighbouring house; the cart passing by on the road was full of contraband; weapons were hidden in every home. His head bowed, Bruno held the long ties of her flowing belt in his hands.

'I thought . . .' he finally said sadly. He stopped, hesitated, then continued, 'that you cared for me . . .'

'I thought so too.'

'And you don't?'

'No. It cannot be.'

She took a few steps back and stood slightly away from him. For a moment they just looked at each other. The heart-rending blast of a trumpet sounded: it was curfew. The German soldiers walked through groups of people in the village square. 'Go along now. Time for bed,' they said politely. The women protested and laughed. The trumpet blasted again. The locals went home. The Germans remained. The sound of their monotonous rounds was the only thing that would be heard until daybreak.

'It's curfew' said Lucile impassively. 'I have to go back. I have to close all the windows. I was told yesterday at Headquarters that the light from the sitting room wasn't blocked out enough.'

'As long as I'm here, you don't have to worry about anything. No one will bother you.'

She didn't reply. She held out her hand to him; he kissed it and she walked back to the house. Long after midnight, he was still walking around in the garden. She could hear the brief, monotonous calls of the guards in the street, and beneath her window her jailer's slow, steady walk. Sometimes she thought, 'He loves me, he doesn't suspect anything,' and sometimes, 'He's suspicious, he's watching, he's waiting.

'It's such a shame,' she thought in a sudden moment of honesty. 'It's such a shame, it was a beautiful night . . . a night made for love . . . We shouldn't have wasted it. The rest isn't important.' But she stayed where she was; she didn't get out of her bed to go to the window. She felt bound and gagged – a prisoner – united with this captive land that dreamed and sighed softly with impatience; she let the empty night drift by.

21

The village had been looking cheerful all afternoon. In the square the soldiers had decorated the flagpoles with leaves and flowers, and on the balcony of the municipal hall, red and black banners with Gothic writing floated below the swastikas. It was a beautiful day. The flags and banners billowed in the soft, cool breeze. Two young soldiers with pink faces were pushing a cart full of roses.

'Are they for the tables?' the women asked, curious.

'Yes,' the soldiers proudly replied. One of them picked out a rosebud and, with an exaggerated salute, offered it to a young girl, who blushed.

'It will be a wonderful party.'

'*Wir hoffen es*. We hope so. We're going to a lot of trouble,' the soldiers replied.

The cooks were working outdoors preparing pâtés and cakes for the dinner. To avoid the dust, they had set up beneath the great lime trees that surrounded the church. The head chef, in uniform but wearing a high hat and apron of dazzling white to protect his jacket, was putting the finishing touches to an enormous gâteau. He decorated it with cream swirls and candied fruit. The smell of sugar filled the air. The children squealed with delight. The head chef, bursting with pride but trying not to show it, frowned and scolded them: 'All right, back up a bit, how do you expect us to work with you crowding around?' At first, the women pretended not to be interested in the cake. 'Ugh! . . . It will be horrible . . . They don't have the right kind of flour . . .' Gradually, they moved closer, shyly at first, then more confidently. Eventually they found the audacity to start giving advice, as women do.

'Hey, Monsieur, there's not enough decoration on this side . . . you need some angelica.'

They ended up helping. Pushing back the delighted children, they bustled about round the table with the Germans; one of them chopped the almonds; another crushed the sugar.

'Is it just for the officers? Or will the ordinary soldiers have some too?' they asked.

'It's for everyone, everyone.'

'Everyone except us!' They sniggered.

The head chef raised the earthenware platter holding the enormous cake and with a little salute showed it to the crowd, who laughed and applauded. Then he carefully laid it on a huge wooden plank carried by two soldiers (one at the head, one at the foot) and they all set off for the château. Meanwhile, officers invited from all the regiments billeted in the area began to arrive. Their long green capes floated behind them. The shopkeepers stood in front of their doors, smiling at them. They had been bringing up their remaining supplies from the cellars since morning: the Germans were buying everything they had, and paying well. One officer snapped up the last few bottles of Benedictine brandy, another paid 1200 francs for lingerie for his wife; the soldiers crowded round the shop windows and looked lovingly at the pink and blue bibs. Finally, one of them couldn't help himself and, as soon as the officer had gone, he called the saleswoman over and pointed to some baby clothes; he was very young with blue eyes.

'Boy? Girl?' the saleswoman asked.

'I don't know,' he said ingenuously. 'My wife will write and tell me; it happened during my last leave, a month ago.'

Everyone around him started laughing. He blushed but seemed very happy. He bought a rattle and a little robe. He came back across the road in triumph.

They were rehearsing the music in the village square. Next to the circle formed by the drums, the trumpets and the fifes, another circle formed round the regimental postmaster. The Frenchmen noted the open mouths and eyes bright with hope, and nodded politely, thinking sadly, 'We know what it's like . . . when you're waiting for news from another country. We've all done that . . .' Meanwhile, an enormous young German with huge thighs and a fat bottom that threatened to split his tight riding breeches entered the Hôtel des Voyageurs and, for the third time, asked to look at the barometer. It was still set at fair. The German, beaming with delight, said, 'Nothing to worry about. No storm tonight. *Gott mit uns.*'

'Yes, yes.' The waitress nodded in agreement.

This innocent delight spread to the customers and the owner himself (who supported the British); everyone stood up and went over to the barometer: 'Nothing to worry about! Nothing! Is good . . . nice party,' they said, deliberately speaking in pidgin French so he'd understand them better.

And the German slapped everyone on the back with a wide grin while repeating, '*Gott mit uns.*'

'Sure, sure, *Got meedns.* He's drunk, that Fritz,' they whispered behind his back rather sympathetically. 'We know what it's like. He's been celebrating since yesterday . . . He's a big lad . . . Well, so what! Why shouldn't they have fun? They're men after all.'

Having created a sympathetic atmosphere with his words and appearance, and after downing three bottles of beer one after the other, the German, beaming, finally left. As the day progressed, all the local people began to feel happy and light-headed, as if they too would be going to the ball. In the kitchens, the young girls listlessly rinsed the glasses and every few minutes leaned out of the window to watch the groups of Germans going up to the château.

'Did you see the second lieutenant who lives at the church house? Isn't he handsome with his smooth skin. There's the Commandant's new interpreter. How old is he, do you think? I'd say he couldn't be more than twenty, that boy. They're all so young. Oh, there's the Angelliers' lieutenant. He'd drive me wild, he would. You can tell he's a gentleman. What a beautiful horse! They really do have beautiful horses, by God.' The young girls sighed.

Then the bitter voice of some old man dozing by the stove called out, 'Sure they do, they're *our* horses!'

The old man spat into the fire, muttering curses that the young girls didn't hear. They were only interested in one thing: to hurry and finish the dishes so they could go and watch the Germans at the château. Running alongside the grounds was a path lined with acacias, lime trees and beautiful aspens with leaves that incessantly trembled, incessantly rustled in the wind. Between the branches it was possible to see the lake and the lawns where the tables had been set up and, on the hill, the château, its doors and windows wide open, where the regimental orchestra would play. By eight o'clock, everyone in the village was there; the young girls had dragged their parents along; children that the young women hadn't wanted to leave at home were sleeping in their mothers' arms, or running about shouting and playing with the pebbles; some pushed aside the soft branches of the acacia trees and watched the scene with curiosity: the musicians on the terrace, the German officers lying on the grass or slowly strolling through the trees, the tables covered with dazzling linen, the silver reflecting the last rays of the sun and, behind each chair, a soldier standing as still as if he were at inspection – the orderlies who would act as waiters. The orchestra played a particularly lively, cheerful song; the officers took their places. Before sitting down, the head of the table ('the place of honour . . . a general,' whispered the French) and all the other officers stood at attention, raised their glasses and shouted, '*Heil Hitler!*' It took a long time for the roar to subside; it reverberated through the air with a pure, fierce, metallic echo. Then they could hear the hubbub of conversations, the clinking of cutlery and the sound of the night birds singing.

The Frenchmen strained to see if they could recognise people they knew. Next to the General with the white hair, delicate features and long hooked nose, were the officers from Headquarters.

'That one, over there on the left, look, he's the one who took my car, the bastard! The little blond one with the rosy complexion next to him, he's nice, he talks good French. Where's the Angelliers' German? He's called Bruno . . . pretty name . . . It's a shame it'll be dark soon; we won't be able to see anything then . . . The shoemaker's Fritz told me they were going to light torches. Oh, Mummy, that will be so pretty! Let's stay till then. What will the owners of the château be saying about all this? They won't be able to sleep tonight. Who's going to eat the leftovers? Who, Mummy? The Mayor?'

'Oh, be quiet, you silly thing, there won't be any leftovers, they've got hearty appetites.'

Little by little, darkness spread across the lawns; they could still make out the gold decorations on the uniforms, the Germans' blond hair, the musicians' brass instruments on the terrace, but they had lost their glow. All the light of the day, fleeing the earth, seemed for one brief moment to take refuge in the sky; pink clouds spiralled round the full moon that was as green as pistachio sorbet and as clear as glass; it was reflected in the lake. Exquisite perfumes filled the air: grass, fresh hay, wild strawberries. The music kept playing. Suddenly, the torches were lit; as the soldiers carried them along, they cast their light over the messy tables, the empty glasses, for the officers were now gathered around the lake, singing and laughing. There was the lively, happy sound of champagne corks popping.

'Oh, those bastards! And to think it's our wine they're drinking,' the Frenchmen said, but without real bitterness, because all happiness is contagious and disarms the spirit of hatred.

And of course, the Germans seemed to like the champagne so much (and had paid so much for it!) that the Frenchmen were vaguely flattered by their good taste.

'They're having a good time. Thank goodness it's not all war . . . Don't worry, they'll be fighting again . . . They say it will be over this year. Sure it would be bad if they won, but what can you do, it's got to end . . . Everyone's so miserable in the cities . . . and we want our prisoners back.'

All along the road, the young girls held each other by the waist and danced to the soft lively music. The drums and brass instruments gave the waltzes and tunes from operettas a bright tone that was victorious, happy, heroic and joyous, that made their hearts beat faster; sometimes a low, prolonged, powerful note rose above the lively arpeggios like the echo of a distant storm.

When it was completely dark they started singing. Groups of soldiers sang to one another from the terrace and the park, from the banks of the lake and the lake itself, where boats decorated with flowers drifted past. The Frenchmen listened, delighted, in spite of themselves. It was nearly midnight, but no one would have dreamed of leaving their spot in the tall grass or between the branches.

Only the burning torches and sparklers lit up the trees. Wonderful voices filled the night. Suddenly, there was a long silence. They could see the Germans running like shadows against a background of green flame and moonlight.

'They're going to light the fireworks!' shouted a little boy. 'They're definitely having fireworks. I know. The Fritz told me.'

His shrill voice could be heard down by the lake.

His mother scolded him: 'Be quiet. You're not allowed to call them Fritz or Boches. Not ever. They don't like it. Just be quiet and watch.'

But they couldn't see anything now except the shadows of men scurrying about. From the terrace someone shouted something they couldn't make out; it provoked a long, low commotion, like rumbling thunder.

'What are they shouting about? Could you hear? It must be *"Heil Hitler, Heil Goering! Heil the Third Reich!"* or something like that. We can't hear a thing now. They're not talking any more. Look, the musicians are leaving. Do you think they've had some news? Do you think they've invaded England? Well, I think they just got cold outside and they're moving the party inside the château,' said the pharmacist pointedly; he was worried about the night dampness because of his rheumatism.

He took his young wife's arm. 'Why don't we go home too, Linette?'

But she wouldn't hear of it. 'Oh! Let's stay, just a little longer. They're going to sing again, it was so nice.'

The French waited but there was no more singing. Soldiers carrying torches were running between the château and the grounds as if they were conveying orders. There was even some shouting. Beneath the moonlight, empty boats drifted on the lake; all the officers had jumped out on to the bank. They were walking along, talking to each other quickly in loud voices. Although the French could hear them, no one understood what they were saying. One by one, the sparklers went out. The spectators began yawning. 'It's late. Let's go home. The party's definitely over.'

They made their way in little groups back to the village: the young girls, arm in arm, walking in front of their parents; the sleepy children dragging their feet.

When they got to the first house, they saw an old man sitting on a straw chair, smoking his pipe. 'Well,' he said. 'Is the party over, then?'

'Yes. Oh, they had such a good time!'

'Well, they won't be having a good time for long,' the old man said calmly. 'I've just heard on the radio that they're at war with Russia.' He knocked his pipe against his chair several times to get rid of the ashes, then looked at the sky. 'It'll be dry again tomorrow . . . Not good for the gardens, this weather.'

22

They're going!

For several days they had been waiting for the Germans to leave. The soldiers themselves had announced it: they were being sent to Russia. When the French heard the news, they looked at them with curiosity ('Are they happy? Worried? Will they win or lose?'). As for the Germans, they tried to work out what the French were thinking: were they happy to see them go? Did they secretly wish they'd all get killed? Did anyone feel sorry for them? Would they miss them? Of course they wouldn't be missed as Germans, as conquerors (they weren't naïve enough to think that), but would the French miss these Pauls, Siegfrieds, Oswalds who had lived under their roofs for three months, showed them pictures of their wives and mothers, shared more than one bottle of wine with them? But both the French and the Germans remained inscrutable; they were polite, careful of what they said – 'Well, that's war . . . We can't do anything about it . . . right? It won't last long, at least we hope not!' They said goodbye to one another like passengers on a ship who have reached their final port of call. They would write to each other. They would see each other again some day. They would always remember the happy weeks they'd spent together. More than one soldier whispered to a pensive young girl, 'When the war is over I'll come back.' When the war is over . . . How far away that was!

They were leaving today, 1 July 1941. The French were concerned primarily with the question of whether the village would be occupied by other soldiers; because if so, they thought bitterly, well, it wasn't worth going to the trouble of changing them. They were used to this lot. Maybe the new ones would be worse . . .

Lucile slipped into Madame Angellier's room to tell her that it was definite, they'd received their orders, the Germans were leaving that very night. They could reasonably hope for at least a few hours' grace before any new soldiers arrived and they should take advantage of this to help

Benoît escape. It was impossible to hide him until the end of the war, equally impossible to send him home as long as the area remained occupied. There was only one hope: to get him across the demarcation line. However, the line was closely guarded and would be even more so during the evacuation of the troops.

'It's dangerous,' said Lucile, 'very dangerous.' She looked pale and tired: for several nights she had hardly slept. She looked at Benoît, standing opposite her. Her feelings towards him were an odd combination of fear, incomprehension and envy: his calm, severe, almost brutal expression intimidated her. He was a big, muscular man, with a ruddy complexion; beneath thick eyebrows, his pale eyes were sometimes unbearable to look at. His tanned, lined hands were the hands of a labourer and a soldier, thought Lucile: earth or blood, it was the same to him. Neither remorse nor sorrow troubled his sleep, of that she was sure; everything was simple to this man.

'I've thought about it a lot, Madame Lucile,' he said quietly.

Despite the fortress-like walls and closed doors, whenever all three of them were together, they felt they were being watched and said what they needed to very quickly and almost in a whisper.

'No one will be able to get me across the line. It's too risky. I know I have to leave, but I want to go to Paris.'

'To Paris?'

'While I was with the regiment I had some friends . . .'

He hesitated.

'We were taken prisoner together. We escaped together. They work in Paris. If I can find them they'll help me. One of them wouldn't be alive now if . . .'

He looked at his hands and fell silent.

'What I need is to get to Paris without getting arrested on the way and to find someone I can trust to put me up for a day or two until I find my friends.'

'I don't know anyone in Paris,' murmured Lucile. 'But in any case, you'll need identity papers.'

'As soon as I find my friends, Madame Lucile, I'll be able to get hold of some papers.'

'But how? What do your friends do?'

'They're in politics,' Benoît said curtly.

'Communists . . .' murmured Lucile, recalling certain rumours she'd heard about Benoît's ideas and activities. 'The Communists will be hunted down now. You're risking your life.'

'It won't be the first time, Madame Lucile, or the last,' said Benoît. 'You get used to it.'

'And how will you get to Paris? You can't take the train; your description is posted everywhere.'

'On foot. By bicycle. When I escaped I was on foot. It don't scare me.'

'But the police . . .'

'The people who put me up two years ago will remember me and won't shop me to the police. It's safer than here where plenty of people hate me. It'll be easier.'

'Such a long journey, on foot, alone . . .'

Madame Angellier, who hadn't said a word until now, was standing next to the window, her pale eyes watching the Germans come and go across the village square; she raised her hand to warn them. 'Someone's coming.'

All three of them fell silent. Lucile's heart was pounding so violently, so quickly that she was ashamed; the others could surely hear it, she thought. The old woman and the farmer remained impassive. They could hear Bruno's voice downstairs; he was looking for Lucile; he opened several doors.

'Do you know where Madame Lucile is?' he asked the cook.

'She's gone out,' Marthe replied.

Lucile sighed with relief. 'I'd better go down,' she said. 'He's looking for me to say goodbye.'

'Take advantage of it', Madame Angellier suddenly said, 'to ask him for a petrol coupon and a travel pass. You can take the old car: the one that wasn't requisitioned. You can tell the German you have to drive one of our tenant farmers to town because he's ill. With a pass from German Headquarters you won't be stopped and you could make it safely to Paris.'

'But to lie like that . . .' said Lucile in disgust.

'What else have you been doing for the past ten days?'

'And once we get to Paris? Where will he hide until he finds his friends? Where will we find anyone courageous enough, committed enough, unless . . .'

She was remembering something.

'Yes,' she said suddenly. 'It's possible . . . Anyway, it's a chance we'll have to take. Do you remember the refugees from Paris we helped in June 1940? They worked in a bank, quite an old couple, but full of spirit and courage. They wrote to me recently: I have their address. They're called Michaud. Yes, that's it, Jeanne and Maurice Michaud. They might do it . . . Of course they'll do it . . . but we'd have to write and ask and wait for their reply, or just take our chances and hope for the best. I don't know . . .'

'Ask for the pass in any case,' said Madame Angellier. 'It shouldn't be difficult,' she added with a faint, bitter smile.

'I'll try,' said Lucile.

She was dreading the moment she would be alone with Bruno. Nevertheless, she hurried down the stairs. Best to get it over with. What if he suspects something? Oh, so what! It was war. She would submit to the rules of war. She was afraid of nothing. Her empty, weary soul was almost eager to run some great risk.

She knocked at the German's door. She went in and was surprised to find he was not alone. With him were the Commandant's new interpreter, a thin red-headed boy with a hard, angular face and blond eyelashes, and another very young officer who was short and chubby, with a rosy complexion and a childlike expression and smile. All three of them were writing letters and packing up: they were sending home all those little knick-knacks soldiers buy when they are in the same place for a while, to create the illusion they live there, but which are burdensome during a campaign: ashtrays, little clocks, prints and, especially, books. Lucile wanted to go but he asked her to stay. She sat down in an armchair Bruno brought out for her and she watched the three Germans who, after apologising, continued working. 'We want to get all this in the post by five o'clock,' they said.

She saw a violin, a small lamp, a French–German dictionary, books in French, German and English, and a beautiful romantic print of a sailing boat at sea.

'I found it in Autun at a bric-à-brac shop,' said Bruno.

He hesitated.

'Actually, better not . . . I won't post it . . . I don't have the right box for it. It will get damaged. It would make me so very happy, Madame, if you would keep it. It will brighten up this rather dark room. The subject is appropriate. Look. Dark, threatening skies, a ship setting sail . . . and far in the distance, a hint of brightness on the horizon . . . a vague, very faint glimmer of hope. Do accept it as a memento of a soldier who is leaving and who will never see you again.'

'I will, *mein Herr*,' Lucile said quietly, 'because of this hint of brightness on the horizon.'

He bowed and continued packing. A candle was lit on the table; he held the sealing wax over its flame, placed a seal on the finished package, took his ring off his hand and pressed it into the hot wax. Lucile watched him, remembering the day he had played the piano for her and how she had held the ring, still warm from his hand.

'Yes,' he said, suddenly looking up at her, 'The happy times are over.'

'Do you think this new war will last long?' she said, immediately regretting having asked. It was like asking someone if he thought he would live long. What did this new war mean? What was going to happen? A series of thundering victories or defeat, a long struggle? Who could really know? Who dared predict the future? Although that's all people did . . . and always in vain . . .

He seemed to read her thoughts. 'In any case,' he said, 'there will surely be much suffering, much heartache and much bloodshed.'

He and his two comrades were getting everything organised. The short officer was carefully wrapping up a tennis racket and the interpreter some large, beautiful books bound in tan leather. 'Gardening books,' he explained to Lucile, 'because in civilian life', he added in a slightly pompous tone of voice, 'I design gardens in the Classical style of Louis XIV.'

How many Germans in the village – in cafés, in the comfortable houses they had occupied – were now writing to their wives, their fiancées, leaving behind their worldly possessions, as if they were about to die? Lucile felt deeply sorry for them. Outside in the street there were horses coming back from the blacksmith and saddle maker, all ready to leave, no doubt. It seemed strange to think about these horses pulled away from their work in France to be sent to the other end of the world. The interpreter, who had been watching them go by, said seriously, 'Where we're going is a really wonderful place for horses . . .'

The short lieutenant made a face. 'Not so wonderful for men . . .'

The idea of this new war seemed to fill them with sadness, Lucile thought, but she didn't allow herself to dwell too deeply on their feelings: she feared to find, in the place of emotion, some spark of their so-called 'warrior mentality'. It was almost like spying; she would have been ashamed to do it. And anyway, she knew them well enough by now to know they would put up a good fight. 'What's more,' she said to herself, 'there's a world of difference between the young man I'm looking at now and the warrior of tomorrow. It's a truism that people are complicated, multifaceted, contradictory, surprising, but it takes the advent of war or other momentous events to be able to see it. It is the most fascinating and the most dreadful of spectacles,' she continued thinking, 'the most dreadful because it's so real; you can never pride yourself on truly knowing the sea unless you've seen it both calm and in a storm. Only the person who has observed men and women at times like this', she thought, 'can be said to know them. And to know themselves.' She would never have believed herself capable of saying to Bruno in such ingenuous and sincere tones, 'I've come to ask you a great favour.'

'Tell me, Madame, how can I be of service to you?'

'Could you recommend me to someone at Headquarters who could get me a travel pass and petrol coupon as a matter of urgency? I have to drive to Paris . . .'

As she was speaking she was thinking, 'If I tell him about some sick tenant farmer he'll be suspicious: there are good hospitals in the area, in Creusot, Paray, or Autun . . .'

'I have to drive one of my farmers to Paris. His daughter works there; she's seriously ill and is asking for him. The poor man would lose too much time if he went by train. You know it's the harvest. If you could grant me permission, we could do the entire journey there and back in a day.'

'You don't need to go to Headquarters, Madame Angellier,' the short officer said quickly; he'd been shyly glancing at her from a distance, lost in admiration. 'I have full powers to grant you your request. When would you like to go?'

'Tomorrow.'

'Oh, good,' murmured Bruno. 'Tomorrow . . . so you'll be here when we leave.'

'When are you leaving?'

'At eleven o'clock tonight. We're travelling at night because of the air raids. It seems a bit ridiculous since the moon is so bright it's almost like daytime. But the army works on tradition.'

'I'll be going now,' said Lucile, after taking the two pieces of paper the short officer had written out: two pieces of paper that symbolised a man's life and liberty. She calmly folded them up and slipped them under her waistband without allowing the slightest sense of urgency to betray her nervousness.

'I'll be here when you go.'

Bruno looked at her and she understood his silent plea.

'Will you come and say goodbye to me, *Herr Lieutenant*? I'm going out, but I'll be back at six o'clock.'

The three young men stood up and clicked their heels. In the past, she had found this display of courtesy by the soldiers of the Reich old-fashioned and rather affected. Now, she thought how much she would miss this light jingling of spurs, the kiss on the hand, the admiration these soldiers showed her almost in spite of themselves, soldiers who were without family, without female companionship (except for the lowest type of woman). There was in their respect for her a hint of tender melancholy: it was as if, thanks to her, they could recapture some remnant of their former lives where kindness, a good education, politeness towards women had far more value than getting drunk or taking an enemy position. There was gratitude and nostalgia in their attitude towards her; she could sense it and was touched by it. She waited for it to be eight o'clock in a state of deep anxiety. What would she say to him? How would they part? There was between them an entire world of confused, unexpressed thoughts, like a precious crystal so fragile that a single word could shatter it. He felt it too, no doubt, for he spent only a brief moment alone with her. He took off his hat (perhaps his last civilian gesture, thought Lucile, feeling tender and sad), took her hands in his. Before kissing them, he pressed his cheek against hers, softly and urgently both at the same time. Was he claiming her as his own? Attempting to brand her with his seal, so she wouldn't forget?

'Adieu,' he said, 'this is goodbye. I'll never forget you, never.'

She stood silent. He looked at her and saw her eyes full of tears. He turned away.

'I'm going to give you the address of one of my uncles,' he said after a moment, 'he's a von Falk like me, my father's brother. He's had a brilliant military career and he's in Paris working for . . .' He gave a very long German name. 'Until the end of the war, he will be the Commandant in greater Paris, a kind of viceroy, actually, and he depends on my uncle to help make decisions. I've told him about you and asked that he help you as much as he can, if you ever find yourself in difficulty; we're at war, God alone knows what might happen to all of us . . .'

'You're very kind, Bruno,' she said quietly.

At this moment she wasn't ashamed of loving him, because her physical desire had gone and all she felt towards him now was pity and a profound, almost maternal tenderness. She forced herself to smile. 'Like the Chinese mother who sent her son off to war telling him to be careful "because war has its dangers", I'm asking you, if you have any feelings for me, to be as careful as possible with your life.'

'Because it is precious to you?' he asked nervously.

'Yes. Because it is precious to me.'

Slowly, they shook hands. She walked him out to the front steps. An orderly was waiting for him, holding the reins of his horse. It was late, but no one even considered going to bed. Everyone wanted to see the Germans leave. In these final hours, a kind of melancholy and human warmth bound them all together: the conquered and the conquerors. Big Erwald with the strong thighs who held his drink so well and was so funny and robust; short, nimble, cheerful Willy, who had learned some French songs (they said he was a real comedian in civilian life), poor Johann who had lost his whole family in an air raid, 'except for my mother-in-law,' he said sadly, 'because I've never had much luck . . .'. All of them were about to be attacked, shot at, in danger of dying. How many of them would be buried on the Russian steppes? No matter how quickly, how successfully the war with Germany might finish, how many poor people would never see the blessed end, the new beginning? It was a wonderful night: clear, moonlit, without even a breath of wind. It was the time of year for cutting the branches of the lime trees. The time when men and boys climb up into the beautiful, leafy trees and strip them bare while, down below, women and girls pick flowers from the sweet-smelling branches at their feet – flowers that will spend all summer drying in country lofts and, in winter, will make herbal tea. A delicious, intoxicating perfume filled the air. How wonderful everything was, how peaceful. Children played and chased each other about; they climbed up on to the steps of the old stone cross and watched the road.

'Can you see them?' their mothers asked.

'Not yet.'

It had been decided that the regiment would assemble in front of the château and then parade through the village. From the shadow of doorways came the sound of kisses and whispered goodbyes . . . some more tender than others. The soldiers were in heavy helmets and field dress, gas masks hanging from their necks. The awaited drum roll came and the men appeared, marching in rows of eight. With a final goodbye, a last blown kiss, the latecomers hurried to take their pre-assigned place: the place where destiny would find them. There was still the odd burst of laughter, a joke exchanged between the soldiers and the crowd, but soon everyone fell silent. The General had arrived. He rode his horse past the troops, gave a brief salute to the soldiers and to the French, then left. Behind him followed the officers, then the grey car carrying the Commandant, with its motorcycle outriders. Then came the artillery, the cannons on their rolling platforms, the machine-guns, the anti-aircraft guns pointing at the sky, and all the small but deadly weapons they'd watched go by during manoeuvres. They had become accustomed to them, had looked at them indifferently, without being afraid. But now the sight of it all made them shudder. The truck, full to bursting with big loaves of black bread, freshly baked and sweet-smelling, the Red Cross vans, with no passengers – for now . . . the field kitchen, bumping along at the end of the procession like a saucepan tied to a dog's tail. The men began singing, a grave, slow song that drifted away into the night. Soon the road was empty. All that remained of the German regiment was a little cloud of dust.

Appendix I

APPENDIX I

Irène Némirovsky's handwritten notes
on the situation in France and her plans for
Suite Française, taken from her notebooks

My God! what is this country doing to me? Since it is rejecting me, let us consider it coldly, let us watch as it loses its honour and its life. And the other countries? What are they to me? Empires are dying. Nothing matters. Whether you look at it from a mystical or a personal point of view, it's just the same. Let us keep a cool head. Let us harden our heart. Let us wait.

21 June.[1] Conversation with Pied-de-Marmite. France is going to join hands with Germany. Soon they will be calling up people here but 'only the young ones'. This was said no doubt out of consideration towards Michel. One army is crossing Russia, the other is coming from Africa. Suez has been taken. Japan with its formidable fleet is fighting America. England is begging for mercy.

25 June. Unbelievable heat. The garden is decked out with the colours of June – azure, pale-green and pink. I lost my pen. There are still many other worries such as the threat of a concentration camp, the status of Jews etc. Sunday was unforgettable. The thunderbolt about Russia[2] hit our friends after their 'mad night' down by the lake. And in order to [?] with them, everyone got drunk. Will I write about it one day?

28 June. They're leaving. They were depressed for twenty-four hours, now they're cheerful, especially when they're together. The little dear one sadly

---

[1] This was thought to be an entry from 1941 but the reference to the Japanese fleet suggests that at least part of IN's note dates from 1942. (Unless indicated, footnotes are the translator's.)

[2] Germany invaded the USSR on 22 June 1941.

said, 'The happy times are over.' They're sending their packages home. They're overexcited, that's obvious. Admirably disciplined and, I think, no rebellion in their hearts. I swear here and now never again to take out my bitterness, no matter how justifiable, on a group of people, whatever their race, religion, convictions, prejudices, errors. I feel sorry for these poor children. But I cannot forgive certain individuals, those who reject me, those who coldly abandon us, those who are prepared to stab you in the back. Those people . . . if I could just get my hands on them . . . When will it all end? The troops that were here last summer said 'Christmas', then July. Now end '41.

There's been talk here about de-occupying France except for the no-go area and the coasts. Carefully rereading the *Journal Officiel*[3] has thrown me back to feeling the way I did a few days ago,

> *To lift such a heavy weight*
> *Sisyphus, you will need all your courage.*
> *I do not lack the courage to complete the task*
> *But the end is far and time is short.*

> *The Wine of Solitude*
> by Irène Némirovsky for Irène Némirovsky

30 June 1941. Stress the Michauds. People who always pay the price and the only ones who are truly noble. Odd that the majority of the masses, the detestable masses, are made up of these courageous types. The majority doesn't get better because of them nor do they [the courageous types] get worse.

Which scenes deserve to be passed on for posterity?
  1 Waiting in queues at dawn.
  2 The arrival of the Germans.
  3 The killings and shooting of hostages much less than the
    profound indifference of the people.

---

[3] The *Journal Officiel* reported all laws, decrees, decisions etc. adopted by the government. At this point in time, Marshal Pétain had already been given constitutional powers. See Robert O. Paxton, *Vichy France, Old Guard and New Order 1940–1944*, Knopf, 1975, p. 32.

4 If I want to create something striking, it is not misery I will show but the prosperity that contrasts with it.

5 When Hubert escapes from the prison where the poor wretches have been taken, instead of describing the death of the hostages, it's the party at the Opera House I must show, and then simply people sticking posters up on the walls: so and so was shot at dawn. The same after the war and without dwelling on Corbin. Yes! It must be done by showing contrasts: one word for misery, ten for egotism, cowardice, closing ranks, crime. Won't it be wonderful! But it's true that it's this very atmosphere I'm breathing. It is easy to imagine it: the obsession with food.

6 Think also about the Mass on Rue de la Source, early morning while it's still completely dark. Contrasts! Yes, there's something to that, something that can be very powerful and very new. Why have I used it so little in *Dolce*? Yet, rather than dwelling on Madeleine – for example, perhaps the whole Madeleine–Lucile chapter can be left out, reduced to a few lines of explanation, which can go into the Mme Angellier–Lucile chapter. On the other hand, describe in minute detail the preparations for the German celebration. It is perhaps *an impression of ironic contrast, to receive the force of the contrast. The reader has only to see and hear.*[4]

Characters in order of appearance (as far as I can remember):
The Péricands – the Cortes – the Michauds – the landowners – Lucile – the louts? – the farmers etc. – the Germans – the aristocrats.

Good, need to include in the beginning: Hubert, Corte, Jules Blanc, but that would destroy my unified tone for *Dolce*. Definitely I think I have to leave *Dolce* as is and on the other hand reintroduce all the characters from *Storm*, but in such a way that they have a momentous affect on Lucile, Jean-Marie and the others (and France).

I think that (for practical reasons) *Dolce* should be short. In fact, in comparison with the eighty pages of Storm, *Dolce* will probably have about sixty or so, no more. *Captivity*, on the other hand, should make a hundred. Let's say then:

---

[4] These words appear in English in the notebook.

STORM	80 pages
DOLCE	60 "
CAPTIVITY	100 "
The two others	50 "

390[5], let's say 400 pages, multiplied by four. Lord! That makes 1,600 typed pages! *Well, well, if I live in it!*[6] In the end, if the people who have promised to come arrive on 14 July, then that will have certain consequences, including at least one, maybe two sections less.

In fact, it's like music when you sometimes hear the whole orchestra, sometimes just the violin. At least it should be like that. Combine [two words in Russian] and individual emotions. What interests me here is the history of the world.

Beware: forget the reworking of characters. Obviously, the time-span is short. The first three parts, in any case, will only cover a period of three years. As for the last two, well that's God's secret and what I wouldn't give to know it. But because of the intensity, the gravity of the experiences, the people to whom things happen must change (. . .)

My idea is for it to unfold like a film, but at times the temptation is great, and I've given in with brief descriptions or in the episode that follows the meeting at the school by giving my own point of view. Should I mercilessly pursue this?

Think about as well: *the famous 'impersonality' of Flaubert and his kind lies only in the greater fact with which they express their feelings – dramatising them, embodying them in living form, instead of stating them directly?*

Such[7] . . . there are other times when no one must know what Lucile feels in her heart, rather show her through other people's eyes.

1942

The French grew tired of the Republic as if she were an old wife. For them, the dictatorship was a brief affair, adultery. But they intended to cheat on their wife, not to kill her. Now they realise she's dead, their Republic, their freedom. They're mourning her.

[5] The mistake in addition comes from the manuscript. (Editor)

[6] These words appear in English in the notebook.

[7] The reference to Flaubert and this word appear in English in the notebook.

APPENDIX I

For years, everything done in France within a certain social class has had only one motive: fear. This social class caused the war, the defeat and the current peace. The Frenchmen of this caste hate no one; they feel neither jealousy nor disappointed ambition, nor any real desire for revenge. They're scared. Who will harm them the least (not in the future, not in the abstract, but right now and in the form of kicks in the arse or slaps in the face)? The Germans? The English? The Russians? The Germans won but the beating has been forgotten and the Germans can protect them. That's why they're 'for the Germans'. At school, the weakest student would rather be bullied than be free; the tyrant bullies him but won't allow anyone else to steal his marbles, beat him up. If he runs away from the bully, he is alone, abandoned in the free-for-all.

There is a huge gulf between this caste, which is the caste of our current leaders, and the rest of the nation. The rest of the French, because they own less, are less afraid. If cowardice stops stifling the positive feelings in our souls (patriotism, love of freedom etc.), then they can rise up. Of course, many people have recently built fortunes, but they are fortunes in depreciated currency that are impossible to transform into concrete goods, land, jewellery, gold etc. Our butcher, who won five hundred thousand francs in a currency whose exchange rate abroad he knows (exactly zero), cares less about money than a Péricand, a Corbin[8] cares about their property, their banks etc. More and more, the world is becoming divided into the haves and the have nots. The first don't want to give anything up and the second want to take everything. Who will win out?

The most hated men in France in 1942: Philippe Henriot[9] and Pierre Laval. The first as the Tiger, the second as the Hyena: around Henriot you can smell fresh blood, and around Laval the stench of rotting flesh.

[8] Characters from *Storm in June*. (Editor)
[9] Catholic delegate for the Gironde region, Philippe Henriot (1889–1944) was one of the Vichy government's most efficient and influential propagandists. A member of the Milice – the infamous French political parapolice force that recruited some 45,000 pro-Nazis to crush the Resistance – from its creation in 1943, he entered into the government of Deputy Prime Minister (Vice-Président du Conseil) Pierre Laval at the beginning of 1944 and preached total collaboration. Henriot was killed by the Resistance in June 1944. Laval was tried and subsequently shot after the Liberation of Paris in 1945. See Robert O. Paxton, *Vichy France* . . . p. 298.

Mers-el-Kébir	painful stupor
Syria	indifference
Madagascar	even greater indifference

All in all, it's only the initial shock that counts. People get used to everything, everything that happens in the occupied zone: massacres, persecution, organised pillaging, are like arrows shot into mire! . . . the mire of our hearts.

They're trying to make us believe we live in the age of the 'community', when the individual must perish so that society may live, and we don't want to see that it is society that is dying so the tyrants can live.

This age that believes itself to be the age of the 'community' is more individualistic than the Renaissance or the era of the great feudal lords. Everything is happening as if there were a fixed amount of freedom and power in the world that is sometimes divided between millions of people and sometimes between *one single person* and the other millions. 'Have my leftovers,' the dictators say. So please don't talk to me about the spirit of the community. I'm prepared to die but as a French citizen and I insist there be a valid reason for my death, and I, Jean-Marie Michaud,[10] I am dying for P. Henriot and P. Laval and other lords, just as a chicken has its throat slit to be served to these traitors for dinner. And I maintain, yes, I do, that the chicken is worth more than the people who will eat it. I know that I am more intelligent, superior, more valuable where goodness is concerned than those men. They are strong but their strength is temporary and an illusion. It will be drained from them by time, defeat, the hand of fate, illness (as was the case with Napoleon). And everyone will be dumbfounded. 'But how?' people will say, 'They were the ones we were afraid of!' I will truly have a communal spirit if I defend my share and everyone else's share against their greed. The individual only has worth if he is sensitive to others, that goes without saying. But just so long as it is 'all other men' and not 'one man'. Dictatorship is built around this confusion. Napoleon said he only desired the greatness of France, but he proclaimed to Metternich,[11] 'I don't give a damn if millions of men live or die.'

---

[10] A character from the novel. (Editor)
[11] Austrian statesman and ambassador to Paris under Napoleon I.

Hitler:

FOR STORM IN JUNE:

What I need to have:

1 An extremely detailed map of France or Michelin Guide
2 The complete collection of several French and foreign newspapers between 1 June and 1 July
3 A work on porcelain
4 June birds, their names and songs
5 A mystical book (belonging to the godfather) Father Bréchard

Comments on what's already been written:

1 Will – He talks for too long.
2 Death of the priest – schmaltzy.
3 Nimes? Why not Toulouse which I know?
4 In general, not enough simplicity!

[In Russian, Irène Némirovsky added: 'in general, they are often characters who have too high a social standing.']

April 1942. Need to have *Storm*, *Dolce*, *Captivity* follow on from one another. Replace the Desjours farm by the Mounain farm. I want to place it in Montferroux. Dual advantage: links *Storm* to *Dolce* and cuts out what is unpleasant in the Desjours household. I must create something great and stop wondering if there's any point.

Have no illusions: this is not for now. So mustn't hold back, must strike with a vengeance wherever I want.

For *Captivity*: the changing attitudes of Corte: national revolution, necessity of having a leader. Sacrifice (everyone agrees about the necessity of sacrifice just as long as it's your neighbour's), then the lapidary phrase[12] which makes him famous, for in the beginning Corte is rather frowned upon: he takes an attitude that is too French but he realises through subtle and menacing signs that this is not what he should do.

---

[12] Paxton mentions Pétain's 'lapidary formula' for defeat in his speech of 20 June 1940: 'Too few allies, too few weapons, too few babies' (Robert O. Paxton, *Vichy France* . . . p. 21) and in his speech of 17 June 1940, Pétain stated: 'the spirit of enjoyment has won out over the spirit of sacrifice' (ibid., p. 33). Similar sentiments are expressed in *Dolce* through the Perrin ladies (ch. 13) and the Viscount and Viscountess de Montmort (ch. 16).

Yes, he is patriotic but only afterwards: today the Rhine is flowing over the Ural mountains, he has a moment of hesitation but, after all, that is understandable given all the geographical fantasies which have become realities these past few years – the English border is at the Rhine and to top it all off the Maginot Line[13] and the Siegfried Line[14] are both in Russia, Horace's final creation *(down him[15])*.

On L.:[16] It must be him because he is a crook. And in the times we are living in, a crook is worth more than an honest man.

Captivity – keep it simple. Tell what happens to people and that's all.

Today, 24 April, a little calm for the first time in a very long time, convince yourself that the sequences in *Storm*, if I may say so, must be, are a masterpiece. Work on it tirelessly.

Corte is one of those writers whose usefulness will become glaringly obvious in the years following the defeat; he has no equal when it comes to finding euphemisms to guard against disagreeable realities. E.g.: the French army was not beaten back, it withdrew! If people kiss the Germans' boots it is because they have a sense of reality. Having a communal spirit means hoarding food supplies for the exclusive use of the few.

I think I should replace the strawberries with forget-me-nots. It seems impossible to bring cherry trees in blossom and ripe strawberries together in the same season.

Find a way to link Lucile to *Storm*. When the Michauds stop to rest one night during their journey, this oasis and the breakfast and everything that must seem so wonderful – the porcelain cups, the dewy roses in thick bouquets on the table (roses with black centres), the coffee pot giving off bluish steam etc.

Send up the so-called writers. E.g. A. C., the A. R. who wrote an article 'Is the *Tristesse d'Olympio*[17] a masterpiece?' No one has ever sent up certain so-called writers like A. B. etc. (there is honour among thieves).

[13] The Maginot Line was the line of defence built between 1927 and 1936 along the north-eastern border of France and Germany to prevent German attack.

[14] The Siegfried Line was the line of defence built between 1938 and 1940 along the western border of Germany. It was destroyed by the Allies in 1944–5.

[15] These final two words appear in English in the notebook.

[16] This initial undoubtedly refers to Laval. (Editor)

[17] Famous Romantic poem by Victor Hugo.

To sum up, chapters already finished by 13 May 1942:

(1) Arrival (2) Madeleine (3) Madeleine and her husband (4) vespers (5) the house (6) the Germans in the village (7) the private school (8) the garden and the Viscountess's visit (9) the kitchen (10) departure of Mme Angellier. First look at the Perrins' garden (11) the day it rains.

TO DO:

(12) the German ill (13) the Maie woods (14) the Perrin ladies (15) the Perrins' garden (16) Madeleine's family (17) the Viscountess and Benoît (18) the denunciation? (19) the night (20) the catastrophe at Benoît's place (21) Madeleine at Lucile's house (22) the celebration at the lake (23) the de[parture].

Still to do: 12, half of 13, 16, 17, and the rest.

Madeleine at Lucile's house – Lucile in Mme Angellier's room – Lucile and the German – celebration at the lake – the departure.

FOR *CAPTIVITY* FOR THE CONCENTRATION CAMP THE BLAS-PHEMY OF THE BAPTISED JEWS 'MAY GOD FORGIVE US OUR TRESPASSES AS WE FORGIVE YOU YOURS' – Obviously, martyrs would not have said that.

To do it well, need to make 5 parts:

1 *Storm*
2 *Dolce*
3 *Captivity*
4 *Battles?*
5 *Peace?*

General title: Storm or Storms and the first part could be called Shipwreck.

In spite of everything, the thing that links all these people together is our times, solely our times. Is that really enough? I mean: is this link sufficiently felt?

Therefore Benoît, after having killed (or trying to kill) Bonnet (for I still have to decide if it might not be better to let him live for the future), Benoît escapes; he first hides in the Maie woods, then, since Madeleine is afraid of being followed when she goes to bring him food, at Lucile's house. Finally, in Paris, at the Michauds' where Lucile sends him. Pursued, he escapes in time, but the Gestapo search the Michauds' house, find notes made by Jean-Marie for a future book, think they are political tracts and arrest him. He meets Hubert there [in prison] who had got himself arrested for some stupidity or other. Hubert would have no trouble getting out, because his powerful family who are total collaborators can pull strings, but out of childishness, his taste for adventure stories etc., he prefers risking his life by escaping with Jean-Marie. Benoît and his friends help them. Later, much later, because in the meantime Jean-Marie and Lucile have to fall in love, they escape and flee France. That should end *Captivity* and as I've already said:

– Benoît	Communist
– Jean-Marie	Middle class

Jean-Marie dies heroically. But how? And what is heroism these days? Parallel to this death, must show the death of the German in Russia, the two full of sorrowful nobility.

Adagio: Must rediscover all these musical terms (*presto*, *prestissimo*, *adagio*, *andante*, *con amore*, etc.)

Music: Adagio from Op. 106, that immense poem of solitude – the twentieth variation on the theme of Diabelli, the sphinx with the dark eyebrows who contemplates the abyss – the Benedictus of the *Missa Solemnis* and the final scenes of *Parsifal*.

He [Hubert] gets out: those who truly love each other are Lucile and Jean-Marie. What should I do with Hubert? Vague plan: Benoît escapes after killing Bonnet. He's hidden at Lucile's. After the Germans leave, Lucile is afraid to have him stay in the village and suddenly thinks of the Michauds.

On the other hand, I want J. Marie and Hubert to be thrown in jail by the Germans for different reasons. That way it would be possible to have the German die afterwards. Lucile could think of going to him to save J. Marie? All this is very vague. Think about it.

On the one hand, I would like a kind of general idea. On the other . . . Tolstoy, for example, with one idea spoils everything. Must have people, human reactions, and that's all . . .

Let's make do with important businessmen and famous writers. After all, they are the real kings.

For *Dolce*, a woman of honour can admit without shame 'these unexpected emotions that reason can tame', as Pauline would say (Corneille).

2 June 1942. Never forget that the war will be over and that the entire historical side will fade away. Try to create as much as possible: things, debates . . . that will interest people in 1952 or 2052. Re-read Tolstoy. Inimitable descriptions but not historical. Insist on that. For example in *Dolce*, the Germans in the village. In *Captivity*, Jacqueline's First Communion and Arlette Corail's party.

2 June 1942. Starting to worry about the shape this novel will have when finished! Consider that I haven't yet finished the second part, and I see the third? But that the fourth and fifth are in limbo and what limbo! It's really in the lap of the gods since it depends on what happens. And the gods could find it amusing to wait a hundred or even a thousand years, as the saying goes[18]: and I'll be far away. But the gods wouldn't do that to me. I'm also counting a lot on the prophecy of Nostradamus.

1944 – Oh, God![19]

While waiting to see the shape . . . or rather I should say the rhythm: the rhythm in the cinematic sense . . . how the parts relate to each other. *Storm*, *Dolce*, gentleness and tragedy. *Captivity*? Something muffled, stifled, as vicious as possible. After that I don't know.

What's important – the relationship between different parts of the work. If I had a better knowledge of music, I suppose that would help me. Since I don't know music, then what is called rhythm in films. All in all, make sure to have variety on one hand and harmony on the other. In the cinema, a film must have unity, tone, a style. E.g.: those street scenes in American films where you always have skyscrapers, where you can sense the hot, muffled, muggy atmosphere of New York. So unity for the film as a whole but variety between the parts. Pursuit – people in love – laughter, tears etc. It's this type of rhythm I want to achieve.

Now for a more basic question and one to which I cannot find an answer: won't people forget the heroes from one book to the next? It is to avoid this problem that I would like to create one large volume of 1,000 pages rather than a work made up of several volumes.

3 July 1942. Definitely,[20] unless things drag on and get worse as they go! But please let it be over one way or the other!

[18] Undoubtedly a reference to the German statement that the Third Reich would last a thousand years.
[19] These words appear in English in the notebook.
[20] Refers to previous paragraph regarding one large volume.

Only need four movements. In the third, *Captivity*, collective destiny and personal destiny are strongly linked. In the fourth, whatever the result may be! (I UNDERSTAND WHAT I MEAN!), personal destiny is extricated from the other. On one side, the fate of the nation, on the other, Jean-Marie and Lucile, their love, the German's music etc.

Now, here is what I pictured:

1. Benoît is killed in a revolution or fight or an attempt at resisting, according to what seems realistic.
2. Corte. I think this might be good. Corte was very afraid of the Bolsheviks. He is extremely collaborationist but, following an attack on one of his friends or out of wounded pride, he gets the idea that the Germans are finished. He wants to commit himself to the extreme left! He first thinks of Jules Blanc, but after seeing him, he finds him [illegible word in Russian], he turns resolutely to a young activist group, that has formed . . . [unfinished sentence].

For *Captivity*:

Begin with: Corte, Jules Blanc visiting Corte.

Then a contrast: Lucile perhaps at the Michauds'.

Then: the Péricands.

As many meetings as possible but not historical, rather the masses, social events or battles in the streets or something like that!

Arrival

Morning

Departure

These three episodes must be stressed even more. The movement of the masses must give the book its worth.

In the fourth part, I only know the death of the German in Russia.

Yes, to do it well, should have five parts of 200 pages each. A 1,000-page book. Ah, God![21]

Remark. The theft of Corte's dinner by the proletarians must have, for the future, a great influence. Normally, Corte should become extremely pro-Nazi, but I could also if I want, if I need to, do it in such a way that he says to himself: 'There's no point kidding myself; that's where the future lies, the

---

[21] These words appear in English in the notebook.

future belongs to this brutal force which stole my food from me. Two possible positions then: fight against it or, the opposite, from now on be a leader of the movement. Let himself be carried along by the wave, but on the front line? Even better, try to lead it? The official writer of the party. The great man of the Party, ha, ha, ha!' even more so since Germany is on good terms with the USSR and will come to tolerate it more and more. As long as the war lasts, this in fact will be madness on the part of Germany etc. Later on, it will be different . . . But later on people will see. They'll fly to the aid of the strongest.

Could someone like Corte have such cynical ideas? Of course, at certain times. When he's been drinking or after making love his favourite way, a way that a mere mortal could barely begin to understand, and even if he did understand, it would cause only amazement and panic. The difficulty here is, as ever, the practical side of things. A newspaper, a kind of radio. Freedom, the Germans secretly paying him a subsidy.[22] We'll see.

All action is a battle, the only business is peace.[23]

The pattern, is it less[24] a wheel than a wave that rises and falls, and sometimes on its crest appears a seagull, sometimes the Spirit of Evil and sometimes a dead rat. Accurately reality, *our* reality (there's nothing to be proud about there!).

The rhythm must be here in the movements of the masses, everywhere where the crowds appear in the first volume, the exodus, the refugees, the arrival of the Germans in the village.

In *Dolce*: the arrival of the Germans, but it must be re-examined, the morning, the departure. In *Captivity*, the First Communion, a demonstration (the one that happened on 11 November '41), a fight? We'll see. I haven't got there yet and I'll approach it realistically.

If I show people who 'influence' events, that would be unacceptable. If I show people act, that is certainly more realistic, but at the expense of keeping it interesting. Nevertheless, must limit myself to that.

It's quite fair (though banal, but let's admire and embrace banality), what

---

[22] 'Some of the most notorious figures of the occupation were the Frenchmen who led political groups or published newspapers in Paris in return for the high life of the occupied capital and, in many cases, direct subsidies from the German Embassy' (Robert O. Paxton, *Vichy France . . .* p. 49.

[23] These words appear in English in the notebook.

[24] These words appear in English in the notebook.

Percy says – that the historical scenes are the best (see *War and Peace*), the ones that are seen from the perspective of the characters. I tried to do the same thing in *Storm*, but in *Dolce*, everything to do with the Germans, all that can and must be separate.

What would be good all in all (but is it doable?) is to *always* show the advance of the German army in the scenes not seen from the perspective of the characters. It would therefore be necessary to begin *Storm* with an image of people rushing around in France.

Difficult.

I think that what gives *War and Peace* the expansion Forster[25] talks about, is quite simply the fact that in Tolstoy's mind, *War and Peace* is only the first volume that was to be followed by *The Decembrists*, but what he did unconsciously (perhaps, for naturally I really don't know, I'm imagining), in the end what he did consciously or unconsciously is very important to do in a book like *Storm* etc., even if certain characters are wrapped up, the book itself must give the impression of only being one episode . . . which is really what is happening in our times, as in all times of course.

22 June 1942. I discovered, a while ago, a technique that has been really useful to me – the indirect method. On absolutely every occasion when I encounter a problem in how to deal with something, this method saves me, gives freshness and strength to the entire story. I use it in *Dolce* every time Mme Angellier is in a scene. But this method of showing something that I haven't used systematically is open to infinite development.

1 July 1942. Find this for *Captivity*:

By unifying, always simplifying the book (in its entirety) must result in a struggle between individual destiny and collective destiny. Must not take sides.

---

[25] 'Music, though it does not employ human beings, though it is governed by intricate laws, nevertheless does offer in its final expression a type of beauty which fiction might achieve in its own way. Expansion. That is the idea the novelist must cling to. Not completion. Not rounding off but opening out. When the symphony is over we feel that the notes and tunes composing it have been liberated, they have found in the rhythm of the whole their individual freedom. Cannot the novel be like that? Is not there something of it in *War and Peace*?' (E. M. Forster, *Aspects of the Novel*, Penguin, 2000, pp. 149–50).

My option: England's style of government by the middle classes, unfortunately impossible, at least wishes to be revived, for in the end its essence is immutable; but it definitely will not happen until after I die: therefore left with two types of socialism. Neither of them appeals to me but *there are the facts!*[26] One of them rejects me, therefore . . . the other . . . But that is out of the question. As a writer, I must state the problem correctly.

The struggle between the two destinies, this happens each time there is an upheaval, it's not logical; it's instinctive; I think a good part of oneself dies when this happens, but not all of oneself. Salvation, in general, is when the time allocated to us is longer than the time allocated to a crisis. Contrary to what is believed, what is general passes, the whole remains, collective destiny is shorter than the destiny of the simple individual (that's not exactly right. It's a different timescale: we are only interested in the upheavals; the upheavals, either they kill us, or we last longer than them).

To get back to my subject: At first, J. Marie has a thoughtful and detached attitude towards this great number of defeats. Naturally, he would like France to have its revenge but he realises that this is not a goal because whoever speaks of revenge speaks of hatred and vengeance, eternal war, and the Christian is upset by the idea of hell and eternal punishment; he is upset at this idea that there will always be someone stronger and someone weaker; he therefore looks to unification . . . What he desires, what he yearns for, is harmony and peace. And collaborationism as it is currently practised disgusts him, and on the other hand he sees communism, which suits Benoît but not him. Therefore he tries to live as if the great, urgent, collective question isn't being asked, as if he only has to solve his own personal problems. But then he learns that Lucile has loved and perhaps still loves a German. He immediately takes sides, for the abstraction has suddenly been transformed into hatred. He hates a German and, because of him, through him, he hates or thinks he hates, which is the same thing, a way of thinking. In reality, what happens is that he forgets his own destiny and confuses it with someone else's destiny. For practical purposes, by the end of *Captivity*, Lucile and J. Marie are in love with each other; this love is sad, unrequited, undeclared, completely conflicted! J. Marie runs away to fight the Germans – if that is still possible by the end of 1942!

The fourth part must be the return, if not the triumph of the chapter when

---

[26] These words appear in English in the notebook.

J. Marie appears. Never forget that the public likes having the life of the 'wealthy' described to them.

To sum up: struggle between personal destiny and collective destiny. To finish, stress Lucile and Jean-Marie's love and stress eternal life. The German's musical masterpiece. There must also be a reminder of Philippe. Which all in all would correspond to my deepest conviction. What lives on:

1 Our humble day-to-day lives
2 Art
3 God

Maie woods: 11 July 1942. The pine trees all around me. I am sitting on my blue cardigan in the middle of an ocean of leaves, wet and rotting from last night's storm, as if I were on a raft, my legs tucked under me! In my bag, I have put Volume II of *Anna Karenina*, the diary of K. M. and an orange. My friends the bumblebees, delightful insects, seem pleased with themselves and their buzzing is profound and grave. I like low, serious tones on voices and in nature. The shrill 'chirp, chirp' of the small birds in the trees grates on me . . . In a moment or so I will try to find the hidden lake.

Captivity:

1 Corte's reaction.
2 Assassination attempt by Benoît's friends which horrifies Corte.
3 Corte learns something from the talkative Hubert . . .
4 Through Arlette Corail etc.
5 Her coquettish ways.
6 Denunciation. Hubert and J. Marie are locked up with many others.
7 Hubert, thanks to the actions of his rich and right-thinking family, is released, J. Marie is condemned to death?
8 Here is where Lucile intervenes, the German. J. Marie is pardoned (compact description of the prison here or something of the sort).
9 Benoît helps him escape. Sensational escape.
10 J. Marie's reaction to Germany and the Germans.
11 He and Hubert flee to England.
12 Benoît's death. Brutal and full of hope.

Interspersed in all this must have Lucile's love for Jean-Marie.

The most important and most interesting thing here is the following: the historical, revolutionary facts etc. must be only lightly touched upon, while daily life, the emotional life and especially the comedy it provides must be described in detail.

Appendix II

Appendix II

Correspondence 1936–1945

Irène Némirovsky to Albin Michel   *7 October 1936*

Thank you for the cheque for 4,000 francs. Regarding this, may I please remind you of my visit to you last spring when I asked if it would be possible for you to work out some arrangement for the future, for you will understand that the situation has become very difficult for me now. You told me then that you would do your very best to comply and that I should put my trust in you. Up until now, you haven't wanted to tell me how you proposed to arrange things, but you promised to make a decision within two months at the latest. You still haven't written anything to me about this since our meeting, which was nearly four months ago. I am therefore asking what you intend to do, for alas you understand the necessities of life for someone who, like me, possesses no great wealth and only lives by my earnings as a writer.

Editions Genio (Milan) to Albin Michel   *10 October 1938*

We would be extremely grateful if you could tell us if Mme I. Némirovsky is of Jewish descent. According to Italian law, anyone who has one parent, either mother or father, of Aryan race, is not considered to be Jewish.

Michel Epstein[27] to Albin Michel   *28 August 1939*

My wife is currently in Hendaye (Villa Ene Exea, Hendaye-Plage) with the children. I am worried for her in these difficult times, for she has no one to come to her aid if she needs help. May I count on your friendship to send me, if you possibly can, a letter of recommendation she could use if necessary

---

[27] Irène Némirovsky's husband. Like her, a refugee who fled Russia during the Bolshevik Revolution to live in Paris, where he was a bank manager at the Banque des Pays du Nord. (Editor)

for the authorities and the press in this area (Basses-Pyrénées, Landes, Gironde)?

Albin Michel to Michel Epstein   *28 August 1939*

The name Irène Némirovsky should make it possible for her to open many doors! In spite of that, I would be more than pleased to give your wife a letter of introduction for the newspapers I know, but I will need certain details that you alone are in a position to provide. I would therefore ask you to please come and see me this evening.

Robert Esménard[28] to Irène Némirovsky   *28 September 1939*

We are currently living in terrifying times which could become tragic overnight. Moreover, you are Russian and Jewish, and it could be that people who do not know you – though they must be few and far between given your fame as a writer – might cause problems for you, also, as we must try to anticipate everything, I thought that my recommendation as an editor might be useful to you.

I am therefore prepared to confirm that you are a writer of great talent, which is also obvious, moreover, by the success of your works both in France and abroad where some of your works have been translated. I am also happy to confirm that since October 1933, the year you came to me after having published some books with my colleague Grasset, including *David Golder*, which was a resounding success and gave rise to a remarkable film, since then, I have always had the most cordial of relations with both you and your husband, apart from our professional relationship.

21 December 1939

Temporary Travel Pass from 24 May to 23 August 1940
    (for Irène Némirovsky)
    Nationality: Russian
    Authorised to travel to Issy-l'Évêque
    Authorised mode of transport: train
    Purpose: to see her children who have been evacuated

---

[28] Director of Albin Michel Publishers and son-in-law of Albin Michel who, at this time, no longer managed the publishing house alone for health reasons. (Editor)

Irène Némirovsky to Robert Esménard　　　　　　　　*12 July 1940*

It's only been two days since the post is more or less back in service in the little village where I am. I am taking a chance and writing to your Paris address. I hope with all my heart that you have made it through these terrible times safe and sound and that you have no cause to worry about any of your family. As for me, even though military operations took place very close to here, we were spared. Currently my most serious concern is how to obtain some money.

Irène Némirovsky to Mlle Le Fur[29]　　　　　　　　*9 August 1940*

I hope you have safely received my letter confirming receipt of the 9,000 francs. Here is why I am writing to you today. Just imagine that in a small local newspaper, I read the short announcement that I am sending you:

Pursuant to a recent directive, no foreigners may contribute to the new newspaper.

I would very much like to have the details of this directive and I thought you might be able to provide them for me.

Do you think it applies to a foreigner who, like myself, has lived in France since 1920? Does it apply to political writers or to writers of fiction as well?

In general, you know that I am completely isolated from society and am unaware of all the recently adopted directives regarding the press.

If you think there is something that might be of interest to me, would you be so kind as to let me know. There's also something else. I am again going to ask your help, as I recall how very kind and obliging you are. I would like to know which writers are in Paris and who is being published in the current newspapers. Could you find out if *Gringoire* and *Candide*,[30] as well as the bigger magazines, intend to return to Paris? And what about the publishing houses? Which ones are open?

Irène Némirovsky to Mlle Le Fur　　　　　　　　*8 September 1940*

As far as I am concerned, there are persistent rumours here which lead me to believe that we might be part of the Free Zone one of these days and I wonder how I would then get my monthly payments.

---

[29] Robert Esménard's secretary. (Editor)
[30] Both newspapers which published Irène Némirovsky's works.

Law on Jewish Residents   *4 October 1940*[31]

From the date of the dissemination of this current law, foreign residents of Jewish descent may be interned in special camps by decision of the *Préfet* in the department where they reside.

All residents of Jewish descent may at any time be forced to live in a specified location by decision of the *Préfet* in the department where they reside.[32]

Irène Némirovsky to Madeleine Cabour.[33]

You now know all the problems I have had. What's more, we have been living with a considerable number of these gentlemen for a few days now. This is painful for all sorts of reasons. I am therefore looking forward with great pleasure to the little village you've told me about, but may I ask you for some information.

1 How big is Jailly in terms of inhabitants and local retailers?
2 Is there a doctor and a pharmacist?
3 Is it being occupied?
4 Can you get any food, on the whole? Do you have butter and meat?

This is particularly important to me now because of the children, as one of them has just had the operation you know about.

---

[31] The sections quoted here are Articles 1 and 3 of this law. It immediately followed the famous law of 3 October 1940 which 'excluded Jews from elected bodies, from positions of responsibility in the civil service, judiciary, and military services, and from positions influencing cultural life (teaching in public schools, newspaper reporting or editing, direction of films or radio programmes)'. It also defined 'Jews racially as anyone with three Jewish grandparents, whatever the religion of the present generation'. See Robert O. Paxton, *Vichy France* . . . pp. 174–5.

[32] France is divided into regions known as '*départements*', similar to the British 'counties'. These in turn are subdivided into 'cantons' and 'communes'. Each department has a central government representative called the '*Préfet*', with several '*Sous-Préfets*' in the cantons. Note that a distinction is being made between foreign Jews and French Jews. French Jews believed they would remain exempt from such laws. Irène Némirovsky was never granted French citizenship.

[33] Madeleine Cabour, born Avot, was a great friend of Irène Némirovsky, with whom she corresponded regularly as a young girl. After the war, her brother, René Avot, took care of Elisabeth Némirovsky when the legal guardian of the two girls went to the United States. Elizabeth lived with his family until she came of age. (Editor)

Irène Némirovsky to Robert Esménard   *10 May 1941*

Dear Monsieur, you will recall that, according to our agreement, I was meant to have 24,000 francs on 30 June. I do not need this money at the moment, but I admit that the recent laws regarding the Jews make me fear that difficulties might arise by the time this payment is made in six weeks' time, and that would be disastrous for me. I must therefore appeal to your kindness and ask you to bring forward this payment by immediately giving a cheque in that amount to my brother-in-law, Paul Epstein, made payable to him. I have also asked him to telephone you to come to an arrangement about this. Of course, he will sign a receipt to release you fully from your responsibility towards me. It distresses me to have to trouble you yet again but I am sure you will understand the reasons for my concern. I hope you still have excellent news regarding A. Michel.

Irène Némirovsky to Robert Esménard   *17 May 1941*

Dear Monsieur Esménard, my brother-in-law told me that you gave him the 24,000 francs you were to send me on 30 June. Thank you so much for your extreme kindness towards me.

Michel Epstein to the Sous-Préfet *of Autun*[34]   *2 September 1941*

I have received a letter from Paris informing me that anyone categorised as Jewish may not leave the village where he resides without permission from the authorities.

I find myself in this situation, along with my wife, since, even though we are Catholics, we are of Jewish descent. I therefore am taking the liberty of requesting that you please authorise my wife, born Irène Némirovsky, as well as myself, to spend six weeks in Paris where we also have a home, 10 avenue Constant-Coquelin, for the period from 20 September to 5 November 1941.

This request is made as my wife needs to sort out some business with her publisher, visit the ophthalmologist who has always treated her, as well as seeing the doctors who care for us, Professor Vallery-Radot and Professor Delafontaine. We intend to leave our two children, aged four and eleven, in Issy and, of course, we would like to be sure that there will

---

[34] Since the department of Saône-et-Loire was divided by the demarcation line, it was the *Sous-Préfet* who took the place of the *Préfet* in the occupied section, where the village of Issy-l'Evêque was located.

be no problem returning to Issy, once we have attended to our affairs in Paris.

Doctor in Issy: A. Bendit-Gonin.

From the Progrès de l'Allier *no. 200*   *8 August 1941*

SOVIET, LITHUANIAN, ESTONIAN AND LATVIAN RESIDENTS ORDERED TO REPORT TO REGIONAL GERMAN HEADQUARTERS

Every male resident over the age of fifteen of Soviet, Lithuanian, Estonian or Latvian extraction, as well as those who are stateless but who previously held Soviet, Lithuanian, Estonian or Latvian citizenship, are ordered to report in person to their Regional German Headquarters with their identity papers no later than Saturday 9 August 1941 (noon). Anyone who does not report in person will be penalised according to the decree concerning this order.

The Field Commandant.

Irène Némirovsky to Robert Esménard   *9 September 1941*

I have finally rented the house I wanted here, which is comfortable and has a lovely garden. I am moving in on 11 November if these Gentlemen don't get there first for we are once again expecting them.

Irène Némirovsky to Robert Esménard   *13 October 1941*

I was happy to receive your letter this morning, not just because it confirms my hope that you will do everything possible to help me, but also because it reassures me that someone is thinking about me, which is a great comfort.

As you can imagine, life here is very sad, and if it weren't for my work . . . Even the work becomes painful when the future is so uncertain . . .

Irène Némirovsky to André Sabatier[35]   *14 October 1941*

My dear friend, I was very touched by your kind letter. Please do not think that I underestimate either your friendship or M. Esménard's; on the other hand, I perfectly understand the difficulties of the situation. Up until now, I have shown as much patience and courage as I could possibly muster. But, what can you do, there are moments which are very difficult. These are the facts: impossible to work and must be responsible for four people's lives. Added to that are stupid humiliations – I cannot go to Paris; I cannot have

---

[35] Literary Director of Albin Michel Publishers. (Editor)

even the most basic necessities sent here, such as blankets, beds for the children etc., my books. A general and absolute prohibition has been declared regarding the apartments inhabited by people like me. I'm not telling you this to make you feel sorry for me, but to explain to you why my thoughts can only be dark [. . .]

Robert Esménard to Irène Némirovsky   *27 October 1941*

I have explained your situation to my father-in-law and have also shown him the letters you recently sent me.

As I have told you, A. Michel only wishes to be of service to you in any way possible and he has asked me to offer you a monthly payment of 3,000 francs for the year 1942 which is the same amount he was sending you when it was still possible to publish your works and sell them regularly. Please be so kind as to confirm your agreement.

However, I must point out to you that in accordance with very precise instructions we received from the Syndicat des Éditeurs (Publishers' Union) regarding the interpretation of directives included in the German Decree of 26 April, article 5, we find ourselves in the position of being required to send all royalties received from the sale of Jewish authors' works to their 'blocked account'. According to this principle, it is stated that 'publishers must pay royalties to Jewish authors by sending them to their bank account after receiving confirmation from the bank that the account is blocked'.

In addition, I am returning the letter you received from GIBE Films (a copy of which I have kept). According to information I received from a reliable source, a project of this type can only be undertaken if the author of the book to be adapted to the screen is of Aryan origin, both in this zone and the other.[36] I can therefore only be involved in such a project when the author whose work is to be made into a film provides me with the most formal guarantee on this point.

Irène Némirovsky to Robert Esménard   *30 October 1941*

I have just received your letter offering me a monthly payment of 3,000 francs for the year 1942. I greatly appreciate Monsieur Michel's attitude towards me. I am truly most grateful both to him and to you; the faithful friendship you both have shown me is as precious to me as the material

[36] Reference to the Free Zone and the Occupied Zone.

support you wish to give me by doing this. However, you know that if this money must be held in a blocked bank account, it would be of no use to me whatsoever.

I wonder if under the circumstances, it would not be simpler to send the monthly payments to my friend, Mlle Dumot,[37] who lives with me and is the author of a novel entitled *Les Biens de ce Monde*[38] whose manuscript is with Monsieur Sabatier. [. . .]

Mlle Dumot is definitely Aryan and can give you any proof of this you may require. I have known her since I was a child and if she could come to an agreement with you about the monthly payments, she would look after my interests. [. . .]

Telegram from Michel Epstein to R. Esménard and A. Sabatier   *13 July 1942*

Irène suddenly taken today destination Pithiviers[39] (Loiret) – hope you can intercede urgently – trying to telephone no success.

Michel Epstein.

Telegram from R. Esménard and A. Sabatier to Michel Epstein   *July 1942*

Just received your telegram. Immediately making joint effort by Morand, Grasset, Albin Michel. Yours.

Irène Némirovsky's final two letters:[40]

Toulon S/Arrox 13 July 1942 – 5 o'clock [written in pencil and legible]

My dearest love, for the moment I am at the police station where I ate some blackcurrants and redcurrants while waiting for them to come and get me. It

---

[37] Irène Némirovsky and her husband, Michel Epstein, had brought Julie Dumot to Issy-l'Évêque in case they were arrested. She had been the live-in companion of the children's maternal grandparents. (Editor)

[38] This work was actually written by Irène Némirovsky and was published in instalments in the newspaper *Gringoire* in 1941 without mentioning the author's name. Published in novel form in 1947 by Albin Michel with Irène Némirovsky as author.

[39] Pithiviers, near Orléans, was one of the infamous concentration camps where children were separated from their parents and imprisoned, while the adults were processed and deported to camps further away, usually Auschwitz.

[40] The first letter was undoubtedly generously passed on by a policeman and the second by someone she met at the Pithiviers train station. (Editor)

is most important to stay calm, I believe it won't be for very long. I thought we could also ask Caillaux and Father Dimnet for help. What do you think?

I shower my darling daughters with kisses, tell Denise to be good and sensible . . . You are in my heart, as well as Babet, may the good Lord protect you. As for me, I feel calm and strong.

If you can send me anything, I think my second pair of glasses are in the other suitcase (in the wallet). Books please, and also if possible a bit of salted butter. Goodbye my love!

Thursday morning – July 1942 Pithiviers [written in pencil and legible]

My dearest love, my cherished children, I think we are leaving today. Courage and hope. You are in my heart, my loved ones. May God help us all.

Michel Epstein to André Sabatier   *14 July 1942*

I tried to reach you by telephone yesterday without success. I have sent both you and Monsieur Esménard a telegram. The police took my wife away yesterday. It appears she is going to the concentration camp in Pithiviers (Loiret).

Reason: general order against stateless Jews between the ages of sixteen and forty-five. My wife is Catholic and our children are French. Can anything be done to help her?

André Sabatier's reply

In any case will need several days. Yours Sabatier.

André Sabatier to J. Benoist-Méchin,   *15 July 1942*
Secretary of State to the Vice President of the Council of Ministers

Our author and friend I. Némirovsky has just been taken to Pithiviers from Issy-l'Évêque where she was living. Her husband has just informed me of this. A white Russian (Jewish as you know), never been involved in any political activities, a novelist of very great talent, having always paid the greatest tribute to her adopted country, mother of two little girls aged five and ten. I beg you to do everything you can. Thank you in advance and yours very truly.

Telegram from Michel Epstein to R. Esménard and A. Sabatier   *16 July 1942*

My wife must be at Pithiviers by now – Think useful to intercede at the regional police headquarters in Dijon – *Sous-Préfet* Autun and authorities Pithiviers. Michel Epstein.

Telegram from Michel Epstein to Robert Esménard   *16 July 1942*
Thank you dear friend – I put my hope in you. Michel Epstein.

Telegram from Michel Epstein to André Sabatier   *17 July 1942*
Counting on you to send telegram with news good or bad. Thank you dear friend.

Lebrun[41] to Michel Epstein – Telegram   *17 July 1942*
Pointless sending package as haven't seen your wife.

Telegram from Michel Epstein to André Sabatier   *18 July 1942*
No news of my wife – Don't know where she is – Try to find out and tell me truth by telegram – with advance notice can phone me day or night. ISSY-L'ÉVÊQUE.

Telegram from Abraham Kalmanok[42] to Michel Epstein   *20 July 1942*
Did you send Irène's medical certificate – must do so immediately. Send telegram.

Michel Epstein to André Sabatier   *22 July 1942*
I have received a letter from my wife, from the Pithiviers camp, dated last Thursday, telling me she would probably be leaving for an unknown destination, which I assume is far away. I have sent a telegram, and prepaid reply, to the commandant of the camp, but I have not heard from him. Would your friend possibly have more success, perhaps he could obtain the information they are refusing to give me? Thank you for everything you are doing. Keep me informed, I beg you, even if it's bad news. Yours truly.

Reply
Have personally seen my friend.[43] Will do everything possible.

---

[41] A Red Cross intermediary. (Editor)
[42] Great-uncle of Denise and Elisabeth Epstein. (Editor)
[43] The content of this letter implies he is talking about Jacques Benoist-Méchin. (Editor)

André Sabatier to Michel Epstein   Saturday 24 July 1942

If I haven't written to you it is because I have nothing precise to tell you at present and I can only bring myself to tell you the kind of things that might lessen your suffering. Everything necessary has been done. I saw my friend again who told me that all we can do now is wait. I pointed out, after receiving your first letter, that your children are French citizens, and after receiving the second letter, of [Irène's] possible departure from the Loiret camp. I am waiting and this waiting, please believe me, is very *painful* to me as a friend ... I say this to assure you that I am putting myself in your place! Let us hope that very soon I will have some definite good news to tell you. My heart goes out to you.

Michel Epstein to André Sabatier   26 July 1942

Perhaps we should point out that in my wife's case they are dealing with a White Russian who never wanted to accept Soviet citizenship, who fled Russia after a great deal of persecution, with her parents whose entire fortune was confiscated. I myself am also in the same position and I am not exaggerating when I calculate that about one hundred million pre-war francs were taken from my wife and myself in Russia. My father was President of the Syndicat des Banques Russes (Union of Russian Banks) and Executive Director of the Bank of Commerce of Azov-Don. The authorities concerned can therefore be assured that we haven't the slightest sympathy for the current Russian regime. My younger brother, Paul, was a personal friend of the Grand Duke Dimitri of Russia and the Imperial Family living in France was often received by my father-in-law, in particular, Grand Duke Alexander and Grand Duke Boris. Moreover, I would point out to you, if I have not already done so, that the German non-commissioned officers who spent several months living with us, in Issy, left me the following document when they left:

O.U. den I, VII, 41
*Kameraden. Wir haben längere Zeit mit der Familie Epstein zusam-
mengelebt und diese sehr anständige und zuvorkommende Familie kennen-
gelernt. Wir bitten Euch daher, sie damitsprechend zu behandeln. Heil Hitler!
Hammberger, Feldw, 23599 A.*[44]

---

[44] O.U. 1 July 1941. Comrades. We lived with the Epstein family for a long time and got to know them and they are a very respectable and obliging family. We therefore ask you to treat them accordingly. Heil Hitler!

I still don't know where my wife is. The children are in good health, as for me, I am still standing.

Thank you for everything, my dear friend. Perhaps it would be helpful if you could discuss all this with the Count de Chambrun[45] and Morand. Best wishes, Michel.

? to Michel Epstein   27 *July 1942*

Are there in your wife's works, apart from the scene in *Vin de Solitude*, passages from novels, short stories or articles that could be pointed out as clearly anti-Soviet?

Michel Epstein to André Sabatier   27 *July 1942*

I received your letter of Saturday today. Thank you so very much for all your efforts. I know that you are doing and will do everything you can to help me. I have patience and courage. I just pray that my wife has the physical strength necessary to bear this blow! What is very difficult is that she must be horribly worried about the children and me, and I have no way of communicating with her since I don't even know where she is.

Please find enclosed a letter which I insist be sent to the German ambassador as a matter of URGENCY. If you could find anyone who could approach him personally and give it to him (Count de Chambrun perhaps, who, I believe, is prepared to take an interest in my wife), that would be perfect. But if you cannot find anyone able to do it QUICKLY, would you be so kind as to take it to the embassy or just post it. Thank you in advance. Of course, if this letter will upset the steps already taken, then tear it up, otherwise, I really wish it to be sent.

I fear the same thing might happen to me. In order to avoid material concerns, could you send Mlle Dumot an advance on her monthly payments for '43? I am afraid for the children.

Michel Epstein to the German ambassador, Otto Abetz   27 *July 1942*

I know that I am taking a great liberty in writing to you personally. Nevertheless, I am taking this step because I believe that you alone can save my wife, my only hope lies with you.

Allow me therefore to explain to you the following: before leaving Issy,

[45] Count René de Chambrun was a lawyer and son-in-law of Pierre Laval, whose only daughter, Josée, he married. (Editor)

the German soldiers who were occupying the village gave me, in gratitude
for the way we treated them, a letter which reads:

> O.U. den I, VII, 41
>
> *Kameraden. Wir haben längere Zeit mit der Familie Epstein zusam-
> mengelebt und diese sehr anständige und zuvorkommende Familie kennen-
> gelernt. Wir bitten Euch daher, sie damitsprechend zu behandeln. Heil Hitler!*
> *Hammberger, Feldw. 23599 A.*[46]

And yet, on the 13 July my wife was arrested. She was taken to the concentration camp at Pithiviers (Loiret) and, from there, sent somewhere else, but
I do not know where. This arrest, I was told, was a result of general instructions given by the occupying authorities regarding the Jews.

My wife, Madame M. Epstein, is a very famous novelist, I. Némirovsky.
Her books have been translated in a great many countries and two of them
at least – *David Golder* and *Le Bal* – in Germany. My wife was born in Kiev
(Russia) on 11 February 1903. Her father was an important banker. My father
was President of the Syndicat des Banques Russes (Union of Russian Banks)
and Executive Director of the Bank of Commerce of Azov-Don. Both our
families lost considerable fortunes in Russia; my own father was arrested by
the Bolsheviks and imprisoned in the Saint-Peter and Paul Fortress in St
Petersburg. We had the greatest of difficulty in finally managing to flee
Russia in 1919 and we then took refuge in France where we have lived ever
since. All this must satisfy you that we feel nothing but hatred for the Bolshevik
regime.

In France, not a single member of our family has ever been involved in
politics. I was a bank manager and as for my wife, she became a highly
esteemed novelist. In none of her books (which moreover have not been banned
by the occupying authorities), will you find a single word against Germany
and, even though my wife is of Jewish descent, she does not speak of the Jews
with any affection whatsover in her works. My wife's grandparents, as well
as my own, were Jewish; our parents practised no religion; as for us, we are
Catholic and so are our children who were born in Paris and are French.

If I may also take the liberty of pointing out to you that my wife has
always avoided belonging to any political party, that she has never received
special treatment from any government either left-wing or right-wing, and

[46] For translation see note 44 on p. 377.

that the newspaper she contributed to as a novelist, *Gringoire*, whose director is H. de Carbuccia, has certainly never been well-disposed towards either the Jews or the Communists.

Finally, for many years my wife has been suffering from chronic asthma (her doctor, Professor Vallery-Radot can attest to this) and internment in a concentration camp would be fatal for her.

I know, Ambassador, that you are one of the most eminent men in your country's government. I am convinced you are also a just man. And it seems to me both unjust and illogical that the Germans should imprison a woman who, despite being of Jewish descent, has no sympathy whatsoever – all her books prove this – either for Judaism or the Bolshevik regime.

André Sabatier to Count de Chambrun   *28 July 1942*

I have received this very moment a letter from the husband of the author of *David Golder*, a copy of which I have taken the liberty of enclosing for you. This letter contains details which might prove useful. Let us hope that they will allow you to bring this matter to a positive conclusion. I thank you in advance for everything you are trying to do for our friend.

André Sabatier to Mme Paul Morand [47]   *28 July 1942*

I wrote to Monsieur Epstein yesterday saying what we had agreed, thinking it would be better to write than to send a telegram. This morning I received his letter in the post. It clearly contains some interesting details.

Michel Epstein to André Sabatier   *28 July 1942*

I hope you received the letter I wrote yesterday and that the one intended for the ambassador has been given to him, either by Chambrun or by someone else, or directly by you. Thank you in advance.

In reply to your note of yesterday: I think that in *David Golder*, the chapter where David does a deal with the Bolsheviks to buy oil rights cannot be seen as very kindly towards them, but I don't have a copy of *D. Golder* here, could you check? You have a copy of the manuscript of *Les Échelles du Levant* [48],

---

[47] Paul Morand was a French writer and diplomat who retained his post under the Vichy government. In 1958 he was refused entry into the Académie Française but was eventually admitted in 1968.

[48] This novel appeared in instalments in *Gringoire* beginning in May 1939. It was published in 2005 by Editions Denoël under the title *Le Maître des Âmes*.

which appeared in *Gringoire*, and which is more savage towards the hero, a charlatan doctor who comes from the Levantine, but I can't remember whether my wife specifically made him Jewish. I think so.

I see in chapter XXV of her biography of Chekhov, the following sentence: 'The short story "Ward 6" contributed greatly to Chekhov's fame in Russia; because of it, the USSR claimed him as their own and stated that, had he lived, he would have joined the Marxists. The posthumous fame of a writer is filled with such surprises . . .' Unfortunately, I can't find anything else and this is very little.

Is there really no way at all to find out from the French authorities whether or not my wife is still in the camp at Pithiviers? Ten days ago, I sent a telegram, with a prepaid reply, to the commandant of the camp and have had no reply. Is it possible that just knowing where she is would be forbidden?

I was told that my brother Paul is in Drancy,[49] why am I not allowed to know where my wife is? Alas . . .

Goodbye, dear friend. I don't know why I have faith in my letter to the ambassador. Michel.

André Sabatier to Mme Paul Morand   *29 July 1942*
Here is the letter I told you about on the telephone. I think you are better placed than anyone to decide if it is best to send this letter to the person its author wants to have it. On the content, I can hardly comment, as for the details, it seems to me there are certain sentences which are rather unfortunate.

Mavlik[50] to Michel Epstein   *29 July 1942*
My dearest. I hope you have received my letters but I fear they may have been lost for I wrote to Julie and our aunt misunderstood her name on the telephone. My dearest, once again I beg you to stay strong for Irène, for the girls, for everyone else. We do not have the right to lose heart since we are believers. I was mad with grief but I am in control again, I spend all day long trying to find out some news and seeing people in the same situation. Germaine[51] got back the day before yesterday, she will be leaving for Pithiviers as soon as she has everything she needs. Since it seems that Sam is at Neaune-la-

---

[49] Concentration camp to the north-east of Paris.
[50] Michel Epstein's sister; she would be arrested and deported to Auschwitz. (Editor)
[51] A French friend of Samuel Epstein, Michel Epstein's older brother. (Editor)

Rolande, near Pithiviers, she is desperate to try to get some news to both him and Irène. We've heard nothing except that Ania is at Drancy and she is asking for some clothes and books. There have been several letters from Drancy where people say they are being treated and fed properly. My darling, I beg of you, have courage. The money is late because the name was misunderstood. I'm going back to see Joséphine[52] tomorrow. Germaine saw the gentleman whose maid is at Pithiviers. I must also see Germaine before she leaves. She had a note from Sam but it was still from Drancy. I will write to you the day she leaves but I would like to hear from you, my dear. As for me, I don't know how, but I'm still standing and still hoping. I send you and the girls my love always.

Mme Rousseau (French Red Cross) to Michel Epstein   *3 August 1942*
   Dr Bazy[53] left this morning for the Free Zone where he will spend a few days; he is going to look into the case of Mme Epstein once there and will do everything in his power to intervene on her behalf. As he didn't have time to reply to you before leaving, he asked me to let you know he received your letter and that he will do everything possible to assist you.

Michel Epstein to Mme Rousseau   *6 August 1942*
   I was happy to hear that Dr Bazy is taking steps to help my wife. I wonder if it might not be a good opportunity to coordinate his efforts with those already taken by:

   1 My wife's publisher, Monsieur Albin Michel (the person who is
      dealing with this matter is Monsieur André Sabatier, one of the
      company directors).
   2 Mme Paul Morand.
   3 Henri de Régnier.
   4 Count de Chambrun.

Monsieur Sabatier will be receiving a copy of this letter and he can give you any information you might need (tel: DAN 87.45). It is particularly painful not knowing where my wife is (she was at the Pithiviers camp –

---

[52] Irène Némirovsky's maid. (Editor)
[53] President of the Red Cross. (Editor)

Loiret, on 17 July and since then I haven't had a single word from her). I would like her to know that the children and I have not been affected by recent directives and that we are all in good health. Could the Red Cross get the same message to her? Is it allowed to send parcels?

Michel Epstein to André Sabatier   *6 August 1942*

Enclosed is a copy of the letter I sent to the Red Cross. Still not a word from my wife. It's hard. Was it possible to contact Ambassador Abetz and give him my letter? Michel.

P.S. Could you send me the Count de Chambrun's address?

Michel Epstein to André Sabatier   *9 August 1942*

I have just learned, from a very reliable source, that the women (and men and even the children) interned at the Pithiviers camp were taken to the German border and from there sent somewhere further east – probably Poland or Russia. This is supposed to have happened about three weeks ago.

Up till now, I thought my wife was in some camp in France, in the custody of French soldiers. To learn she is in an uncivilised country, in conditions that are probably atrocious, without money or food and with people whose language she does not even know, is unbearable. It is now no longer a matter of getting her out of a camp sooner rather than later but of saving her life.

You must have received the telegram I sent yesterday; I pointed out one of my wife's books, *Les Mouches d'Automne*, first published by Kra, deluxe edition, and then by Grasset. This book is clearly anti-Bolshevik and I deeply regret not having thought of it sooner. I hope it is not too late to stress this new piece of evidence we have to the German authorities.

I know, dear friend, that you are doing everything you can to save us, but I beg of you, find, think of something else, speak again to Morand, Chambrun, your friend and in particular to Dr Bazy, President of the Red Cross, 12 rue Newton, tel: KLE 84.05 (the head of his section is Mme Rousseau, same address) pointing out the new evidence of *Les Mouches d'Automne*. It is absolutely inconceivable that we, who lost everything because of the Bolsheviks, should be condemned to death by those who are fighting them!

Alas, my dear friend, I am launching one final appeal. I know that it is unforgivable to impose on you and the rest of our remaining friends this way but, I say it again, it is a question of life and death not only for my wife but also for our children, not to mention myself. The situation is serious. Alone here, with the little ones, virtually imprisoned since it is forbidden for me to move, I cannot even take solace in being able to act. I can no longer either sleep or eat, please accept that as an excuse for this incoherent letter.

10 August 1942

I, the undersigned, Count W. Kokovtzoff, former President of the Council of Ministers, Finance Minister of Russia, hereby certify that I knew the late Monsieur Efim Epstein, Administrator of the Bank of Russia, member of the Union of Banks that operated in Paris under my chairmanship, that he had the reputation of a banker of irreproachable integrity and that his actions and sympathies were clearly anti-communist.

[sworn at the Police Station]

André Sabatier to Michel Epstein   *12 August 1942*

I received your telegram and letters. I am replying before leaving Paris for the suburbs for a few weeks. If you need to write to me between 15 August and 15 September, send it to the [publishing] house where it will be dealt with immediately, they will do whatever is necessary if they can and keep me up to date. Here is what I've done: many initiatives without much success as yet:

(1) No reply from the Count de Chambrun to whom I have written. Since I don't know him, I can't chase him up, as I don't know whether his silence is a sign that he doesn't wish to get involved. His address is 6 bis, place du Palais-Bourbon, VII.

(2) On the other hand, Mme P. Morand is displaying tireless devotion. She is increasing her attempts, she has your letter and its essence will be sent very soon, along with a medical certificate, by one of her friends who is also at the embassy. *Les Mouches d'Automne*, which she read, does not seem to her to be at all what she was looking for: anti-revolutionary, of course, but not anti-Bolshevik. She suggests that you do not take any unsystematic and pointless initiatives, as she sees it. The only door you should be knocking on, again according to her, is the Jewish Union who alone, through its network, could tell you where your wife is and perhaps get news to her about the children. Here is her address: 29 rue de la Bienfaisance, VIII.

(3) My friend told me straight out that his attempts led him to conclude there was nothing he could do.

(4) Same reply, just as categorical, from my father, after approaching the French regional authorities.

(5) I asked a friend to contact the author of *Dieu est-il français?* (Friedrich Sieburg) who promised to see [what could be done], not to have her released, which seemed doubtful to him, but at least to have some news of her.

(6) Yesterday, I telephoned the Red Cross where I spoke to Mme Rousseau's stand-in, who was very kind and knew all about the matter. Dr Bazy is currently in the Free Zone and is making enquiries in high places regarding what might be possible. He is due back on Thursday, so I'll phone him before I leave.

My personal feelings are as follows:

(1) The directive which affected your wife is part of a general order (here, in Paris alone, it seems to have affected several thousand stateless people), which partly explains why we seem to be incapable of obtaining an order for special treatment, but which also means we can hope that nothing special might happen to your wife.

(2) This directive was ordered by certain German authorities who have total control in this area and in the face of whom the French authorities and other German civil or military authorities, even those in high places, seem to have no influence.

(3) Leaving for Germany seems probable, not to go to the camps according to Mme P. Morand, but to go to Polish cities where stateless people are all being held.

All this is very hard, I feel it only too well, dear Monsieur. You must try only to think of the children and remain strong for them, easy advice to give ... I'm sure you'll say. Alas! I have done everything I can. Your very faithful André.

Michel Epstein to Mme Cabour   *14 August 1942*

Sadly Irène has gone – where? I do not know. You can imagine how worried I am! She was taken away on 13 July and I have had no word of her since. I am alone here with the two little girls who are being looked after by Julie. Perhaps you remember having met her at avenue Président-Wilson. If I ever receive any news of Irène, I will let you know immediately. You wish to help us, dear Madame. I will take advantage of this offer without even knowing if what I ask is in the realm of possibility. Could you get us some thread and cotton wool as well as some typewriter paper? We would be extremely grateful to you.

Irène Némirovsky died at Auschwitz on 17 August 1942, a fact which makes the correspondence that follows this date even more poignant. (Translator)

Michel Epstein to Mme Cabour   20 August 1942

Irène was taken away on 13 July by the French police, acting on orders from the German police, and taken to Pithiviers – because she was a stateless person of Jewish descent, without taking into account the fact that she is Catholic, her children are French and that she took refuge in France to escape the Bolsheviks, who also stole her parents' entire fortune. She arrived at Pithiviers on 15 July and, according to the only letter I received from her, she was due to leave again on the 17th for an unknown destination. Since then, nothing. Not a word, I don't know where she is or even if she is alive. Since I do not have the right to leave this place, I have asked various people to intervene, without success as yet. If there is anything at all you can do, I beg you to do it, for this suffering is unbearable. Imagine that I can't even send her any food, that she has no clothes or money . . . Up until now, I've been left here for I am over forty-five . . .

Michel Epstein to André Sabatier   15 September 1942

Still no sign of life from Irène. As Mme Paul[54] advised, I have taken no new initiatives. I am counting on her alone. I don't think I can bear this uncertainty for long. You said you were waiting for some news from Dr Bazy. I assume you haven't had any? I hope the Red Cross can at least make sure that Irène gets some clothing, money and food before winter sets in.

If you see Mme Paul, would you please be so kind as to tell her I have received a card from His Grace Ghika[55] who, six months ago, was still in good health in Bucharest.

---

[54] Wife of Paul Morand, but to be safe, it was necessary to use ambiguous names. (Editor)
[55] A Romanian bishop prince who often came to see Irène. (Editor)

André Sabatier to Michel Epstein   *17 September 1942*

I telephoned Mme Paul as soon as I got back. I expressed your gratitude to her and told her you had taken her advice. All the steps she has taken, even those with the person to whom you have written a letter, still have not yielded any results. She told me: 'It's like banging your head against a wall.' Mme Paul thinks that the wise thing to do is to wait until these great movements of populations are somehow contained and stabilised.

Michel Epstein to André Sabatier   *19 September 1942*

Our letters have crossed. I thank you for giving me some news, no matter how depressing it may be. Could you please find out if it would be possible for me to be exchanged for my wife – I would perhaps be more useful in her place and she would be better off here. If this is impossible, maybe I could be taken to her – we would be better off together. Obviously, it would be necessary to speak to you about all this in person.

André Sabatier to Michel Epstein   *23 September 1942*

Ever since the 14 July I told myself that if a trip to Issy were necessary, I wouldn't hesitate to go. I do not think that, even now, this could lead to any definite viable decision. Here is why.

To exchange places is currently impossible. It would only mean one more inmate, even though the reason you give for it is obviously well-founded. Once we know exactly where Irène is, that is to say once all this is 'organised', then and then alone, it might be possible to make this proposal.

Together, in the same camp! Another impossibility, as separation between men and women is strict and absolute.

The Red Cross has just sent me a telegram this morning asking for a detail that I do not know and that I am in turn asking you for in a telegram. I will send it immediately. Let us hope we are on the way to having some news.

Michel Epstein to André Sabatier   *29 September 1942*

I promised I would be asking for your help and I am keeping my promise. This is what I need. My Alien Identity Card, valid until next November, has to be renewed. This depends on the *Préfet* of the Saône-et-Loire, Mâcon, and I must send him a renewal request soon. I do not wish this request to cause us any new problems. I am therefore asking if you could approach the *Préfet* of Mâcon. Everything is perfectly in order, but the scarcely propitious circumstances for people in my category lead me to fear problems from the Ministry of Justice etc. May I count on you? I will do nothing until I hear from you but the matter is pressing.

André Sabatier to Michel Epstein　　　　　　　　　　　*5 October 1942*

I have just received your letter of the 29th. I read it and had someone else read it. There is no doubt, my response is clear: stay where you are, doing anything at all seems to me extremely foolhardy. I am expecting Dimnet to come and see me and will be happy to discuss it with him.

André Sabatier to Michel Epstein　　　　　　　　　　　*12 October 1942*

This morning, I received your letter of the 8th as well as a copy of the letter you sent to Dijon. I am writing to tell you the following:

Our friend also had everything perfectly in order but you must realise that didn't prevent anything from happening.

As for the children, they are French and, to use your own expression, I do not get the impression that a change of scene is essential, but that is only my opinion. It seems to me that the Red Cross would be best placed to give you more detailed and concrete information.

Michel Epstein to André Sabatier (Creusot Prison)　　　　*19 October 1942*

[letter written in pencil]

I am still at Creusot, being treated very well and in perfect health. I do not know when we will continue our journey or where we are going. I am counting on your friendship towards my family. They will need it. I am certain you will look after them. Apart from that, there is nothing I can tell you except that I am keeping faith and I bid you farewell.

Michel was first imprisoned at Creusot, then taken to Drancy. On 6 November 1942 he was deported to Auschwitz and sent immediately to the gas chamber. There is then a two-year gap in the correspondence. (Translator)

Julie Dumot to Robert Esménard　　　　　　　　　　　*1 October 1944*

I am writing to ask you to continue sending the monthly payments. You know that I have had many worries. For seven months I have had to keep hiding them in different places. I hope this nightmare is now over. I have gone to get the children to put them into boarding school. My eldest girl is in the third year of secondary school,[57] they are happy finally to be free for Denise will be able to do her schoolwork more calmly as her future is also at stake.

Julie Dumot to André Sabatier   *10 October 1944*

I have received the 15,000 francs. I have been worried about my children since last February. I had to hide them again. That is certainly the reason why Sister Saint-Gabriel did not reply to you. They couldn't go to school for seven months. I hope we will be more settled now and that they will work hard. I have put them back in boarding school. Denise is in the third year of secondary school and Babet in the fourth year of primary school.[58] They are very happy to see their friends again and the good Sisters who helped me so much in our time of need. I hope that now nothing else will happen to torture us while we wait for the return of our family in exile. Is it possible to sell any author's work now or are sales still being regulated?

Robert Esménard to Julie Dumot   *30 October 1944*

Thank you for your letter of 1 October. I can see that you have had to suffer through many cruel days of anguish. Now you can finally put your mind at rest regarding the girls' future who will be able to pursue their studies in peace; we can only hope that this terrifying nightmare will soon come to an end and that in the very near future you will receive some word of their parents. This is, as you know, one of my dearest wishes . . .

André Sabatier to Julie Dumot   *9 November 1944*

I read with great trepidation the fears you recently had regarding your children. I can only rejoice now in knowing that you are safe from all the measures of the type to which you allude. All we can do now is pray for the swift return of those who have been taken from us.

Monsieur Esménard has, of course, given the necessary instructions for the remaining copies of Mme I. Némirovsky's works to be sold. As for me, I have been wondering if now would be the time to publish the two manuscripts of hers that I have, her novel *Les Biens de ce Monde* and her biography of

[57] Age thirteen to fourteen.
[58] Age eight to nine.

Chekhov. Like myself, Monsieur Esménard considers it would be preferable to postpone such publication, for it would perhaps be dangerous to attract attention to her at a time when her situation does not protect her from potentially dreadful reprisals.

Robert Esménard to Julie Dumot   *27 December 1944*
May 1945 finally bring us peace and the return of your dear absent family.

Albin Michel to Julie Dumot   *1945*
9000 francs (June–July–August 1945).

Reply of Robert Esménard to R. Adler   *8 January 1945*
We received the card dated 13 October 1944 addressed to Mme Némirovsky, but alas! we have not been able to forward it to her. In fact, Mme Némirovsky was arrested on 13 July 1942 at Issy where she had been living since 1940 and taken to the concentration camp at Pithiviers, then deported the same month. Her husband was arrested a few weeks later and also deported. All attempts to intervene on their behalf were futile and no one has heard from either of them since. Fortunately, their two little girls were saved thanks to a loyal friend with whom they are living in the provinces. Please believe that we deeply regret having to be the bearer of such news.

Reply of Albin Michel to A. Shal   *16 January 1945*
Thank you for your card dated 6 November 1944 addressed to Mme Némirovsky. Alas! it will be impossible for us to forward this card to her for our author and friend was taken away in 1942 and marched to some camp or other in Poland. Since then, in spite of many various efforts, we have never been able to learn anything. Her husband had the same fate a few months after his wife. As for the children, they were fortunately entrusted to friends of the family in time and are currently doing well. I deeply regret having to be the bearer of such sad news. Let us not lose hope . . .

Marc Aldanov to Robert Esménard   *5 April 1945*
(Found[ation] for the relief of men of letters and scientists of Russia – New York)
We have just learned the tragic news regarding Irène Némirovsky from Madame Raïssa Adler. Madame Adler has also told us that her two daughters were saved by one of their grandfather's former companions. This woman, Mlle Dumot, we understand, is a completely trustworthy person, but unfor-

tunately is lacking in financial means and cannot, therefore, take responsibility for their education.

The friends and admirers of Mme Némirovsky in New York met to discuss how we might be able to help the children. But they are neither numerous nor rich here. As for our committee, today we number about one hundred men of letters and scientists. We have been unable to do enough. This is why we are contacting you, dear Monsieur, to find out if Mme Némirovsky has any funds with her French publishers from royalties and if so, to see if it would be possible for you and your colleagues to place a portion of these fees at the disposal of the two children. We will send you their address.

Robert Esménard to Marc Aldanov   *11 May 1945*

Mme Némirovsky was, alas! arrested on 13 July 1942, taken to the concentration camp at Pithiviers, then deported. Her husband, a few weeks later, met the same fate. We have never heard from them again and we are terribly worried about them.

I know that Mlle Dumot, who saved the two little girls, is raising them perfectly well. In order for her to do so, I must tell you that since Irène Némirovsky's arrest, I have sent Mlle Dumot large sums of money which come to nearly 151,000 francs and that we are continuing to provide her with a monthly payment of 3,000 francs.

André Sabatier to Julie Dumot   *1 June 1945*

I have been thinking of you and your children often since the camp survivors and prisoners have begun to return to France. I am assuming that for the moment you haven't heard anything or you certainly would have let me know. As for me, I have been unable to find out anything at all. I asked Mme J. J. Bernard[59] who knew Mme Némirovsky and who is currently with the Red Cross trying to take the necessary steps to find something out. Naturally, if I hear anything at all, you will be the first to know. There is one question I wanted to ask you: what happened to the manuscripts that were at Issy when Mme Némirovsky was arrested? I heard that there was a long novella she'd finished. Would you happen to have the text? If so, could you send it to me so we could possibly publish it in our journal *La Nef*.

[59] Mme Jean-Jacques Bernard, wife of the writer Jean-Jacques Bernard, son of [the writer] Tristan Bernard. (Editor)

André Sabatier to Father Englebert   *16 July 1945*

My reason for writing to you will come as a surprise. Here is what it is about: you will surely know I. Némirovsky by name and reputation, one of our greatest novelists of France in the years preceding the war. Jewish and Russian, I. Némirovsky was deported in 1942, as was her husband, and undoubtedly sent to a concentration camp in Poland; we have never been able to learn anything more. Even today, there is total silence and we have, alas! lost any hope of finding her alive.

I. Némirovsky left her two little girls, Denise and Elisabeth Epstein, in France in the care of a friend. I have just seen the woman who has looked after them; she told me that she had managed to get the girls accepted as boarding students with the Dames de Sion [Sisters of Zion]. It was all agreed when, at the last minute, the Mother Superior changed her mind, on the pretext that there were not enough places, which was both a disappointment and a terrible problem for the good woman who is looking after these two little girls. Would it be possible for you to find out exactly what is going on? And if you have influence with these Sisters, could you use it to ensure that Denise and Elisabeth be admitted to the Dames de Sion for the beginning of the school year in October at the latest.

We care a great deal about these two little girls, as you can understand; whatever happens, even if you can do nothing, thank you in advance for your consideration of this request.

Telephone call to André Sabatier   *23 July 1945*
Chautard (Union Européenne Industrielle et Financière
[European Union of Finance and Industry])

Monsieur de Mézières of the U.E.[60] is willing to do something to help Irène Némirovsky's children, in conjunction with our firm.

[manuscript note on transcript of call: wait until he contacts us]

Would be willing to send 3,000 francs per month.

Has found a religious boarding school near Paris for 2,000 francs per month per child.

---

[60] Banque de l'Union Européenne (formerly the Banque des Pays du Nord where Michel Epstein was Manager). (Editor)

Omer Englebert to André Sabatier   *7 August 1945*

    I am pleased to inform you that the Russian Jewish novelist (I can't recall her name!) whose daughters you wanted to help and whom Monsieur Sabatier recommended to me on your behalf, have been accepted at the Dames de Sion, in Grandbourg near Evry-Petit-Bourg. The Mother Superior has just told me that they can attend at the beginning of the coming academic year.

Julie Dumot (46 rue Pasteur, Marmande) to A. Sabatier   *29 August 1945*

    I do not know how to thank you for your extreme loyalty. I am very happy for the children, especially for Babet who is only eight years old and has her entire education ahead of her. As for Denise, who is doing very well now, she can improve herself in this first-class establishment, as her mother wished. This is why I am so very grateful to you, for having made their parents' wishes come true. If Denise cannot continue her studies, she must have her Certificate of General Education to be able to work, we'll find out about that in a few days. Your kind letter reached me here where I have brought the children for their holidays. Denise is completely cured. She had an X-ray which showed that all signs of the pleurisy had disappeared. As for Babet, she is going to have her tonsils and adenoids out next week. I couldn't have it done sooner, as the doctor is on holiday, which means I'll get back to Paris a week later than expected.

    Yes, Monsieur Sabatier, there was the possibility of the Société des Gens de Letters (Society of Men of Letters) doing something for the children. Monsieur Dreyfus, to whom I explained my situation, saying that I couldn't manage with my 3,000 francs per month, that Denise had been under medical care for six months, took the matter to his friend, Monsieur Robert, asking for something to be done for the children. The very same day, I informed Monsieur Esménard, who knows all about it. If you need any information about me, Tristan Bernard has known me since I was sixteen.

Albin Michel Publishers to Julie Dumot   *3 October 1945*

    12,000 francs: Sept – Oct – Nov – Dec 1945.

Robert Esménard (note for Mlle Le Fur)   *7 December 1945*

    Friday afternoon, I went to see Mme Simone Saint-Clair who is a member of a committee whose purpose is to come to the aid of I. Némirovsky's children. Certain individuals and groups are going to deposit a monthly amount to a notary who has been appointed to retain the money until, in theory, they have finished sitting the exams for their *baccalaureat*. Once Denise, the eldest, has passed it, I assume this matter will be reviewed.

Apart from that, these gifts will be received in such a way as to constitute a capital sum for I. Némirovsky's daughters, which they may use however they wish when they are no longer minors. There is already a certain sum, which includes a payment by the Banque des Pays du Nord where M. Epstein was employed, something in the region of 18,000 francs, corresponding to 3,000 francs a month with a certain number of back payments.

Mlle Dumot will have at her disposal, through the auspices of the notary, X amount to reimburse her for her expenses, then each month an amount to be decided. As for our firm, I have said that from the date of our last monthly payment – the sum of 2,000 francs per month will be paid, without, of course, this amount being deducted from I. Némirovsky's royalties. In addition, I shall allocate the sum of 2,000 francs per month from Mme Némirovsky's royalties, dating from the month when I began sending these monthly payments, in other words, these monthly payments will be calculated retrospectively from the date of the first payment.

Widespread announcements will be made in the press to raise money.

W. Tideman to Irène Némirovsky   *7 December 1945*
I am a journalist working for a newspaper in Leyden (Holland) for whom I have offered to translate a novel or short story from French, in instalments. They have just informed me that they agree in principle to publish whatever I suggest or send them. I explained to them that there would be royalties to pay, which would undoubtedly be much greater for a novel already published here, as the publishers would claim their share, than for a new, unpublished short story, for which they would only have to deal with the author. And I thought of you even though I am only familiar with your novels.

Albin Michel's reply to W. Tideman   *29 December 1945*
I have seen the letter sent to my offices addressed to I. Némirovsky and am alas! unable to pass it on to her.

Mme I. Némirovsky was, in fact, arrested in July 1942 then deported to Poland, we think. Since the date of her arrest, no one has heard anything from her.

Preface to the French edition*

In 1929 the French publisher Bernard Grasset was so enthusiastic about a manuscript he had received in the post that he immediately decided to publish it. It was only as he was about to send a contract to the author of the novel, entitled David Golder, *that he realised no name or address had been given - just a post office box number. He put an advertisement in the newspapers asking the mysterious author to make contact.*

When Irène Némirovsky arrived to meet him a few days later, Bernard Grasset was astonished: how could this fashionable, cheerful young Russian woman, who had lived in France for only ten years, have written a book that was so brilliantly daring, cruel, and mature? He questioned her carefully to make sure she wasn't standing in for a famous author who wished to remain anonymous, but as he did so his admiration grew. Her French was impeccable (although born in Kiev she had learned it from her governess); as well as Russian, she knew Polish, Basque, English, Finnish and a little Yiddish (a language she would make use of in her novel Les Chiens et les Loups, *published in 1940).*

David Golder *was an overnight success, unanimously acclaimed by the critics and admired by other writers. However, the twenty-six-year-old Irène Némirovsky refused to be carried away by her sensational entry into the literary world. She was surprised that so much fuss was made over* David Golder, *which she considered, without false modesty, a 'minor novel'. On 22 January 1930 she wrote to a friend, 'How could you think I could possibly forget my old friends because of a little book which people have been talking about for a few weeks and which will be forgotten just as quickly, just as everything is forgotten in Paris?'*

Irène Némirovsky was born 1903 in Kiev, then part of the area known as Yiddishland to which Russian Jews were confined. Her father's family came from the Ukrainian city of Nemirov, which had been an important centre of the Hassidic movement in the eighteenth century. Léon Némirovsky had the misfortune to be born

* This is an edited version of the preface that appeared in the French edition of *Suite Française* published by Editions Denoël in 2004.

in 1868 in Elisabethgrad, the city where the great waves of pogroms against the Jews began in 1881. However, his family had prospered, becoming wealthy by trading in grain. As a young man Léon had travelled widely before making his fortune in finance, going on to become one of the richest bankers in Russia. His business cards read, 'Léon Némirovsky, President and Managing Director of the Bank of Commerce of Vorononej, Administrator of the Union Bank of Moscow, Member of the Private Commercial Banking Committee of Petrograd'. He bought an enormous private house overlooking St Petersburg, on a quiet street lined with gardens and lime trees.

Irène was not a happy child. Her mother, who liked to be called Fanny (after her Hebrew name, Faïga), saw the birth of her daughter as the first sign of her declining youth and beauty. She felt a kind of aversion to Irène, for whom she never showed the least sign of love, and would spend hours in front of the mirror pampering herself, or away from home in search of extramarital affairs. She could not bear the idea that her looks would fade, or that she might turn into the kind of older woman who kept young men. She forced Irène to dress like a schoolgirl well into her teens in order to convince herself that she wasn't growing older.

Léon, whom Irène adored and admired, was always busy with his work and most of the time was away, or betting large sums of money at the casino. A lonely, solitary child, entrusted to the care of her governess, Irène took refuge in books, and fought off despair by developing a ferocious hatred of her mother. This violent and unnatural relationship between mother and daughter would be at the heart of many of her novels, as would her disdain for her mother's wealthy Jewish milieu.

In Russia the Némirovskys led a life of luxury. Every summer they would leave the Ukraine for the Crimean coast, Biarritz, Saint-Jean-de-Luz, Hendaye or the French Riviera. Irène's mother would take up residence in a villa, while Irène and her governess were sent to lodge with a family. At fourteen, after the death of her French teacher, Irène began writing. Settled on the sofa, a notebook on her lap, she developed a technique inspired by Ivan Turgenev. As well as the narrative itself, she would write down all the ideas the story inspired in her, without any revision or crossing out. She filled notebook upon notebook with thoughts about her characters, even the minor ones, describing their appearance, their education, their childhood, all the stages of their lives in chronological order. When each character had been detailed to this degree of precision, she would use two pencils, one red, the other blue, to underline the essential characteristics to be retained; sometimes only a few lines. She would then move quickly on to writing the novel, improving it, then editing the final version.

In 1917, the Némirovskys were still living in the large, beautiful house in St Petersburg they had occupied since 1914. Némirovsky described the house in her autobiographical novel Le Vin de solitude*: 'The apartment . . . was built in such a way that from the entrance hall, you could see all the way back to the other rooms – a series of white and gold reception rooms that were visible through the large, open doors.' For a number of Russian writers and poets, St Petersburg is a mythical city; to Irène Némirovsky it was nothing more than a collection of dark, snow-covered streets, swept by the icy wind that rose from the disgusting, polluted canals of the Neva. When the October Revolution broke out, Léon Némirovsky thought it expedient to move his family to Moscow since he frequently went there on business and had sub-let an apartment from an officer of the Imperial Guard who had been assigned to the Russian embassy in London. His plan proved misguided. Moscow was where the more violent fighting took place and the family were trapped in the apartment for five days, their only food a bag of potatoes, some chocolate and sardines. Wedged in between other apartment blocks and surrounded by a courtyard, the house was hidden from the street. While battles raged outside, Irène explored the officer's library. There she discovered Huysmans, de Maupassant, Plato and Oscar Wilde (*The Portrait of Dorian Gray was her favourite book*). When the street was deserted she would quietly go down to pick up the empty cartridges.*

During a lull in the fighting, the Némirovskys went back to St Petersburg, but the Bolsheviks had put a price on Léon's head and he was forced into hiding. In December 1917, taking advantage of the fact that the borders had not yet been closed, Léon Némirovsky made arrangements for his family to travel to Finland, disguised as peasants. Irène spent a year in a little hamlet consisting of three wooden houses in the middle of a snowfield. She still hoped to return to Russia and the wait seemed long. While they were there, her father returned to Russia several times in disguise to try and rescue their belongings. Yet despite the uncertainty and lack of comfort, Némirovsky experienced for the first time a period of serenity and peace. She was absorbed by her writing, composing prose poems inspired by Oscar Wilde.

With the situation in Russia deteriorating and the Bolsheviks drawing danger-ously nearer to them, the Némirovskys moved on to Sweden, finally reaching Stockholm after a long journey. They spent three months in the Swedish capital, where Irène would always remember the mauve lilacs growing in the courtyards and gardens. Then, in early 1919, the family took a small cargo boat for France, sailing for ten days through a terrible storm, which inspired the dramatic final scene in David Golder*. Safe in Paris, Léon Némirovsky took over as director of a branch of his bank and so managed to rebuild his fortune.*

Irène had always loved France and, in Paris, her life changed utterly. She enrolled at the Sorbonne, where she graduated with a distinction in literature, and began sending stories to magazines. In 1927 she published a novella called L'Enfant génial, *about a young Jewish boy from the slums of Odessa who seduces an aristocrat with his poetry.*

The Némirovskys were soon assimilated into French society and led the glamorous life of the wealthy upper-middle class: *fashionable soirées, champagne dinners, balls, luxurious holidays. Irène adored dancing. She dashed between parties, living, as she herself admitted, 'the high life'. Sometimes she gambled at the casino. On 2 January 1924 she wrote to a friend, 'I have had the wildest week: one ball after another, and I'm still a bit heady and finding it difficult to get back into the routine of work...' Another time she wrote from Nice, 'I'm behaving like a madwoman, it's shameful. I dance all night long. Every evening there are very chic entertainments in different hotels, and as my lucky star has blessed me with a few handsome young men, I'm enjoying myself very much indeed.' A further letter, written just after a return from Nice, reads: 'I haven't behaved very well . . . for a change . . . The evening before I left, there was a grand ball at our hotel, the Negresco. I danced like a mad thing until 2 a.m. and went outside in the freezing cold to drink champagne and flirt.' A few days later she wrote: 'Choura came to see me and lectured me for two hours: it seems that I flirt too much, that it's bad to upset boys like that . . . I broke off with Henry, you know, and he came to see me the other day looking pale, wide-eyed and evil, with a revolver in his pocket!'*

In the whirlwind of one of these parties she met Mikhaïl – Michel Epstein – 'a small dark-haired man with a very swarthy complexion', who wasted no time in courting her. He had a degree in Physical and Electronic Engineering from the University of St Petersburg, and worked as a senior banking executive at the Banque des Pays du Nord, Rue Gaillon. She liked him, flirted and, in 1926, they were married. They moved to 10 avenue Constant-Coquelin, a beautiful apartment on the Left Bank whose windows looked out over the large courtyard of a convent. In 1929 Irène gave birth to Denise (Fanny sent a teddy bear). By the time her second daughter, Elisabeth, was born in 1937, David Golder *had been turned into a film, and she had published nine novels. She and Michel moved in high circles and took holidays in fashionable spa towns for Irène's asthma.*

In spite of her fame, and though clearly very attached to her new country, Irène still didn't have French citizenship. In 1939 Irène decided that she and her children should convert to Catholicism. This decision should be seen in the context of the obsessive fear of war in 1939, and the previous decade of violent anti-Semitism during which Jews had been portrayed as evil invaders and power-hungry warmongers – a race of bourgeois merchants and revolutionaries. She and her family were baptised early in the morning of 2 February 1939 in the Chapel of Sainte-Marie in Paris, by a family friend, Prince Ghika, a Romanian bishop.

When war broke out in September, Irène and Michel took their two small daughters, Denise and Elisabeth, to the safety of Issy-l'Evêque, in Saône-et-Loire, the village where their nanny, Cécile Michaud came from. There, they were left in the care of Cécile's mother, Madam Mitaine.

For the first months of the war, Irène and Michel stayed in Paris, making frequent journeys to visit their children. Then, in June 1940, the Germans occupied Paris and the Némirovskys decided to leave Paris altogether, taking up residence in a hotel opposite the house of Cécile Michaud, the Hôtel des Voyageurs. From then on life became increasingly difficult. On 3 October 1940, a law was passed giving Jews inferior legal and social standing. Most important, it defined, based on racial criteria, who was to be considered Jewish in the French State. The Némirovskys, who took part in an enforced census in June 1941, were both Jewish and foreign: their baptism certificates were useless. Michel no longer had the right to work at the bank; the publishing houses were 'Aryanising' their personnel and authors, so Irène could no longer be published. Further race laws passed in October 1940 and June 1941 stipulated that Jews could be placed under house arrest or deported and interned in concentration camps. Issy-l'Evêque was now in the occupied zone and the Hôtel des Voyageurs was full of German soldiers. Irène, her husband and her daughters all openly wore the Jewish star.

Irène Némirovsky watched what was happening with pitiless clarity: she had no doubt that these events would result in tragedy. But life went on. Denise celebrated her first Communion, despite going to the local school with the Jewish star sewn prominently on to the front of her coat. Michel amused himself by writing a multiplication table for Denise in rhyme. The family were finally able to find a large house to rent. Irène read and wrote constantly. Every day, after breakfast, she would go out, sometimes walking for ten kilometres before finding a spot she liked. Then she would start working. Between 1940 and 1942, the publishing house Albin Michel and the director of the anti-Semitic newspaper Gringoire *agreed to help her publish her short stories under various pseudonyms. She also wrote a life of Chekhov and a novel,* Les Feux de l'automne, *which would not be published until 1957. But, most important, in 1941 she started work on an ambitious novel to be called* Suite Française.

Némirovsky began Suite Française, *as was her habit, by writing notes on the work in progress and thoughts inspired by the situation in France. She created a list of characters, both major and minor, then checked that she had used them correctly. She dreamed of a book of a thousand pages, constructed like a symphony, but in five sections, according to rhythm and tone. She took Beethoven's Fifth Symphony as a model.*

On 12 June 1942 she began to doubt she would be able to complete this huge endeavour. She had a premonition that she didn't have long to live. But she continued work on her book, simultaneously writing notes. She called these lucid, cynical remarks Notes sur l'état de France *(Notes on the State of France). They prove that she had absolutely no illusions, not about the attitude of the inert French masses − 'loathsome' in their defeat and collaboration − nor about her own fate. As she wrote at the top of the first page:*

> *To lift such a heavy weight,*
> *Sisyphus, you will need all your courage.*
> *I do not lack the courage to complete the task*
> *But the goal is far and time is short.*

In her writing she denounced fear, cowardice, acceptance of humiliation, of perse-cution and massacre. She was alone. It was rare to find anyone in the literary and publishing worlds who did not choose to collaborate with the Nazis. Every day, Irène would go to meet the postman, but there were increasingly few letters from her publishers. She did not try to escape her fate by fleeing − to Switzerland for example, which was taking in a small number of Jews coming from France, especially women and chil-dren. She saw the situation in such bleak terms that on 3 June she wrote her Will and gave it to the children's governess, asking that she take care of Denise and Elisabeth if necessary. She gave precise instructions, listing all the possessions she had managed to save, which could be sold to provide money to pay the rent, heat the house, buy a stove, hire a gardener who would tend the vegetable garden to provide food while rationing lasted; she provided the addresses of her daughters' doctors, and details of their diet. Not a word of revolt. A straightforward understanding of the situation exactly as it was − hopeless.

On 3 July she wrote, 'Just let it be over − one way or the other!' She saw the situation as a succession of violent shocks that could kill her.

On 11 July she was working in the pine forest, sitting on her blue cardigan 'in the middle of an ocean of rotting leaves drenched by last night's storm, as if on a raft, my legs folded beneath me'. That day she wrote a letter to her editor at Albin Michel that left no doubt about her certainty that she would not survive the war: 'My dear friend …think of me sometimes. I have done a lot of writing. I suppose they will be posthumous works, but it helps pass the time.'

On 13 July 1942, the French police knocked at the Némirovskys' door. They had come to arrest Irène. On 16 July, she was interned in the concentration camp at Pithiviers in the Loiret region. The next day she was deported to Auschwitz in Convoy number 6. She was registered at the extermination camp at Birkenau, and as she was very weak, was sent to the Revier.* She died on 17 August 1942.

When Irène was taken away, Michel did not understand that to be arrested and deported meant certain death. Every day he expected her to come home and insisted, at mealtimes, that her place be set at the table. In complete despair, he wrote to Marshal Pétain to explain that his wife had a delicate constitution and to request permission to take her place in the labour camp.

In October 1942, the Vichy government responded by arresting him. He was first imprisoned at Creusot, then Drancy, where his search document shows that 8,500 francs were taken from him. On 6 November 1942, he too was deported to Auschwitz and was sent straight to the gas chamber.

Immediately after arresting Michel Epstein, the police went to the village school to get Denise, but her schoolteacher hid her behind her bed. The police did not give up and continued their hunt. The Nemirovskys' governess had the presence of mind to remove the Jewish star from their clothes and flee the village with the little girls. They spent the rest of the war moving between hiding places. The first was a Catholic boarding school where two of the nuns knew the little girls were Jewish. There Denise was given a false name but she never managed to get used to it, so she was often scolded in class because she didn't reply when she was called. But the French police – who it seems had little better to do than hunt down two children so they might share the same fate as their parents – picked up their trail. The girls were forced to leave the convent to hide out in a series of cellars in the region of Bordeaux. Whenever they boarded a train to move in, the governess would tell Denise to hide her nose. When Denise caught a chest infection, the people who were hiding her didn't help her to see a doctor.

The war over, the two girls returned to Paris and went to their grandmother's house to ask for help. Fanny had spent the war years in Nice, living in great comfort, but when the children rang the doorbell she refused to let them in, shouting through the closed door that if their parents were dead they should go to an orphanage. (Fanny died in 1972, in a large apartment in Paris on the avenue Président Wilson. The only things found in her safe were two books by her daughter: Jezebel and David Golder.) Each day, wearing a sign with their names written on it, Denise and Elisabeth would make their way to the platform of the Gare de l'Est, where trains carrying the survivors of the concentration camps were beginning to arrive.

---

*The infirmary at Auschwitz where prisoners who were too ill to work were confined in atrocious conditions. The SS would periodically pile them into trucks and take them to the gas chambers.

They would also go to the Hôtel Lutétia, which had been turned into a reception centre for returning deportees – once, Denise began to run down the street after a woman because she thought she recognised her mother – but eventually it became clear that their parents were not coming back.

That the manuscript of Suite Française *should have survived in such circumstances is extraordinary. It was Denise who put it into a suitcase as she and her sister fled Issy l'Evêque. She had often watched her mother writing – in tiny handwriting to save ink and paper – in the large leatherbound notebook. She took it as a memento of her mother. The suitcase accompanied Denise and Elisabeth from one precarious hiding place to another. After the war, they couldn't bring themselves to read the notebook – having it was enough. Once, Denise tried to look inside to see what was there, but it was too painful. Many years passed, and she and her sister Elisabeth, who had become an editor in a publishing house under the name Elisabeth Gille, agreed they should entrust their mother's notebook to the Institut Mémoires de l'Edition Contemporaine, an organisation dedicated to documenting memories of the war, in order to preserve it. Before giving it up, Denise decided to type it out. With the help of a large magnifying glass, she began the long, difficult task of deciphering the minuscule handwriting. Soon she discovered that these were not simply notes or a private diary, as she had thought, but a violent masterpiece, a fresco of extraordinary lucidity, a vivid snapshot of France and the French – spineless, defeated and occupied: here was the exodus from Paris; villages invaded by exhausted, hungry women and children battling to find a place to sleep, if only a chair in a country inn; cars piled high with furniture, mattresses and pots and pans, running out of petrol and left abandoned in the roads; the rich trying to save their precious jewels; a German soldier falling in love with a French woman under the watchful eye of her mother-in-law; the simple dignity of a modest couple searching amidst the chaos of the convoys fleeing Paris for a trace of their wounded son . . .*

Denise Epstein sent the manuscript to the publisher Denoël. Sixty-four years after Nemirovsky's death, we are finally able to read the last work of a writer who had held a mirror up to France at its darkest hour.

When Denise Epstein entrusted the manuscript of Suite Française *to the archives, she felt tremendous sadness that her sister Elisabeth Gille, who died in 1996, had not been able to read it. Elisabeth had, herself, written* Le Mirador *(The Watchtower): a magnificent imagined biography of the mother she never had the chance to know. She was only five years old when Irène Némirovsky died in Auschwitz.*

Myriam Anissimov

Acknowledgements

My thanks go to Olivier Rubinstein and everyone at Editions Denoël who welcomed this manuscript with enthusiasm and emotion; to Francis Esménard, President and General Director of Albin Michel, who showed great generosity in allowing the publication of a piece of the past of which he was the guardian; to Myriam Anissimov, the link between Romain Gary, Olivier Rubinstein and Irène Némirovsky; and to Jean-Luc Pidoux-Payot, who helped read the manuscript and gave me his valuable advice.

Denise Epstein

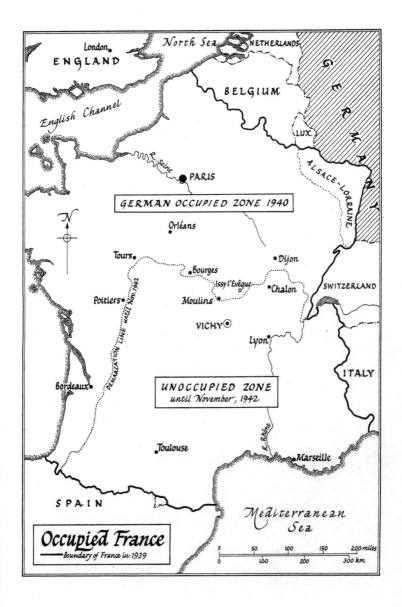

London •
ENGLAND

North Sea

NETHERLANDS

BELGIUM

G E R M A N Y

English Channel

LUX.

R. Seine

ALSACE-LORRAINE

PARIS

GERMAN OCCUPIED ZONE 1940

N

Orléans •

Tours •

• Dijon

• Bourges

Issy l'Evêque •

• Chalon

SWITZERLAND

Poitiers •

DEMARCATION LINE until Nov. 1942

Moulins •

VICHY ⊙

Lyon •

ITALY

Bordeaux •

UNOCCUPIED ZONE
until November, 1942

R. Rhône

• Toulouse

• Marseille

S P A I N

Mediterranean
Sea

Occupied France
—— Boundary of France in 1939

0   50   100   150   200 miles
0   100   200   300 km